A Story Like Truth

Barbara —
Can't thank you
enough for all
your kindness and
support.
Herbert M. Padgett

The Sea in Winter

A Story Like Truth

A Novel

Deborah McWatters Padgett

LULU.COM

A Story Like Truth

LULU.COM
Published by Lulu.com.

First published in 2012 by Lulu.com
3101 Hillsborough St | Raleigh, NC 27607-5436

Author's note: This is a work of fiction. Names, characters, places and incidents either are the product of the author's imagination or are used fictitiously, and any resemblance to actual persons living or dead, establishments, events or locales is entirely coincidental.

ISBN# 978-1-105-74780-9

The Sea in Winter

<u>Also by Deborah McWatters Padgett</u>

<u>Fiction</u>

SOLVING LONELY, A Novel
&
THE SEA IN WINTER, A Novel

A Story Like Truth

Dedicated with all my love, respect and gratitude to my true life's love Michael Padgett. He has been my champion, my true believer and my hero for all the years of my healing. I adore you Michael.

A Story Like Truth

As I thrust my hand deeper into the swirl of this stream — history, nightmare, accountability — I feel the current angrier and more multiform than the surface shows: There is fury here, and terror, but there is also power, power not to be had without the terror and the fury. We need to go beyond rhetoric or evasion into that place in ourselves, to feel the force of all we have been trying — without success — to skim across.

and

We therefore have a primary obligation... not to undermine each others' sense of reality for the sake of expediency...Women have often felt insane when cleaving to the truth of our experience. Our future depends on the sanity of each of us, and we have a profound stake, beyond the personal, in the project of describing our reality as candidly and fully as we can to each other.

Adrienne Rich, On Lies, Secrets, and Silence: Selected Prose. W.W. Norton, 1995

Author's Introduction

In the summer of 1989, two years after Dr. Susan Forward's publication of Men Who Hate Women and the Women Who Love Them, one year after Ellen Bass's and Laura Davis's publication of The Courage to Heal, two years prior to Dr. Carol Tavris's Beware the Incest Survivor Machine and three years prior to Dr. Renee Fredrickson's publication of Repressed Memories: A Journey to Recovery from Sexual Abuse, my third marriage ended with my admittance to the psyche ward of Fairview Riverside Hospital.

The diagnosis was post-traumatic stress syndrome tied to childhood sexual, physical and emotional abuse. Three times I had married, unconsciously seeking the love, comfort and safety I was denied, but knowing only to put the name love to chaos, denigration and abuse.

Outwardly, my life appeared a life of significant achievement. I espoused feminist ideology, raised two lovely daughters, put myself through school, climbed the corporate ladder, contributed to honorable causes and became an outspoken visual artist and sometimes writer. My life was a race to live, to outdistance the past. Without conscious acknowledgement of the truth, or even conscious awareness of the truth, I lived the life common to many survivors of childhood brutality. It was a life without rest and peace. It was a life of desperation to establish that it was too okay for me to be alive, that I was not either worthless.

In each subsequent marriage, as my self-hatred at my failure mounted and I tried to keep up appearances, I grew more weary and frantic. The more weary and frantic I became, the more self-hating and self-destructive I became. I began to believe the words my husband shouted in my face and shook into my body while he gripped me in a rage: "You deserve what you get. You have no right to expect…"

Finally, mostly wanting to die, but fearing it too, I picked up the phone and asked for help. In the dozen or more years since that ending – that ultimately proved to be a beginning, I've asked myself, more times than I can say, if the journey from there to here was worth the pain. Mostly I answer "yes."

I long sometimes for the peace of oblivion, for the days past when I ignored the truth of my own experience. But it's an oblivion that I now know results in sickness, fear, drug and/or alcohol addiction or ends in death at one's own hands or at the hands of a batterer. I am determined to do everything in my power to avoid any of these as the final truth of my experience.

In the 1980's and 1990's numerous books, fiction and non-fiction, were published telling stories of childhood abuse. Initially these stories shocked, surprised and inspired the outrage of the reading public. Soon the marketplace was inundated and book reviewers and audiences alike grew tired of these same old, same old horror stories. As a matter of fact, it began to look as if nearly everyone, if they looked hard and long enough at all the skeletons in the family closets, could claim a horror story of their own. By 1992 voices telling the truth of survival and recovery were, to a large extent, silenced. Stories of rape, domestic violence, incest and child abuse were no longer marketable. Books and articles after 1992 held such stories up for ridicule.

The various forms of help offered to would be and/or real victims ranged from the silly, obnoxious and syrupy to hard-nosed "lock 'em up and throw away the key" court cases, to honest-to-God, legitimate psychotherapy offered by professionals who know the pervasiveness of child abuse and the life long debilitation and, yes, threat to society such abuse poses.

One of my writing heroines, Louise Erdrich, was interviewed a few years back about her characters. She talked about the life long effect on children who are abandoned, neglected, un-cared for and abused by those they should have reason to trust. She said she invented, "recognized" the childhood rape that formed the stories in the life of her character June. "It's a great treasure to me that I had a secure childhood." Erdrich said. "But I see in people who are my age now great gaps and absences because they haven't . . ."

"June [Erdrich's character] is an intelligent woman but she is unable to make up for what she missed as a child to heal herself. She is a wounded person all through her life. She has enormous wells of 'rage and despair'. . . The thing that becomes apparent throughout life is that when you have terrible things happen to you, sometimes people don't really recover." [Erdrich by Kay Miller, Variety, Star Tribune]

So, there, in the mid-1990's, sat thousands upon thousands of women, men and children. They were in support groups, in psychotherapy, in the psychiatrist's office. They searched for a source of wisdom that would tell them how to bring their own stories to a place beyond mere survival to a sense of arrival and peace with themselves and the past.

In one short decade we had come full circle from ignorance, shame and silence to full-voiced declaration of harm done and accountability demanded then back around to ignorance shame and silence.

Though therapists offered advice, suggestions, medication and ritual, they couldn't assure that following these rituals would result in health and renewal. The diagnosis was too new. The treatments, experimental. Would be survivors were urged to forgive themselves for not forgiving their abusers, were induced to relive the horror of the past and stand strong and alone, facing their families with the awful truth. In the blackest most sorrow-filled moments of my own search, I felt tortured by a question no one could answer: Will I ever be all right or will this pain be endless? I grew ashamed of my own need for answers, for healing.

There were no stories yet of recovery and subsequent thriving to hang on to for hope. There hadn't been time for the therapies and medicines to be tested. The whole nation, it seemed, was on Prozac and it and the whole idea of recovery from childhood abuse had become a subject for jokes and ridicule.

I felt stranded and having finally looked at the truth of my childhood, no longer wanted to claim it. I wanted nothing more than to go back into hiding, take back my demand for accountability and return to the comfort of my lie of a life. I left therapy. I went off Prozac and I shut up, already! and began to doubt everything I knew to be true.

A STORY LIKE TRUTH is fiction. It is my attempt to show, through an imagined life, a truth very much like my own and to answer that vital question for myself and others like me—Will I ever be all right, or will this pain be endless?

Deborah McWatters Padgett

Chapter One

In the days and nights preceding hurricane Beth in late August 1949 the ocean taunted Tampa's inhabitants with a vertigo of swells and calms. Heat weighed heavy on the arms and legs and even children stopped their play to watch and wait. Shopkeepers, brows spewing sweat, hammered a lethargic beat on mildewed sheets of plywood against windows and doors. Heat trapped the scent of over ripe citrus and too sweet coconut. Gulls mewed and circled low under the ceiling of heat. Pedestrians staggered like drunks with nausea. A serpent of traffic snaked its way north and inland.

At five o'clock in the afternoon, on August twenty-nine, the sky a green black calm in the distance, Reverend Earl Blackwell drove his laboring seventeen-year-old wife Elizabeth toward, rather than away from, Tampa's coast. The twenty four-year-old Earl, straight black hair pomaded short and slick against his scalp, black frame glasses disguising his fierce and sullen gaze, silently cursed his fate and that of the baby whose birth was imminent.

Elizabeth, tensed delicate features, black hair in a crimped frenzy around her face and shoulders, moaned and writhed on the seat beside Earl. Her labor pains gave her brief reprieve and in the seconds available she lifted the edge of her maternity blouse to wipe the sweat from her face. So thin, so depleted of energy was this girl it was inconceivable she would bear a child in the hours ahead.

She depended on Earl for everything. Had since the day they met. To Elizabeth, Earl was a mature man of God. She was a young girl in his thrall. Her fingers, nails bitten into the surrounding skin, clutched her husband's thigh.

On a blue sky day the preceding October, Earl and Elizabeth came this same route to Tampa Municipal Hospital where Elizabeth made her husband the proud father of their first baby girl, Ariana.

Came this route too in mid-December, the baby Ariana sleeping quietly in the back seat while Elizabeth hemorrhaged onto a diaper wadded between her legs — her womb a fist beating from her body a too soon conceived second child.

That day in December, while Elizabeth mourned the child the doctor pronounced dead, Earl praised God for sparing him another mouth to feed.

Then, at five o'clock suppertime, on a day late in March, Earl returned home from his work as pastor of the Baptist church in Waverly, a poor rural community about an hour inland of Tampa's coast. He'd spent the afternoon in his study at the white washed sheet metal church preparing a sermon he called "Blessed Tragedies." Elizabeth had already fed the six-month-old Ariana who played and cooed in her playpen within reach of the dinner table.

While Elizabeth served Earl his supper he boasted. Fork in one fist, knife in the other he made a pulpit of the table.

"People," it was a shout, a question, a command Earl issued to the dinner table as if to the multitudes.

"People," he said, "Get ready!"

"Get ready for the visitation of the Lord … ." He leaned now, eyes fastened on those of the sparrow salt and pepper shakers just beyond the edge of his plate. He smirked self-satisfaction thinking of what he was about to say.

"His eye … oh, people, yes … his eye … is on … the sparrow. His eye is on the sparrow and …" Now he closed his eyes and lifted his head toward the white glass ceiling fixture his wife bought for a dollar at Woolworth's some time ago. But he wouldn't notice the flies who died flying into that light. It was another light that visited Earl and urged his voice to whisper this curse, "and I know… I know …" he looked again at the sparrows, signaling the sheer depth of his knowing, "He watches," Earl pointed his fork at the upturned faces of the bird shakers, held their gaze, then leveled his pronouncement "… You." He nodded his head yes and smiled looking at his plate.

"Oh, Honey," his voice lifted in exaltation that held not a hint of humility, "I'm going to give it to them this Sunday. You just wait. This sermon…" he forked food into his left cheek, chewed quickly but didn't have the patience to swallow before he went on, "tells the Lord's truth as spoken through his enlightened witness."

Elizabeth sat opposite her husband, not looking his direction, unnecessarily fearing he might look her way and see her eyes betray the secret she carried. She dangled a teething ring over the rail of the playpen toward Ariana's uplifted face.

"That's good, Earl. That's real good." She knew she should show more interest, urge him to tell more, but she knew, too, he wasn't likely to notice one way or the other.

As Earl continued to pontificate Elizabeth watched the fork in her hand capture, then release the glue-like canned meat and scalloped potatoes she'd prepared for supper. She was grateful her husband had returned home so full of himself because, at these times, she had reason to hope she'd be spared his wrath concerning their poverty-stricken state and the resulting meals she was able to scrape together.

Earl's moods had become increasingly unpredictable lately and it was not uncommon for him to make instant and dramatic shifts between adoring, nearly lovesick husband, to loud and violent demonstrations of rage.

Though Earl was in a good mood now, Elizabeth shuddered to think how he'd react once she found a way to say that the baby whose death he'd celebrated and she'd mourned, was still alive. She struggled to find a way to tell him she still carried this child.

She finished eating, occasionally nodding or showing a faint smile to her husband who had only ceased in his self-adulation for the brief moment required to fill his own mouth with dinner.

When she came close to Earl to take his empty plate from him, he grabbed her around the hips and pulled her near making snapping and chewing sounds as he buried his face in her belly. More distressed than aroused she pretended pleasure and amusement as she pushed his face from her in a manner she hoped he would see as playful.

"Earl … the baby!" she said, then caught herself from holding her arms to cover her abdomen. She recovered quickly and referred to Ariana.

"You watch her for a second now, while I clean up these

dishes." She took refuge then in the kitchen, gazing from the window at the barren dessert of their yard, her hands in the soapy water.

From the other room she heard Earl change his tone to baby talk. Heard him telling Ariana how proud she would be of her daddy on Sunday when he delivered "the good news." Ariana giggled at the words and Earl lifted her into the air, laughing above his head.

"The good news!" he repeated and with each repetition the baby would laugh with greater glee. "The good news!"

Returning from the kitchen Elizabeth found Earl on his back on the bare linoleum of the living room floor bouncing his still laughing daughter in front of him on his chest. The sight of Earl, so happy with his baby girl, encouraged her. Surely he would love any child of his as much. Elizabeth smiled and lifted Ariana, calming her laughter with a caressing hand and kissing her fragrant scalp.

Once Ariana was bathed and put to bed, Elizabeth prepared herself to join Earl in their bedroom. She knew now that the way to deliver her not-so-good news, was to show him first how irresistible she found him. Nothing pleased Earl more than unadulterated adoration, real or feigned.

She stopped first by the dresser and ran a brush through her dark hair. Earl rose from the bed and came to take her in his arms. He lifted the hair from her neck and placed a kiss there then looked into her eyes in the mirror they faced. She lifted her hand to caress his hair and he reached to unbutton the front of her dress.

Later that night, as she lay naked and trusting in her husband's arms she found the courage to tell him.

"Sweetheart," she said, tracing a finger along the muscles of his chest that rose and fell in a rhythm slowing for sleep.

"Hmmm?" He alternately lifted and dropped strands of Elizabeth's hair from her head resting against his chest.

"The baby… um … well, the doctor … Earl, are you listening?"

"What? Oh, yes… 'the baby,' you said. She's fine, honey." He turned to her, propping himself on one arm as she moved away from him on the bed. "What's this about a doctor? You're worrying about nothing again, aren't you?" He ran his hands over her shoulders and back.

"Look at me, Elizabeth."

But she couldn't. She faced away from him summoning courage.

"Earl," she said, "Earl. Listen to me." Brave now, she faced him and cupped his chin in her hand. "I don't mean Ariana."

"What do you mean you don't mean Ariana?" Earl took her hand from his face. "What's going on here, Liz? You sound so…"

"Earl. I'm still pregnant. That's the baby I mean. I'm talking about the baby I miscarried in December…"

Earl was silent and Elizabeth continued.

"I didn't. That's what I'm trying to say."

"'Didn't' what?" Now Earl was sitting up on the bed. He used his strength to turn her toward him.

She kept her eyes low. "Earl, I didn't miscarry the baby. I'm still pregnant. We're going to have another child."

Earl reached to clasp Elizabeth's chin in his hand. He squeezed hard and forced her to look in eyes. He said nothing, just focused the full force of his rage at her eyes.

"How could you? Just — exactly — Tell me, Liz…" he shook her by the shoulders. "How could you? You — we… That miscarriage! That was a blessing. Why, we can no more afford another child now than … than… I don't know what." He clenched her shoulders in his hands then pushed her away.

He left their bed, pulled on a pair of pants. She heard the door close behind him and the sound of the car engine turning over.

Abandoned there in a kaleidoscope, she imagined that if she let her fingers search the bed's surface she would find herself lying in a blanket of shattered glass. It seemed a sudden force of nature determined to simultaneously fill her with life and suck the life from her. It occurred to her then, that if the fetus lived to term, the baby would be born in the coming hurricane season.

By the time Earl and Elizabeth arrived at the hospital the night of the storm the streets of Tampa were nearly empty. A deep quiet, like a breath too long held, penetrated the evening calm with something akin to frenzy. An occasional hot and low gust of wind swirled paper wrappers along sidewalks under flickering street lamps.

Elizabeth Blackwell labored for hours alone as her preacher husband Earl paced the waiting room drinking from paper cups the tepid brown water that passed for coffee. Outside palm trees bent double to protect their limbs from the hurricane's inevitable onslaught. Sea swells rose and glided to shore. The former calm became a rumble and a roar that suffocated the cries of sea gulls.

Late in the night as hurricane Beth spent her fury on Tampa's shores, yet another storm brewed, simmered, nearly retreated, then burst forth in her rage to live. From between the numb and emaciated thighs of the poor white child bride of a preacher who'd mourned her baby for dead near five months before, came a child as unwelcome to the world as a Tsunami. The hurricane foretold the destiny of the newborn Miriam. Foretold her fierce refusal to accept death.

* * * * *

On another storm-tossed shore, two-thousand miles away, Julia Rousseau, fifty-two years old and childless now for more than two decades was wakened from a dreamless sleep by the cries of a newborn baby girl.

She rose from her bed and, dressed only in her thin cotton gown, followed the cries, first seeking the child in all the warm and protected spaces of her home — then, outside on the rocky cliffs above the sea where clouds hid then revealed the moon. There, the child's cries pierced the night and silenced all other sounds.

The winds tore at Julia's gown, plastering it transparent against breasts unsuckled all these years. She raised her arms, opened them wide to the night sky above the foaming sea. The cries subsided and this child, too, eluded her grasp. She held herself in her own embrace and climbed the rocks to the door that, carried by the wind, battered her home's entrance.

Julia returned to her bed but could not sleep. She opened the drawer of a bedside table and took from it a locked diary. Taking the tiny golden key from beneath her mattress, she opened it and read the words she wrote on a day in October, twenty-four years before.

Monday, October 24, 1925
Cornwall on Hudson

Can you bear, dear diary, to hear the story of the months and weeks just past? Will you listen as a true friend can be trusted to do? I am so utterly alone today. Only you and my very own soul can know my grief. My sin. My sorrow.

I've returned here to my parents home — home of my birth

— only a few hours ago. Returned after what I hope will be the most harrowing experience in all my life. I lied to everyone regarding my whereabouts these last five months. I fear I've returned to a friendless state. I've left all who love me in the dark concerning this, my secret sorrow.

But you, dear diary, you already know my heart's truth, don't you? I tell you nothing you did not suffer with me. You know I've shunned conventional morality. Know I never wished to marry. Never felt the pressure so many of my peers experience.

You know my recent love is gone — returned to Paris where he lives and writes and where his wife and children keep a home for him knowing nothing of my existence. I do not blame him. I knew he lived only for the moment's passion, much as I've been content to live. He was not my first love, nor is he likely to be my last. He is, without knowing it though, the father of a son he will never meet. Will never know.

My father and mother are away for my return home. And though they would not judge, I will not tell them I have loved and lost a son, a baby boy. I haven't the courage to raise a child. Such upbringing can only do him harm. But, forever I will know a profound loss at having carried and birthed a child. A profound shame that I could not call him mine.

As I let him go — let the nurse take him from me, I felt myself the lost child. I wanted to run with the baby, hide him, pretend I could be the mother he needed. But in my soul, I knew the stigma he would suffer. "Bastard," my son's name. No. I cannot give him what any child deserves. I cannot name him. Can say only… goodbye.

All words said.
No embrace.
Hunger unending.
You on distant shores
Only goodbye.

One singular poignant moment
Touch a sky of brilliant color —
Then, nothing
Only goodbye.

Forever watching you leave —
Imagining —
You become.

.

Unable to grieve
Unable to love,
So brief communion.
On fire with the knowing of you.

My son ...
Only goodbye.

Chapter Two

Earl Blackwell looked at his baby daughter through the window of the hospital nursery, unable to generate the least feeling of tenderness. Miriam's face was pinched, misshapen and bruised from the forceps that had been used to pull her forcibly from the womb. Already she had a mysterious rash and would need costly medication and a lot of special attention. Who, he thought, would care for Miriam's sister, Ariana — his much loved first child, still only a baby herself at just over ten months old — with this new baby requiring so much? Where was the money going to come from to feed, clothe and care for these children?

He left the hospital early in the morning when the storm broke and made his way over the debris-strewn miles between Tampa and Waverly. The white cinder block house he shared with his wife, Elizabeth and the baby Ariana was outside of town along a dirt and gravel road. It was one of five or six similar houses that lined one side of the street. Across the street was an abandoned and dying citrus orchard where trees felled by last night's storm lay like so many bleached out corpses.

He pulled his rusted black 1941 Ford along side the house where there was no discernible driveway — just a yard of tufted grass in sandy soil where several hibiscus shrubs bloomed to spite their barren surroundings. He was relieved to find no apparent damage to the house. He climbed the steps to the front porch, weary with the effort and wondering where he would find the strength to care for Ariana until Elizabeth and the new baby returned home.

He went to the kitchen, thirsty for a good, strong cup of coffee. He insisted, no matter their poverty, that Elizabeth never let the coffee supply run out. He demanded she have it ready, hot and strong when he came to the kitchen in the morning and when she served him supper at night. Now, alone in the kitchen, he opened the cupboard above the stove thinking that might be where Elizabeth kept it. A cockroach scurried into the dark recesses behind white paper bags and cardboard boxes of flour, rice and oatmeal, lettered with the word "Relief" in black ink.

He cursed, careful not to use the Lord's name in vain. "That mouthwash they call coffee at the hospital … baah!" When Earl seethed and cursed he was vigilant in avoiding common swear words. Swearing was a sin against God a preacher couldn't commit. He made his way through the tiny kitchen opening and slamming cupboard doors, his anger rising with each failure to find a can of coffee.

He threw the cabinet door closed but the force was too much and it bounced against the clasp and hung open hovering above his head, threatening to pierce his skull should he stand too quickly after searching the lower cabinets. He just cleared its point when he stood and noticing the dagger, gave it another smack that bounced it, crack against the cabinet then up against the side of his face. Furious now he lifted the empty aluminum percolator from the stove and flung it across the room. The glass top shattered, assuring he couldn't make coffee even if he'd been able to find some.

The truth is he wouldn't have known how to make a pot of coffee anyway and was too proud to ever ask anyone for help or directions. "Ah blast! That's woman's work anyway!" He stormed around the room, "blasting" this, "blasting" that. He gave up on coffee and kicked the pot on his way to the bathroom from the kitchen.

He was an arrogant young man who held sturdy opinions about woman's role as subservient to man's. He sought counsel from no one even in those matters he knew little or nothing about. He was a dictator in his home and in his church.

Returning home after Miriam's birth and realizing he would have to fend for himself, a fury rose in him. The coffee was just the beginning. He shouted his rage through the empty house, blaming and cursing everyone but himself and God.

"Elizabeth should have known better than to get pregnant again so soon after having Ariana. Women and babies," he spit the words. "What a curse you bring on the world! I've been nothing but messed with my whole life 'cause of women and their over-active wombs! Oh, all except for Mother, of course. My mother couldn't have a baby — couldn't, that is until she'd adopted one (namely me) who she didn't know how to take care of — then produced that brat of a sister of mine long after she thought that was a possibility. Timing — Nuts! You'd think it was the thirteenth century the way women don't pay any attention to timing and just go ahead and get pregnant without thinking how it's going to effect somebody else …" On and on he alternately muttered and roared his disgust. He was mad at the world and pitied himself that there was no one there to take care of him as he believed a man deserved to be cared for.

In the bathroom he splashed cold water on his face noticing the scrape of his beard against the skin of his hands. His were not the hands of a workingman. Slight calluses from regular pencil use were the only mar on these limp flower petals. He looked in the mirror expecting to admire his own good looks but saw there, instead, the red and tear-streaked face of a frightened kid. He felt self-conscious and it occurred to him the neighbor, Mrs. Brook, who took Ariana so they could go to the hospital, would probably be expecting him soon. He imagined, by now, she'd noticed his car out front.

Earl, unaware how easily his voice and slamming doors and cabinets could be heard across the yard, liked to think he was good at keeping up an appearance of mature professionalism. He tried to pull himself together; shaved quickly, ran a comb through his hair and put on a clean shirt. He checked himself in the mirror before crossing the yard to Mrs. Brook's house and, except for looking a little droopy around the eyes, was satisfied his disguise was in place.

He shoved his hands in the pockets of his trousers and watched his feet as they shuffled a slow pace across the barren yard scattered with debris from the storm. He thought about the new baby and knew he shouldn't, but he wished she had just died back in December when the doctor said she did.

He climbed the three low steps to Mrs. Brook's front porch and lifted his fist to knock on the screen door.

"Come on in, young daddy." She opened the door, catching him off guard, before he could knock. He nearly fell into her soft square bosom, but righted himself by catching the doorjamb with his hand. Ariana, oblivious to her father's presence and fingering a small stuffed toy chick, rode the flowered, skirt-covered hip of Mrs. Brook.

"You look bushed young fella. Come on in here and sit down on the sofa." She led the way to the living room and signaling him to sit, put his daughter in his lap.

He welcomed the closeness of his daughter's warm body against his own. He wondered how long she would be content with the little he had to offer. How long before she'd notice there wasn't enough of anything to go around in their bleak little world. Resting for the first time in how many hours he didn't know, there in the house of a near stranger, the reality of his young family's circumstances washed over him, and he couldn't help himself, he broke down and cried.

Embarrassed by his outburst but too tired to keep up a front, Earl set Ariana on the floor at his feet and put his head in his hands. Mrs. Brook tried to help him save face. "Let me fix us a cup of coffee, shall I?" She turned from him and walked toward the kitchen.

In a few minutes Mrs. Brook returned with a tray of steaming coffee cups, spoons rattling on their saucers. Earl regained his composure and reached to lift a cup of fragrant coffee from the tray as Mrs. Brook bent to set it on the table between them.

Mrs. Brook sat in a chair facing the sofa. "Tell me about your new baby. Got yourself a boy or a girl?"

"Girl. Another … girl." He didn't meet Mrs. Brook's gaze. Said, "Something's wrong though."

"Oh? Wrong? What do you mean? Is the baby all right? Is Elizabeth okay?" She leaned closer and stroked Ariana's hair, worried a little now.

"I don't know." Now he looked at her hand on his little girl's head. "No one said anything. I mean, that is … the doctor didn't say anything. I just, well, she doesn't look right. Not at all right …" His voice trailed off.

"Oh well, now. You know how odd newborn babies can look, Reverend. You sure it's not just you've forgotten how this one here looked a few months ago?" Now she was sure he was imagining a problem.

"Maybe. Maybe you're right. Doesn't feel right though. Doesn't seem like it was with Ariana."

"Listen, Reverend Blackwell — I'm probably gonna stick my nose where it doesn't belong here, but, far as I'm concerned, there's enough at stake here for me to take the chance."

Earl stirred cream into his coffee and lifted the cup to his lips, looking at Mrs. Brook as he took his first grateful sip.

"Soon as your young missus and that new baby of yours come home from the hospital — well, soon as they're up and around I mean — I want you to send them across to me for a little visit, you hear?"

She watched the young man fighting further tears through his exhaustion and thought to herself he required the same kind of care a third child would. It was clear to her his wife wasn't going to be able to be everything to two babies and this child masquerading as a grown husband beside.

Earl nodded his head but she couldn't tell if he was really listening or not. He finished his coffee and left with the baby in his arms.

Mrs. Brook stood holding the door for him and he turned to say, "And thanks. I mean, for taking Ariana for us."

"Anytime. And, don't you forget what I said. I'm happy to help."

* * * * *

Elizabeth couldn't produce milk for her new daughter and Miriam wouldn't tolerate cow's milk formula. It made her sick every time she ate and projectile vomiting became the aftermath of every meal. She cried incessantly and wasn't growing at all. Earl found more and more excuses to stay longer at the church. When the sick baby cried he became enraged and stomped out of the house slamming the back door and yelling at Elizabeth.

"Can't you do something to shut her up? You're a mother. You're supposed to know how to take care of her!"

Six weeks after they came home from the hospital, Mrs. Brook came over on an afternoon when she could no longer stand to hear the crying of both the baby and Elizabeth across the distance of their sandy yards. Earl either hadn't conveyed her message to his wife or she was just too scared to ask for help.

Elizabeth dabbed at her red nose with a dingy handkerchief and held the screaming baby Miriam against her chest with one arm as she opened the door to her neighbor. The smell of stale milk and messy diapers was quieted momentarily by the warm breeze through the open door. The breeze filtered through the odorless hibiscus and carried a sense of flowers that freshened the room.

"I know it's not my place, and —you know my husband Jim —, well, he said I should keep my nose out of other people's business. . ." Mrs. Brook spoke rapidly into the young mother's tear-stained face as she reached to lift Miriam into her own arms, "but, I was absolutely furious to think of you here day after day, alone with those two babies and your young husband apparently doing nothing to help—if you don't mind my saying so—just going about his business as usual. Must feel like you got three babies, doesn't it?"

Elizabeth burst into fresh tears and attempted a few words in defense of her hard-working husband, but found herself feeling strangely understood in her heartache. Nodding yes through her tears, she didn't resist as Mrs. Brook took the baby from her. She backed further into the room beyond the door and sat, letting an old, worn easy chair swallow her in her distress.

"I can't nurse her," she sobbed. "She gets sick every time I feed her from the bottle. I feel like such a failure. I'm so unhappy and I should be grateful . . ." Her voice trailed off as she cried harder and louder. Ariana, a year old now and walking, poked her small face around the corner and into the darkness of the late afternoon living room where she could see her mother crying and her baby sister breathing exhausted breaths against the breast of the neighbor lady.

Mrs. Brook walked toward Ariana and kneeled down to face-level, reaching to stroke her soft brown hair. Ariana looked sad, confused and afraid, so Mrs. Brook explained, "Oh sweetie, you are so precious! I bet you wonder what's going on out here, don't you?" Ariana eyed the neighbor with suspicion and stood back to get a clearer look at the woman holding her sister.

"Well, honey—I mean, Ariana, you remember me don't you? Remember when you came to my house before your new baby sister came home?" Ariana didn't understand but inched closer to Mrs. Brook. She didn't seem to mind when, still kneeling and holding the baby in one arm, Mrs. Brook reached the other arm around her waist to talk to her.

"Ariana, honey, your mommy has her hands full here with your little sister so sick. I thought to myself she could use some help from somebody who knows a thing or two about babies." She looked down at Miriam in her arms. "See now, she's stopped crying. Makes everybody feel better, doesn't it?"

"Mrs. Blackwell," she said, standing to leave, " How about I take this tiny one over to my place. I've a notion she might be allergic to cow's milk and might react better to the kind that comes from goats. I've got a can in the kitchen. Here, can I take this bottle right here?" She reached for the bottle Elizabeth put on the lamp table by the door when she'd answered Mrs. Brook's knock.

Elizabeth instinctively trusted this friendly neighbor who seemed to have a magic touch with the previously never silent baby Miriam. She stood and opened the door, smiling a weak thank you through the screen as Mrs. Brook carried her baby across the yard between the houses.

When Mrs. Brook left with the baby, Elizabeth lay down on the floor next to Ariana who, by that time, was playing with the pan lids from the kitchen cupboards. She wrapped herself around her playing little girl and cried herself to sleep.

This was a scene her husband could not overlook upon arriving home expecting his dinner to be ready at five o'clock. Without saying a word he lifted Ariana from the floor and carried her to the crib in her bedroom, closed the door and returned to the kitchen. Elizabeth, startled awake by his arrival, and embarrassed at the state he'd found her in, poured out her grief and sense of inadequacy to her husband.

"I never should have had another baby when I couldn't even take care of Ariana or my husband. Or myself! What are we going to do, Earl? What are we going to do? I can't—I just can't cope any more." Still she sat on the floor where Earl found her when he came in. She sobbed, pulling fiercely at her hair. Her face was slick with tears and her body jerked and coughed with each fresh sob.

He reached down and grabbed her in the soft part of her arm just above the elbow.

"Get up. Get up right now before someone sees you!" He whispered, muffling a yell. "I can't believe I married such a sniveling cry baby."

She staggered to her feet, pulled by the pain and force of his grip on her arm. Elizabeth tried to control her tears and reached toward her husband for comfort and support. He pushed her away, flinging her arm back toward her face. She fell into the chair and sat rocking forward and back, still crying, her hands covering her face in shame.

He looked around the sparse, dilapidated kitchen his wife did her best to keep clean and tidy. It was 5 o'clock and Earl had prayer meeting to cover at seven that evening. He was hungry, tired and fed up. He thought the last thing he needed was to come home to what he'd just come home to. He loved his beautiful girl of a wife but he knew better than to put up with her self-pity.

"Look, honey," he said. He knelt in front of her and put his hands gently on the smooth round pads of flesh where her arms joined her shoulders. "Look at me, Liz." She looked up through her tears. He reached to un-stick a strand of her hair from beneath her eye, and couldn't help but feel moved by her beauty.

"Liz, you know it's not been a good day for me either … but, but you can't act like this. You just can't act like this. What will people think? If I can't keep my own family in line, how am I supposed to run a church?" He pleaded with her to understand.

"Oh, Earl, I know. I know. I just feel so helpless sometimes. So overwhelmed. I won't do it again. I didn't mean to make you mad. It's not your problem, I know. The kids are my responsibility. You're right to be angry with me. And look at me. All a mess when my handsome husband gets home." She stood, straightening her dress over her bare legs, smoothing her hair back behind her ears.

Earl looked at her. Looked at her legs and feet, bare on the cold, pitted linoleum. Looked at her tan arms and neck, the soft, dark hair that framed her face in waves. The sad, tear streaked face that looked bee stung but tried, anyway, to smile for him. He lost all thought of anger.

Overcome with desire, he pulled her to him and kissed her hard. He needed to bury himself so deep inside her that hunger and time and responsibility were obliterated, if only for a moment, in the single drug a Baptist preacher was allowed, marriage sanctioned lust.

Holding her face close to his with one arm, he reached the other to pull her chaste cotton dress up and her white cotton briefs down in one swift movement that landed his hand, middle finger searching, digging, as he breathed the words, "Come on woman, I need you..." He thrust and tore at her in that place she knew was his and not her own. She gasped and tried to pull her mouth away from his probing tongue. Now he held her face in one hand, his fingers pressing her jaw, forcing her lips apart and around his tongue.

She did want to be held. Wanted the comfort of him. Was frightened by his anger. What would she do if he ever got so mad he left her? She needed him. He was all she had. She thought if she could relax, make him feel welcome to every part of her in every way he wanted, maybe it wouldn't hurt. He couldn't really mean to hurt her. She knew that. He loved her, didn't he? Loved her the way a married man of God was entitled to love his wife.

No, he wasn't doing anything wrong here. What was wrong with her, she wondered, that she was so tense, so much wanted him to wait, to slow down, give her more time. He reached his hand to caress her thigh and when he took his mouth off hers for a brief gasp of air, she put her hand softly on his lips and looked at his hungry eyes. She reached under her skirt and took his hand and led him to the bedroom and opened to him for the immediate taking.

When her husband finished with her he stood over her.

"Hurry up and get decent," he said. "It's time you fixed dinner."

He left the room tucking in his shirt and zipping his fly. Elizabeth rolled herself to a sitting position on the edge of the bed and reached a hand to retrieve her under pants from the rug on the floor. Ravaged and confused, she told herself it was her fault. Some inadequacy that kept her from understanding her husband's way of showing his love. "He can't help himself. He loses control. Maybe it's because he loves me too much."

Chapter Three

With Mrs. Brook's help Miriam's physical health and disposition improved greatly. She was still a handful, always wriggling and wanting to be held. Loaded with curiosity, wiry and active, she got into everything from the time she could crawl. Increasingly, Elizabeth depended on Mrs. Brook for Miriam's care and life with Ariana was relatively calm and peaceful for a time.

Elizabeth recovered sufficiently from her heartache and self-hatred to begin to teach an after-school Bible class for elementary children in the neighborhood and she took Ariana along with her. She learned how to juggle two little girls and a demanding husband and began to demonstrate some sense of competence in her role as preacher's wife. Her cooking improved, as did her timing, and she seldom failed to have her husband's dinner ready by the five o'clock deadline. She developed a certain skill at reading his sexual moods and now prided herself on her ability to submit to him with something he was willing to interpret as joy.

Earl's temper began to give him problems with his deacons and congregation. They told him he seemed to get more arrogant and power hungry all the time and didn't have the caring, pastor-ly manner so desired by the congregation. When Miriam was nearly four years old the deacons submitted a vote of no confidence in this young pastor and he was forced to resign.

He was devastated—felt blind-sided. He raged loudly, rubbing the back of his head and shouting, walking in circles around the kitchen while Elizabeth folded the laundry or ironed the clothes after bathing the children and tucking them, without her husband's help, into bed each night.

Instead of this whole fiasco serving as a lesson in humility for Earl he blamed his situation on his parishioners and on his wife. The church should have provided for them better.

"Earl, Earl, listen to me." Elizabeth tried to calm him. Tried to interrupt his rant before he said something they'd both regret.

"No — sense — of — timing ... Then there are those women who just don't have morals. Women like whoever got pregnant with me when she wasn't married and never intended to marry I'll bet. And look where it's left me. Just look, I'm running around trying my best, in spite of a floozy of a mother, to lead people to Jesus — lead people to morals, for cripes sake. Oh nuts, anyway. Nobody wants to listen to what a man of God has to say anymore. And look at you Elizabeth. I mean, look at the sickly little life-sapper we've got on our hands with Miriam. Geez," he said, "I know you're young, honey, but I didn't expect you to be a fool."

He was becoming increasingly critical toward Elizabeth. Never once did he claim any responsibility for the difficult situation they were in. If he were less arrogant he could have asked for advice and guidance in matters of income and money and pursuing better circumstances for his family. He called names, blamed this person and the other. It was all someone else's fault. Most often it was the fault either of the mother who adopted him, who he never felt deserved him, or the fault of the woman who gave him his illegitimate birth and marked him forever with the name "bastard." He knew very little about his birth mother, but spent his whole life trying to live down his innate sense that doom was his birthright and a woman with loose morals was the source of that doom.

"They couldn't appreciate a gift from God if it stood right up and bit them."

Finally, raged-out and with only one more paycheck to count on, Earl did the only thing he could think to do. He called his mother and father and asked if he and his family could come home. He would have to find a church that paid him enough to support his family and there was nothing immediately available in Florida. It was humiliating to him to have to rely on his parents. They had warned the young couple of the hardships they would face with him expecting the Lord to provide and him not finishing school and Elizabeth only a young and inexperienced girl who had never been away from home.

But, of course his mother didn't turn them away. She agreed they could come home but she insisted Earl find some kind of work and make a contribution to expenses, whether or not he received another Call.

It was through his mother that an old friend of the family heard of their dire circumstances and made the offer of a temporary residence. They were offered, free of charge, a cabin in the north woods along the shore of Lake Superior. Earl was greatly relieved he would not be living under his mother's and father's constant critical gaze. He took his family north.

* * * * *

Miriam was four years old when her poverty-stricken family headed to Minnesota's North Shore. There, on Lake Superior's volatile shores, she was to make her first discovery of the essential nurturing and sense of home the woods, wild and waves offer. Gale force winds alternating with mirror lake calms sustained her then as now, like the essential blood in her veins.

Earl's initial plan was to spend a week or two in prayer and supplication at this little place up by Lake Superior while he got his specific bearings about this job God probably had in mind. As soon as they got to the cabin he unpacked two boxes of theology books and a ream of notebook paper onto the only table next to the only window view in the filthy little cabin.

The only place to sit down was an old shiny green vinyl couch whose stuffing, where it was exposed, looked to have been turned into some kind of a nest for rodents. There was a bedroom with two sets of bunk beds and one bare light bulb with a dangling three-inch turn-on chain poking out of the ceiling. The beds were noticeably pee-stained from previous tenants but any odor had long since been blown fresh by lake breezes.

The place itself had been somewhat of a Godsend, so Elizabeth knew she should be grateful—should always be grateful, to even have a roof over her children's heads.

She just took out the broom and managed to sweep herself into a quiet fit of tears within the hour. Ariana, precocious and not wanting to be in the way, took her copy of whatever book she was reading and climbed to the far corner of the top bunk. She leaned out to pull the tiny light chain in her resourceful, five-year old way, and established her lake side routine for the duration.

Miriam climbed out of the car that day into the crisp, cool, sun-speckled shade which bordered what appeared to be a stage jutting out over the water. This stage, a huge platform of rocks shaped by an ancient glacier, stopped and dropped steeply into an endless, foaming, smashing, blue-green lake the size of an ocean. Not able to take her eyes from the sight before her, she absently lifted the skirt of her cotton dress, that kind with the big tie-bow in the back, pulled her panties down, and peed on the base of a huge tree.

Having spent the first few years of her life mostly in the care of the harmless yet heathen Mrs. Brook, or one of her two sets of Grandma/Grandpa's, she now found it easy to make herself scarce where her family was concerned. She couldn't help but notice they didn't like her around much. It seemed to her that if her dad noticed her at all, he noticed she needed punishment of one sort or another. She sensed both he and her mother tried to hide or shush her as often as possible. So she just developed a knack for hiding or disappearing when she thought she could get away with it.

The little Miriam felt such freedom there by the cold waves of Lake Superior. She felt refreshment unlike anything she'd ever experienced before. Even after dark, when it was necessary to come into the cabin, she would press her face to the open window and take great gulping breaths of the wind coming through the trees and off the lake. Sometimes there were warnings a bear had been sited. She wasn't afraid though. She was more afraid of the dangers inside the cabin than outside. In truth, she just couldn't rest easy unless she was out there in the wild — holding private witness to the secrets the waves and woods whispered and roared to her.

Often she felt like a wild flower or an animal when she would go alone to what seemed her very private and holy, holy place. That place of the high ceiling cathedral-nave where the song of the organ moans and whistles from the wind blowing off the lake consumed her hungry spirit. Sometimes, there by the lake, she would swear the gentle voice of a woman came to her riding a glistening wave to shore. The woman talked to her of embrace, safety and treasuring.

She could almost see her kind face in the water where the river meets the lake and ripples black, gold and silver and the sun makes transparent stained glass window colors through the leaves of the trees. Sometimes she imagined God urging the bears, the deer, the wolves and the coyote to stop their instinctual pursuits to watch her, their fellow-animal dance. She imagined their smiles. Maybe they even cried for joy to see her find this place God made especially for her. As summer turned to fall she had the supreme pleasure of living, briefly, among the changing colors of her cathedral on the shore.

Just in time for winter Earl was offered a position at a developing church in Maple Grove, Michigan and Miriam started kindergarten in a red brick schoolhouse near the treeless parsonage by the Calvary Baptist Church. The vacant lot next door to their house had a single weeping willow tree circled by a patch of deep green grass. She took every available chance to lie on her back in that soft grass and look at the sky through the shade of the weeping willow leaves. It wasn't her lake. It wasn't her cathedral or her rippling river, but it was the closest she would come to sanctuary for some time. The gentle voice of rescue was silent for now.

Over the years, the scrawny, rash-bitten baby Miriam grew to noticeable beauty. Hers was a dangerous beauty, though — a beauty that shamed her parents. A beauty she wasn't supposed to know existed because of the grave dangers of pride and vanity.

The family went less and less often to the Lake. She began, increasingly, to be seen only for her beauty and rebellious spirit and to receive punishment for these sins.

Chapter Four

Miriam sat on her knees, elbows bent, small hands, one on each cheek, supporting her head. She was six years old. It was a bleak winter day in the Blackwell family's yellow, pre-fab house in suburban Lansing, Michigan, where Earl was pastor of a church in a basement with no building on its foundation. She sat on the shiny green vinyl sofa, looking out the picture window, watching for the rusted blue Ford station wagon to turn onto Swift Road. Her mother sat next to her on the couch. She didn't look out the window like Miriam. She looked down at her feet and faced into the room. She held a tear-drenched handkerchief to her face. The black and silent phone on the stand between the wall and the end of the sofa was her sole focus. She looked past it to the white and black specks in the pattern of the linoleum tiles of the living room floor.

Miriam's mom was worried sick about her husband. Miriam, therefore, was worried sick about her mom.

Her dad left home that morning to fly a single engine Cessna up North to check on some land the church was thinking of buying for a summer camp for kids. He borrowed the small plane from a parishioner who ran a nearby airstrip. He was supposed to be home hours ago. Elizabeth called the airports up north and out on Highway 20 as well as the guy Earl borrowed the plane from but nobody knew where he was. They told her he hadn't filed a flight plan so they couldn't tell her a thing.

"He'll turn up ma'am. You just wait and see." One guy told her not to get her "undies in a bunch" which Miriam thought sounded silly and funny but it made her mother burst into hot, fresh tears.

That's when she turned around to start keeping watch out the picture window. She felt hungry, cold and afraid. Her Mom hadn't moved from the couch, so she hadn't fixed lunch and there were no cooking smells to warm the gray atmosphere of the living room. She felt her mom's fear all through her. "Mommy hates it anyway, that Daddy is so stubborn about being such a fly boy," she thought as she watched car after car pass by on the street outside the window.

Elizabeth hated flying. It scared her. Those little tiny planes way up there among all the huge, jet propelled ones and with such thin walls they shook and felt like they were going to rip wide open with every move of the throttle. Though she rarely refused him anything, believing it her duty to obey her husband, she refused to fly with Earl anymore and had hoped her refusal would make him decide it wasn't worth it to cause her such fear. He only did it, she thought, to satisfy some adventurous whim he'd had ever since she'd known him. He'd learned to fly in the air force but didn't qualify to be a fighter pilot because of his bad eyesight. He didn't get to be a hero and go overseas to fight a war either — another issue he had with his birth mother's sense of timing. His untimely birth meant he was too late to fight the big war and by the time Korea came around he was entrenched in his life as a minister, husband and father.

"What does that man expect me to do if he goes off and gets himself killed?" Elizabeth cried into her hanky. What was she supposed to do with two little kids and no home to call her own, she wondered.

Their home was a parsonage provided by the church. Elizabeth had never worked a day in her life. There was no insurance, but her husband continued to dismiss her fears as childish and foolish, then insist on flying somewhere it's just as easy to drive to. And what's worse—to not even bother filing a flight plan. If she wasn't sure he had crashed and was dead already she'd want to kill him for putting her through this.

Elizabeth was dependent on this fly-boy, body and soul, ever since she was sixteen years old. She loved him madly and unreservedly and didn't even usually mind that he didn't listen to her opinion on things. But, this one thing… Why couldn't he compromise on this one thing and give up flying at least until they could afford a house or insurance in case something awful should happen?

Miriam prayed all to herself and into the hands in front of her face. Her dad had beaten her with the belt last night before bed because she didn't scrub the ring off the bathtub. She left puddles on the floor when she got out of her bath—oh, and left her wet towel all wadded up on the back of the toilet too, and "who do you expect to clean up your messes, anyway, young lady?" He guessed he'd have to teach her a lesson about being considerate. After the beating, she cried herself to sleep. When she got up that morning her dad was already gone and what if he was dead and here she had been so naughty and would never have a chance to make it up to him.

The sky had not changed color even slightly all day long. It was a white, unbroken shade of gray — the same white as the old snow that was just beginning to melt. As it melted it revealed patches of black mud in the yard that her parents hadn't time to seed for grass before winter came in that year. She sat there, watching for Daddy, feeling terror for Mommy and shouldering a heavy sense of guilt. She thought about the "Father Knows Best" TV program she watched before her bath the night before. Watched it before the beating. She thought about Bud and Kathy and how, when their dad came home from work every day, they just couldn't wait to see him. They would run to the door, Kathy in the lead—because she was littlest and cutest. Kathy would leap into her father's arms and he'd give her a big bounce and smile right into "Puddin's" face—he called Kathy "Puddin". She'd wrap her fat little arms around his neck so tight and squeeze his head and he'd just smile all the harder. Miriam could tell Bud would have loved to jump into his dad's other arm or jump on him piggy-back style to be carried into the living room. But Bud was a boy and he was too big for that. She could just tell he wanted to, though, and Father would have loved it too if he did. There in the living room all three of them would fall in a soft heap on the sofa and they'd catch each other up on their day apart. They always seemed to actually be excited or concerned about each other's success or disappointments.

She must have closed her eyes picturing this perfect family dream, thinking about how, if her Daddy ever did come home, she would be different. If she could be more like Kathy Anderson then her daddy would be just like Puddin's daddy, Jim Anderson . . .

Miriam jumped when she heard a car door shut out in the driveway. Her Mama didn't move. Just sat there paralyzed or in some kind of fear-filled daze. She saw her chance. Miriam would make everything all better.

She climbed down from the couch and went to stand in the doorway between the dining room and kitchen so she'd be ready as soon as her daddy came through the door.

She saw the door handle turn and took off at a dead and smiling run. She jumped, arms stretched out, expecting her daddy's arms to reach out and swing her to him the way Kathy's daddy's arms did on the TV last night. Her jump caused the top of her head to smack right into her dad's glasses and send them all crooked on his nose. She fell "slap" on the kitchen floor as she heard Daddy's first, fully alive, angry, loud — not dead in a plane crash — words.

"Oh nuts! What are you trying to pull now, Miriam? Get out of here. Now! Go to your room. I'll deal with you later. As if I haven't got enough to put up with, I have to walk into a house where you're just waiting to break my glasses. As if I'm made of money and can afford new ones."

She stared up at him from where her fall landed her on the floor. Unbelieving. Confused. Did he mean it? He was really mad and she had to go to her room and couldn't even tell him about how she prayed he was alright and that she wasn't going to be naughty anymore and was going to make him proud and happy?

Her father walked on through to the living room where her mom was still staring at the specks in the floor tiles. She watched the back of him as she slunk off to her room to try to figure out what she'd done wrong and how to fix it.

Once in her room she walked past her bed and dresser, past her toy box and shelf of books and paper dolls and games. She bent to pick up her doll, Milly, from her cardboard box bed. She took her into the closet with her and pulled the door shut behind them. She held Milly extra close and cuddled them both into the extra blankets that were piled under the hanging dresses, blouses and jackets in the dark closet. She'd been so sure her plan would work and her house could feel just like the house on "Father Knows Best." Now she was thinking really bad thoughts. She couldn't help it. Except for how worried she was about her mommy and how sad she would be if her daddy hadn't come home, she really thought life would be a lot easier and happier if he hadn't come home. She knew this was a very, very bad thing to be thinking. She decided to sing a Jesus song. She hoped singing about the wonderful Jesus would take away her bad thoughts.

"Jesus loves the little children," she sang in a whisper, "All the children of the world . . ." She tucked her knees up under her stomach and knelt forward with her forearms on the floor and bent her head to her prayerfully clasped hands. Milly was crunched right up to her between her stomach and her knees as she crouched on the closet floor. She told Jesus she was sorry again and please could she not die and could she please not go to hell?

After a while she was done praying and sat stroking Milly's soft curly blond hair and she felt quite a lot better. She started to get hungry and wondered if Ariana was in the living room watching the Mickey Mouse Club without her. She opened the closet door and went to see where everybody was.

Her daddy read the newspaper like it was any other day—the lamp making a yellow triangle around the shape of him sitting in his chair. He looked lit up like Jesus in the picture in the dining room. Guilt for wishing he wouldn't have come home made her shiver as she looked at him in his Jesus light. Ariana was lying on her stomach on the floor in front of the TV set. She could smell good food smells coming from the kitchen and could see her mommy opening the oven door to pull out the Spanish rice casserole.

She went to the kitchen and put her arm around her mommy's legs and pressed her face real quick against the fresh outdoor smell of her cotton skirt. Elizabeth reached down and touched Miriam's hair and she felt relieved that everything would be all right and her mommy still loved her.

"Go get washed for dinner now, Princess. It's almost ready and you know Daddy hates it when you come late to supper."

* * * * *

The falling ice cream bowls sounded like the triangle, cymbals and tambourine her teacher gave them to make music with at school, as they tumbled from her hands and hit the bare asbestos floor in the dining room. Glass broke and shattered every which way under the picture of Jesus in his triangle of golden light. She and her dad, mom and sister were having ice cream in the living room the night her dad's plane hadn't crashed.

No one said anything when she dropped the bowls. No one

dared speak. She felt the fear and awkwardness in the room. It was like how totally quiet the world gets just before a heavy summer storm. She had quietly gotten up off the floor where, always on these ice cream occasions, she sat stirring her ice cream into a "milkshake" with her legs pointed out backwards from her knees. She had wanted to help somehow, wanted to feel a part of something. One by one, she picked up her family's empty ice cream dishes and stacked them in her arms. As she reached the far side of the dining room, just past the oak table, it happened. There was a bright blue toy dump truck she'd been playing with earlier in the day. Daddy had already yelled at her once to put it away. As the bowls crashed and splintered around her bare feet she stood paralyzed. She held her hands pressed against her mouth to stifle the cry that was beginning to rumble up from deep inside her. She heard her father's loud steps. He grabbed her hand away from her mouth and yanked her by the arm, squeezing her wrist painfully in his hand that was covered with rough black hairs.

His voice, "Now look what you've done young lady. As if I need anymore trouble from you. Now you'll get what you've been working toward all day."

Earl grasped her arm by the wrist and pulled her toward her bedroom. She caught a glimpse of Ariana, her legs curled under her skirt at the far corner of the couch, her face close to the book she was reading. Whatever feelings or awareness she had, disguised in a posture of intense childhood studiousness.

Once in the bedroom Miriam's father gave her a shove, his hand at her back, that reeled her across the room and landed her face down on the bed. The floor was covered with toys and he fumbled and slipped as he unbuckled his brown leather belt. Furious and screaming at her with every breath he took, he jerked the belt fast as it came out of its loops making a cracking sound like a horse whip. He folded it in half, end to end and held it by the buckle and the tip. She garnered all her strength and courage and squirmed as fast as she could, whimpering and sobbing to a sitting position in the far corner of the bed and up against the wall. She thought if she could get her bottom and her legs under her and somehow hide her bare arms he might not be able to find a good spot to hit. He lunged at her trying to grab an arm or a leg out from under her and bring her closer. She held on to the knob at the top of the bedpost with one fierce little Herculean hand

"Daddy, no . . . I'm sorry, Daddy. I didn't mean to . . . No, Daddy, please don't give me the — no, Daddy, no . . ." He jerked her loose from her hold on the bed and brought her, backside up, head and face almost hitting his knees to a stretched out position across the bed. "Thwack." The belt hit her bare legs just above the back of her knees where the tender skin burned and stung from the impact. She put her hands behind her and tried to cover the entire length of her legs and bottom but the belt came down a second time catching her across her fingers, and raising another welt where her hands couldn't protect her. She pulled her hands in close under her tummy and braced herself. She couldn't get her breath to cry and had quit yelling her pleas for mercy.

"Where is Mommy? Where is my Mommy?" her brain screamed. She started to count. He wouldn't hit her more than ten times, would he? If she could just hold still, hold her breath and pretend she was somewhere far, far away until she could count to ten, maybe he'd quit and she'd be okay.

She left then — sort of drifted somewhere away from the body that her daddy was beating. She lost count of how many times he hit her. She came back into her bare-legged, bare-footed, bruised and torn body when he yelled at her to get her rear end out there and help her mother clean up the mess.

She felt weak, angry, bitter and alone, in her attempt to help her mom clean up after the disaster that left spilled ice cream and broken shards of the white glass bowl all over the floor right under Jesus whose eyes she could feel on her. It took her a minute to realize that the red circles making polka dots on the chocolate soup and bowl shard mixture were raining down from her bleeding thumb. It made her ashamed. She was just adding to the mess. She wished she could disappear. Had Mommy noticed yet? The faster she tried to mop up the blood drops the more they appeared. She stopped and looked up at her mother who, it was clear, had just that moment realized she was bleeding.

She knelt down and turned Miriam to her so she could examine the jagged cut that went nearly to the bone in her right hand. "You've cut yourself pretty bad haven't you? Come on with me. Let's go get you cleaned up."

Her mother's hand holding hers felt warm and the skin was its own mother-safe kind of rough from the housework she did.

She loved it when her mother touched her even though she never came to her rescue before or during the beatings, or came to hold her in her arms and comfort her. Still, she was not unkind to Miriam at these times and that meant a lot. Meant the only comfort she knew in those desert places away from the woods and shore.

The lack of cruelty from her mom and the ministrations of gentle cut-washing and bandaging filled her with hope and the belief that she was loved. She thought her mom was probably scared that Daddy would hurt her too if she interfered in any way. Really, her mother was playing the same guessing game as she about what would send her husband into another rage against her little girl. It was an exhausting effort and took any energy she might have otherwise used to stand up to her husband and tell him what he was doing to their daughter was cruel, wrong and monstrous. Besides, she trusted him to know better than she how to properly discipline the children. She thought he was probably right that this spirited and strong-willed little girl's rebelliousness should be broken to avoid her behavior threatening his ministry and livelihood. "How can he lead a church to obedience when he can't make his own child obey"? He often quoted Scripture in support of his brutality and the Word of God lent considerable credibility.

After she bandaged Miriam's hand, Elizabeth didn't make her go back to clean up the dining room. She walked her to her bedroom, her hand resting on her back to guide her. She sat down on the bed and turned her little girl to face her and helped her take her dress off over her head. She pulled her PJ's from under the pillow and helped her into them. Miriam climbed gratefully between the sheets. Mommy tucked the blankets up close under her chin. She put her hand on Miriam's forehead, brushing the soft, nearly black bangs from her face and placed a goodnight kiss just above her eyebrows.

"Don't forget to say your prayers, Princess." She turned off the light and closed the door behind her.

Though Miriam was usually afraid of the dark; tonight she was more afraid of the light outside her room — the light where her father sat, reading his paper, waiting, resting up, for the next requirement fatherhood would make of him.

Her curtains were open to the night sky. Her doll Milly was there in bed with her. She held her close and talked to her. She could see a sparkle of white gleaming stars in the early evening sky.

Their glow lifted her spirits until she remembered that Jesus was out there too and would be looking at her and wondering why she hadn't prayed to him yet, like her mom said to, to ask his forgiveness.

She put her head under the covers and crawled way under the sheet and blanket and sat up forming a little tent for herself. She didn't think she should have to ask for forgiveness tonight. It wasn't her fault. She had tried so hard to be nice and to help.

She sat in her blanket tent and told Milly, "No, no, I won't say I'm sorry. I won't. I won't. I won't. I'm going to run away, Milly. I really am. First chance I get. What? Oh no, I won't leave you sweetie. I'll take you with me and we'll always be together no matter what."

When she heard Ariana coming into the room and preparing for bed she curled up on her side and pretended sleep until, with exhausted resignation, she fell asleep in the warm embrace of Milly in their own private blanket-tent.

She dreamed that night that she was a huge and graceful white-winged bird. She soared and swooped over sun-drenched beaches, dived nose first into the white caps of the peaks of ocean waves and rose again, nose in the sky and laughing as she soared toward the warmth of the sun. She flew over tree lined neighborhoods where children rode their two-wheelers, skated on sidewalks and ran through lawn sprinklers giggling and squealing their mingled joy and distress. She alighted on the back of a gleaming mahogany stallion gliding wind-like, over and through country lanes and pastures. The air around her smelled of summer. The dry earth scent mingled with the briny, intoxicating fragrance of oceans, lakes and rivers. Summer was hers. She soared high above it all and admired her possession. She swooped low and brushed and caressed it in its every detail.

The dream shifted and she became a small child sleeping in the tall grass of a lakeside meadow. She felt scratchy, prickly and hot and couldn't adjust her body to avoid the pounding heat of the sun or the pierce of small rocks against her legs and side as she lay curled, baby-like and alone in the grass. The sun was so bright she couldn't open her eyes without a stinging pain shooting them instantly full of tears. She reached out a hand and something rough, jagged and leathery moved under her touch. She sprang to a sitting position and found herself surrounded by gaping mouthed alligators. She tried to scream but found she had no voice. Her legs folded under her like cotton filled tubes as she tried to lift them to run. Her legs finally found their strength and she stepped on the green-black backs and heads of the creatures whose mouths were red with blood. She woke sweating and screaming "Mommy, Mommy . . . Mommy!" with every ounce of strength she could muster.

"Shhhh. Shhh. Princess. It's all right. It's all right. I'm here now." Her mommy stroked her shaken daughter's head and climbed into bed beside her, cradling her body against her own. She had no idea what possible explanation there could be for this little girl's extreme fright in her own home and bed. Her screams defied description. Bone chilling came close. Her mother fell asleep cradling her tiny daughter and hoping Earl would let this one go and not seek retaliation against Miriam for yet another night's interrupted sleep.

Chapter Five

Uncle Jack's limp and muscular body — he had been a weight lifter in prison — pulled heavily on the glistening silver chain of the child's swing that held him by his lifeless neck. He hadn't meant to die. Just meant to "get the goat," of his young wife, Miriam's Aunt Ellen. Wanted only to worry her somehow — call attention to his need for her. Would he have cared — would it have stopped him from his childish and deadly act of defiance had he known his niece, Miriam — his niece to whom he was a hero and a star — was the child, running eagerly to the park to play in the early morning summer sunshine, who found him useless, spent and gone forever? Would he have cared that he ruined for her forever, the sight, the feel, the soaring and lifting heaven, of a ride on a swing?

It was June 1955 and her Uncle Jack's suicide was a devastating loss to her. She was nearly six years old and had learned to live much of her waking life in the world of fantasy and daydreams. Even at her tender age she had absorbed enough of the Cinderella and the handsome prince myth to fuel a belief that, if you could just manage to hold on tight and stay alive until you were grown-up and beautiful, a handsome man would love you and marry you. You would never have to go home again if you didn't want to and the strong, handsome prince would protect you and wouldn't ever let anyone hurt you again.

Miriam's Uncle Jack was her Aunt Ellen's handsome prince. Aunt Ellen was in high school when Miriam was real little. She met Jack when he joined her church after turning over a new leaf upon release from prison for petty theft and vandalism. Aunt Ellen married Uncle Jack right after she graduated from high school.

Miriam had watched in awe as her Aunt Ellen prepared for the wedding. She was as real a princess to Miriam as Cinderella was in her picture books. She got to dress like a princess herself so she could walk down the aisle tossing pale yellow rose buds from a white basket with an ivory bow on top. She memorized every detail of Aunt Ellen's fairy tale wedding. The prince was tall and tan. His near black eyes sparkled and his teeth shone white against his skin.

Flowers and candles were everywhere. The music in the church was so romantic. An angel-voiced friend of Aunt Ellen's, Kate was her name, sang "I Love You Truly." Even Daddy sang a song for his sister. His voice sounded so sweet when he sang that Miriam was able to keep from feeling afraid of him on that made-in-heaven day.

Oh, and the kiss! When Uncle Jack took Aunt Ellen in his arms and they pressed themselves close together and closed their eyes . . . she tried hard to imagine what that would feel like. She closed her own eyes and moved her lips around the way she imagined Aunt Ellen's lips moving against Uncle Jack's. Her eyes were surprised open by the trumpet and piano serenading the new husband and wife in their march from the church. She pushed angel-voiced Kate, the maid of honor, out of her way to get a view of the back of them. The train of Aunt Ellen's gown swished in harmony with the music as she leaned on her Prince's arm and grinned her way to the vestibule.

After the wedding and a reception that resembled a Prince's Ball, the happy couple drove away in Uncle Jack's two-toned, red and white Renault convertible and headed for their honeymoon paradise in the Pocono Mountains. Aunt Ellen confided in Miriam that their very own cabin had a giant, heart-shaped bathtub and just oodles and oodles of bubble bath fit for a princess's luxurious soak. All that night Miriam lay awake in Aunt Ellen's bed remembering the wonder and magic of the day and dreaming of the day her handsome prince would come to carry her away to happily ever after.

It surprised her, when they visited again at Thanksgiving, to find her Uncle Jack and Aunt Ellen living in the same house with Grandma and Grandpa Blackwell. Aunt Ellen even had her same bedroom and still argued all the time with Grandma. Grandma still did all the cooking and cleaning. Aunt Ellen had a job now and every day after work she would bring a girl friend home to have supper with the family and just expect Uncle Jack and Grandma and Grandpa and everybody to adjust. Life didn't look like a fairy-tale marriage had changed it much for Aunt Ellen. Miriam had imagined they would have a cute little house of their own and that, when she came to visit, she would see a lot of kissing and cuddling and Aunt Ellen and Uncle Jack holding hands and smiling a lot.

Still, her Aunt and Uncle were a lot of fun to be with. They took her to the toy store and let her pick out anything she wanted. She wanted a turn of the century farm set with its own barn, fence and pioneer family figures she could play with to create the imaginary life of her ancestors. Milly needed some new outfits so Miriam could dress her up like a pioneer baby. Aunt Ellen spared no expense in making Miriam's toy store dreams come true. They took her to Kiddy-Land and let her ride the kid-sized roller coaster as many times as she wanted. The giant swirling teacups were her favorite carnival ride. They bought her chocolate milkshakes she didn't have to share with anybody. They gave her quarters and told her which buttons to push on the juke box so she could hear songs like "Blue Moon" and "Love me Tender" and some by the Everly Brothers too.

One thing that turned out to be an advantage of the happy couple not wanting much privacy for mushy stuff was that she still got to sleep with Aunt Ellen sometimes when she visited. Then Uncle Jack slept in the bedroom that used to be her daddy's. Turned out he was used to sleeping there because Aunt Ellen still invited her girl friends over to stay the night some times, just like when she was in high school. Uncle Jack slept in Daddy's old bedroom when that happened. Since Aunt Ellen had always had her girlfriends around a lot, Miriam didn't think much about it being unusual now that she was married. She guessed she really hadn't expected the girlfriends would always be there whenever her Aunt and Uncle did something together or took Ariana and her out to do fun things, though.

When she and her family saw them at Christmas that year everything was as it had been at Thanksgiving but her Aunt and Uncle were talking about trying to adopt a baby. She was never told the reason they didn't or couldn't have their own baby but she wondered about it and created imagined mysteries in her head to explain everything that puzzled her. She didn't know the specifics about where babies come from but she did know her own mother's stomach was huge right then and it was because she was carrying a baby who would be born soon. She knew this meant her mommy was going to give birth to a baby and that was different from adopting where you get your baby from someone else. She wondered if having babies had anything to do with people who are married sleeping in the same bed — something about "sleeping together." She thought probably if Aunt Ellen and Uncle Jack would sleep in the same bed maybe they could make their own baby. But maybe they thought it would be nicer to have a baby right away without having to carry one around in your own tummy for what seemed, from watching her mother, like an awfully long time. She asked Aunt Ellen why she wanted to adopt a baby that was somebody else's and didn't that other person want the baby from her own tummy but her answer was that Miriam wouldn't understand until she was older.

When Miriam got home after the Christmas visit she asked her mom some of the same questions and it didn't seem like she knew any answers either. She overheard her mom and dad talking about Aunt Ellen and Uncle Jack and it turns out they thought it odd that so many girlfriends were still around and that the happy couple didn't seem to cuddle or laugh or sleep together or anything. There was talk about how they thought it would be better for the marriage and for Grandma and Grandpa, too, if Jack and Ellen got their own place. Maybe they would when their baby came. "Oh well" — seemed to be the conclusion her parents reached.

It seemed a long time until she heard that the new baby had come to live with everyone at Grandma's house. They named the little girl Linda. They didn't get their own place because who would take care of the baby if they didn't live in Grandma's house. Miriam had a new little sister by this time and in the summer the whole family took a car trip to show off Stephanie — Miriam called her Steve — and to meet Linda.

Aunt Ellen and Uncle Jack were still at their jobs when they arrived at Grandma and Grandpa's house. Grandma brought the little pink bundle named Linda from the bassinet in the dining room and laid her down next to the little yellow bundle named Steve on the gray wool brocade arm chair in the living room. Miriam's mom and grandma snapped pictures with their Brownie cameras of the two babies side by side and about the same age and size. By the time her Aunt Ellen and Uncle Jack got home from work both the babies had been given their bottles and put to bed.

Aunt Ellen and Uncle Jack came in and gave all the relatives big hugs. Aunt Ellen asked Miriam what she thought of her cousin Linda. "Isn't she the cutest?" she said, and then started tickling Miriam and rolling her around on the floor, playing with her just like old times.

Grandma said that supper was ready so go get your hands washed and stop your "wrastling" around before you wake up the babies, and get yourselves to the table. Aunt Ellen made a face that Grandma couldn't see, a funny face with her tongue sticking out and Miriam laughed. They both jumped up and raced up the stairs to the bathroom to wash their hands.

At dinner her Aunt Ellen said, "Kate's coming over after supper to go to youth night with Jack and me. We'll probably go out for ice cream later so don't wait up for us."

Uncle Jack said, "Ellen, I thought we agreed it was just going to be you and me tonight and we would come home early to have some time with our new baby."

"I changed my mind, though. What was I supposed to do? Kate called and asked if we were going. I couldn't just tell her we wanted to be alone. How would she feel? She is my best friend you know Jack. You and I can be together anytime."

Jack looked down at his plate and squeezed his lips together real hard and breathed kind of heavy through his nostrils that got bigger when he did that. His fists were clenched on either side of his plate. "Fine. Sure Ellen. Whatever you say." He pushed himself away from the table and Miriam could hear him walking back and forth on the front porch while the family ate in silence.

Miriam sat on her grandpa Blackwell's lap in his chair while he brushed her hair after supper. She was starting to feel pretty confused in her daydreams about growing up and getting married and having her own babies. When she dreamed of her future it wasn't like what she saw happening between her Aunt and Uncle. It was still like in the storybooks about Cinderella or Snow White or Rapunzel and their handsome princes.

She sat day dreaming as Grandpa brushed her hair. In her daydreams her handsome prince was her best friend. He was her hero and her rescuer. They would laugh and play together with their cuddly little babies in their very own house in the forest by the water.

She jumped off Grandpa's lap and went to look at the pudgy

and peaceful faces of her brand new cousin named Linda and her baby sister, Steve.

Later that night, Grandma helped her into a bubble bath in the old footed tub she loved. She played house with her toy dishes and Milly. Milly was her little baby and she talked to her and sang to her while she fixed an extra fancy supper for the baby's daddy. He would come home from work and take Miriam in his arms like Uncle Jack did with Aunt Ellen on their wedding day. He would say, "I love you and Milly so much, Cinderella. What's for supper? Let's eat!"

Her mom tucked her in that night next to Ariana. They slept on the floor wrapped in sheets and blankets in their daddy's old room where Mommy and Daddy would share the single bed. Steve was in the corner of the room in her red plaid car bed.

Miriam hadn't been awake to see her aunt and uncle come home but she figured they must be sleeping in their room together now, since she didn't see Uncle Jack on the couch. Their bedroom door was closed when she got up just after sunlight. No one was up yet. She tried to be super quiet. It was summer and hot outside even in the early morning. She picked up Milly and tiptoed down the stairs and out the back door of the house.

The park was just down the street and around one corner and she knew she shouldn't go alone but she felt big and brave and she planned to be home by the time the rest of the family woke up. It was a beautiful, sunshiny morning and she and Milly couldn't wait for those lazy bum grownups before going for a ride on the swings.

When she found her Uncle Jack on the swing set she couldn't move her legs or cry out or anything for awhile. It was like in those dreams where her legs were limp and useless and her voice wouldn't make a sound when she tried to scream. When she was finally able to move, it was more of a fall that left her lying there in the dry dirt on the playground with Milly next to her just out of reach of her outstretched hand. Her Aunt Ellen and Mommy and Daddy had come looking for her when they found she wasn't anywhere in the house. They found her there in the park with her Uncle Jack.

* * * * *

Miriam's family had to extend vacation that summer because of Uncle Jack's death. She and her sisters were rushed off to

Grandma and Grandpa Barrett's across town from the Blackwell's. There were so many questions she wanted to ask but no one seemed to have time for answers. It had been really scary to see Uncle Jack hanging there in the park. She wondered who would take him down. Her mom said the police were taking care of "things," whatever that meant. She didn't get to talk to Mommy or Aunt Ellen or anybody until a few nights after she found her dead uncle. Her Grandma Barrett helped her get dressed up and fixed her hair and Mommy and Daddy picked her and Ariana up to take them to the funeral home to see Uncle Jack.

The building was white and had pillars all across the front like she'd seen in pictures of some other country. It looked sort of like a church but not exactly. There were candles just like at Aunt Ellen and Uncle Jack's wedding and soft, sad music could be heard through speakers in the ceiling. She had never seen so many flowers in all her life even at the Botanical Gardens and she couldn't understand why, with all those flowers there was a scent so piercing and sweet she could hardly breath. It was that overwhelming sticky, sweet odor, worse even than hot cotton candy, the smell of which always made her wretch and feel tight in the throat. Her mom said it was just the smell of so many different kinds of flowers with all their different scents in one room. Miriam has never before or since smelled anything like that except where death is involved.

She knew it would be rude to hold her nose so she just put the skirt of her dress up against her face and breathed into it whenever she felt no one was looking. She looked beyond all the people gathered in the doorway and saw Uncle Jack lying down in a polished mahogany casket with flowers under it, next to it and behind it on a table. She walked the aisle between the chairs that led to Uncle Jack. He was all dressed up just like for his wedding. He looked like a sleeping prince. She wished so much that Cinderella would come and give him a magic kiss to wake him up and put everything back the way it was supposed to be.

Earlier that day she'd heard Mommy and Daddy talking about Linda's adoption papers not having been signed yet, and that with Jack dead, Aunt Ellen would not get to keep her new baby and how that would probably just about kill Grandma to lose that little girl. Miriam felt sad and very small. She crawled behind the flowers at the base of the casket and sat underneath Uncle Jack until she could quit crying. In a while the room began to fill with people walking past Uncle Jack and mostly saying nice things to him about how much they would miss him and how they would pray for his soul's salvation. Some people seemed really mad at him. Aunt Ellen stayed in the foyer and wouldn't come close to the casket at all. After everyone had said goodbye to Uncle Jack, she heard her mother calling her name. She came out from under the casket and ran to bury her face in her mother's skirt. Her mom patted her head.

"Come on honey," she said, "we're all going over to the church for a supper the Ladies Aid is making for our family and the other people who knew Uncle Jack".

"Mama, please can't we just go back to Grandma and Grandpa Barrett's? It's too sad here and, anyway, I'm not hungry."

Her mom and dad dropped her back at the Barrett's but Ariana went ahead to the church for supper. The next day was the funeral and after the service they would all go to the cemetery and put Uncle Jack's casket under the ground. Miriam didn't think she could stand to be around to watch something so sad as that. She would try to talk her mom into letting her stay home and play.

She and her baby sister were allowed to stay with Grandpa Barrett while everyone else went to the funeral. Everyone said the baby was too little and, if Miriam would rather not come, maybe she could help Grandpa with Stephanie. Anyway, they conceded she would probably just be in the way and wouldn't know what was happening anyway. Everyone on both sides of the family was going, but Grandpa Barrett said he didn't know Jack that well and he would be happy to stay with Steve and Miriam if they wanted to drop them off at his house.

* * * * *

Grandpa and Grandma Barrett were Elizabeth's parents. Elizabeth Barrett Blackwell was born to George and Anna Mae Barrett in 1932 while the nation struggled in the throws of the Great Depression. She was their first-born in a marriage that was quite new. Circumstances were pretty bad for most people and Elizabeth never remembered feeling particularly or uniquely deprived as a child. She did remember wishing her parents would stop their constant bickering and fighting. She wished her Dad wouldn't make her Mom cry.

She had no memory of her Dad drinking and running around with other women but remembered her Mother's cries and screams and accusations. She remembered being sent to spy on him, whatever that meant.

Elizabeth only and always wanted to make everything better. In her family, her neighborhood, at school and ultimately for her country and the world. She was a good girl. She was tall and thin and pretty. She was bright and quick and funny and kind. She seldom had a grade below A level at any time in her schooling. She dreamed of one day becoming a nurse. She loved to hear and tell stories. If her Dad was a bounder and a player it wasn't apparent to her. What was apparent was his love for music, song, and stories. He was a handsome and strong man. Did he belittle her mother? Was he unfair to her or was her mother really all those things he said she was? A weak, sniveling, nag and a fishwife? Her mother was so often crying, tired and unhappy that Elizabeth found it hard to be around her. Found it hard to see her more endearing qualities.

Her mother took too many opportunities to tell Elizabeth with great embellishment and self-pity (at least that's how Elizabeth saw it) about her hard childhood. Her mother's dad, Elizabeth's great grandpa, had been a coal miner who drank too much and beat his wife and his daughters, sparing only his sons from his wrath.

Cowering, sniveling and fearfulness seemed qualities honestly come-by among the women in Elizabeth's family genealogy.

Anna Mae told her daughter Elizabeth all about her harsh treatment in school where her knuckles were beaten daily because she could not help using her left hand rather than her right. Grandma Barrett dropped out of school after the eighth grade having never mastered reading or writing — skills which came so easily to Elizabeth that she felt her mother to be quite stupid and unworthy of much respect.

As most children do, though, Elizabeth absorbed the trials and shortcomings and even the finer qualities of her parents and her home life, for the most part, on a subconscious level. Elizabeth was an active and energetic child surrounded by aunts and uncles who lived nearby with their hoards of children. These cousins were playmates for Elizabeth.

Elizabeth avoided home and hearth to a large extent and filled her days with adventures with friends and cousins. She was accepted proudly among her all-boy cousins as one of the few girls whose company they would tolerate. She had a brother, Elmer, four years her junior, who she teased, taunted, tortured and generally looked after. She had a sister, Susan, the same age as Aunt Ellen. She and Aunt Ellen were friends and went to the same church and to high school together.

Aunt Susan wasn't married yet, like Aunt Ellen, and Miriam liked to look at her sketchbook and lie on her stomach on her bedroom floor under the eaves listening to her collection of 45 rpm rock and roll records. Aunt Susan went out on lots of dates and wasn't often home when Miriam was there visiting. She liked to daydream about the dates Susan went on with all the good-looking boys she knew. Maybe, Miriam thought, Aunt Susan will fall in love and get married and things will work out better than they have for Aunt Ellen and Uncle Jack. She was no where near ready to give up her fantasies of married love and romance.

Miriam's mother's parents, Grandma and Grandpa Barrett lived in a house with a front porch that had a glider couch on it. The front yard was long and narrow and bordered on one side by trees and brush that seemed like a deep and enticing forest to her. She would play there for hours dreaming herself back to the forest by Lake Superior.

There was a hedge as tall as she was that Grandpa kept well trimmed. It separated the front yard from the street and on summer nights Grandpa would show her and the other children how to catch lightening bugs, which were especially abundant out by the hedge.

Inside the house there was a four-foot square heat vent between the living room and dining room with the bathroom on one side and the cellar door on the other. She loved to stand on the vent when the fan was blowing the heat up from the basement furnace and let it blow her skirt into a big bubble all around her as it warmed her legs with its blast of hot air.

The kitchen was at the back of the house and had a door that closed against the noise of the rest of the house. Grandpa spent a lot of time in there with the door closed after he came home from work at night and before work in the mornings. At night, before bed, he would have graham crackers soaked in a bowl of warm milk. In the morning, before work, he ate Wheaties — the breakfast of champions. When he wasn't in the kitchen he would sit in his lazy-boy chair and smoke his pipe and read a book or magazine.

He was quite the reader and passed his love of reading on to his daughter, Elizabeth. He especially loved history and seemed particularly interested in who and where his birth parents might be. His adoptive parents had taken him from an orphanage when he was already twelve years old and made it clear they only wanted him because they needed help with the work on the family farm. He was a lonely boy who gained friends and comfort through making up stories and songs. Miriam used to pretend her toy farm was the home where her grandpa lived and worked as a boy. She tried to imagine a better life for him than the one he really had.

The day of Uncle Jack's funeral Grandpa Barrett was singing a silly song while he trimmed the front hedge and cut the grass with the rotary mower. Miriam sat on the glider on the front porch with Milly. She watched her grandpa work and thought about how sad it would be if someday her own handsome prince hung himself on a swing set.

The rocking motion of the glider made her drowsy so she went inside and lay down on her grandma and grandpa's bed in their bedroom just off the living room.

The bedroom window stood open to the summer afternoon breeze that blew Grandma Barrett's white chiffon curtains across her bare legs as she lay sleeping on the pink chintz covered double bed. It was the bedroom her grandparents had shared since her own mother was a baby. It was a small room with one window and walls that were far too pink. Pink like Pepto Bismal is pink. Inside the closed wooden door a cotton house coat, hanging from a hook, echoed the pink of the walls in its flowers and exhibited jarring yellow/green swirling leaf shapes. The robe was torn under one of its elbow length sleeves.

When Miriam went to lie down for her nap she couldn't take her eyes from the torn house coat. She watched it hang there, limp and lifeless and imagined in horror her grandma's body hanging there in the robe, just like Uncle Jack hung, fully dressed, from the chain of the swing set in the park.

One by one she imagined the people in her family hanging there on the hook of the door, the silver chain of a swing wrapped around each one's neck. Her mother, her eyes open, pale, transparent blue in their death gaze. She wore a mint green cotton house dress with buttons up the front and slash pockets with white piping trim. Her mouth hung open, but, as in life, no words spoke her horror or dismay. Next, she pictured Daddy; white shirt, black tie and his black preaching suit. His black oiled hair stood in a point straight up off his forehead. She couldn't look at his eyes. His hands reached out as if to grab her.

She was afraid now and turned onto her back to face the closet door and wall at the foot of the bed, trying to shake the awful images that invaded her nap. Over the dresser — her grandma called it the "bureau" — and just to the right of its attached mirror was a picture of Jesus — a decoupage on an oval shaped circle cut from the trunk of a tree. It was that picture of Jesus where he looks right at you with the sweetest eyes and you can't help but notice his halo. His hands don't show but you know they are palms up and reaching out to you. She liked this picture of Jesus. He wasn't at all like the Jesus her daddy described who always seemed to be mad at her for one thing or another.

Lying there with the breeze on her legs and looking at Jesus, she lost herself in his sweet eyes and tried to imagine heaven. She wondered if Uncle Jack was up there right now with Jesus and was Jesus mad at him for what he did, or does he just feel sad, like she does, that the handsome prince's life is over?

* * * * *

Was it minutes or hours later she felt a chill wind cross her bare legs? Her feet were cold though she'd kept her white bobby sox on after removing her shoes and climbing into bed. The room had been warm when she lay down and she hadn't felt the need for a blanket.

Groggy with sleep and without opening her eyes she reached to pull her skirt down over her legs that were beginning to feel cold. She guessed the wind had blown her skirt away from her legs. She turned over in her near-sleep and reached, eyes closed to pull the corner of the bed spread around her.

It wouldn't come loose. Something held it in place. Someone was there on the bed next to her. Still, only half awake, she did not open her eyes. Whoever was there offered no warmth or comfort. Was it her grandpa? Her memory flashed quickly to a time she'd completely forgotten until that moment. A time when her grandpa had been alone with her and didn't seem at all like her silly, singing grandpa. She had been alone in the bathroom. He frightened her as he opened the door and it slammed against the towel rack on the wall. His face was red and his eyes blazing as he unbuckled his belt. She'd covered her face, whimpering "No."

He wasn't going to belt her like Daddy did, was he? He didn't take his belt off though and she uncovered her eyes to see him, pants unzipped, holding something brownish gray, like the body of a mouse — like a turnip just pulled from the ground, in his hand. He pushed it in her face as he whispered harshly, bending near her. "Get out of here. I have to use the toilet."

But she couldn't seem to move. She was frozen there. She doesn't remember leaving the bathroom. Doesn't remember anything after that. Just a tear-filled, hot, sticky, exposed sort of shame that made her want to throw up even as she remembered.

She tried to tell herself it was just her imagination. She feared something but wasn't sure what. She could tell it was her grandpa there in the room with her. She felt frozen there on the bed, unable to open her eyes or mouth. Maybe it would be okay. Maybe he just wanted a nap too, and, after all, it was his bedroom.

She felt him move and could hear him breathing. Now he was at the bottom of the bed. A fresh chill ran through her and she reached again to try to pull the covers over her. He held the cover in place with his hand and lifted her skirt up over her stomach. It was like one of those nightmares where she couldn't scream and she couldn't move. Grandpa must have thought she was sound asleep. She froze and tried not to breathe or let on she knew he was there. He was watching her. She could tell. Would he hurt her if she showed signs she knew he was there? The cold, dry pads of his finger tips prodded her stomach as he, with great care not to wake her, pushed under the elastic of her underpants and gathered the fabric together to pull them in a circle from under her dress. She felt blue cold, freezing and burning and red with embarrassment and sick all at the same time. Her closed eyes burned with tears and her cheeks with shame. Now he opened her most private place with his fingers and put his face up close between her legs.

His tongue was huge and felt rough like a cat's tongue. She tried to pretend she was still asleep and dreaming as she pushed with all her might against his forehead to make him stop — make him go away. His forehead was slippery with sweat and all her strength wasn't enough to make him go away. She couldn't make him move so she told herself it wasn't really happening. It was just a dream.

She let her mind carry her away to the woods by the lake where she felt safe and warm and loved and where God would never let anyone, even the wild animals, hurt her.

She didn't know how long Grandpa stayed or even what he did after she left for the Lake. Sometimes, after that, and even now, as an adult, she had flashes of images and feelings she didn't understand. Poking, piercing, feelings of pressure. Feelings like a dull edged vice-grip squeezing her flesh to the bone. It happened sometimes in dreams and she felt she would die from the torture but she couldn't get him to let go. Couldn't get him to realize he was killing her. She never knew if these agonizing feelings were about what her grandpa did or if her tortured feelings came from some other source.

Sometimes she felt herself suffocating with something big and soft and smooth against her nose and mouth. She felt the presence of a bare-bellied animal of some kind, much bigger than she was, covering and crushing her small body. She didn't know what to make of the feelings and did her best to put them out of her mind.

She couldn't say how long her grandpa stayed there on the bed with her that day. She left her body and let the lake rescue her. Sometime later she heard the front door open and the voices of the funeral attendees coming into the house. Grandpa was gone. She scrambled down from the bed and pulled herself quickly into her white cotton panties. She pulled the covers down on the bed, climbed under them and pulled them over her head. She didn't dare leave the room. Didn't dare look into Jesus' sweet eyes.

Chapter Six

On the way home to Michigan from Grandma's and Grandpa's house she begged to sit in the front seat so she could put her head in her mother's lap and feel the comfort of her hands caress her hair and face. She had to take turns because, of course, Ariana wanted to sit up front too. Each of them had to share their mother's lap with the tiny Stephanie who Mom held close to her chest. Miriam leaned over the front seat, standing on the hump of the floor in the back seat, and pressed herself as close to her mother as she could. She rested her head on her mother's shoulder and quietly listened to the conversation between her mom and dad as Ariana slept, her head in her mother's lap.

Something was said about Grandpa Barrett being sick. She thought to herself that this maybe was because of the dirty potty things he liked to do. Her skin chilled and she shivered with fresh goose bumps remembering this most recent embarrassing experience with her otherwise sweet and funny grandpa. This hadn't been the first time he had taken access to her in ways she couldn't understand and that sometimes hurt and sometimes didn't. Neither would it be the last. She chose to put it out of her mind. It upset her to think of it and she believed it must be her fault. She knew she would get punished severely if her daddy ever found out. She reached her arm around her mother's shoulders and put her hand on her neck under her rich black hair where it's waves covered her soft skin. She rested her cheek against her mommy's head, hoping it would soon be her turn in the front seat.

They were headed home to Maple Grove in suburban Lansing, where her dad was still pastor of Calvary Baptist Church — the church that was nothing but a basement with a flat, tar roof at ground level. There were piles of dirt all around with some areas smoothed over to serve as a parking lot. The only way you could tell it was a church was a white sign out front with brown letters saying the church's name and a picture of a cross painted in the same brown paint. There were no flowers or trees anywhere in sight. In their yard next door to the church a swing on two metal chains hung from the clothesline poles in the back yard, but Miriam didn't have the stomach for swinging once she was home from Uncle Jack's funeral.

She had come to like her neighborhood and had several friends within easy walking distance of her house. She liked it that there were so many boys living near by. Some of them were older than she was but they would still play with her if she would go into the bushes with them and play doctor or take her panties down for them. She often asked them to return the favor and show her their penises. She would come home flustered and excited and feeling funny in her stomach. She knew she had to be very careful to keep secrets about where she'd been and what she'd been up to.

It was in this house that she and Ariana each had serious bouts of chicken pox that forced them to stay inside and in bed for so many days she thought she would die of boredom. She and Ariana shared a bedroom and played Superman by flying from one bed to the other across the chasm of approximately twelve inches that separated one bed from the other.

It was in this house, too, that she experienced a serious increase in night terrors. To this day she can't explain how real those tigers, lions, rattlesnakes and alligators were who inhabited her sleep and woke her screaming in the night. She was afraid to sleep alone. Afraid to let her hand or foot outside the bedcovers for fear of whatever fierce animal, serpent or knife-bearing intruder might lurk there under the bed ready to grab and devour her. She often dreamed a beautiful collie dog, who looked like Lassie, standing far off in an endless meadow of golden & swaying grass. She was alone walking in slow motion toward the lovely animal. As she approached the collie suddenly snapped huge, fang like teeth at her and bit her hard, clamping her jaw tight into her side. The pain was unbearable and Miriam carried the pain with her long after she awakened from dreaming.

Because of her nightmares, her parents were not getting any sleep. She sobbed loudly when denied access to their bed. Sometimes her dad would belt her in a rage and drag her by one arm and screaming to the corner in the dining room outside the bedroom hallway, where she was told to stand quietly, while everyone else in the house was still in bed. How she craved the comfort of a loving touch. It had become dangerous for Miriam even to dream.

* * * * *

One night in early Spring, 1956, when Miriam was almost seven years old, her mother was out preparing the ground for a flower garden when the telephone rang. Her dad picked up the phone and his mother told him that his father, Miriam's dear, dear Grandpa Blackwell, was dead. He died suddenly from a severe asthma attack.

No one understood what Miriam's Grandpa Blackwell meant to her. He meant the only safety and friendship she had ever known with a man as a child. Grandpa Blackwell adored her and made no bones about it. She remembered vividly, Grandpa picking her up under her arms and swinging her in a full circle and then hugging her to him, laughing with pleasure and greeting when she ran to him.

She only got to see Grandpa a few times a year when her dad and mom packed their children up in the car and drove right through the night to New York State where both their families lived. She stood in the back seat, face smashed against the window or the window rolled down and her head sticking out as far as she dared, to catch the first glimpse of her grandpa sitting there on the front porch of the house on Fowler Avenue. She couldn't get out of the car fast enough. He'd come down the porch steps and descend the four foot incline of the front yard — which always seemed a huge hill to her as a little girl trying to climb up it on roller skates — and she was always the first to reach his arms. He'd carry her up the steps and into the house, holding her there while he held the door for everyone else to file in. They'd kiss his cheek or say "Hi, Pop" as they passed.

Grandpa Blackwell's house was a two story wood-frame house, painted white. A couple of evergreen bushes stood sentry duty at the sides of the front porch steps but Miriam didn't remember ever seeing flowers in the front yard. The living room seemed so tidy and the smell of Grandpa's menthol cigarettes, the vague odors of the last meal that was cooked in the kitchen, the laundry being done in the basement, always refreshed her and made her feel happy to be home. Her own house had asbestos tile floors, bare of rugs or carpeting and the furniture was upholstered in stiff, skin-grating fabric sort of like burlap in its look and feel.

She thought her grandpa and grandma had such nice things. The stairs to the second floor and even the bedrooms were carpeted in a velvety gray, the color of a baby bunny. Much of the furniture was very old and had belonged to people who lived a long time ago. She loved to imagine life before cars and running water. She relished all things old fashioned.

She loved the old pedestal sink in Grandma and Grandpa's bathroom with its separate faucets for hot and cold. She especially loved the old footed tub that represented hours of bath time fun for her, a child who relished the sight and feel and smell of water in any form. She couldn't wait to shed her clothes and sink into the comfort of the warm bath, surrounded by bobbing aluminum cups, bowls and a set of measuring spoons from her Grandma's kitchen.

The house had three bedrooms, a dining room, kitchen, living room, pantry and one bathroom. Outside, in the back yard there was a hose neatly rolled around a metal wheel set up close to the house. The very back of the yard was filled with flowers grown on tiers of rock against a high fence. Out by that fence stood a brick and mortar charcoal grill her father built for his mom. Ariana used to roast hot dogs and marshmallows and things out there after dark. Miriam didn't like hot dogs or marshmallows when she was young and was usually inside, lost in the comfort of the warm water against her skin, by the time the back yard roasting was going on.

Those summer nights after supper she ran up the stairs to her grandmother's bedroom and reaching on tiptoes took the gold and silver handled hairbrush, its face inlaid with flower painted porcelain, and ran to find her grandfather. She found him in his gray chair in the corner of the living room near the arched doorway to the dining room or on the front porch in one of those folding chairs with nylon straps woven alternately green, yellow, and white. She climbed up on his lap and he took the hairbrush from her hand. She folded her arms across her chest with satisfaction and reclined, her back to his front, and awaited his strokes with the hairbrush. In those evenings all talk was grown-up talk. Sometimes the voices came out in pained, hushed, concerned tones and Miriam listened, afraid someone was hurt or angry.

Her dad bragged or complained, went on and on about himself and how great he is and how everybody else was to blame that he had to leave this or that church, lost this or that job. Mostly, she was aware of the crickets and felt the warm night air blowing the scent of summer flowers from the back yard out into the street lit with deep yellow globes against the darkening sky. She heard the voices of children playing, out on their bicycles and roller-skates and heading home, having stayed out later than they were supposed to. Mothers' voices crooned, "Jon-a-thon, Maaar-y . . . It's time to come i-i-n now. . ." Later she would hear the screen door close at some far off house down the block as a child, answering the mother's call, returned home.

After awhile Grandpa Blackwell's hands slowed their rotation: one hand smoothing Miriam's hair, the next brushing the place he smoothed; brush, smooth, brush, smooth. His breath came slow and deep and had a soft snoring, scraping sound to it. His head nodded to one side and his mouth hung open to release the sounds of sleep. His left hand, the smoothing one, rested on her head but his right hand dangled at the side of his chair from the weight of the hairbrush.

Her dad talked on. Grandma suggested ice cream and Grandpa bolted awake, tickled Miriam's waist and said, "Watch out! Ice cream!" He spread his knees so she squealed and fell with a soft thump right through his legs and onto the floor of the porch. Grandpa stepped over her saying, "Last one to the ice cream's a rotten egg," and bolted for the kitchen, Miriam flat on his heels, letting the screen door slam behind them.

But now, what was Miriam going to do without her Grandpa? It would just be Aunt Ellen and Grandma and a steady flow of Aunt Ellen's girlfriends now when she went to visit. Aunt Ellen was no longer playful. She lost her little baby, her husband and her dad all in such a short period of time.

Grandma would be more lonely and unhappy than ever now. Miriam wished she could see her grandfather one last time and tell him he was her favorite man ever and she loved him very much. Wished she could kiss his rough cheek and smell the menthol cigarettes on his clothes. Wished he would brush her hair once more. She wanted one last chance to tell him goodbye.

The day her grandma called and told her dad his father was dead Miriam was rushed off, along with Ariana, with no explanation, to stay for a week with a woman she knew her mom and dad thought was a terrible sinner.

The woman's name was Blanche. Miriam's mom told her she had to call her "Mrs. Blanche." She wore make-up and had bright red hair piled high on her head. She kept a pair of spare glasses on a rhinestone chain around her neck and Miriam loved to watch that chain sparkle as Mrs. Blanche's great breasts jiggled when she moved. Mrs. Blanche's husband was Harold, a short, bald man who always dressed in a brown and tan tweed sports coat, brown slacks, a white dress shirt — gray from too many washings — and a brown necktie with tan and mustard curlicues on it. Everyone in the church felt sorry for Harold because his wife was a heathen floozy. Harold would get up in church and give his testimony and ask everyone to pray that Blanche would come to know Christ as her personal Savior. He was in a real fix, because as long as he stayed married to her in her un-faith, he was in a state of sin, but, if he divorced her, he would, of course, be in a state of sin. Miriam thought Harold was pretty funny-looking and a little bit creepy and she tried to picture Harold and Blanche kissing or making babies but it was an image that just didn't work.

The colorful Blanche and her collection of grown-up lady dolls were the only bright spots in Harold and Blanche's dingy little brown house. Bright, shiny, metallic, emerald green always flashed before Miriam's eyes when she remembered Blanche and her dolls.

Mrs. Blanche's doll collection was a wonder of historical dress. She had dolls from the Flapper era and dolls in long, full-skirted dresses with bustles and choker necklines from the Victorian era. Some of her dolls wore clothes from the 1930's or from the days of World War II. Blanche had book after book of old fashion catalogues and historical figure paper dolls. She showed Miriam Harold's books with pictures of horse-drawn buggies and Model A and Model T Fords. To Miriam the olden-days looked much more colorful and interesting than now days and she began to create fantasies and imagine how life had been for her ancestors and the ancestors of her friends.

During that week she barely gave a thought to her sister Ariana. She was there in the house when Mrs. Blanche showed

Miriam how she made paper-dolls and when she walked and sat knee deep in scraps of fuscia, gold, and royal blue fabric preparing to sew another costume for one of her dolls, but she didn't participate.

Ariana spent the bulk of the week reading on the bed in the darkened bedroom off the dining room where she could see Miriam and Mrs. Blanche absorbed in dolls and paper dolls. Though Ariana and Miriam were so close in age there was a distance between them. Ariana felt danger in alliance with this sister who inspired such wrath from their father. She knew, too, her father would not appreciate his daughter's attraction to the colorful Mrs. Blanche. She kept her distance, and if she too was grief stricken, she showed no apparent signs.

Perhaps she, like Miriam was afraid to even think of it. The few questions Miriam asked before her mom and dad left, were ignored. Elizabeth was absorbed in taking care of her husband and didn't want him to be bothered or upset by the children — least of all Miriam, with her uncanny ability to send him into a violent rage under almost any circumstance. There certainly wasn't time for that now.

Miriam tried to ask some questions, just like she had about Uncle Jack's suicide, but she couldn't get anyone's attention. She was forced to sit there in the background trying to guess the depth of the tragedy before her.

Ariana appeared to be fine. Grandpa, however, was gone forever and no one ever talked about him. Miriam wondered if she was the only one who loved him? Wondered too, if he was the only one who loved her? She felt alone in her grief. Felt her dead grandfather was the only grown up who might understand her sorrow but she feared he was too far away in heaven to hear her call to him. She worried he might not even be in heaven. Her dad never came right out and said his dad was going to hell but he did believe he was a sinner because he smoked cigarettes.

All that week, with the help of Mrs. Blanche, Miriam imagined and day dreamed herself into a world peopled with highly costumed paper dolls. She asked Mrs. Blanche to tell her what kind of clothes people wore when her grandpa and grandma were young people. Together they made up stories of life in the 1920's and the 1930's.

Mrs. Blanche told her about world events of the time and

what the lives of women were like. She told her what kind of houses, furniture, jobs and transportation people had.

Miriam's future as a historian was born in those childhood experiences. Her interest in history was born of desire to live in another world. A desire to live in the world where her beloved grandpa who protected, comforted and loved her, was very much alive. Now Miriam had two very important places she could go when she craved safety — the woods by the water and back in time where the dolls she made lived.

The week she spent with Mrs. Blanche offered her a sense of peace and refuge in a time of deep sadness and confusion. It gave her a chance to come to terms, to some extent, with the loss of her dear grandpa.

Out back of Mrs. Blanche's house the yard ended in a short stone wall the other side of which towered a stand of pine trees with a soft forest floor. Though the pine forest was nowhere near endless like the forest by the lake, it offered her a place to feel fresh breezes and breathe in the scent that took her to all the forests of her young life. There she played for hours among the trees, piling the pine cones and needles in ledges to make dividing walls between the various rooms of the dream house she created. Throughout her childhood the smallest stand of trees and greenery and the tiniest of lakes or streams represented a compelling draw to refuge and to undiscovered answers she hoped would some day be hers.

* * * * *

Calvary Baptist Church eventually got its above ground walls and windows and a great brown cross on its rooftop. Miriam's parents yearned for life in a home of their own out from under the watchful eye of the coming and going church congregation. The family moved from the parsonage next to the church and Miriam's day to day contact with the children who lived on her street was severed and she was left without her weeping willow tree.

Except for those losses she was delighted to move to the brand new house across the street from the school yard. Her own back yard in the new house was practically an orchard. There were apple trees, pear trees, plum, peach and cherry trees. She and Ariana had the job of picking up the fallen fruit and checking it over to see if it should be discarded or could be used in Mother's canning. She still saw some of her old neighborhood friends at school and was often invited to their birthday parties. The bedroom she shared with Ariana in this house was painted baby blue and was bigger than their last room. It had a large window looking out on the trees in the back yard. She loved the way the sun beams shone and lit up the tiny particles of dust when she was in her room on sunny afternoons. She tried to believe a good angel was nearby in the glow of that beam.

Just down the street from the new house was a heavily wooded lot that became her treasured woodland playground. Milly was her constant night time companion still, but she was getting too old to carry her with her everywhere. During the daytime when she could be outside she would run to her woodland or play with friends in the playground of the school yard. On rainy days, in the evening and in the winter time she continued her beloved creation of paper dolls and their life stories.

The church her dad pastored was still the same one that had been a basement when they first came to town, but now the years of congregational fund raising had resulted in a bright white stucco building on top of the old basement foundation. The parishioners had planted flowers and grass where the piles of dirt used to be. The work of building the new church kept her father away from home quite a lot and she could almost forget, at times, his unpredictable rages. Forgetting though, was dangerous, because she failed to keep her guard up and sometimes stumbled into behavior that invited his wrath and left her, once again, beaten and humiliated.

It wasn't long after the new church was built before Earl got himself into trouble with his temper again. This time he became dissatisfied with the caliber of the congregation and the lack of financial success the church was experiencing. He thought he could do better and was getting itchy for a place that would appreciate him more and pay him commensurate with that appreciation. There was an open pastorate at a church sixty miles from Maple Grove and he was hired there after a couple of candidate sermons and interviews with the Board.

This time the family moved during Christmas break into a parsonage with a fireplace and golden hardwood floors. It was the fanciest house the family ever lived in, but it was still a parsonage and was located right next to the church and across the street from a dilapidated and abandoned barn.

Elizabeth thought the house was beautiful but was worried sick about the parishioners, who owned the house, looking over her shoulder, to be sure she took proper care of the lovely floors and kitchen cabinets. She felt exposed and ill at ease among these prosperous people and was particularly concerned that her children behave well so the church family would think well of her as a wife and mother.

The former pastor's wife had run away with a muscular, tan member of the congregation and left her husband and children to fend for themselves. The deacons had kicked the pastor from the church for being an ineffective head of household, believing that his inability to manage his family was indication he couldn't lead the church. Elizabeth was anxious about the house and her children. She buried her feelings of neglect. Her husband hadn't included her feelings at all in his decision to leave their treasured orchard home and the community where she had finally settled in and developed friendships. She was concerned too about pulling the children out of school in the middle of the school year. When she tried to talk to Earl he simply let it be known that he was the man of the house and that his family, and that included her, had to abide by his wishes. After all, he said, "I'm not required to consult you when it comes to following the will of the Lord."

Chapter Seven

It was the middle of the school year but Miriam's first day of the fourth grade at the new school. She was terrified. She didn't know anyone yet. Ariana had met a friend named Sylvia at their daddy's new church and she lived just down the street. She was in the same fifth grade class as Ariana and she came by early to walk with her and show her the way.

Napoleon Elementary School was down one street, turn right by the restaurant and go up another street. Elizabeth told Miriam she was a big girl and should be brave.

"Miriam, you are nine years old now. You're plenty big enough to walk to school alone." She said she couldn't take Miriam to school because she had Stephanie to look after. Besides she was going to have another baby soon so she insisted Miriam had to be a big girl.

At breakfast that morning Miriam didn't touch her sugar pops or orange juice, even though her father yelled at her and told her she had to sit there until she finished every bite. She tried, but she just couldn't do it. She felt sick with fright and knew if she ate she would throw up. She kept trying to eat, though. She'd pick up her spoon and put two sugar pops on it, bring it close up to her mouth and then shut her mouth just at the tip of the spoon so no food could get past her lips. She sat paralyzed. Now her dad was yelling she was going to be late for school and what a fine start that would be. That her teacher would think her parents couldn't control her and about how that would hurt his ministry. Miriam could tell he was getting really mad.

She got up from the table, took her Cinderella lunch box from the counter top, walked out the back door and lay down in the dirt driveway between the house and the church. It was the same driveway that led to the road she had to walk to the fourth grade at her new school. She couldn't seem to make herself get up and walk alone to that unfamiliar school. She put her head in her arms there in the dirt and tried to disappear before Daddy got there with the belt.

"Thwack!" She felt nothing but red-hot hatred.

"Thwack!" Numb — wanted nothing but sleep.

"Thwack!" Still she didn't cry.

He pulled at her, trying to lift her by his free hand and his rough grip tore her dress. Her legs were noodles and she fell in a rag doll heap in the dirt. She didn't want to give him the satisfaction of seeing her cry but knew he would keep hitting her if she didn't break down. She crawled away from him looking over her shoulder. The tears came. She crawled on all fours until the driveway reached the road. She went up one road and down the other until she reached the school yard.

At the door to the school Mrs. Beach knelt down and put her gentle hands on Miriam's waist. Mrs. Beach had thick long brown hair pulled back in a pony tail. She wore a soft peach-colored sweater over her large breasts where a string of pearls fell and hung right between the two of them. She wore dark red lipstick and her eyes were the biggest and bluest Miriam had ever seen. She touched the dirty streaks that lined Miriam's face, stood up and took her hand to lead her to a little room just outside the fourth grade class. As she sponged Miriam's face clean with a warm wash cloth she talked to her.

"Oh, honey. I've been looking for you," she said. "The Principal told me we would have a new little girl in class today and when you weren't here yet when the bell rang I asked Caroline to sing some songs with the class while I went to look for you. The whole class is so excited. We don't get many new children in the middle of the year. We've been thinking of you as a sort of after-Christmas present."

Mrs. Beach stood up from the kneeling position she'd adopted to talk to Miriam and wash her face. She bent over and turned her face up to her own by putting one hand under Miriam's chin.

"There now. Is that better? You sure are a pretty after-

Christmas present. Do you like to sing songs? Let's go see what song Caroline and your classmates are singing. I'll bet. . . Let me think ... Oh, I know. They'll have gotten all the way to "On Top of Spaghetti" by now. We'd better hurry. It's one of my favorites."

Mrs. Beach was right about "On Top of Spaghetti." She helped Miriam find a place to sit among the circle of children on the floor on the round rug made of purple, green and blue rags. She didn't know the words to the song so she just listened at first feeling too shy to join in the singing. The next song was a clapping song that kept going faster and faster until some children fell backwards out of breath and laughing, unable to keep up.

Miriam felt much better now. Already she felt she could be happy at this school and dreaded the school-bell that would signal her return home.

Mrs. Beach stood in front of the circle of children, her hands clasped in front of her at stomach height. She smiled through her bright lips.

"Boys and girls, I am pleased to introduce to you Miss Miriam Blackwell. She and her family just moved to our town and we are happy to welcome her to our class. Let's give her a warm welcome so she'll feel at home here with us." She smiled and clapped. The children joined her and twisted and turned their faces and bodies to see their new classmate.

Lunch time came and she felt a bit awkward not knowing the way to the lunch room or the routine for this new school. She watched her classmates go to their cubbies and followed them to collect her Cinderella lunch box from the cubby Mrs. Beach said was hers. She was surprised to see her name already on the wooden box when she arrived at school that morning. The cubbies were in colors red, green, blue and yellow and each had the student owner's name in two inch high block letters that looked like little people with grinning faces. Their limbs were posed in various positions acrobatic or stationary depending on the letter's shape.

She carried her lunch box back to her desk as she saw the others doing. Mrs. Beach called the names of children row by row and they filed out and down the hall to collect their milk and find a seat in the lunchroom.

A fat girl with dark, greasy and stringy chin-length hair and bangs that poked in her eyes, stood up from her desk behind Miriam.

"Hi Miriam. My name is Paula Brown. Do you want me to show you how to get your milk? I'll sit with you too if no one else has already asked you."

Miriam was grateful she would not be all alone and gave Paula a quick, relieved nod "yes." She followed her from the room when their names were called. At first, neither one of them could think of anything to say. As more children joined them at the table and began to question each other about the contents of their lunch boxes. Some traded Twinkies for Hostess Snowballs and bananas for oranges, and Miriam began to feel right at home. Paula asked her what was in her lunch and the whole table seemed curious to know. Did she like bologna or was peanut butter her favorite? Did she want those raisins or would she trade for this oatmeal cookie "cause I only like chocolate chip"? What was her old school like? Did she have any pets? The lunch hour flew by and Miriam was sure she gained any number of new friends.

After lunch when they were working at their desks on their timetables, Paula leaned forward to Miriam.

"My house is only a little way from your house. We watched the moving men bring all your stuff and, I hope it's all right; I snooped to see if any of the new kids looked close to my age. I was so excited when Mrs. Beach said the new girl would be in our class and would sit right near me in the B row."

Mrs. Beach looked up from her desk, looked at Paula and put her finger to her lips to signal her to quit talking and go back to work on her timetables. Paula was quiet for a minute then said in a whisper right next to Miriam's ear, "Will you walk home with me?" Miriam smiled down at her worksheet and nodded her head twice.

On their way home Paula taught her all the words to "On Top of Spaghetti." Paula showed her a different way home from the one Miriam took that morning but it was almost the same distance.

They stopped by Paula's house so she could show her mom her new friend and so Miriam would know where Paula lived. Paula's house didn't have much paint at all on its wooden siding. There was a tree stump in the front yard. In the gravel driveway which was rutted with muddy tire tracks rested a rusted-out car that was missing one wheel.

Mrs. Brown looked exactly like her daughter except she was taller with a face that was puffier and showed little round lips smeared with pink lipstick. When she smiled, Miriam could see she was missing the tooth just to the left of her two center front teeth. The missing tooth did not, however, deter Mrs. Brown from laughing and welcoming both Paula and her new friend.

"Hi there girls! How was school today? Can I fix you some cocoa with marshmallows to warm you up?"

The girls had come in the back door and had to step over a big, shaggy, tan mutt named Cynthia to get into the kitchen that smelled of cold garbage.

The only light in the house that afternoon came from the blaring TV set where Gary Moore laughed along with a celebrity guest. All the windows wore yellow/brown paper shades pulled down against the daylight. Mrs. Brown said it was because she couldn't see the TV with all that light coming in the windows.

In spite of the darkness and how poor it seemed Paula's family was, Miriam felt warm and safe in that house where Mrs. Brown served her the best cup of cocoa she ever tasted. She felt completely welcome in their home.

Miriam and Paula became close friends — always walking to and from school together. She spent as much time as she could at Paula's house instead of her own. Only three people lived at Paula's house: her brother, Phil, Mrs. Brown and Paula. Paula said her dad left soon after she was born and she didn't miss him since she never really knew him. Her mom got by with a part time job behind the counter at the dry cleaners in town and they got most their food from the government Relief program. Their only extravagance was the big TV in the living room and the electric bill they paid to keep it running almost all day, every day. They didn't wash their hair or clothes as often as some families because they wanted to keep the water bills reasonable. That explained Paula's greasy hair.

Lots of times Mrs. Brown would still be at work when the kids got home from school — a fact Miriam kept a secret from her parents so they wouldn't tell her she had to come home if she didn't have adult supervision. Miriam, Paula and Phil fixed after school snacks of boxed macaroni and cheese or made their own cupcakes from a Duncan Hines cake mix.

"My dad won't let my mom use cake mixes." Miriam told Paula one afternoon when they were licking chocolate cupcake batter from their fingers. "He says they leave an awful taste in his mouth."

She put her hands on her hips, made her face into a fierce grimace and imitated her father's low voice dictating household cooking policy. "Cake mixes, Elizabeth, are the work of the devil. They taste of pure laziness." He wouldn't allow macaroni and cheese either and it was Miriam's favorite. She told Paula about the time her mother had made the mistake of serving it for dinner. Again she imitated her father. She sat then stood, slamming her fist on the table, knocking the chair over behind her as she rose and stomped from the room. "This gummy goo is not a fit meal for a man and I won't have it!" She fell laughing onto the threadbare brown sofa. As she landed a small cloud of dust puffed around her. Paula joined her, making her own cloud of dust and they laughed falling against each other in a heap of giggles. Later Paula told her she always thought she was missing something to not have a dad around, but having a dad didn't sound like it was so much fun at Miriam's house.

Miriam felt so grown up on those days they had the house all to themselves. Paula even taught her how to make fudge. There was a feeling of freedom and happiness Miriam felt so rarely in her own home. She could hardly believe it that when Mrs. Brown came home those afternoons after school she wasn't mad at all about the mess the children made. She just acted happy to see them and seemed like she couldn't wait to be with her children and her dog and hear all the details of their day apart.

* * * * *

The public library in Napoleon was on the same street as The First Baptist Church and handy enough for Miriam to walk to by herself. She was delighted with this freedom to continue the exploration of history she'd begun in Maple Grove. After Grandpa died and she spent the week with Mrs. Blanche she craved all the information she could get about the way people lived in the early part of the century. Now that she was old enough to have a bit of independence she developed a habit of walking to the library close to their house. There she would look for picture books and stories that would show her what life had been like for people who lived when her grandparents and great and great great grandparents lived. There were stories of Caddy Woodlawn, Anne of Green Gables, Louisa May Alcott and Laura Ingalls Wilder and she honed her young reading skills and stretched her imagination to encompass these lives so different from her own.

When she found pictures of women and children in period costume she'd bring them home. With her colored pencils and crayons, she made paper dolls and fashioned clothes for them like the ones she saw in the books. With these dolls she enacted fantasies and stories and pretended she was her own grandmother or great grandmother as a girl or a young woman. Though she made up these life stories, she felt she was coming to understand something of her own history.

Such play was a comfort to her. By this time she had several good friends, boys and girls, and they spent hours together pretending to be adults in another place and time.

She gradually came to accept the death of her grandfather and uncle. Her growing independence and ability to read and go off alone on her bicycle kept her away from home on weekends and after school. Still, she was home for supper and bedtime and had to go to church twice a day on Sundays and to Wednesday night prayer meeting with her family.

She was impatient with the chores required of her at home and her belligerence about washing dishes, folding the laundry and sweeping the kitchen got her into considerable trouble.

Her growing confidence led her to show off her imagined power when her friends were around. Sometimes she tempted fate by mouthing off at her dad. He raged and threatened but rarely did his furor result in Miriam getting a beating. The common punishment was to deny her a visit to a friend's house or a trip to the library. Or, she couldn't use her bike or go swimming for a week.

Miriam would go wild with rebellion when these restrictions were applied. Her mouth said things that meant — could only mean — more trouble for her. But she couldn't stop herself and seemed destined to bring down on her head more and prolonged punishment. She never felt remorse. She became capable, at these times, of feeling only hatred and rage. Life at home between Miriam and her father was perpetually tense and miserable. What worse punishment than to be trapped at home with a father toward whom and from whom, she felt only hostility?

She couldn't stand it. She sneaked out of the house, lying about what she was going to do and where she would be. Thus, more punishment, more rage, more fury and ultimately an increased sense of unwelcome, entrapment and loneliness in her own home whenever her family was around.

* * * * *

One afternoon when Miriam was not allowed to leave the house she was in her room alone working on a cardboard stage set for her paper dolls. Her mom took Stephanie and the new baby, Rebecca for doctor's appointments. Her father was at the church in his study working on Sunday's sermon. Ariana was at school helping with the school newspaper. Miriam had permission to leave her room but if she left the house she would not be allowed to go to Theresa's pajama party that coming weekend.

She enjoyed having the whole house to herself so didn't even consider defying her parents on this one — plus she felt she'd rather die than miss a pajama party. She spent the day lost in her work on the stage-set for "The Day of the New Doll." It was a historical piece she made up about a girl whose mother was an artist during the 1920's and was a wild and rebellious Flapper who smoked long skinny cigars and sat in smoky cafes with famous writers who told each other poems and stories.

She sat in her bedroom facing away from the bedroom door, legs out to the sides and on her knees as she worked on the floor. Words and music floated from her as she worked to create another make believe history.

She was completely absorbed in her task and unaware of any sounds inside or outside the house. If her family had returned home, if hours and hours had passed, she was unaware of it.

Lost in her imagination she didn't hear anyone open the door. She had no idea how long Roger had been standing there like that, watching her.

"What you up to, Miriam?"

She jumped, startled to hear a voice other than her own. She turned to see him in his pose, one arm head-height and holding the doorframe to support his body; he leaned in a complete diagonal across the entire threshold. He looked like he owned the place. His other hand was shoved deep in the pocket of his tight blue jeans. He wore a white crew-neck sweater that hung below the waist of his jeans and a replica of a WWII brown leather bomber jacket. When Miriam jumped and looked up at him he un-leaned himself from the door and walked in a slow stride toward her, both hands in his pockets now.

She slid her seated body as far away from him as the surrounding furniture would allow.

"Roger, what are you doing here? Did my Mom let you in"?

"No, cutie. Far as I can see nobody's home but you — and me, of course." He leaned over Miriam and pinched her cheek playfully between his thumb and forefinger.

Miriam blushed. She wasn't afraid of Roger. Just surprised to see him in her house. He was sixteen years old and lived in the house behind hers. She'd seen him lots of times, hanging out with his buddies down at the corner store, or working in the driveway on his bike. She thought he was very handsome but knew he had a reputation as a kind of troublemaker and tough-guy teenager. His hair was light brown and cut in a flat top. He appeared to have a nice suntan even in the winter.

She thought the way he dressed was cool and hoped, when she got older, she would have a boyfriend as cute as Roger. Still, he had never paid much attention to her before, except to tease and whistle at her to make her blush sometimes when she was out in the yard or on her way to school. His family went to her church so they knew each other's names though they were never put together in social situations because of their age difference.

He and his older sister and parents had been over for the house warming when the Blackwells moved in, but Miriam couldn't think of another time he had been in the house. Certainly, he had never tried to engage her in a conversation before.

"How come you're here alone without a baby sitter, Miriam? You too big for baby-sitters now?" He squatted near her and pulled his arms from his bomber jacket and tossed it on the bed behind her. He looked around him at all the paper dolls, cardboard, crayons, scissors and paste that cluttered her bedroom.

"So. What's all this?" He fingered a paper doll and reached to attach a dress with little tabs to this flat paper body that wore only a camisole and underpants that went nearly to her knees.

"Roger, I don't think you are supposed to be in here. I'm being punished, if you must know. I can't leave the house or have anybody over to play. If my parents find out I let you in they won't let me go to Theresa's pajama party on Friday, so I think you should go now."

"But this looks like fun to me. Can't I stay and play? Don't you have any boy paper dolls so I can pretend to be in your story too? What exactly are you doing here? If you tell me I can play too, can't I"?

Miriam was flattered by his attention and welcomed having someone want to be in her play.

"I'm making a play Roger. It's about the life of a Flapper. Flappers were women who loved to dance and go to parties and they smoked little thin cigars and wore different kinds of dresses than we do now. Sometimes they even wore suits like men. They were young women when my grandma was a young woman. I like to pretend I live in different times in history and I make up plays and paper dolls about it."

"Hmmm. That so? This is good, Miriam. Really. I think we could have a real good time together here. Hey, any boys in your play? Because your Flapper here will need a boy to dance with, won't she?"

"Yes. I have boy paper dolls too. Here, you can be this one." She handed him a slender male paper doll whose black hair was combed straight back from his forehead and slicked to stay in place with pomade. He had a handlebar mustache and wore a man's sleeveless undershirt and boxer shorts.

"But Roger, we have to listen very closely to be sure no one comes home and finds you here. You have to be sure to hide or sneak out if anyone comes in, okay? I will be in awful trouble if my parents find out you've been here."

"Sure." He said. "I can do that. If they come in the front I'll go out this back window. If they come in the back I'll duck out the front door before they can see me. But it wasn't long ago I saw everybody leave so we probably have lots of time, don't we? I've noticed they leave you alone to play quite a lot, considering your age and all. Don't they like you much?"

"Roger, I just seem to get in trouble a lot. Okay? I don't know if they like me or not and I don't care, either. So let's just change the subject. I have a perfectly fun time here making up imaginary lives. They don't have to take me with them. I just get yelled at all the time anyway."

"Okay. Okay." He put his hands up as if she was a real tough talker and he had to protect himself. "Didn't mean to touch a sore spot. Got you all riled up didn't I? Let's get back to this paper doll thing."

Now she relaxed into this. It made her laugh when he acted scared of her. This was going to be such fun. She was thrilled that Roger wanted to play with her. She didn't know boys liked this kind of thing, and especially someone so handsome and grownup as Roger.

It was great to have him there acting out the boys part and making it up as he went along. He said he could really help her out with her story because, since she was a girl, she wouldn't know as much as he did about what boys are like and what they like to do with girls.

"Not to get you all weird again, Miriam, but I don't get why your parents left you all alone here. I mean, I know it's a pretty safe neighborhood and it's only a small town — but I thought your parents watched all you kids like hawks. I hear your dad yelling at you about do this, don't do that all the time. I'm surprised he lets you out of his sight with how strict he is."

"Yeah, well I guess he figures I have to be punished and everybody else had other things to do this afternoon. I don't really mind having to stay home if the rest of the family isn't here to boss me around. I hope they don't come home for a long time." Especially now that you're here, she thought.

"Well, gee, just let me know when you're alone here. I think you're a real cute girl, even if you are kind of young. I can teach you a lot about boys that will help you make up more realistic stories."

"I just don't think my parents want me to have friends in the house when they're out. I can't let them know you were here and don't you tell anyone either, okay?"

"Oh yes. That's important. We'll just keep it a secret between the two of us." He crossed his heart, aimed his fingers at his head like a gun, and poked at his eye. She mimicked his motions and laughed.

Roger was good at making things up and she was thoroughly flattered and pleased to have him for a secret playmate. She could hardly believe he was really here with her — that he thought she was cute and really seemed to want to be her friend.

He said some more about all he could teach her about boys and could help her so she wouldn't feel so young and inexperienced when she got to be a teenager. All this was so romantic and fed nicely into her fantasy world.

Roger wondered did she have a boyfriend in her class at school.

"No. Not exactly a boyfriend. I like Timothy Otto and I think Billy Williams is cute. Sometimes boys come over when we have pajama parties if we have it at somebody's house whose parents aren't real strict. The boys can never stay over though. They go home pretty early. Then all we talk about is what fun it would be if they could stay and dance with us and what would it be like to kiss them on the lips." She felt hot in her face and giggled behind her hand when she said this.

"Oh. Kissing, huh? Do you think it would feel good to kiss a boy?"

"Oh no. Roger! I shouldn't have said that. Now I'm embarrassed. I shouldn't have said anything."

"It's okay Miriam. Everybody feels that way. You don't have to be shy with me. I can show you how a kiss would feel if you want me to. It would have to be another secret though. We'd have to be sure never to tell anybody. Do you think you would like me to kiss you?"

"No. I can't. I feel funny. I never even kissed a boy my own age and you're all grown up and everything. I know you've kissed lots of girls, haven't you?"

"Well, maybe I have, but that's what I'm saying. I can help you so you won't feel so funny when the time comes and you have a boyfriend you want to kiss. There's lots of stuff girls should know about boys so they don't mess up — things they can do to make boys really love them. Here, come here." He took her hand in his.

His hand felt soft and warm and she was touched by this gesture of affection, but felt funny way down in her stomach too. Something in her felt uncomfortable but, at the same time, he was so handsome and he was being so sweet to her. She couldn't bring herself to resist or to tell him she felt a little bit creepy.

He pulled her a little closer to him. "Come sit closer to me, Miriam. Like this. Like boyfriends and girlfriends do."

She moved in next to him and he placed her hand on his thigh under his hand. He spoke to her in a soft voice about what good friends they would become. He told her about places he would take her and fun things they could do in secret together. He put his arm around her shoulder and pulled her head to his chest. "I like you very much Miriam. I really do. Don't you like me?"

"Oh yes." She could hardly get the words out. Her throat was closed with a feeling that felt part like great happiness and part like she was going to cry. It felt good to be so close to him. It was so rare anyone held her close or touched her softly. A strange feeling filled up her insides. She had only daydreamed how it would be to have a boy friend. She didn't know boys as big as Roger liked little girls like her.

He stroked her hair and touched her face and neck with his warm fingers. "Do you want to know what a kiss is like?" He touched her chin gently and lifted her face to his and kissed her light and slow on her mouth. His lips were soft and full and she felt she couldn't breathe the whole time his lips were on hers.

"Close your eyes, Miriam. Like this. This is how teenagers kiss." He moved her face away to show her how to close her eyes and brought his lips to hers again. She kept her eyes closed and tried to get her breath when he took his lips from hers.

He told her she could make him the happiest boy in the world if she would put her hand "here, under my sweater, like this." He placed her hand where his sweater covered the waist of his jeans and there she felt the firm, warm, silky part of him she instinctively knew she was not supposed to touch. She started to pull her hand away. She felt confused and curious at the same time. She was afraid he would leave if she didn't make him happy. He held her hand against him and told her not to be afraid. He wouldn't ever tell anybody so she wouldn't get in trouble or anything. He said this is a special thing she should know about boys and how girls can tell when a boy really likes them a lot.

He went on talking to her with such gentleness and she knew, somewhere inside her that something wasn't right, but she so much didn't want her new friend to go away. She wanted to make him happy.

He helped her move her hand up and down and squeeze the smooth tip of his penis. She felt shocked and curious at how hard and big and warm it was in her hand. He asked her if she'd like to kiss it. She was so confused and by this time she was about to cry. She didn't know how to say no. She quickly bent her head to kiss him. It was the warmest thing she'd ever put to her lips.

"That was so sweet of you, Miriam. Oh, don't be scared. Oh, now I've made you cry. Don't you like me, Miriam?" She looked up into his face and shook her head "yes."

."Don't cry. It's all right. You don't have to do anymore if you don't want to." He put a handkerchief over his penis and stroked himself quickly. She watched as the muscles in his face tensed and his skin flushed. Suddenly it was as if something had silently burst and Roger's face relaxed into a smile. He looked at her but didn't seem to really see her as he pulled himself back together and tucked himself in.

"I promise I won't tell anybody what you did, Miriam. Because I really do like you and I wouldn't want you to get punished or not be able to go to Theresa's pajama party or anything. I better go now before someone catches us. You'll keep this our secret won't you? Because I can't be your friend anymore if you tell anyone. They wouldn't understand. Okay? You promise?"

Her sad and tear streaked face managed an "I promise."

Roger threw his jacket over his shoulder and left the room saying, "Bye, Miriam. Maybe we can play again some time, huh?"

After he left she didn't feel like playing anymore. She ripped the man with the handle-bar mustache in six pieces and used her scissors to cut the stage set apart. She felt sick to her stomach and so cold and alone as she knelt to vomit in the toilet in the bathroom of the empty house.

When everyone came home and her mother called for supper she pretended she was asleep. She heard her dad say to her mom he would have to punish her in the morning because "Look at the mess she's made in her room."

Chapter Eight

During the night she lay awake formulating her plan of escape. She would run away. Maybe they would be happy to not have to bother with her. She knew she would get lost if she tried to go very far. She could only take with her the few things she might hide in her lunch bucket and inside her coat. She knew where she could go to hide and nobody would tell on her.

Paula told her she could come to her house anytime, even when nobody else is home. She would leave school when the bell rang as usual, and no one would miss her until supper time. When they came to look for her Paula and her mom and brother would tell mother and father that they hadn't seen her since school got out. She knew she wouldn't be able to stay with Paula forever, but maybe just long enough to get an idea where to go next. She wished so much that her Grandpa Blackwell was still alive and she could go and live with him. He would have understood. And lots of kids live with their grandparents don't they?

She got out of bed the next morning when her mom came into the room to tell Ariana and her it was time to get up. She thought her mother gave her a warning and tender glance. She averted her eyes from her mother's so she wouldn't detect her daughter's guilty plan or ask her about yesterday. Her mom put her hand on Miriam's forehead wondering if she was coming down with something that had caused her to sleep so much yesterday. There was no apparent fever but she looked a little faded around her eyes, her mother said. When her mother left the room Miriam kicked the debris from yesterday under her bed and made the bed neatly.

She was determined this day would start out smoothly and without trouble to interfere with her departure. She collected her crayons, scissors, a couple special paper dolls and a few items of clothing and put a sweater over the top of everything on the shelf in her closet. After breakfast she would get them so she could take them with her to her new home. She dressed quickly and went to the kitchen to find her mom so she would button up and tie the back of her dress and help her with her hair.

Elizabeth had made French toast for breakfast. Miriam's favorite. She wanted to run to her arms and tell her everything. She wanted to believe her mom would keep her safe and protect her from her dad. She felt full of shame, though, knowing she was going to run away without telling her mother, that she couldn't bring herself to ask her to button and tie her dress and comb the snarls from her hair. She fairly slunk into her chair, her face nearly level with her plate and sat waiting for her dad to arrive to say the blessing.

During the blessing she kept her eyes open and stared at her dad. Looking at him there, his eyes closed, going on about "thank you Lord for the food you in your great wisdom so graciously provided to our humble and sinful family — we who are not worthy to wipe your feet or the sweat from your brow. . . May we live this day in fear and worship before you. Knowing that at any hour, any moment, you may return to judge those who are in sin before you. . ." she felt doubly guilty because she could think only of how very much she wanted to be as far away from him as she could get. And, if that wasn't a sin, she thought, what is?

"Amen." Her dad pulled his napkin from under his fork and shook it out and lay it across his lap in one smooth, snapping sort of movement. He looked at Miriam. "No French toast for you young lady. Yes. You. Miriam. No French toast for you."

She didn't want to fight. She could feel hot tears welling up in her eyes but didn't want to give him the satisfaction of seeing her cry. She was mad though and she just knew her mom had made the toast especially for her. It was her quiet way of saying she noticed Miriam and cared even if she wasn't going to all out put her own safety on the line and stand up to her husband and tell him to lay off their little girl. She slid from her chair and reached for her lunch box from off the kitchen counter on her way out of the room. She was barely able to control her rage.

"Expect to be severely punished young lady, when you get home from school today. Your mother and I don't appreciate your disobedience. I don't know what you think you're doing leaving your room in the mess we found it in last night. You, with nothing to do all day yesterday but behave yourself. This time you'll get a lesson you won't forget."

Ariana, Stephanie, Rebecca and Mommy all went right on putting jelly and butter and syrup on their French toast. Nobody said anything. They didn't look at each other or at Miriam or their dad. They ate, each as if they were completely alone and they didn't hear or see anything unusual.

"Oh no you won't," Miriam turned on her father, risking everything. "You won't punish me when I get home from school. You won't ever punish me again because I'm going to run away from home." She ran to her room to the sounds of her dad's chair crashing to the floor as he rose in a rage from the kitchen table, upsetting coffee cups and orange juice — the table cloth caught in his belt buckle.

"Don't you dare tell me what you will and won't do, little miss." He followed her, reaching to unbuckle his belt on the way. The uproar in the kitchen slowed him down and she ran past him and out the back door listening to the thunderous clap of his voice behind her. When she reached the end of the driveway, she heard the back door close and turned to look. He'd gone inside. He didn't follow her.

She stopped just past the driveway and put her coloring crayons and scissors in her lunch box. She rolled up several sheets of paper and slid them down the front of her dress and into the elastic waistband of her underpants so they wouldn't fall through her dress. She put on her jacket and walked the back way to school. This morning she walked alone. She figured, once she got to school; she'd apologize to Paula for not stopping by to pick her up.

* * * * *

Awakened by the warm, stinging flow of urine in her underwear, she lifted her head to see her teacher standing over her. Hot urine ran down her bare legs into her bobby socks. She'd been working at her desk in class on a floor plan for her dream house but hadn't been able to keep her eyes open.

"Miriam? Are you alright?" She could hardly lift her head to look at Mrs. Beach. She was so embarrassed. So ashamed. All the kids would see.

"Here, Miriam, let's put this around your dress so you won't be cold." Mrs. Beach spoke softly and wrapped her cardigan sweater around Miriam's waist to help hide the damage and to help her with her embarrassment.

"Class, continue your work please. Miriam isn't feeling very well. I'll help her to the nurse's office and then come right back." She led Miriam from the classroom.

Once in the hallway Miriam said, "No, that's okay Mrs. Beach. I can go myself."

"Well, if you're sure, I… Honey, what's wrong? Something must be the matter. This isn't like you. You've seemed so tired all day."

Oh how she wanted to say "Please hide me. I can't go home again. I did something awful and I can never go home and I need someone to take care of me until I'm old enough to take care of myself." But she couldn't do it. There was really nothing Mrs. Beach could do to help. Miriam was alone in this and would have to figure out how to manage by herself. "I'm okay. I'm sorry I made such a mess. You won't tell my parents will you?"

"Don't you want me to call your Mom and Dad and see if they can come get you? I think you should just go home and let them take care of you until you feel better honey."

"No, don't, please don't call them. I'll be fine. I'll just go to the nurse. I'll be fine." She walked toward the nurse's office and Mrs. Beach turned and shut the classroom door behind her.

When she figured out no one was looking she walked out the double glass doors at the far end of the school building and headed for safety.

* * * * *

The sky was overcast and a drizzle accompanied her escape. The house was dark when she let herself in through the unlocked kitchen door. Paula's mother was more afraid of locked houses than unlocked ones for the danger they present to firefighters and policemen coming to her children's rescue in her absence.

Miriam knew she would have no trouble getting inside and was pretty sure she would be alone. No one would be home for hours and she desperately needed the sanctuary and solitude this old and damp house could provide.

She stepped over Cynthia the dog, there in her usual posture blocking the doorway. Cynthia lifted her head and groaned a recognizing hello of sorts as Miriam passed over her. She made her way through the kitchen and living room and turned right entering Paula's bedroom just off the living room. She closed the door behind her.

Paula's room was musty and a place where no one ever has to pick up their toys or make the bed. Miriam unwrapped Mrs. Beach's sweater from her waist, slipped out of her urine soaked underpants, removed her socks and shoes and found a pair of dry pajama bottoms rolled in a heap on the closet floor.

She slipped them up under her dress and climbed under the mounds of covers on Paula's narrow bed. She wrapped the covers close around her, looked up at the browned and yellowed, water-stained ceiling where pictures formed themselves in the shapes of the characters who would people her dreams as she slept. She fell asleep to the sound of the rain pelting the roof overhead. The wind made a sound like the low whistle of a train leaving for a place some people call home.

She dreamed a floating, drifting, soaring, flying dream that took her right up to the very face of the full moon, striped in gray and silver streaks of cloud in a near black sky. Face lifted, she turned and twirled effortlessly, warmed by the moon's glow. She dived, eyes wide open, arms close to her sides, her feet undulating in a graceful swim across the sky. Carried upward by a current of wind, she flew, dancing a full circle that landed her splay-legged on a four foot diameter, jagged edged ice platform in the center of a bottomless lake surrounded by snow covered mountain peaks. She wore the red and brown plaid dress she wears in so many of her dreams. She rode the white float alone and unafraid and came to shore on a sun heated sand beach, washed with cresting waves from some far off storm. She stood very near the shore as the waves came closer and rose and swelled and retreated.

The waves talked to her. There was something they wanted her to know. Something they had to tell her. She stayed to listen though the powerful water threatened to carry her away. She went very close to understand what was being said. A massive curving shine of a wave wrapped itself over her head and pulled her into its embrace. It was not cold like she thought the sea would be. It felt like shelter. Felt like the warm and loving embrace of her Grandpa Blackwell. There was a voice though, and it wasn't her grandpa's voice. It was the voice of a woman there on the shore, reaching out to her. The voice talked to Miriam of rescue, safety, rest.

She waked to find herself warm in her mother's arms. Her mother found her sleeping and dreaming run-away child. She wrapped herself around Miriam's sleeping body and pulled the covers close around them. Miriam felt her mother's desire to protect her, but could feel her anger too, for worrying her so. Her mom was so focused on her husband — had been for so long — she hadn't seen the seriousness of her daughter's distress. Here in Paula's bed she realized her daughter's hurt but all she could offer was a few minutes of mutual hiding before she carried her back into the storm, the place in which they both live.

Chapter Nine

The white raft swayed gently back and forth and a pattern of circles rippled the glass of the iron-rich lake where Miriam's perfect, arrow-straight, slow motion dive took her far below the surface. If someone was watching from shore they would have begun to fear for her safety when, after what seemed an interminable time, her face hadn't broken the water's surface. An underwater camera would have caught her in a slow and grateful swoon; hair flowing smoothly back from her face and forehead and creating around her shoulders a silken black aura. Slowly she ascended through the water, eyes closed, lips in self-satisfied smile, her face toward heaven.

Water streamed from the slippery contours of her face. She took great, hungry gulps of the air that filled her nostrils with the scent of fresh, musty seaweed. A slightly acrid smell of the lake's muddy bottom all washed clean by the clear, cool water of the spring fed lake hung in the air.

She gave a little bounce when she reached the surface and lunged forward in a sprint-like breast stroke toward the raft. The rusted chrome rails of the steps reached out to her like a mother's waiting arms and pulled her in one smooth motion to the raft. A sun-toasted towel she'd brought with her when she rowed the boat out and anchored it to the raft, warmed her fingers as she bent to grasp it. She wrapped the towel around her dripping and goose-bumpy shoulders. She breathed deeply and did a little dance step to keep her balance on the rocking raft and to help her contain her overwhelming pleasure.

Skinny, sun-browned and shedding sheets of lake water, she

embraced herself and lifted a corner of the towel to wipe the moisture from her face. This, for Miriam, was a moment of supreme peace. Supreme joy. She was eleven years old and this whole lake, which might have been the whole Universe, was hers. Only hers.

After the first hurdles of starting to attend a new school in the fourth grade, she had made a lot of friends. Her bike took her everywhere — at least that's how it seemed to her. There were numerous lakes around that community so a lot of her friends lived close to or even right on lakes. Billy, Linda, Timmy, Tommy, Cindy — they all had lake homes and were allowed to have friends over all the time. She loved the water. The town she lived in was in a rural area and some of her friends lived on farms and had horses. Her friend Marvin would come by on his pony and pick her up to go out to the lake where Billy lived.

There had been lots of parties and over nights over the year and a half when she lived in the parsonage. Rebecca, the baby of the family was just about a year old when Earl came home one day announcing to the family that they would have to find another place to live.

He and a pastor from Jackson were starting a new church. The Deacons and Earl had been at odds on issues of dogma and church policy nearly from the day he accepted their offer to come as pastor. Problems had reached a near breaking point and neither side was willing to bend to the other. There was no point in fighting it. He would have to find another pastorate. Miriam was afraid she would have to leave the school and friends she'd come to love.

As it turned out her mom and dad bought a little cottage right on Sweezy Lake, with a dock out front and a raft in the middle. The house was in Miriam's same school district so she didn't have to leave any of her friends.

The house was meant to be only a summer home. It was tiny and didn't have insulation or a good heating system. The family of six crammed into the two bedroom with sun porch, lake home. The move to the little red house on Sweezy lake marked the beginning of the greatest year of Miriam's childhood.

There was a big stone fireplace with a raised hearth in the living room and a screen porch that went all the way across the front of the house. Ariana, Stephanie and Miriam shared one of the bedrooms. Their parents kept Rebecca in a small crib in their room.

This house was and to this day remains Miriam's idea of the perfect dream house. Times she was there on her lake alone she almost felt she'd found her true home. In the spring and summer she never missed a chance to be out in that lake. Early in the morning she would row out and hook up to the raft and swim and dive and soak up the sun, the scent of the cool, refreshing water and watch birds of every kind soar over head. Her mom would call her in at lunch time and she'd row in, pack a picnic, maybe pick up a friend from down the lake a short way, and row back out to the raft.

She had a boy friend now. Marvin. The one with the pony. He lived near by and would sometimes ride his pony over to go swimming with her. She had crushes on Ronny and Bruce and Billy too, but Marvin was her designated boy friend. The first summer at the lake felt like an uninterrupted dream come true. The family seemed pretty happy. Her dad was preoccupied and wasn't paying much attention to her either way, good or bad, so she hardly ever got the belt anymore. Her mom and dad threw barbecues and badminton parties for the youth group from the church and the yard was always filled with family and friends.

The other pastor that Earl signed up with to start a new church had two daughters the same ages as Ariana and Miriam, but they looked and acted like grown women. They were, respectively, eleven and twelve. They both wore bras and had breasts to fill them. They wore nylon stockings, straight skirts and pointed toe shoes. They lived in a beautiful house in the city and had ruffled and canopied beds with matching curtains on their windows. They had so many clothes and so much lipstick and makeup that Ariana and Miriam both envied them.

Miriam still wore dresses with full cotton skirts and a tie at the back. Was still very much the flat-chested little girl. Oh, how she wanted to look like Joanna. Oh, how Ariana wanted to look like Charlene.

Both Dads/Pastors were asked to speak at Maranatha, a Christian conference complex on Lake Michigan. It was a Youth Conference. Miriam watched from an awed distance as the boys all drooled over and flirted with Joanna and Charlene. She stood looking up at the faces of the teen aged girls leaning over the bathroom sink, looking into the mirror as they applied their lipstick. On the beach the couples paired off and she watched them kiss, rolling on the sand in each others arms. Miriam sat alone in the sun. Its heat, cooled slightly by a breeze off the white caps, heightened her awareness of her skin. The smell of life and decay was everywhere rich and present and reminded her of her own body. All day and into the evenings at Maranatha the young people were subjected to lectures on modesty, chastity, piety and purity. She felt sinful merely living in her own skin. She loved and hated her body at the same time. She knew it was wrong to long so for the touch, the kiss of the older boys rolling in the sand with their teenaged lovers. The longing inspired near physical pain for Miriam.

At night, in the main hall of the conference center, trumpets sounded ecstatic messages of revival. Miriam stood along with the others, singing an anthem of praise.

Maranatha, Maranatha!
Hope of all the blood-bought throng.
Maranatha, Maranatha!
It's the theme of this our song.
Coming soon, the Savior, who we long to see ...
Maranatha chimes ...
Keep ringing ...
Mel-o-dyyyy!

A thirty-something tenor, with hair like Elvis, but wearing a navy blue suit like Miriam was used to seeing in church, was the lead singer, lead trumpet player whose performances each night stirred the crowd to a confusing and lustful frenzy for Christ.

On the last night of the conference Miriam, frenzied and craving more, more, ever more of Christ and his trumpet sounds and his songs straight from heavens gates, overcome with remorse for her sinful thoughts, for her lying and talking back to her father — all her many years of behavior that certainly was sin or wouldn't have inspired his rage — stumbled forward, crying as the horns moaned and the choir sang.

Just as I am without one plea
But that thy blood was shed for me.
And that Thou bid'st me come to Thee
O Lamb of God, I come! I come!

She was not alone at the altar at the foot of the stage. Young people poured from their seats, moved to tears and confession. They fell on their knees in prayer and already saved adults came to lay hands on their heads and shoulders and pray over the repentant ones.

Just as I am and waiting not
To rid my soul of one dark blot.
To Thee whose blood can cleanse each spot
O Lamb of God, I come! I come!

The trumpets quieted, the choir and congregation continued to hum as more children left their seats awash in guilt and came forward to receive Christ. Miriam cried quietly, eyes closed. She held her shame filled head in her arms at the altar.

Above the sound of the hums rose a powerful male voice it took Miriam only a moment to recognize as the voice of her father. She raised her head and saw his face, bent low to the microphone, one hand raised over the heads of the congregation beneath the stage, eyes pinched closed in the intensity of his passion for their lost souls. He prayed then began to sing, leading the congregation

Only trust Him, only trust Him
Only trust Him now.
He will save you, He will save you
He will save you now…

Miriam buried her face in her arms again. Now she sobbed. Not only had she sinned against Christ, but against this powerful messenger of Christ — her own father, who, if she were to cease her sinful lying, she would be forced to admit, she hated.

Miriam felt lost. She was irredeemable.

Elizabeth came to the altar at the close of the service and helped Miriam to stand and walk the distance to their cottage on the conference grounds.

"It's not what you think, Mother." Miriam confided. "I mean I'm not saved, if that's what you think."

"Why Princess, what do you mean? Of course you are." Elizabeth and Miriam entered the cabin through the orange light that showed through the windows and door and had served as a subtle beacon as they made their way along the dirt path.

Elizabeth sat on Miriam's bed and watched as her daughter turned her back to her to undress and pull a summer nightgown over her head. She was struck by her daughter's beauty. Her young body was brown from the sun and her hips just beginning to take on the swell of a woman's hips. When Miriam turned to face Elizabeth, her gray eyes seemed lit from within and her black hair shone in the glow of the bedroom lamp.

Elizabeth often marveled at the beauty of this daughter over that of her other children, but she never told her little girl that this was true. Once she confessed to Earl her surprise at Miriam's growing beauty, especially given this child's frightening appearance as a newborn and as a baby. Earl turned on her and denounced her for her pride. He forced her to promise she would not turn Miriam's head by idle flattery that could lead only to vanity. He never confessed he saw anything lovely in their daughter. Elizabeth had long been troubled by the animosity between her second child and her husband, and believed, as he did, that it was not his doing, but the very nature of the child that inspired his rage.

"Her will must be crushed, Liz. The Lord will not tolerate a willful child. Certainly, you're not too blind to see it's true. I won't have you encouraging her." Earl had made this belief perfectly clear more than once.

"What, Mom?" Miriam noticed her mom watching her. "Why are you looking at me like that?"

Elizabeth lowered her gaze and offered a smile to her daughter. She extended her hand and pulled Miriam to sit beside her on the bed. The two of them had shared so few moments like this, un-threatened by the presence of the man of the house.

"Tell me what you mean — about 'not being saved.'"

"I just can't be. That's all. If I tell you why, you won't understand. How could you?"

"Honey, it just can't be true that you can't be saved. Anyone who wants to accept Jesus can be saved. You want to don't you?"

"I thought I did. Tonight, with that music being so beautiful … well, this whole place and everything… I just wanted to be so good. So different, you know. I wanted to change. To finally change so Dad would love me and trust me."

"Miriam! What are you saying? Are you saying you don't think your daddy loves you? Now — you know that's not true!"

"See, Mom. That's just what I mean. You won't understand! You only see what you want to see ..." Miriam stood and walked across the room to sit in a wooden chair under the open window. She turned her back on her mom and tried to see the waves on the lake but the night was too dark.

"Now you listen here, young lady ..."

Miriam turned to face her mother again. "I'm sorry Mom. That didn't come out right. I just mean ... Oh, I don't know what I mean. Only ..."

"Miriam, I guess you're right. I don't understand. You are a fortunate little girl as far as I'm concerned. You have a mother and a father who love each other and who love the Lord. Now. It's about time you got that through your head. Maybe you should try to see things more through your father's eyes. Maybe that would make you a little less selfish." She stood and turned the covers down and Miriam let her mother tuck her in, fluffing the pillow behind her so she could sit, and pulling the sheet and blanket up over her chest. She rested her hand on her daughter's chest and began her attempt to educate her daughter about the child and the man, Earl Peter Blackwell.

"Your father hasn't had a particularly easy life, Miriam. He needs our love and understanding. He doesn't hurt you because he wants to. No parent would hurt a child on purpose. It's just his way of showing how much he loves you. If he didn't love you, he wouldn't hit you. He wouldn't care enough what becomes of you to take the time and trouble to yell at you and punish you to correct your behavior."

Miriam listened as her mother told her the hurt her father felt growing up in a house where both parents worked and were away more than they were home. He was left to his own devices and had to figure out young how to fend for himself.

She told Miriam about how her father learned of his adoption when he was seven years old and his mother yelled the truth through her rage at discovering another of his vandalous boyhood pranks that had left her ashamed and humiliated in the face of her neighbors.

Earl hadn't felt close to either his father or mother and throughout his adult life talked very little about his ancestry. He said he knew almost nothing. His mother had been illegitimate and never knew who her father was. She was too ashamed to talk about her mother or family. His dad had been chronically ill and a stoic, closed-mouth, working class man who very much felt children should be "maybe seen, but definitely not heard" and who was rather silent in the upbringing of this son of his.

It was hard for Miriam to understand her father's dad was the same Grandpa Blackwell who showed her such delight and kindness.

She wondered why her grandparents, in what her mother described as a nearly loveless marriage had adopted her father anyway.

Though their marriage was not one of great warmth and affection, they may have felt a baby could help them create a feeling of family — that part of why the marriage was so cold was because they'd been unable to have a child. It wasn't so much that Earl's parents were terribly nasty and abusive to him. They both had to work long hours at tedious factory jobs and were forever exhausted from their daily tasks. Neither of them was able to create a sense of family they hoped would happen through adopting this boy.

Elizabeth described parents who grew increasingly separate from each other and left the little boy — her husband, Miriam's father — with a sense of being pretty much alone in the world except when he was out on the streets and making up his own adventures. He'd never said he felt un-liked or unloved in particular — maybe he felt largely invisible except at the hand of his father's sister who cared for him while his parents worked.

"Your father's aunt was a mean woman who was very cruel to him when he was in her care."

"Mean how, Mom?" Miriam wondered if his aunt hit him with the belt and how her mother would explain that it was love when her dad hit her, but cruel when his aunt hit him.

"Oh, well, I don't know specifics, honey. Your dad doesn't like to talk about it. He thinks the past is the past and would prefer to ignore it for the most part."

Miriam went to sleep that night having been asked to understand things that confused her horribly. She determined her mother was probably right, though, and she ought to try harder to appreciate and show respect to her father.

What was she supposed to think? How was she supposed to feel? Here at Maranatha her emotions were in constant conflict. In the Bible classes and sermons she heard over and over again the threat of hell

The last day of the conference, out of the clear blue sky and in front of the entire congregation, her dad announced the new church in Jackson wasn't going to make it. It couldn't support two pastors. He was moving his family to Johnson City, his family home in upstate New York, where he would sell real estate. He asked for their prayers.

Miriam was devastated. She would lose the first place she'd ever really called home. She would have to leave all of her friends. She would not have her beloved lake outside the front door of her house.

Everything changed after the Bible Conference. Joanna and Charlene were moving to Miriam's school district and Joanna had co-opted Ariana's boyfriend. The eyes that had been on Miriam and voted her sixth grade homecoming queen, were now focused only on the beautiful, the sexy, the so grown up Joanna.

The family wasn't scheduled to leave for New York until early fall so Miriam could have taken advantage of the whole summer ahead to hang onto her dream home. Her dad was going to go out to New York at the end of July and try to find the family a place to live. They were moving to the town where her mom and dad grew up so it wasn't a completely unfamiliar place to her. She knew of a park near her grandparents' house and far from the park where, years earlier she'd found her Uncle Jack hanging from the chain of a swing. This city park had a roof top swimming pool and a carousel that played rock and roll music. All the teenagers hung out there on summer nights until dark when they were expected home. She saw an opportunity to change her image completely and without her mother looking over her shoulder. She volunteered to go early to New York with her father, gritting her teeth against the thought of a long road trip with him that she saw as offering freedom and escape at the road's end. She would use this opportunity to try to love and appreciate the father her mother was so convinced hurt her only out of the depth of his love. Besides, she reasoned, he would be busy looking for a house and starting a new job.

Miriam had no memory of the sexual abuse she suffered at the hands of her mother's father and knew both her grandma and grandpa to be lenient disciplinarians. She would live in their house and feel free to grow into her idea of a teenager sooner rather than later.

Miriam had learned to sew when she was seven years old

and by the time she was twelve and ready to leave for New York she had the skills to make herself a wardrobe of straight skirts and tight shorts with sleeveless tops just like the ones Joanna and Charlene had. She shopped for pointed toe shoes and had her hair cut and styled in a bouffant hairdo. She bought lipstick, an eyelash curler and a padded bra. By the time she arrived in New York she was a new woman. She was, to all appearances, a full-fledged teenager and she was out to prove it to the boys at the park! What use did she have for little boys who rode ponies anyway? She was practically grown up. Her hormones were raging. She was ready for a change. Ready for whatever independence she could grab.

Chapter Ten

In 1945, at war's end, Julia Rousseau built her home on the rocky cliffs of a peninsula that jutted into the Atlantic Ocean off Owl's Head, Maine. The talented, rule-breaking Julia, who came to adulthood in the early years of the twentieth century, experienced the influence of the industrial revolution. She was a dedicated writer who chronicled the lives of her contemporaries in the political and arts realms of Greenwich Village and followed their expatriate exploits overseas to London and Paris in the days between the wars. Twenty years earlier Julia had given birth to a baby boy. She'd delivered him to the hands of a nurse who subsequently offered him to the arms of Ginny and George Blackwell. The Blackwells were a working class family. Ginny and George earned their living as factory workers at Endicott-Johnson Shoes in Binghamton, New York and neither had any idea of the skills required to raise a son.

In the years that followed Earl's birth, Julia had no reason to doubt her decision to avoid the dangers of an illegal abortion in favor of giving her baby to a family she believed would love him better than she could. She was vigilant in the keeping of her diaries and if she made any concession to the reality that she was a woman who was in some way a mother, it was in the record keeping she did in a subconscious attempt to leave for her son and his probable children the details of the circumstances of her life, should they ever seek to know them.

Though Julia was twenty eight years old and a mature woman at the time of Earl's birth there was about her a quality of recklessness. She was a rule breaker, beholden to no one. She never understood why society demanded that a woman, no matter her inclination or intelligence, be relegated to the role of household drudge and near slave. Her own mother lived a life of privilege as the wife of a railroad baron, and though there were certain freedoms inherent in such a social station, still, she knew her bounds and did not overstep them. Shackled herself, she encouraged in her only child Julia, a spirit of rebellion and emancipation. Julia's father saw that she wanted for nothing so there was no need to marry and become dependent on a husband, or to serve as governess or maid in the house of someone else's husband.

It was fitting that Julia retreated to a safe-home in the Catskills in upstate New York during the months of her pregnancy. Upstate New York had served as focal point for a national conference on Women's Emancipation as early as the 1870's. Julia felt herself a privileged daughter to these courageous women who paved the way for her freedom. She knew, though, there was a long road ahead to true freedom and equality for women and made the fight for that freedom her raison d'etre in the years after her son's birth.

In 1929 Julia and a number of her contemporaries established the "Society for the Preservation of Women's Experience" and opened offices on the third floor of a brick storefront on a corner in Greenwich Village. One result of The Society's efforts on behalf of women was the publication in 1955 of a small book, Sisters of These Shores, compiled and edited by Julia. It was no coincidence the book was published by a woman owned and operated New York independent book press and, no coincidence either, that it's publication marked the thirtieth anniversary of Julia's son's birth. What was coincidence, however, was Miriam Blackwell's happening on a signed copy of that very same book, on the shelf in the lodge of the Catskill resort on a dreary summer day in 1962.

For Julia her involvement in the Suffragette movement —her labors to make women's lives and words visible — her commitment to that work and its importance, justified her choice to remain free of the bonds of marriage and parenthood. Many of her peers who lived lives similar to hers in the proclamation of women's right to free choice, had born children out of wedlock or chosen abortion at great peril to their survival. She did not quarrel with the decisions they made. In giving birth rather than having an abortion, though, she believed it more likely her life would be spared and she would be able to achieve the purpose to which she felt called. She did not feel this same call to motherhood or possible death at the hands of an abortionist.

In the summer of 1962, Miriam Blackwell would find her grandmother's book on the shelf in the lounge of a summer resort in the Catskills Mountains of New York State where she stayed on rainy weekend with her Aunt Ellen and her partner, Deirdre Hope who had been her constant companion since the suicide of Ellen's husband Jack. If not for the rainstorm that interrupted Ellen, Deirdre and Miriam's plans to sun bathe and swim in the cool waters of the resort's spring-fed lake, Miriam might never have seen the little book.

Why Miriam's hand reached automatically for that particular book will remain forever a mystery. Perhaps there was some force at work in the world that guided her fingers. She had no way of knowing, of course, that the book was written by her own grandmother. No way, either, to know that Julia's was the voice of comfort and acknowledgement that reached her sometimes in those quiet, solitary moments near the water.

Miriam curled her thin legs beneath her on the soft leather of the chair in the lounge of the resort. Comforted and warmed by the flames and scent of the wood fire that relieved the chill of the afternoon rain, Miriam reminisced about the lake home she'd so recently left behind. The book fell open on her lap, revealing page after page of aged and worn photographs of women of her parents' parents' generation.

Women posed together in a Paris café, at a picnic along the Seine, on the banks of the river at Cornwall on Hudson or at a desk in Greenwich Village. One woman smoked a thin, tapered cigar, another lifted a glass of red wine in salute to the photographer. Under each picture the date of the photograph and the name of the woman pictured. Miriam recognized these women, dressed in either ankle length skirts with high collars, or sheer and short dresses, neck and throat draped with beads and scarves, or even, in some instances, man style suits, as the women who peopled her paper doll plays and fantasies. She stared hard at the pictures, trying to read all she could into the expressions on the women's faces. She recognized the women with the dark, painted lips, finger crimped curls and short hair and skirts as the Flappers who were the wild women of her grandmothers' generation, and not a bit like Grandma Blackwell or Grandma Barrett.

Miriam sat alone in the lounge under its ceiling beamed in Adirondack timbers. This was not a resort typically attractive to children. Her aunt and Deirdre had decided on a nap after lunch. Other guests were presumably in the dining room or napping too.

Miriam counted fifteen pages of photographs and looked at each one with a near microscopic eye trying to discern from the pictures what the captions could not tell her. The women laughed with heads thrown back, legs kicking the air. She turned the book to look at the back cover and saw there the picture of the author standing on the rocks above a wave-blasted shore. Julia Rousseau wore a man's black suit and what appeared to be a soft white blouse, open at the collar. Her black hair was clipped at the back of her head in the traditional suffragette style but strands of it escaped and blew wildly about her face. She stood looking out to sea and Miriam found her beautiful and at once familiar and strange.

Chapter Eleven

After Roger and the paper doll day, Miriam lived sometimes in those feelings he awakened in her. They served as refuge, though a shame-filled one, when there were no waves or breeze-swaying trees to calm her spirit. Oh, she relished the times spent with girlfriends but increasingly realized she had insight beyond that of other little girls. Her fantasies took on an overt tone of sexuality. They were filled with an intensity, a desperation. She felt a compulsion to include boys in all the parties and social events of her life. A need to find a way to be in the dark and alone with a boy.

Though her father became less brutal toward her physically as she got older he seemed to attain great satisfaction from grilling her endlessly about her every thought and activity. He exercised a strangle hold on her mind from which she escaped at great peril. She felt her only freedom, her only salvation, was to defy her father and was unable to discern between responsible, self-respecting behavior and dangerous, frivolous and irresponsible involvement.

No one could reach her. No one could get close. It was too late. Her sole aim was to survive and to have that survival feel good, feel exciting. Danger and deceit put her at risk and she'd come to feel most fully alive in the face of that risk and danger.

Once she'd left Sweezy Lake and settled into her life as a teenager in New York, she concentrated on creating for herself a fully-modern appearance designed to attract attention. In the seventh grade she won considerable reputation as a ratted-haired, white-lipped, tight-skirted floozy. She built this reputation pretty much on appearance alone in the sense that no actual sexual activity — beyond making-out like a banshee with six or eight of the cutest boys in her class and a few in her older sister's class — took place.

Mornings before school her mom would come at her face with a hot, soapy washcloth and attempt to scrub away the mascara and white lipstick. She would scream in her mother's face, push her away and run from her cries of sorrow and outrage. Run from Elizabeth's insistence her daughter was running headlong down the devil's path to fornication.

Miriam's early adolescence, and the freedom she demanded at her peril, in the town where her father tried his hand at real estate, didn't last long. After a year and a half of trying to make ends meet and falling steadily into dept, Earl was forced to admit he was a failure at selling real estate. He decided his true calling remained the ministry and, after making inquiries and interviewing for the few available pastorates, was offered a church in a back woods township in the Finger Lakes Region. He was promised a salary of fifty dollars per week as a part time preacher which he intended to supplement with substitute teaching in a nearby Christian school. Faced with little choice and less real opportunity, and with mortgage foreclosure a distinct possibility, Earl moved his family to the false brick, asbestos sheeted house with the water-soaked wall paper, the blackened, torn linoleum floors and the rickety front porch that shook and threatened to fall onto the ground beneath it during the slightest of storms.

When the family moved in the middle of Miriam's eighth grade year, she made the best of the situation by becoming yet another version of herself. She padded her bra, smoothed her hair and styled it like the models in Seventeen Magazine. She sported Bobby Brooks-like separates on her make-believe curves.

The first day of school the boys lined up, their heads, one on top of the other, stretching to see through the small square window of the classroom door, "the new girl". Her tan stocking covered legs were crossed provocatively under a short red wool pleated skirt. Her white sweater with red trim softly draped her freshly laundered breasts.

She was not allowed to date boys or go to dances. She developed close friendships with girls and every day after school there was legitimate cause to stay in town and hide her liaisons with boys under the pretense of homework, study, shopping and gabbing with one girlfriend or the other. She became ever more adept at sneaking and lying. Sports activities of all types were acceptable to her parents, so she was often found on the Friday night spectator bus, an avid sports fan, making out with Bill, Tim or Tom.

By the time she was fourteen years old she met and fell in love with Johnny Angel. Jonathan Paul Walters.

Miriam and Johnny knew just enough about sex to scare them away from intercourse, both because of the threat of hell-fire and teen pregnancy. Neither of them could stand the thought of the humiliation of either of these consequences. They risked everything but that in their exploration of the limits of Miriam's parents' patience and each others hungry lips and bodies.

Johnny and Miriam sat on the bleachers in the gymnasium, hand in hand, looking in true anguish into each others eyes and talking their desire to run away together, cross state lines to a place where no parental permission was needed to marry. That was the ninth grade for Miriam.

She wanted nothing in life so much as the drug-like ecstasy of a man's hands on her body. Life at home was a constant screaming match between Miriam and her father. He no longer used the belt but chased and cornered her, sometimes swinging the full force of his arm and slapping her hard across the face. She learned to apply make up over the mark of his hand on her face, as she did to cover the hickeys Johnny's kisses left on her throat. If anyone ever noticed she was hurt they never said a word. Sometimes at night her mother would come to her and sit on her bed pleading with Miriam to please quit her enraging behavior. That her daughter was out there for all the world to see, flaunting in the faces of the congregation who were her teachers and her school mates and their parents, her blatant disregard for the Scriptures mandate of chastity, was a source of extreme vexation for her parents. Yet another situation where they felt her as a threat to Earl's ministry and livelihood.

In the tenth grade Miriam's family moved again and she left Johnny's side to attend a school some twenty miles away. By that time Johnny had his driver's license and she was permitted to go on group or double-dates. For a time she and Johnny maintained their passion and the belief they were meant for each other, but the boys at her new school had greeted her arrival with the same level of enthusiasm she'd received when she moved to Johnny's school. She wanted her freedom so she broke up with Johnny.

She became infatuated with a star soccer and basketball player whose family was devout Catholic as well as prosperous, and who thought she and her backwoods, country preacher family were clear examples of poor white trash. The boy's name was Bill Parks. He was smart, strong, handsome, sweet, innocent and in love for the first time. He came from a good childhood and a happy home. He hated to lie to or disappoint his parents, but in order to see Miriam, he had to.

When she first came to town she was given a small part in the school play, "Papa was a Housewife" and she and Bill would meet up at the Laundromat or up in the cemetery after rehearsals and after his soccer practice, to do some necking and heavy petting. They were beside themselves with lust but with the same impediments to satisfaction she and Johnny encountered. It all ended sadly when Bill's dad discovered their secret necking sessions and insisted Bill put an end to this immediately or forfeit his soccer championship possibilities and the ski trip to Colorado over break. Really, infatuated as Bill was, the relationship with Miriam was far too intense.

It divided his loyalties in such painful ways, it came to be something he felt was destroying him. He was, in truth, relieved to have to say goodbye. He later fell in love with the Principal's daughter, a Catholic too, and an acceptable match. There was considerable heartbreak for both Bill and Miriam in the break-up. She pursued and was pursued by other boys and indulged quite freely in the flattery of it all, but, underneath, she felt hurt and loss and knew that Bill did too.

Johnny was there, always had been, ready to come back at a moment's notice. Her family had taken to Johnny as if he was a son and he was at her house more than she was since their break up.

He had a sense that if he couldn't have Miriam, perhaps Ariana would find him acceptable. Miriam's desire for a "steady" coincided with the incident of finding Johnny and Ariana kissing in her bedroom. Well, it was Ariana's bedroom too. Not only did she see them kissing but she overheard them talking about Johnny's desire to go to college and seminary and become a minister.

For Miriam, this talk of a career and the possible

disappearance of Johnny into her sister's arms represented a challenge. She determined to commit to Johnny. She had one year left of school. As soon as she graduated, she would marry him, leave home and help him through school in some place far, far away.

* * * * *

Junior High and High School had presented Miriam with a wild roller coaster ride between the respect and admiration she sought from teachers and her aching need for romance and sexual approval. For her, because of her early childhood experiences, these needs had a heightened and intensified quality far beyond the already staggering pressure for popularity the usual teenager craves.

She was a highly capable student who couldn't knuckle down to her studies unless some love interest was involved. She flirted shamelessly with the two male teachers she encountered during her teenage years. They were both English teachers. The interest she took in this area of study and her response to the romance and intrigue of literature, in spite of her recognizable emotional problems and her incredible neediness, caused each in turn to do what some would describe as letting her "get away with murder."

Her need for male attention drove her to extremes of showing off. She wanted to be center stage and did all she could to make an impression on these teachers by reading heady novels, poetry and classical literature far beyond the level of her peer group. She grabbed lustily after all controversial issues of the day, the kind of things no one talked about in a Baptist minister's home; abortion, free-love, pacifism, nuclear disarmament, birth-control. She took these subjects on as topics for reports, speeches and classroom demonstrations, making a name for herself as a loud-mouth and a trouble maker with those who felt a young girl should listen and not talk and whose talents should be put to more subtle engagements.

Mr. Strong, Miriam's sophomore English teacher and the high school drama coach saw through her tough girl cover and offered her the comfort and rescue of words. He gave her his own dog-eared copy of Truman Capote's <u>Other Voices, Other Rooms</u>. It took her many years to understand the value of what began in that one tender act of this tall, serious-faced teacher, who quietly asked her to stay after class one day and placed in her hands a book that would open worlds to her. After the day of that tender gift, her need to understand history was nurtured by Shakespeare, Thornton Wilder, Thomas

Mann, Tolstoy, William Styron, Evelyn Smith and James Baldwin. Her curiosity was insatiable for all areas of life that had been withheld from her.

Maybe what she read in fiction was all made up and offered no truth concerning the lives and time and place in which the stories were set. But to her, the places, scents, passions and beliefs she encountered in literature were a homeland, another place of refuge. A place too, where she began to learn some answers to questions that plagued her.

Her early forays into history had come about through curiosity and play. The jump into the past that was perhaps the true impetus for her ultimate career as historian was being chosen, by Mr. Strong, to play the part of Emily in Thornton Wilder's, "Our Town." By the time she played the part of Emily, her family had moved three additional times since leaving her dream home on Sweezy Lake.

She became Emily. She couldn't tell where Emily left off and she began. She lived the part of the nineteenth century, small town girl, with the tragic and blessed life, for all the many months of preparation for two nights of glory under the lights on the high school stage. Being Emily changed her in ways that many years later she would realize as rescue. Being Emily fed her a grain, a seed really, that would grow somewhere deep within her during all her years of reaching and yearning for rest and peace.

During the decades of her life when she sought comfort and caress in the arms of so many people, not recognizing the danger the immediate gratification held for her, Emily was there in her. She whispered at first, then ultimately tried to scream above the chaos and din of her life. "Pay attention," she said. "Take notice of life as you live it. Take care with your life for the sake, not only of yourself, but for all those who will come after."

Emily sowed the seed in Miriam that would lead her to look backward in time, not at her own life at first, but to the lives of women at the time of "Our Town."

Not that she knew any of this at the time she was actually living Emily Gibbs/Webb. No, for her, being chosen for this part and being given the chance to live someone else's life for the months of her sixteenth year, represented escape and fulfillment.

Throughout high school Miriam's desire to leave her father's house accelerated. Her unladylike, ungodly behavior did not go unnoticed and she was at constant battle with her dad. He seemed to show interest only in what she was doing wrong, the ways in which she was breaking the rules and defying his power. He gave up on Miriam's amounting to anything and didn't encourage any of her interests or abilities. It was assumed she would fall into early marriage. He only prayed she would not humiliate him by becoming pregnant.

During high school she was under constant restrictions and sometimes grounded for months at a time. She mastered lying and sneaking around and, finally, there was no way the restrictions could get any greater because they exceeded the time remaining to her graduation from high school and her eighteenth birthday.

Johnny bought her a small diamond ring and proposed to her in the front seat of his 1963 VW Bug. The engagement was a relief to her father because he felt he could trust and control Johnny and, before long, he would take Miriam off his hands and out of view of his congregation. Finally, he would be free of this rebellious and willful child who had so negatively colored his life.

Chapter Twelve

Miriam's final years of high school and her decision to find her freedom from home by an early marriage, coincided with national events of great significance. In 1963, the young, Catholic, Democrat President of the United States was gunned down in the streets of Dallas. President John Fitzgerald Kennedy — handsome husband of the fashionable Jackie O., father of two adorable children — whose years in office would be eulogized as the "Days of Camelot." The years following the death of the young hero saw the resurgence of the Women's Movement as well as the entry of the United States in the war in Southeast Asia and with it the birth of anti-war sentiment and the sexual revolution. The birth control pill was introduced and, for the first time in history, women were free to express themselves sexually without fear of unwanted pregnancy. The conservative values of the post World War II era saw challenge and confrontation and life for the generation just coming to adulthood, Miriam's generation, seemed to offer the possibility of freedom never before realized by modern society.

But Miriam, by leaving home and marrying at age seventeen, was only superficially aware of the world changing around her. Unwittingly Miriam was repeating the pattern set by her parents' early marriage. She continued to live in a world of fantasy, picturing for herself a future in which, she herself the image of Jackie O., would sit with her two beautiful children, in the front pew of the church, while her husband Johnny, following in Earl's footsteps, would lead a congregation to godliness. Hers was a fantasy of vindication. No longer would she be the unwelcome child, the black sheep. She would follow the lessons her parents taught and she would make them proud by living a new and improved version of the life they lived.

Johnny avoided the draft by his decision to train for the ministry. His selection of a school in Minnesota meant Miriam would once again have access to the waves of Lake Superior. His choice of career meant she would be free of the worry of losing her husband to a death in the jungles of Vietnam.

Johnny started classes in the fall of the 1967 and he and Miriam lived briefly in a haven of their imagined future while all around them the world expanded in a successive explosion of fireworks. Before a year passed, another Kennedy son would fall prey to an assassin's bullet; the brilliant Janice Joplin and Jimmy Hendrix of the new era of drugs, sex and rock and roll would lie dead as a result of the excesses of the new American freedom they claimed. The war in Vietnam would go on and on and, ultimately, more than 50,000 young Americans would die, not a few of them the victims of the police and National Guard who tried to silence the voices of anti-war protest on the streets and campuses of American soil.

In the early days of marriage Miriam pretended a level of confidence and satisfaction she did not feel. She lived her life on the surface, making all the motions she believed proper to her role as future preacher's wife. She had no ambitions other than to help Johnny get through school and to make a home for him and the family they would build.

One weekend the first fall they were in Minnesota, Miriam and Johnny took advantage of an opportunity to visit Lake Superior's shore. There in proximity to the waves she was visited by a sense of discomfort — a reminder of something she'd either lost or never found. A professed and actively evangelical Christian now, she chalked the discomfort up to a lack of diligence in her prayer life. She didn't want to acknowledge all she might risk in a loss of faith. But something there on the shore, something she felt as a voice, urged her toward that risk of questioning, delving deeper to discover the root of her discomfort. She determined it was dangerous to let this voice speak her name and didn't return to the shore again until Johnny finished college.

By the fall of 1967, Julia Rousseau, living now these many

years on the cliffs above the sea, had seen and felt keenly the richness of the changes in her country. Her diary still her confidant, she wrote these words on the forty-second birthday of the son who was never hers.

Thursday, October 12, 1967
Owl's Head, Maine

Dear Diary,

Threats of war, again and again and again in my life time. And, oh it was easier to bear in my youth, my young womanhood…

All the leavings and letting go of a lifetime have entered again my aging (oh, but you know it's thriving!) seventy year old heart. But I do not regret. No, life for me has been blessed, rich, thrilling, to say the least. I've prospered in all ways. An occasional heartbreak or loss has only added richness to the depth of my experience. Over the years, and especially in October of each year, my thoughts go to the little boy, who is of course now a man living somewhere in the same world as me. And now, forty two years after his birth, it is in many ways a very different world — but, too, in the essential way of the human animal — much remains the same.

There is serious and deadly turmoil now in Southeast Asia. My boy, unless he's a career military man, will likely escape being sent to those jungles. That is, if he is living still — and, if he survived World War II — and my prayer is he was spared that horror as well as the war in Korea.

Oh, dear diary, what generation has existed upon this earth since the beginning of mankind that has not, at one time or another, believed it possible to change the fate of humankind? Repeat. Repeat. Birth and wide-eyed bliss. The sunshine, lovely flowers, feel of the sand under your curling toes as a wave-pushed breeze brushes your hair from your face. And yes. Yes. Hope is necessary. Hope as well as a belief that hatred, war and killing are not inevitable, this belief is necessary too. At what point, I've wondered often, does holding to this hope and belief simply become an essential pretense — a delusion to keep us from giving up? Oh I don't mean giving up in a suicidal sense. Not "I might as well be dead." No. But the kind of giving up, giving in, acquiescence that makes the artist silent. The kind of giving up that says to the desperate artist its all been said, painted, sculpted, written, danced and sung before and what good has it ever done? I think of what I know of the life of Anais Nin, Henry Miller and, yes, my Maine muse and grace visited companion, May Sarton. These, my contemporaries are not naive. They have not given up or given in. Did anyone of them ever think to change the direction of all human kind by offering up one, true and certain philosophy or belief system? No. Each has forged a personal path for navigating this world of horror and wonder. I've just read again Thomas Wolfe's You Can't Go Home Again. I wondered as I read deeper and deeper into the pre-sentient (yet telling only the true present) novel, published in 1938: wondered if Wolfe really thought he was the first one to say it in a way that might be heard. That might stop the hatred and the killing. . . Then I started thinking how much he could just as easily be describing our world now and the generations of people now living on this planet we can't seem to stop ourselves from destroying. No matter how many or great the wise ones who issue warnings. We all deceive ourselves and that's perhaps the common human thread that keeps us loving life, believing in its goodness. I've often held to Nin's reasoning about the contribution we make to peace by living individual lives of peace and tolerance and a faith in some kind of cosmic or Universal Whole that we're all an essential part of. When asked what I'm doing for world peace, world hunger. What am I doing to stop the harm? I'm trying not to add to the harm. Trying to be tolerant of differences. Trying not to be violent or greedy or unkind. I feel so helpless when I take on the entire world picture, or U.S. picture, or New York or even my little neighborhood here in Maine. I always have to come back to what I can and can't control. What I can and can't contribute. I will be about peace. I will be about kindness. I will share the wealth. These are the examples I (perhaps) set. Maybe my way of living is seen and makes a difference for those who follow me, for others around me. A quiet contemplation. Taking my own life seriously enough to perhaps not add to the killing — this seems important to me.

You Can't Go Home Again caused me to think of the parallels between the life of George Webber, my contemporary, Nin's and Henry Miller's too, and the times in which we now live. George lived in a world he perceived as never before having been at such a cross roads — each powerful country at the time racing, racing to make the first weapon of mass destruction. Hitler coming to power along with Stalin, Mussolini, the industrialization of nations, the possibility of ease of travel one continent to the next and everyone, everywhere fighting to be first, lay claim to the biggest prize, the greatest power and control. Any everywhere the suppression of human truth and creativity wrecking havoc with the genuine genius heritage of Germany who gave us Mozart, Beethoven, Goethe, Proust (the list is endless. . .) And in our own country at the time there was a sense of isolationism. A naive nationalism that led this, the richest nation in the world, to believe nothing could harm our contentment and our wealth and our power. The Banks fell (the mighty fell), a socialistic (dare I say communistic) touch might have fed the hungry, clothed the naked, housed the homeless. But, no, such a spirit of sharing the wealth and concern for all people rather than the covering of one's own ass — to borrow a phrase from the youth of today — was a philosophy held suspect. People who cried their outrage at the greed, at the capitalist system were blacklisted and censored and silenced in this, our would-be democracy.

Wolfe's book cried outrage at censorship and greed and fierce, self-protective nationalism. If Wolfe had lived to see the 1940's he no doubt would have been tried for treason or at best, been censured for pro-Communist leanings. But he's saying again what Ecclesiastes said hundred's (thousands?) of years before him. And we don't hear it now, don't see it now any more than we did those thousands of years ago or when Wolfe 's book was published. The few cry their outrage in each generation; the helpless masses grab onto hatred, bitterness, self-defense or simply live in quiet, impoverished desperation. I have wracked my brain for what my role should be in stopping this inexorable march to human doom. It saddens me horribly to be aware of history, of the present, of the inevitable future. "If you're not part of the solution, you're part of the problem." — you know that one, I'm sure, dear diary. And maybe it is a self-delusional thing I do to act my grain-of-sand part by living peace, acceptance for others; that sort of thing. Right now, though, it still seems the course for me. I am little by little coming to believe mine is a life well-lived, and this I will leave as legacy.

Oh, but, truest confidant, where is he now? Where is my boy? You would think, after all these years I would cease to wonder. But that's not the way for me. At seventy years old, I desire more than ever before to leave a legacy, a part of me that will somehow go on in someone else. I fantasize, (expect?), imagine there are children now.

Imagine my son, in the age of traditional and conservative values that overtook America after WWII, married, became a traditional family man. Over the years I've written songs or poems, or danced a heartfelt wish toward my son and toward his children, wherever and whoever they may be. I've kept confidence with you, dear diary, but imagined that someday, perhaps after my death, my well-wishing will reach beyond these shores and touch the life of my son and his children and their children.

But now, dear diary, the confidence I must share with you today … I've made a dramatic step. I've hired a legal representative to do a little spy work. I've sensed a growing need across the years and miles for my presence. Perhaps I'm completed demented, delusional, but my soul tells me I am sane to feel this. I'm not certain if it's my boy who seeks me or a child of his. My heart and soul feel the pull, the reaching. There's a treasuring that's needed. A rescue perhaps. I've felt it most keenly in the years since I built my home here on the cliffs of this peninsula off the coast of Maine. And sometimes, when my mind and spirit are locked in the motion of the waves, I swear I hear a voice. It's the voice of a girl child. Sometimes it comes in a sweet song and I feel as if a soft prayer has entered me and I whisper it on a breath and send it back across the waves.

Oh, I've told you, dear diary, of these days by the sea when she reaches out to me. I tell no one else. Friends would think me crazy. And, perhaps it's all just wishful thinking, but a girl grown to woman in these times in our world needs her history, needs all the sense of connection and clarity she can get to allow her the freedom to claim her place and move forward.

And yes, perhaps it is the effect of old age. Perhaps I'm wishing for the impossible. But I've prospered so and learned such valuable lessons in the life I've lived. I now seek an heir. I long for the possibility that my blood and spirit flow in the life of a woman.

I'll know soon enough. I've hired a firm in Cornwall on Hudson, the firm that settled my parents estate and handled all their affairs, to help me find the source of the voice coming to me with the waves.

Can I Write?

Can I write your face?
Your eyes,
Your scent?
The cadence of your song —
Heartfelt, wrung with sorrow
Through and through.

The music of your voice
A tune so mellow as to melt my
Stone enshrined heart.
Flowing lava I become.
Surround you with my heat.
Your face, your eyes, your scent…
Sorrow in song
The music of communion.

Chapter Thirteen

"Pastor Paul," Miriam confided. She was eighteen years old and had been married to Johnny for a full year. "I need your help. I don't know where to turn. I'm afraid and lonely and I don't think Johnny loves me anymore."

Pastor Paul was a chaplain at the local hospital. He was considered a counselor. He had some background in psychology. Christian psychology. She believed at the time it was important to steer clear of secular or "lay" psychologists. Such a person might give far too much permission to just trust herself, be herself, believe in herself, an approach that left Jesus out of the equation, and that was not at all acceptable for a young Christian in training for becoming a Baptist minister's wife. She hadn't dared to tell anyone in the church that she and Johnny attended how desperate and alone she felt. She searched the yellow pages under "Counseling Services" and came up with a listing for this chaplain.

Pastor Paul didn't seem to understand why Miriam would come to him. His specialty was comforting the bereaved, frightened, suicidal and/or tragically diagnosed, when they or their loved ones were in and around the hospital. She was doing a trial and error thing to avoid having to confess to anyone who knew her just what was troubling her.

Pastor Paul sat behind a golden finish maple desk. It was rather small, its right side pushed against the wall of the little office at the far end of the hospital chapel. A green glass-shaded lamp sat next to the wall and was the only item on the desktop. Pastor

Paul, it was obvious, did not use this desk or office as his place of work. It appeared to be a place various chaplains could schedule when they needed a quiet space to consult with someone. The pastor looked entirely uncomfortable and out of place in this setting. His appearance was a bit off-putting. Pale, transparent skin through which rivulets of reddish/blue veins could be seen under a dusting of rust colored freckles. His hair was extremely sparse and the same color of pale rusty gold as his freckles. He wore glasses that kept sliding forward on his nose and he had the nervous habit of constantly adjusting them. His features were essentially nondescript. One of those kinds of faces whose features would come off with the glasses and be just a blank concave circle shape with his mottled skin stretched smoothly around it. A face she now thinks of as Muppet-like. He was probably in his late twenties, maybe early thirties and had a tendency to produce a fine, mist-like sweat in Miriam's presence.

His face registered bright red shock when she described to him the circumstances that brought her to his office. It was a fight she'd had with Johnny. For the third or fourth night in a row, and they were newly-weds, he had refused to make love to her. It wasn't the first time. They had waited — she with great impatience for completion and fulfillment — to consummate their relationship until they were officially married the week after she graduated from high school.

The actual event, intercourse, had been a great disappointment for Miriam after all the anticipation. Their nights and afternoons of heavy petting and non-stop making out all through high school held much more excitement.

What she wanted was all the feeling of those groping, illicit — "we have to wait — no, no, please don't stop — oh, but we can't, we can't. . ." — experiences, followed by the ecstasy and transport she'd come to believe would be hers when, at last and finally, engorged penis entered willing — pleading, begging — vagina and all the rewards of waiting, holding out, would be realized in glorious, God-approved orgasmic release.

Miriam and Johnny, after settling into their honeymoon cabin, went straight for the "real thing" they'd only been able to dream of in the weeks and years that preceded their wedding. Miriam tried to relish the experience, embrace it and hold it in her memory. She'd waited so very long. Her life-long ache would disappear in the arms of her husband.

She thought something significant like pain or a little tear and bleeding might punctuate the moment. They skipped over the long, intense, probing kisses. Skipped over the caresses that made her crazy with desire. Oh, they kissed and touched but there simply was no necessity for these substitutes any longer. Johnny slipped right inside her without a single hitch. There wasn't the slightest wince of pain or sense of a virginal barrier. She just felt fuller than she ever felt with his finger inside her, that's all. Johnny moved around in there for awhile, but, since he'd had the luxury of coming all along during their heavy petting sessions, it didn't appear that actual intercourse was any big deal to him. He came. Miriam didn't. They did it again. He came again. She didn't.

She started her period the next day and was bloated and irritable. Married one full day and already she felt wrung out and foolish in her belligerent insistence on getting married so young.

Bent double with cramps and sweating with the fierce humidity of the June weather she was attracting biting black flies and mosquitoes in record numbers as she attempted to grill their long-planned romantic, first married meal, steak with baked potatoes and peas. For their honeymoon they'd rented a cabin on a quite lovely, if man-made, reservoir in Ohio.

By the second night of marriage she was covered with red welts from the bug bites, bleeding like a stuck pig and feeling sweaty and exhausted. They tried to make love in spite of her condition but she felt ugly and the whole bloody process disgusted her. She spent the remainder of her honeymoon crying, scratching bug bites and gorging on junk food.

They drove from Ohio, where she'd spent her senior year in high school to their first married home. She was excited that they would live in St. Paul, only a three hours drive from the solace of her much missed, much craved Lake Superior shore. She decided her disappointment during her honeymoon was simply hormonal and approached married life with renewed hope and vigor.

She and Johnny made love often and there was certainly some comfort for Miriam in Johnny's arms. She knew she was missing something, though. Before her wedding she had asked her mom and her aunt for some information about sex.

"Does anything come out when a woman 'comes' like it does for a man?" she asked.

"Oh, I guess you'll just have to wait and see about that." Said her aunt. Like, "That would be telling now, wouldn't it?"

She'd been permitted to read a small pamphlet on married "love" written by some Baptist preacher. It said "to effect satisfactory intercourse, it is advisable for the woman to lie on her back, lift her knees at a slight bend with her legs spread just a bit."

She was horrified! Even with all the groping she and Johnny had done, she didn't expect she'd be in the embarrassing position of spreading her legs and bending her knees right in front of him. She asked her mom about it and she calmed Miriam by saying, "No. At least I never did."

This was it. These were Miriam's role models. This was her preparation for bliss in the marriage bed.

But this couldn't be all there was! "Maybe," she thought, "maybe I did come but I just don't know it. Maybe this is what it's like for a woman. It wasn't at all bad. It actually felt good." Good enough she pretty much insisted it happen several times a day in the early days of her marriage. She became somewhat of an acrobat in her attempts to accomplish the longed-for sense of completion, release and connection. She learned lifting those knees and spreading her legs was merely the beginning of the positions and contortions she would happily go through, naked and right in front of a man.

She became ever more dissatisfied as Johnny became frustrated and disgusted with her. He called her a nymphomaniac. She accused him of impotence. The friction increased between them and one night Johnny cried, "What do you want from me? Just what do you want"?

Punching a pillow she'd thrown across Johnny's stomach, she yelled, screamed and sobbed at the top of her voice, "I want you to fuck me! I want you to fuck me! I want you to fuck me!"

She tore from the room. Johnny chased her and tried to shush her so the neighboring couples in the Christian college housing complex would not hear such profanity coming from the mouth of a future minister's wife. She threw herself face forward on the living room couch in their apartment and sobbed. She felt utter desperation and rage. She wanted to die. She wanted him dead.

Johnny stood in the doorway between the kitchen and living room, back lit by the florescent light that showed her red, white and blue kitchen canisters and American flag curtains just beyond his scrawny and naked, adolescent body. He hung his head, supporting himself by one arm against the door jamb. He looked at Miriam, shook his head and turned to walk back into the dark bedroom alone.

She wanted Johnny to hear her calling the crisis hot line. Wanted him to know she was at her wit's end. She needed a crisis to break the monotony and deprivation of their terribly young married life. She needed him to say he understood how bad it was, how bad she felt. She needed him to say he was a man. He could fix everything for her. He could make it better.

The guy who answered her call acted like he had bigger fish to fry. He suggested talking to a counselor. " Do you have a Pastor? Would your Mom or Dad understand? Don't you have a friend or a sister you could confide in?"

She finally hung up the phone, drained. She climbed back into bed and sidled up close to Johnny, his back to her stomach. She slipped her arm around his middle, enjoying the feel of his warm, smooth flesh. Feeling a rush of hope and love for this boy who was her husband, knowing she'd frightened him, she held him until they both slept. In the morning she looked up Pastor Paul's number in the yellow pages and so began twenty three years in and out of psychotherapy and support groups. So began her education on her past and toward her future.

Needless to say, perhaps, but here it is anyway — Pastor Paul was not a whole lot more help than her mother and aunt had been. He did ask some questions, though, that opened deep wounds for Miriam. He asked about her relationship with her father.

She told him she and her dad fought all the time and she couldn't wait to get away from him. She didn't go into much detail about her childhood or her dad's disciplinary style. Just said something about authoritarian, rigid and dogmatic. Since Pastor Paul seemed to think relationships with men such as fathers, grandfathers and brothers could impact a marriage, she did confide that she recently had an experience that kind of disturbed her a little bit. It was about her grandpa on her mom's side of the family.

She told him she'd been alone one night in the basement apartment she and Johnny shared when they first got married. Johnny was working nights at a paper manufacturing plant in St. Paul. Miriam watched this movie about Sigmund Freud and his work with young women and hysterics. Something was said about childhood sexuality and childhood molestation.

The TV screen and the voices coming from the set faded to a hazy background as Miriam sat frozen and seeing in vivid, three-dimensional color, her Grandpa Barrett quietly entering the bedroom where she napped near an open window when she was very young. She remembered him carefully removing her underpants from under her plaid cotton jumper and, with red face and fumbling, clammy fingers, he licked her and licked her in the place her mom and dad taught her was filthy and dirty.

Seeing and feeling this image, she could hardly breath. She wasn't in pain and didn't remember being in pain when he did it. Then, another image came, of an earlier time; and another when she was nine or ten. She was so embarrassed, so mortified, and so unbearably ashamed. In those few moments her entire sense of her history and relationship to her family was altered. She shook her head and took a few quick breaths to make it all go away, turned off the set and went to run a bath.

She told Pastor Paul that a few weeks after that her mom and dad came for a visit. She told her mom about this strange experience she'd had and that maybe it was all just her imagination or a dream but she wondered had she said anything to them about it when she was little. Her mom stiffened and tears came to her eyes.

She said, "Yes. Yes, Miriam, you did say something. Yes, it did happen. We hoped you would forget it. You didn't seem to be hurt by it."

Miriam calmly accepted all this and never spoke of it to anyone after that. She believed, yes, it hadn't hurt, why make a big deal out of it?

With great care and gentleness Pastor Paul leaned across the desk and looked into Miriam's ashamed eyes.

"Miriam," he said, "you need to know. It did too hurt you and it just so happens — it matters very much."

She wanted more than anything for her forty-five minute session to be over. Maybe Pastor Paul thought it mattered but she didn't feel like it had anything to do with her anymore. Why was he focusing on that when she came to talk about her sexual frustrations with Johnny. She wanted him to give her some instructions to take home that could make Johnny want her and assure her everything would be all right. She certainly hadn't anticipated all this "Did you love your mother? Did you love your father? How was your relationship with your grandfather?" stuff.

She left, dissatisfied and went home, deciding maybe she and Johnny should have a baby and put this all behind them. A change was all they needed, she decided. They would move. She would get a new job and she would try to have a baby.

* * * * *

She started work as a clerk typist in an office at the University. She and Johnny moved off campus and she felt a little more freedom to listen to her rock and roll music and have friends over from work whether they were Christians or not. Johnny was more and more absorbed in his school work and his full time job as a custodian. Miriam developed friendships with the single women who lived in her apartment building and started to feel pretty much like a young, free, single woman herself.

She gave up begging Johnny for attention and sex. She started to have intimate conversations with other young women about their sexual experiences. A woman, maybe ten years older than she, who had a happy marriage and two children, was particularly helpful.

She told Miriam about a book called <u>The Sensuous Woman</u>, by J.— the author obviously wanted anonymity.

Miriam felt extra sneaky, like she was really sinning, the night she went out to Rosedale and bought the book at B. Dalton. She brought it home and hid it under piles of underwear in her top dresser drawer. She didn't dare read it right away. What would this woman say to her? This was the era of the sexual revolution but Miriam, a Baptist minister's daughter and future minister's wife, was not one of its participants. Would this book make her want to participate? Would it lead her to sin and send her on the path to Hell? She was truly frightened and truly mesmerized by the possibilities reading this book might hold.

She waited for a Friday night so she would have the whole weekend to recover or do penance or whatever was going to be needed after opening the pages of this naughty, naughty book. She took a long, leisurely bubble bath and smoothed lotion over her skin, before slipping into her white cotton nightgown. She fluffed her pillows and propped them next to the bedside lamp. She stretched out comfortably on the bed and with hours ahead of her before Johnny would be home. She opened the book and she read.

J. talked about the importance of a woman knowing her own body, how it responds, what it needs to feel satisfied. J. confessed, no, flaunted, her own techniques for sexual fulfillment. She said, "If you don't know your body, how do you expect him to?" She said, "Masturbate."

Miriam could not believe her eyes. She flushed and giggled and twisted her legs together under the covers feeling dangerously titillated. "I couldn't," she thought. "I just couldn't. How would I do that?" But that titillation kept at her.

She was alone. She had absolute privacy and all the right parts and tools. "What if it doesn't work?" she thought. "What if I'm not like other women?" "What if I find out it's no different than what I've been feeling all along and it's just no big deal — there's no such thing as fulfillment?"

She set the book down on the bed beside her, lifting the covers back to reveal her thighs under a soft layer of nightgown. She shyly lifted her nightgown with the fingers of her left hand to reveal the soft, dark curls between her young, married thighs.

She closed her eyes and licked the middle three fingers of her right hand until they were nice and slippery. She used her left hand to open her lips just a little and set her three moistened fingers right where J. said she should. She hesitated, feeling tense, breaths coming in irregular gasps, feeling a warm glow all through her. She moved her fingers, began to tease herself, to try this and that lightness of touch, slippery stroke, all around and over and on that spot from which little microbes of electric charged feelings emanated, emanated, oh God! — emanated! She touched, stroked, teased and played, her face growing hotter, the skin on her shoulders and breasts misting over with moisture. Her nipples stood at full attention and her gown had fallen off her shoulders to reveal just one of her breasts. A cool breeze from the open window blew across the exposed breast and sent a marvelous shiver of pleasure right up through her head and back down to her toes again. Climbing higher and higher, sighing, moaning, grinning like an idiot, she rocked from side to side.

"I can't believe it! I can't believe it! I can't believe it!" She cried, she shuddered, she gasped for air as she came for the first time, and, boy oh boy, she knew it too.

* * * * *

J. will never know how dramatically her little one hundred twenty-nine page book changed Miriam's life. Maybe J. can't be held entirely responsible but it was The Sensuous Woman that set her on a new course of study in womanhood and sexuality. To say Miriam became preoccupied with this new Pandora's Box of sexuality would be an understatement. The Sensuous Woman was about things other than masturbation, of course. Having been set, what felt like, entirely free by following J.'s simple instructions in that particular skill, though, she felt compelled to try out suggestions that would include Johnny in this vast and rich world available at their proverbial finger-tips or whatever-tips.

She decided the only problem with their marriage was that, prior to J., she hadn't known her own body. Now that she was learning, she figured all she had to do was show Johnny what she'd learned. He would, she presumed, be as excited and enthusiastic about this new sport of wild, abandoned sex as she was.

"Maybe," the book said, "maybe your man wants to see you for the sex kitten you are. Get rid of that flannel nightie and the moccasin bedroom slippers. Surprise him at the door completely nude except for a hat and high heels."

Well, she thought this sounded like great fun. Her first attempt to show Johnny the new Miriam happened on a weekend when he didn't have to work the night shift for three nights in a row. He'd pulled a temporary day shift and would be home by four o'clock on Friday afternoon. She took the day off work and concentrated all her energy on setting the stage for a night of complete romance with Johnny. In the morning right after he left for work she ran herself a planning bubble bath. She lay back in the tub and practiced her technique in self-love all the while envisioning how, later that night, she would seduce her young husband and make him love her again (and again, and again . . .).

In the grocery store she picked up strawberries half the size of apples and just brimming with crimson juice she knew would act as a love potion. She spent the longest time in the whipping cream aisle weighing the relative merits of heavy whipping cream vs. ultra thick ultra pasteurized whipping cream vs. double rich whipping cream. She just didn't know. Maybe the spray can would be the most fun. She pictured herself holding the can above Johnny's erect penis. She would squirt a thick coil of the cream in a circle, first around each testicle, then a cord of the tasty stuff in a swirl around his cock and end up in a big question mark shape somewhere up by his belly button. She would then lick and suck until that question mark disappeared.

The thought made her giggle and a little moisture leaked from between her legs. She knew this would be way too much, way too soon, though. She decided on the ultra pasteurized, ultra thick or whatever it was, and set it in the cart next to the juicy strawberries. She visualized herself feeding these dripping morsels to Johnny by holding the stem in her teeth and leaning toward him where his hungry mouth would nibble at the ripe fruit until their lips touched.

When Johnny opened the door to their apartment at four that afternoon she was ready for him. She didn't want to frighten him away by appearing too eager or acting like a brazen hussy. She wore a short dress of soft fabric, a skin colored lace bra and skimpy bikini matching underpants. She greeted him in bare feet. Her long, dark hair was freshly washed, curled and styled. She pulled some of it back and up and tied it in a ribbon, leaving the rest of it to cascade around her shoulders in an attempt to create a sweet, innocent appearance.

She approached Johnny and helped him remove his coat. She loosened his shirt buttons and removed his belt before leading him to the couch where she knelt down and took off his shoes and socks. She rubbed his feet and looked up into his tired face to ask him about his day.

He lay his head back on the couch cushion, closed his eyes and rubbed them with his hand. He said he couldn't believe how long the day was. He'd had to work the night before he reminded her and he'd had hardly any sleep the last few days. He said, when he tried to sleep all he could think about was how far behind he was falling in his school work. He rubbed his eyes. Miriam rubbed his feet. He started to cry. She held and rocked him in her arms until he fell asleep.

There would be no strawberries and whipped cream for this sad and tired man tonight.

* * * * *

In the years that followed her conversion to "sensuous

woman," Miriam led her life skimming the surface of the history she couldn't face. She involved herself in seemingly honorable pursuits but for all the wrong reasons. Everything became a cover and a lie of a successful, purposefully lived life. Her interest in Women's Liberation, the pursuit of her degree (and ultimately her doctorate), an honorable career, motherhood, childbirth education and a commitment to breast-feeding, leadership roles in her children's schools and pre-schools, conferences, lectures so appropriate to her emerging expertise in women's history, masked her continued yearning. At the heart of it all, under the mask, at the black bottom core — was compulsion and desperation. She lied so effectively, she believed herself. She convinced herself she acted for right causes.

But life was chaotic and unpredictable. She was storm tossed and too busy, too caught up in out-distancing her past to realize she was moving further and further from the rest and home she longed for.

Soon after she became the embodiment of the sensuous woman and had tried and failed at all attempts to bring Johnny into sync with her desire for sexual fulfillment, she discovered the re-emergence of the Women's Movement. In the books, articles and lectures of Gloria Steinem, Betty Freidan, Nancy Friday and Germaine Greer, she eagerly sought and found justification for her desire for independence from the confining role of marriage to a depressed and non-participating husband.

The world, she knew, was in the full swing of the sexual revolution and proponents of open marriage and free love filled the media with their message of individual freedom. She enrolled in school, joined a women's support group, came and went from the house she shared with Johnny with little sense she owed him an explanation of her activities.

He worked nights and weekends and had no energy to devote to romance or even shared conversation on the rare occasions their paths crossed. She, more and more, led the life of an unattached college woman whose decisions were, in her mind, a concern to no one but herself.

She pursued her degree in history and a minor in literature and found her heroes among the fictitious and the dead who decried the role of slavery imposed on women by marriage and monogamy. In her classes at the University, she met women who had chosen single parenthood outside of marriage, selecting as their child's father a suitable and willing stranger. She hadn't decided that she no longer loved Johnny. As a matter of fact, she harbored a hope that, once her own life was fulfilled and he established a sense of direction, their interest in each other would be rekindled. She certainly thought him to be the most suitable candidate to father her child.

She was a couple of years into her free-loving, free-thinking life, and still married to Johnny when she determined she was ready to be a mother. She'd been extremely cautious about birth control over the time she'd felt free to engage in casual affairs and liaisons because, though she longed to conceive and give birth to a child, she held firmly to her desire to have Johnny father the baby.

After the rush and excitement of free living, she felt hungry for something she had trouble naming. She longed for the in-depth sensuality and the spiritual aspects of being responsible for caring for the child she wanted to conceive.

She renewed her commitment to Johnny, who behaved over the last few years as if he was oblivious to her infidelity. Miriam and Johnny mutually fantasized about the baby they would make. She stopped her wild, party-girl life and determinedly prepared herself for healthful and loving motherhood.

Both Johnny and Miriam were delighted when they learned she was pregnant. Johnny dropped out of seminary, where he was feeling a particular sense of defeat, and took on a full time job that allowed him to be home with Miriam on weekends and evenings. She continued her classes at the University during her pregnancy. She felt flushed and full of life and its importance in a way she'd never before experienced. She ceased her flirtations and threw herself into her role as pregnant woman and future mother. She felt she knew real and true love for the very first time.

Months into the fantasizing and day dreaming of future bliss with baby shared between Johnny and Miriam, life returned to some of its day to day ordinariness.

Johnny began to feel he'd missed out, in marrying so young, on the freedom other young men in his generation experienced. He sensed Miriam had changed in her need for him and he started to pursue idle flirtations and friendships that involved keeping company with people with little or no academic or intellectual aspirations. Miriam was consumed with her studies and her preparations for her baby's birth and saw Johnny's new diversions from home as a good thing. She didn't want him to depend on her always being there for him or making him the center of her life. Neither of them noticed how far their paths were drifting even as they prepared to bring a child into their lives.

She discovered too, that pregnancy did not quell her desire for romance and affection or her need for affirmation from admirers. Increasingly, in her life as a student she came in contact with people who opened her mind to new and stimulating ideas. She loved to spend time in deep philosophical discussion with students and faculty at the University. As always, she was filled with longing. Filled with an un-named yearning, which her marriage to Johnny, her dreams of her future role as mommy, and her research as a history student didn't answer.

She developed a close and deep friendship with one of her professors, Dr. Al Thomas. He was fourteen years her senior and had been married for seventeen years to a smart and attractive Vassar graduate. He deeply loved his son and two daughters and had been a faithful husband throughout his marriage. Miriam knew, but wouldn't admit to herself, that Al was attracted to her. She knew she loved the attention of this brilliant man. It meant so much to her to have his admiration and she told herself it was an innocent, intellectual connection she felt to him.

By the time Al got around to confessing his interest in Miriam went beyond the intellectual and philosophical, and that he found her beautiful — in her extremely pregnant, less than feeling anything close to lovely state — she had come to depend on the approval he offered.

Her feelings were confused and she tried to trust her own soul, her own sense of right and wrong. She left Johnny, Al and the University, when it came near time to have her baby, and went to her renewing home in the woods by Lake Superior. She gave birth in January to an Aquarius daughter, with the help of a midwife and by the light of the full moon over the part frozen, part storm-tossed waters of her treasured lake. She named her lovely daughter Storm. It was a name that aptly described her own life.

Johnny came north to spend the weekends with his wife and daughter and developed a true and deep love for his baby girl. He admired Miriam's strength and beauty as she cared for their tiny infant. He sat close to her when she nursed their child. During their days together at the lake, Miriam and Johnny both felt a new hope rise that this baby might mean a place of coming together for them as a family.

Al came north to see her. She hadn't expected his visit. She tried to put him and all thoughts of his importance to her out of her mind and focus fully on being, first and foremost, the mother of the tiny Storm. But Al brought through the snow, and in his glove-warmed hand, a dozen glorious yellow roses, hungry kisses and a desire for Miriam no one had ever shown. She loved him deeply. She loved Johnny too. It was unfair to say "yes" to either one of them.

* * * * *

She returned to the city and the university to live a life deeply fragmented by mixed desires. There was a part of her that was completely Madonna-mother, earth-mother, rich with sensual baby love. And when she was fully living that part of her, it was everything. There was a part of her that lived in the relish of the friendship and sense of family she'd had with Johnny since she was fourteen years old, and together they shared a longing for a future of calm loving between them.

Sometimes she was wholly the person Dr. Al Thomas, gentle, brilliant, fascinating, acclaimed professor of history, wanted, desired more than life itself. She was sometimes the budding women's historian basking in new-found knowledge and fascination with her future career. She lived for one and a half years simultaneously and separately in these places and personae.

Chapter Fourteen

Over and over again in Miriam's life she became obsessed with a need, a craving, for the complete attention of one particular man. Al Thomas was the one who finally risked everything that had ever been of great importance to him and gave her what she thought she wanted — all of him.

It perhaps should have taught her a further lesson in taking care what she wished for. After Storm was born she wrestled with conscience, guilt and her out of control desire to have Al and all his love and attention would mean, all to herself. She hated herself for wanting him. She hated him, blaming him for awakening this desire in her in the first place.

It wasn't the case that she had time on her hands. It was impossible to figure how there was space in her life for the loneliness and craving to creep in and gnaw at her as it did. She tried to throw herself full-force into caring for Storm, making Johnny a happy husband. She worked hard at her studies. Al was constantly on her mind. Everything she did was aimed at showing Al she was worthy of him. The meals she fixed for Johnny, the romantic evenings she created, she would describe to Al in great detail to make him jealous. Make him wish she was with him instead of Johnny. The way she nurtured, played with and loved her little baby, had as much to do with showing Al what a wonderful mother she would make for his children and a child they might have together, as it did with her true knack for motherhood.

Even in her studies, she was competing against his Vassar graduate wife who was a pillar of the local feminist community. She played on her strengths, youth and beauty and her ability to satisfy Al's every sexual fantasy. Every errand was an excuse to be near him, even if it was just to shop at the same grocery store as he.

The pressure built and she became openly destructive, taking great chances with Johnny's tolerance and making her presence felt in Al's home life. She believed she had to have him or die. One day on campus she convinced Al to go for a walk with her in broad daylight. She broke down and raged at him, striking her fists against his chest, crying and yelling, begging him to either love her or kill her.

She was lost in an all consuming passion of rage and desire. Al was as caught up in the crisis as she was. He lost control of his carefully guarded emotions and picked her up in his arms and ran with her to a wall at the river's edge.

She held him tight against her, crying, " I don't want to live. I don't want to live. I love you too much." Al stopped his motion toward the wall and dropped to his knees, still holding her in his arms. They held each other, crying and rocking.

"I'll do something, Miriam," he said. "I'll do something. I don't know what. We can't go on like this though. This is crazy."

For Miriam, the craziness just confirmed her belief it was true and essential love she felt for him. The more it was crazy; the more it was passionate and dangerous, the more certain she was, this was love. And, for true love, she would do anything.

She left Johnny and took Storm with her. Al couldn't leave his wife and children. He was sorry.

" I want you," he said. "I don't need you."

Miriam joined a baby-sitting co-op where she and other single mothers took care of the others children so they were free to take classes, study and date. She was careless with these hours of freedom, sometimes bringing a man home with her, smoking dope, drinking, playing music and making love so loud that her baby would wake from sleep and come to see what was happening.

She was ashamed of what her little girl saw, but tried to tell herself Storm was too young to be affected by it. By morning she would make everything all right and it would just be her baby and her and she'd show Storm there was nothing to fear. She promised herself to be more careful in the future, but often her need for danger, and to rid herself of her constant thoughts of Al, would win out, and Storm would wake to find a drunken and lustful stranger in the house.

Storm's birth and existence, taught Miriam, introduced her, really — since Storm was her first child — to the worst kind of terror, the greatest joy and the deepest kind of love. The day she was born and the weeks, months and years surrounding that day, before and after, were times for Miriam of desperation, confusion, rebelliousness, longing to be cherished, trying to be the right kind of grown up — having poor examples — and not knowing how. Some of the ways she was and the things she did and learned about being a mom — some of that she was proud of. She tended to want to dwell on what she did well and right. The truth though is that she did a lot wrong and she caused harm. To say she merely made mistakes makes too light of her selfish, ignorant and harmful behavior.

Her life and the choices she made put Storm in harm's way and she wished she could take that back and have her history be one of solid, non-stop comfort and a sense of deep down safety. She tried so hard when Storm was a baby to escape the frightening influences of her family and her childhood. She thought such escape would come from running fast and hard as well as proving herself a capable student and historian. She lived an extreme, self-indulgent, love-seeking and pleasure-seeking life. She didn't know then what she later learned about the abusive forces that shaped her. That those experiences made her lack conscience and compassion. Made her grab for escape and lack of responsibility for her behavior. She was terrified to sit still and take an honest look at her history and the hurt and damage. She became a tough guy. She would "show them." She knew it was important to care for and protect her baby. In a practical and even an emotional sense she believed she did that rather well. But there was a fair amount, too, of chaos, upheaval, tension and compulsive behavior that Storm lived in the middle of and had to have sensed and absorbed.

It was a sad and stormy end to Miriam's marriage to Johnny. Storm was a baby-sized witness to that. Then, when it was just Storm and Miriam and she was living fully her new-found freedom in the age of the sexual revolution, she did a lot of dating and partying. She and Al were engaged in a tempestuous affair and he was in and out of their lives. A particularly rage-full fight they had when Storm was only two years old scared Storm badly.

Al's desire for Miriam increased with his knowledge of her reckless behavior. He spied on her, standing outside her bedroom window the nights he knew Storm was with her father. One night he heard Miriam's moans of pleasure in the arms of a young, muscular, drug-abusing history student, and his patience snapped. He called Miriam at four in the morning and told her to get ready, he was coming to get her. "This has to stop." He insisted. "I need to be with you."

He picked her up at six o'clock in the morning. He wouldn't speak to her or tell her where her was taking her. Silently, he smoked one cigarette after another, until he pulled up outside a high rise apartment building on the West Bank. He took her to apartment 420, stubbed out his last cigarette and began to caress and undress her roughly.

She was in heaven! All she could think as she participated fully in his near ravishing of her, was "You're mine, now. You're mine now, aren't you?"

He'd left Jan and found a place to live. When he'd spent his lust for Miriam that first morning in his apartment, he cried, holding her face in his hands. "Never, never, never do that to me again. Do you understand? I'll lose my mind. I don't know what I'll do. Do you hear me? I can't share you. I won't." He sobbed his words into her face. She was afraid and more excited than she'd ever been. She was in dangerous territory and it felt strangely like home.

* * * * *

Miriam's marriage to Al never had a chance. Al couldn't forgive himself for leaving the home he shared with his wife of seventeen years and the three children he dearly loved. Miriam and Al bought a house close to the home where his children lived and they came over and spent the night three times every week. Miriam wanted very much to have a second child but Al was concerned about making his other children feel unimportant. He was in his early forties and unsure he wanted to prolong child rearing well into his sixties. Miriam begged and pleaded and argued her heart-felt desire to have another baby — a child who would be theirs, rather than his or hers. Al acquiesced and they learned on their delayed Paris honeymoon that she was pregnant. Two years into their marriage she gave birth to her second daughter, Jane.

The weeks before and after Jane's birth were a wonderful

time for Miriam. So much of the time it was just the two of them and Miriam would day dream her thoughts and wishes for her. Storm was in kindergarten in the mornings and, before Jane was born, there were many days Miriam would sit and rock, looking out the front window, the ground covered with snow, holding her warm inside her, rocking, thinking and loving her already. She felt she already knew who she was, but of course she couldn't have. She didn't know if she would have a son or a daughter. She spent her evenings reading classic novels, her feet in Al's lap. In those days the house was always filled with music. Sometimes it was Handel's Water Music, sometimes Vivaldi, Telleman or The Brandenburg Concertos — often it was Jackson Browne, Linda Ronstadt or Stevie Nicks. She would sometimes go to the nursery where the crib, dresser and a cute little lamp were all ready and waiting for Jane. She would stand there gazing, dreaming and holding her belly. Life felt so right for a time.

Al agreed they would take several weeks and go north to have their baby by the Lake. Storm was with them. Jane's birth was an easy, fulfilling and highly sensual experience for Miriam. By this time she felt Al was completely committed and completely hers. He participated fully in Jane's birth and she hoped they would now have a bond that would allow her to feel welcome and at home as his wife.

Their marriage seemed to strengthen and grow right up to the time Jane was a year and a half old. Miriam began to feel restless to be back in school or working in the school and community. She was still determined to move forward on her degree and hoped to teach one day. As her activities took her out of their home, Al lost faith in her and withdrew.

Al was ashamed to have abandoned his other children for something so frivolous as his passion for a younger woman. He felt shame for creating a child with Miriam — a child his other children might see as taking the attention and love they deserved. He pushed Miriam to the background and essentially ignored her when his children were near. She begged and protested and pleaded but had no true confidence that she deserved better treatment.

In the privacy of their bedroom Al would berate and belittle her as a whiney and belligerent child. When she tried to explain herself or argue in her own behalf, he put her down telling her she was too immature to accept criticism.

She turned to Zoe Baird, a therapist, licensed consulting

psychologist and Stanford Ph.D. Al had become rage-full, jealous and possessive of Miriam's time and presence — all the while pulling further away from any communication or intimacy with her. Miriam was lonely. She began to lie to him so she could spend time with other men. All his professed love and respect for her prior to their marriage seemed to have been drowned in his fear of losing her, and his loss of self-respect for loving her. He was withdrawn and aloof and inattentive when she was around but angry and belittling when she participated in community, school or neighborhood involvement that put her in the company of other men close to her own age.

Finally, she asked Zoe if she thought there was any hope that Al would ever be able to respect her as a peer and love her without all-consuming jealousy. She told Zoe about his jealous rages. About his coldness to her. She didn't admit she was flirting with other men. Didn't say she was seeking response, admiration, laughter, sex and romance in their arms. She described her involvement as platonic — as friendship, nothing more.

Zoe met with Al and he established an ultimatum for continuing in the marriage. If Miriam would cease to have friendships with men he would stay in the marriage. Miriam wanted time to think, to live separate from Al for awhile. A chance to rebuild her confidence in her ability to live as an independent adult.

Al said, "No time off. No separation. You stay here and quit seeing male friends or we'll get a divorce. I won't negotiate on this one."

She felt lonely, invisible and diminished in her life with Al. It was reminiscent of the parts of her childhood where her parents constantly shushed her, didn't dare take her out in public for fear she'd bring some humiliation and shame upon them. She felt mostly worthy of nothing but shame in his presence.

She packed her belongings, took Jane and Storm with her and rented a two bedroom apartment near Storm's elementary school. She told herself it wasn't over. Only temporary. She just needed time. Maybe with time to think — maybe then Al would realize how much he loved her, put her in first place. Maybe Al would go to counseling with her and they could put their marriage back together. It never happened.

When his son asked him if he missed Miriam after she'd gone, he said only this, "I miss the sex".

* * * * *

It was a revelation to Miriam, once she had her own home and bed, how much less lonely she felt than she'd felt so many nights sleeping with Al. She loved him though. Loved him with a passion and fervor that made her willing to sacrifice her own need for companionship, intimacy and respect. She stayed as long as she did trying to hold out hope that he would recover from his guilt and start to see her as something more than a young, fresh body who fulfilled all his sexual desires.

It didn't take long after their divorce for Miriam to determine loneliness terrified her more than mistreatment. She took the leap that landed her in the arms of Roy Berman, a man she knew from her days of volunteering in the school Storm attended. Took the leap that landed her in the most dangerous territory she'd lived in since childhood.

She needed to believe — insisted to herself and everyone around her — the friendships she had with men were based on mutual respect, common intellectual, social, political and spiritual interests. She did get a lot of response from men and it was a comfort to her and helped her gain confidence in the days following Al's departure from her life. She needed too, to lie to herself. Needed to continue to skirt and skim across the issues that were dictating her life and keeping her the claim of this forward, backward, whirlpool motion that dragged her time and again to the black bottom of something she was drawn to, programmed to repeat.

She'd left her parents home and went out into the world at seventeen, but home and all its love lessons followed her everywhere she went. She chose men, one by one, going from bad to worse, until she arrived at the place she began — her father's lessons in love.

Chapter Fifteen

Miriam secured a secretarial position at a local college after not having worked full-time for a number of years. She took on leadership roles at Storm's school and Jane's nursery school. She attended college classes, working now on her master's degree. Since she didn't want to accept any help from Al, who told her she couldn't make it financially without him and tried to hold her to him with that threat, she was able to qualify for food stamps and some public assistance to help pay for medical and child care.

She was fairly happy in her social life and making stabs at realizing her desire to invite people, men and women, in and out of her home and activities without getting caught up in a committed, long-term relationship before she felt ready.

It's true that, at this time, she was pretty much seeing Roy exclusively. She would go to parties, out to dinner, to the theatre and to lectures and musical events with male friends, but there was seldom a question of sexual attraction on her part. She found herself having to push some men away who wanted more intimacy than she had to offer, but, by and large, the friendships were comfortable and platonic in nature.

She liked the idea of what she called sexual-friendship. Liked intimate, all-night conversations, listening to music with a friend, reading aloud to each other. Then, maybe a bath, a massage, and if it felt right, yes, some friendly sex with someone she cared for and trusted. She felt pretty much a failure at marriage by this time and there were, in those days, many socially acceptable ways to conduct the sexual and romantic dimensions of a woman's life.

It was after she took Roy up on his offer to rent her the second floor apartment of a duplex he owned, that, even though he didn't live there at the time, he became possessive toward her. A few months after she and the children set up comfortable residency there, Roy moved in downstairs. Assumptions took over. She found she had little will power to resist his charms and the comfort of lying in his arms at night. It was just too easy. It was, in retrospect, extremely dangerous.

She had been in pain and overwhelmed with guilt over failing in yet another marriage. Felt she couldn't trust her own perceptions. If what she'd had with Al wasn't the stuff of life long love and commitment, then what was? Yet she was so lonely and unhappy in the home they'd shared. She was easy prey to anyone who could make her laugh, make her feel beautiful, visible, smart and interesting.

She couldn't trust her feelings or what any one told her or even what she thought she'd seen and experienced. She needed guidance and support.

She adored her children. Told herself they came first, but took full advantage of their regular visits to their fathers' homes. She claimed, insisted really, how healthy and good it was that they spend at least two nights a week, one of them a weekend night, in their fathers' care and company. And, yes they were well cared for. But in their absence, she was reckless and self-destructive. Deeply needy, never questioning why.

Her reckless behavior during Storm's early childhood had harmful and lasting effects on her. What effect would the break up of her marriage to Jane's dad have on her life? She was never able to provide certainty, during those years, for either of her daughters about where they would be or with whom and how secure/ insecure that place or person would be.

Again, she sought counsel from Zoe.

During her struggle to determine what she felt for Roy she let herself love a man who had been a good friend to her for years and who was the former husband of a close friend. It started out with them simply getting together as single parents.

His name was David and she invited him over with his two

little kids to have pizza and so their kids could play together. It wasn't completely innocent, though. She wanted to explore the possibility of a friendship with him ever since each of their marriages broke up. She was still dating Roy but not feeling, in her saner moments, a commitment to anything long-term was a good idea.

She was still reeling somewhat from her break up with Al. Still felt she loved him but couldn't see a way to put the pieces back together. Since Roy had left his bride of only a few months soon after her marriage to Al broke up — and swore it had nothing to do with his expectations her — she didn't know how much to trust him.

Besides, she truly wanted to be free of a significant relationship until she could sort through what had gone wrong with Al. She felt tons and tons of unrequited stuff in that relationship. She was loaded with unfulfilled longing and had a sense of being unvalued and invisible. The invisibility caused her to reach out in her day dreams and sometimes test the waters of response from other men who seemed interesting to her. She'd played at some flirtation with men when she was studying at the University and when she worked with other young parents at her daughter's school. None of these came to much. Just vague flirtation that affirmed her, her attractiveness, the pleasure of her company and conversation, and kept her blinded to the need for reflection about the direction her life was taking.

She pulled too close to Roy too fast. He offered easy, available comfort for her despair. She was honest with him about her dream of remaining free of commitment for a time. She wanted time to search and explore so her life wouldn't remain one unhappy, unrequited love story after another. Wanted too, to get some solid career training to keep her from financial dependence on men. Her studies were going well and she was gradually gaining the sense she might be able to make a contribution to her field.

The first few times she and David and their kids got together were relaxed and pleasant. David confided in her, sharing his own sadness, fears and disappointments about his lost love. Eventually she told Roy she wanted to explore a deeper friendship with David. That she had, for a long time, felt drawn to him and felt she owed it to herself to see if there was something of significance in her feelings.

Roy blew up. Exploded in a rage. Maybe this was her first experience of his possessiveness and cruelty. He didn't physically threaten her then. He backed her up and yelled in her face holding her shoulders hard against the wall. His rage was familiar and should have tipped her off that she was in danger, but something from the past told her he was right to want to hurt her. Still, she did not want her life controlled by his rage anymore than she had wanted her father's rage to control her. She reverted to her own familiar behavior and began to lie in an effort to protect her independence without making a complete break from Roy. Roy lived downstairs and was aware of her every coming and going. He didn't want her to see or spend time with anyone but him.

As soon as she started to spend time with David, Roy found a woman and brought her home to have sex with him in the bedroom right under Miriam's second floor apartment. Afterwards he came upstairs to confess, cry and beg in her arms. She didn't know what to do. Didn't know what she felt.

She had been intimate with Roy for a long time now and he could make her laugh like nobody's business. She didn't know if she could live without that laughter. She knew that Roy and she played well together and playtime had been in short supply in her previous relationships. His charm extended to the bedroom where he took great pride in his prowess and performance. Miriam worried she couldn't do without his arms around her — couldn't do without the way he made her feel when he made love to her. She couldn't seem to break free of his hold on her. So she lied to be with David.

She lied and told him she was going away for a week alone to do some work, sort through some of her feelings without the distractions and needs of her children, her job, housekeeping and all that. She rented a motel room just a few miles from her house and asked her sister, Steve, to stay with Jane and Storm.

Steve had been her best friend for years now. She'd come to live with Miriam for a time just after she and Al broke up. She had an apartment of her own now but spent a lot of time with her two nieces and Miriam. She told Steve where she was going and what it was all about. She asked her to keep it between the two of them because she feared Roy's reaction should he learn she was spending some time alone with David.

The very first night something remarkable and deeply moving happened between Miriam and David. It felt like they had always known each other. Their bodies as they slept fit so perfectly together.

It was more natural to sleep wrapped together and feeling like one animal than as two separate people.

In the days that followed she learned so much about David. He loved flowers. He was an extraordinary gardener. Both the inside and outside of his home were perpetually flower-filled. Throughout the year giant hibiscus bloomed in his windows alongside a vast array of exotic plants most people in Minnesota never see unless they travel to warmer climates.

He was an excellent and choosy cook and loved to play an equal part in the planning, presentation and indulgence in romantic, candle-lit dinners. Breakfasts in bed were erotic and sumptuous feasts where they moved easily from dining on dripping and leaking fruit, to nibbling and devouring each others ready bodies.

For days they left the bed only to bathe together or prepare. In the bathtub they slid soapy hands everywhere, rubbed each others bodies to a raw, pink/golden sheen with a rough wash cloth. They slid alternately and seesaw style under the water to be pulled by the other's arms in a rocking motion to the surface again and again. They made love even in the way they read to each other from the words of Maya Angelou, Anais Nin, Carlos Castenadas and their own words where they shared their stories, imaginings and dreams.

The actual act of sexual intercourse was just one of the many ways they let themselves leave the world and experience each other fully. She'd left home in an act of exploration but soon felt connected to a full-blown soul mate.

Two thirds of the way through that week of days they hoped to spend together, Roy found out where they were. He called the room and yelled through the receiver beyond Miriam's ears in an attempt to intimidate David too. When they stopped answering the phone he would call and let it ring and ring. He called at all hours of the night and even came to the room and pounded savagely on the door, threatening to break it down at four one morning. The manager had to come and drive him away with the threat of calling the police. Miriam had discovered too much and David had become far too important to her over those few days for her to let Roy's behavior dissuade her from loving her new-found soul mate.

Their connection seemed to go beyond physical proximity so they knew telepathically the words to a song the other was listening to, singing along with in the other's absence. Phone calls at night after the kids were in bed allowed them to double check to see if that message they thought they'd received telepathically was for real.

When she went home she told Roy she didn't want to see him until she figured out if what she'd found with David was meant to be a love she could commit to. By that time Roy had calmed down and come to the conclusion he needed some time away from Miriam.

Miriam knew she had hurt Roy deeply, and she understood the hurt and his sense of betrayal. It came down to a conflict she felt about her need to determine her direction or settling into a relationship she knew deep-down she couldn't trust — just to keep the peace for the time being.

Leaving Roy was painful for her. All she could think of in his absence were the happy times. Roy was a dancer and a lover and an entertainer. David couldn't dance for anything and his love making came more from the soul than from the studied expertise Roy took pride in.

Roy couldn't seem to see outside himself enough to see the setting or rising sun, enjoy a flower's bloom and scent or hear and bask in the words that fell from another's lips. David sent telepathic burning sunsets to her from around the world when his travels kept them apart. He sent Miriam a sunset off Bodega Bay in California the last time she made love with Roy before they separated.

The sunset is what did it. As Roy held her in his arms and reminded her, for the last time, what she would be missing, David sent her a sunset so vivid she cried for the beauty of it. She kissed Roy good bye and flew to California to be with David.

They camped on the shore above great flower covered cliffs overlooking the ocean. She was home for those hours and days by the sea. They camped in a KOA in Petaluma where they cooked fresh scampi, dipping a crisp and chewy sourdough baguette in the garlic butter and swilling bottles of fume blanc they picked up in the wine country. The camper rocked with their laughter, songs and love making. They made their own avocado dip and picked up a daily bag of tortilla chips as they headed off on each leg of their tour.

The next week they had to go home and see what parts of what they had would last, fit in to life back home, and what parts had to be shed day to day and treasured only in their memories. The return to ordinary life presented significant difficulties. Roy's friends and David's friends were the same people. David's ex-wife, Susan, was one of Miriam's best friends and was less than thrilled about his loving her.

Miriam had been the first one Susan told when she fell in love with a younger man and struggled with her conscience and her commitment to her husband and two little children. Miriam had wet-nursed David and Susan's baby son when Susan went back to work. The baby had to have human milk to thrive, and since Miriam was still nursing Jane at the time, she nursed their baby son.

Jane, though only four years old when David and Miriam became lovers, found the relationship confusing. Already she had to adjust to staying alternately at her dad's house and her mom's. She adjusted to Roy's regular presence and now she was being asked to let David and his two little kids become a part of family life.

David's house was just across the street from Jane's father's house, which added further confusion. Half of Miriam's friends were upset with her for hurting Roy and the other half were mad because they were certain she would hurt David.

She and David tried to revert to friendship without sexual contact but couldn't manage it without a feeling of extreme deprivation. Finally, the disruption and confusion got to be too much. She still hadn't completely lost interest in Roy and had to promise not to see David if she wanted him back in her life. Little things about David had started to bother her.

He didn't get jokes and didn't know how to tell them. His inability to dance started to make him seem clumsy to her and his gardening talents turned more and more to raising a prize crop of marijuana and indulging in its pleasures. The risks she'd taken with David were a great escape for her in the short run, but a life of uncertainty and risky adventure and hedonistic pleasure seeking wasn't a life she could accept. She needed to feel safe and wanted to offer safety to her children. She said "Yes" to Roy and "No" to David. She should have said "No" to both of them.

Chapter Sixteen

Roy had two sons from a previous marriage to a still very angry woman. Miriam had no interest in becoming a step parent after the fiasco with Al and what she endured because of his guilty conscience. It was important to her that she and Roy keep their families separate and stay living in separate apartments. She liked his children, but didn't want to get caught in the middle of the endless quarreling and one-up-man-ship that went on between Roy and his ex-wife.

Roy's oldest son was fourteen and, though a really nice kid, pretty severely troubled and prone to depression as well as violence toward his mother. His younger son was quiet and sweet but seemed to be burying some heavy hurt by overeating. He was fat and kids made him feel pretty bad about it. Both boys worshipped their dad. He'd been off and on in his attention to them. Mr. Unavailable, dropping the occasional crumb over which the kids would go "ga-ga" to try to please Dad and maybe make him come around more often. Roy ignored their pleas for time alone with him; time to have him all to themselves, and didn't seem to see how it made them suffer. They just had to take what they could get and be, or at least act, satisfied with it.

Once Miriam set her relationship with David aside and made a commitment to Roy he insisted it was sheer silliness and economic folly for them to be living on separate floors of the same house. With her help he could refinance and remodel the house to make it a large and suitable one-family home. The economy of sharing life with

Roy had its allure. Miriam had finished her dissertation but part-time teaching stints and child-support didn't cover all expenses plus the student loans she had to repay.

.Roy's plans sounded romantic and she wanted to believe they could become a happy family. She thought nothing of it that he refused to put her name on the deed but let her co-sign on the loan. He lied to her about his financial position and his level of indebtedness.

He told her once that she could count on his commitment to her. That he felt about her like he'd felt about no other woman. He said, "You've shown me the real meaning of the word Woman." She hadn't needed these lines. She'd become tired of looking ahead to an uncertain future. She made up lies to convince herself it was safe to commit to Roy. Deep down, she didn't even really believe her own lies.

His lies and half-truths were so constant and so transparent she ceased to question him. Just took what she could get. When she did take the trouble to question his logic or poke holes in some story he told her, she could count on him — here's where the certainty came into their relationship — exploding in a rage. The only uncertainty was what form the rage would take.

What would it be this time? Would he wait until he thought she was asleep and come into the bedroom and throw a full glass of cold water on her face with no explanation? At four in the morning, would he turn on every light, radio and TV in the house and turn the volume up full blast all the while stomping in a circle and yelling, "Now do I have your attention? Now, can I get you to listen to me?"

Maybe they'd be sitting on the bed together and she would tell him she knew he'd lied to her about where he'd spent the evening. He'd maybe say something like, "You never know when to stop do you? You just never quit? Well I'm not going to let you talk tonight. I've had enough of your accusations and I know how to make you quit blabbing."

She would protest, insist it was important to talk this through, get to a place where they could trust each other. One night when circumstances deteriorated and she insisted on making him listen to her, he said, "I told you I wasn't going to listen to you, but you just can't quit talking, can you?" He smashed a pillow across her face knocking her backward on the bed. At first she thought it was some kind of joke, that he'd all the sudden turned playful. She tried to raise her head, get her breath. The full force of his weight was lying there on the pillow over her face. She struggled briefly, then went numb. Her lack of resistance must have made him anxious so he jumped up and lifted the pillow from her face. She screamed, trying to get Jane's attention from her room at the other end of the house, "Jane, Jane!"

"Don't you dare bring Jane into this, you bitch." He tried to put the pillow over her face again. She pushed it away and ran toward the stairs where Jane was coming toward her. "Call 911 Jane. Please, hurry."

"That's right. Make a big deal out of nothing. Make Jane think I'm some kind of a monster. That's all we need. What's it going to be tonight? You gonna go stay at your sister's? Alright go. Maybe I'll get some sleep for a change instead of having to listen to you yapping away at me."

Miriam went quickly to Jane and said, "Never mind, honey. I guess it's all right now. I was afraid Roy was going to hurt me. Come on. Let's you and me go find a place where we can get some rest. I'm so sorry I upset you. I didn't know what else to do".

Jane looked baffled and concerned. "What did he do Mom? What was he doing to you?" She tried to explain what had happened but it didn't make any sense to her. How was it going to make sense to Jane? She felt ashamed for involving Jane in her struggle with Roy. It wasn't fair to her. How do you live in a house, though, where a man as volatile as Roy lives, and keep every upset a secret from the children who live there too? She felt tortured. She was in too deep now to just pack up and walk away. She was afraid to leave. Afraid to stay. She told herself she was fine. He hadn't really hurt her. She'd maybe misread the situation. "He wouldn't really try to do me serious harm would he?"

Morning came and Roy found her sleeping on the couch in the family room. He brought her a cup of coffee and a flower he'd picked from the yard. She felt groggy. Her eyes were puffy and she was exhausted from crying herself to sleep. Roy took her in his arms and confessed to being a fool. He didn't know what made him act so awful last night.

"Surely you know how deeply I love you and I could never stand to hurt you," he said. He just couldn't believe, though, that after all he'd sacrificed for her, she would think he was lying to her.

He was sorry he'd scared her, but he just couldn't let her get away with such accusations.

Miriam said she understood. "Maybe it was my fault," she thought. "Maybe I, like Roy said, over-reacted." She believed he loved her. She knew how much he wanted to be trusted. "It's okay, Roy. I'm alright. But I want you to think about getting some counseling. You really lost it last night and I can't have my kids living in a house where they have to fear for their mother's safety."

"Oh Boy. Here we go again. Drop it, Miriam. Sick little Roy, again, is it? Well, I'm not the sick one here, Miriam. If you want to go crying to some counselor again, go ahead. All you want to do is have a counselor fix me. You never take any responsibility yourself. You know I'd never act the way I did last night if you could just learn to mind your own business and shut your mouth when I tell you to."

Miriam didn't have the energy for this. She took her coffee and went to check to be sure Jane was alright before she went behind the locked bathroom door and let the steaming spray of the shower bring a smattering of strength to the surface of her body and mind. When she came out of the shower half an hour later, Roy had left for work. He was nothing if not punctual — another proof he held over her head of his exceedingly responsible and trustworthy nature.

Weeks would go by and there would be no incidents to make her doubt Roy's love and commitment. She would begin to imagine she had just created a crisis and if she could learn to not do that everything would be all right. She started seeing Zoe Baird for counseling every other week.

For a time life went on with reasonable smoothness. She and Roy remodeled their house making it highly suitable for regular visits with his sons. Mat and Josh had a room to share for the nights they stayed over at their Dad's.

Mat was fourteen years old and off the charts when it came to brilliance. He was, however, extremely unhappy and bored. If he didn't feel like going to school, he didn't go. He would lock himself in his room at his mother's house and not speak to anyone in the family for days on end. When he came to his dad's house he'd focus solely on the TV set. He'd laugh at the jokes his dad told at the dinner table, lie about how he was doing in school and what he was doing with his days, and go home to his mother's only to lock himself in his room again.

Miriam had a position now in the history department at a private college two hours south of the home she and Roy shared. The commute was brutal but she was grateful to be hired given the dry job market, particularly in her field.

Grizzly statistics were a regular topic of discussion for the faculty advising staff that year. Record numbers of extra bright students were attempting suicide. Far too many of them had been successful. The faculty and student service staff was trying to put together a suicide prevention plan and she had done a lot of research on the symptoms of depression and possible suicidal tendencies in teens for her committee work.

From what Miriam had seen of Mat she believed he was a really good kid who was in a great deal of pain. His parents were certainly concerned about him too but they seemed blind to the severity of his symptoms. The school Mat attended suspended him and put the condition on his return to school of his getting some help. He ran away from home.

He was found two days later hiding in the basement of an apartment building where his aunt lived. His aunt never knew he was there. Roy and his ex-wife, Maddy, took Mat to a therapist who had a specialty in working with run-aways. Roy and Maddy invariably let fly at each other during these sessions. They couldn't make Mat go, and when he did go, once there, they couldn't make him stay. During one session he walked out, hailed a cab and went home to lock himself in his room. Now he would talk to no one. Maddy would come home from work and see signs that Mat had eaten something but it was mostly munchies and junk food. Just enough to subsist on.

Miriam was beginning to fear for Mat's life. He had cut himself off from all of his friends. Roy told Miriam Mat was none of her business. When she would try to discuss her concerns with him he said she was over-reacting and to keep her nose out of his parenting. He had it all under control.

She decided she would try to get through to Mat herself. He always seemed to like her, but, lately had kept her at a distance just like he kept everybody else. Mat's depression seemed to her to be despondency and she felt she wouldn't be able to live with herself if he actually committed suicide and she hadn't even tried to reach out to him.

She called Child Protection Services from her office on

campus one morning after Mat had pulled a knife on his mom and retreated to his room again. She explained that her husband had asked her to stay out of his relationship with his son but she just felt the situation had reached crisis proportions and someone needed to get to Mat right away that day.

The agency suggested she call her husband and insist he go to Mat, welcome or not, so that he would not be alone and in danger. Mat had not shown up at school that day or the day before, and now he wasn't answering the phone and there were no signs of life in the house. Roy refused to go and yelled at Miriam over the phone.

"Mind your own goddamn business, Miriam. I mean it. You stay out of this or you'll be sorrier than you've ever been!" After that she called the police, explained her concerns and they sent a squad car to find out if Mat was all right. The police called her at work saying they couldn't get any response from Mat.

Miriam didn't know what more she could do. She was physically two hours away from her own daughters who would just be getting home from school. Roy would not tolerate more urgings from Miriam. She was too far away to go to Mat herself.

She dialed Mat's phone number on the off-chance he may have seen the police at the door and would be curious enough to pick up the phone. Mat answered. She told him she had been thinking about him all day and wondered if maybe, when she got home, he'd go out for some Chinese food with her. Wondered if maybe it was time they got to know each other better. Mat's voice had been gentle and kind when he realized it was Miriam on the phone. He said, "My Dad's he - - -."

"What the hell do you think you're doing?" Roy yelled into the phone, obviously having yanked it from Mat's hand. "Didn't I tell you to stay out of this? Mat is my concern, do you hear me, my concern. How would you like me to butt in on your kids? Huh? How would you like it if something happened to one of your precious little girls?" He slammed the phone down so hard it hurt Miriam's ear. She was upset by Roy's yelling but, frankly, relieved he was there with Mat and that Mat seemed to be alright.

She went back to her work. She was advising a student who was trying to decide between a degree in history or literature. The phone on her desk rang. After a couple of rings it was clear the secretary had picked it up. A minute later the phone rang again. She let the secretary get it and went on working. The secretary slid a pink memo slip under the door with the message, "Roy is on the phone. He says he has to talk to you." Miriam went out to her secretary and confided in her that Roy just wanted to harass her further and that, if he called again, please tell him she'd talk to him when she got home.

The phone rang again. This time the pink note said. "Emergency. It's about Jane."

Miriam quickly called the neighbor's house where Jane stayed after school. Roy had stopped by to pick Jane up and had just left with her in his car. Her neighbor didn't know where he was taking her. Miriam called the police and gave them a description of Roy's car and his license number.

The phone in her office rang again. "Don't bother to call the police, Miriam. It's too late." She heard Roy's ragged and rage-full voice on the other end of a pay phone. He hung up.

She called the police again and told them about Roy's call. She called her neighbor and asked her to be on the look out for Roy. She ran to her car and drove in blind terror for the life of her child, the two hours toward home. She tried to tell herself it was all a hoax. That Roy couldn't be that cruel. He couldn't have hurt or killed her little girl.

"No. No. No. But if he could be cruel enough to terrorize me like this, what isn't he capable of?" she had to ask herself.

"Oh God. He is so very, very sick. So incredibly dangerous. How could I have walked so blindly into his clutches." All the way home she cried and chanted at the same time, "Oh, Jane, Jane, my dream baby. Please, God. Please let her be okay."

Miriam ran into the house stumbling and sobbing. She called out to Jane and to Storm. She heard the sounds of muffled voices coming from Storm's bedroom at the back of the house. She ran to the door and fell through it to find Jane, Storm and her sister Steve huddled together in a corner on the floor by the bed.

"He's upstairs," they whispered in unison.

She took Jane in her arms. She held her back from her a little way so she could see her wonderful face. She put her hands all over her little girl's face and hair before holding her close again.

"Oh, honey. I was so afraid. Are you all right?"

"Mom, what's wrong? Why were the police here? Why is everybody acting so weird? Roy just took me to a bookstore."

"Jane, oh honey, I'm sorry to seem so weird. Roy did something really scary to me. I was afraid he might hurt you. It's okay now, though. You're fine and that's what's important."

She turned to see Steve crouched, head in hands. Steve lifted her head and nodded it slowly and sadly from side to side.

"Miriam, you and the girls had better come and stay with me until you get this thing straightened out. Kathy, next door called me and I came as quick as I could. Roy said 'I'm leaving,' and went upstairs as soon as he brought Jane in."

* * * * *

Two days later Miriam took Roy back. So began her ultimate descent into the hell for which her childhood love lessons had programmed her. Roy agreed to counseling and she agreed to marriage. Again, crisis and passion spelled mad, deep and true love to Miriam.

On the surface of things, she seemed to have life under control. She had earned her doctorate in record time, considering she was working for a living and raising two children. Her research on women's history was becoming recognized by some as a freeing force in women's lives. She worked freelance as a consultant in addition to her teaching responsibilities and traveled the lecture and conference circuit in attempt to increase her visibility and recognition. In short, she was the classic over-achiever, attempting an appearance of normalcy to shroud the chaos of her life.

At home, with Roy, life was a constant roller-coaster of crisis. She had unwittingly entered a downward pulling cycle of abuse that would ultimately threaten her life. The well-read, well-educated woman, Miriam, believed that what attracted her to Roy was his great sense of humor, his light-heartedness, his capable and caring ability as a teacher, his understanding and support of women's issues. She didn't know his charm and wit were the common guise of a manipulative and abusive man.

He made her laugh (often at herself) until she cried and wet her pants. In his peak moments he showered her with compliments and gifts. He flattered her intelligence and professional accomplishment, knowing she'd had enough of idle and greedy acclaim for her beauty.

He saw in her a wounded, vulnerable and needy child who would do anything just to feel she counted — mattered to someone. He used his knowledge of Miriam's need, her yearning to feel safe and treasured, to his brutal advantage. By the time she came to her senses about the danger she was in and the danger to which she'd subjected her children, she felt trapped, ashamed, beaten and utterly broken.

The situation had been intolerable for nearly two years. The episodes of violence escalated, became the norm, when Jane and Storm were visiting their fathers. Miriam tried to cover the hurt and fear and make life seem safe, normal and constant in their home. She was ashamed to be in this situation that others had warned her about before she ever married Roy. She hadn't believed it could happen to her. She'd believed Roy's anger and cruelty were a result of his self-doubt and sense he was unlovable. She thought, like so many battered women think, she could love him to health and happiness. She'd staked her life on this. She nearly lost.

* * * * *

On their third wedding anniversary they went away together for a romantic weekend at a bed and breakfast. At first his insults over dinner came across as jokes. She laughed and responded in the spirit in which she thought Roy was delivering these comments. As the evening progressed, it became apparent he wanted to argue, wanted to fight. Miriam felt trapped and afraid as he baited her with this comment and that, this insult and that. She poured champagne, fed them both strawberries, tried to change his mood and the tone of the conversation. She attempted to casually excuse herself and gain respite in an old fashioned bubble bath.

She thought in the privacy of the tub she might be able to strategize a way to get through the night without being hurt any more than she already was. She settled into the bubbles, closed her eyes and tried to think straight in these few minutes she had to herself. Moments after she settled in the tub she heard him at the bathroom door, trying the handle. He tried again, outraged she'd locked him out. He yelled to her through the door. "Unlock this door Miriam. What are trying to do? Keep me away on our anniversary?"

"Roy, I just need a few minutes here. I'm a little tense for some reason. Thought I'd take a breather so we can be more relaxed together." She scrambled for words that wouldn't enrage him further.

"Well isn't that just so romantic and special?" he sneered. "She wants some alone-time on her anniversary. What am I supposed to do while you're in there spending our anniversary by yourself? I came here to be with you and I spent good money doing it too, so if you know what's good for you, you'll unlock this door right now." He jiggled the handle roughly and banged on the door with his fist.

Miriam couldn't think what to say and was afraid to unlock the door. Roy kicked and banged till the latch swung loose. He came into the room grinning and holding the broken doorknob before her eyes in a gesture of pride. She sat cowering at one end of the tub. This was a position all too familiar from her childhood days. Her face felt hot, her eyes burned, silent cries and an urge to vomit filled her throat.

"Is this how you spent your romantic weekends with David? Huh?" He reached his hand into the tub and scattered the bubbles that covered her shivering body.

"I bet you didn't lock good old Dave out did you? I bet he was right in there with you, wasn't he?" He turned away from her and walked toward the mirror, gaining strength for his next onslaught.

Miriam lunged for a towel at the side of the tub, wrapped it quickly around her body and tried to rush past him out of the bathroom. She couldn't tolerate her own naked vulnerability. She wanted to get to a robe or shirt or anything to cover her nakedness.

Roy turned and grabbed her, pulling her into his arms. "I'm sorry Miriam." He kissed her neck. She pulled at him with all her strength trying to get his mouth away from her. He held on tighter, pushing his face into hers.

She turned her face from side to side, squeezing her mouth and eyes closed in another gesture familiar to her from childhood. He pressed harder. His hands on her back, arms and bottom started to hurt her with kneading and digging caresses.

"Miriam, come on. I said I'm sorry. You know you like it when we kiss and make up. Come on honey." She tried one last time to extricate herself, but knew he'd just catch her again before she could put clothes on and get to safety. She was far too ashamed to yell for the proprietor who knew this was their anniversary celebration. Besides, Roy was unlikely to go so far as to hit her here where he might get caught. She went numb in his arms. Her slack body permitted his kisses and caresses. He carried her to the bed and entered her moaning his sorrow for the things he'd said earlier. Telling her, promising her, he was so sorry, didn't know what came over him, loved her so much...

When she drifted back to her body and conscious mind, Roy was asleep on the bed beside her. He looked innocent. He looked like the sweet and vulnerable man he often was.

This time, though, after all the times she'd managed to survive his attempts to suffocate her, strangle her, twist her arm, badger her, back her against walls to spit insults into her face ... This time she was through. She silently faced the night with him, was quiet and calm at breakfast, and didn't speak a word to him all the way home.

Miriam hired a lawyer the next day and that lawyer encouraged her to stay with Roy. The abuse didn't sound as bad to her as some others she'd heard about. Miriam ignored her advice. She went home and told Roy he had to be gone by bed time or she would call the police. He resisted only slightly for fear of being exposed and the harm it could do to his career.

She called Zoe. She wanted confirmation from this trusted-other that her decision to leave Roy was the right one. If there was any hope she could make it work, she did not want to have a third failed marriage on her conscience

Chapter Seventeen

It was Zoe, this time (and again) who led Miriam to deeper self-awareness, understanding and acceptance.

Miriam always looked forward to her meetings with Zoe. Really wanted to think of her as a peer and a friend, but of course that's not the appropriate professional relationship between a client and a therapist. She sometimes wondered if it wasn't the desire for Zoe's approval and applause that helped her navigate a blitzkrieg path from clerk typist/wife/mother status to that of a self-supporting historian. Zoe thought she could do it and Miriam didn't want to let her down no matter the sense of defeat that paid its regular visits.

Miriam always thought of Zoe as being older than she, but, really, she was probably younger by six years or so. Zoe had great aesthetics. Her office was furnished with comfortable but modern furniture that had something Asian or Oriental about it. The colors were calming, muted but never such dull things as brown or gray. More of a grayed down violet or blue. Her favorite artist was Mark Rothko. The rose, lavender, blue and green colors in his paintings decorated her walls in lavish peacefulness. Hypnotic. That's how the decor struck Miriam. Zoe's office had a lakeside view and often the windows were open to the scent of the trees and water across the way. The rest Miriam found in her company created in her the hope rest would sometime be hers for more than forty-five minutes at a time and for less than $100 an hour.

She always wanted to bring Zoe some treasure of accomplishment or indication of maturity and sanity. She couldn't make her say she cared for her, but how Miriam craved her love. Zoe was a quiet, calm, deliberate woman who didn't reveal personal feelings. She would, at best, indicate a minor degree of something that might be overstated as "pleased," when Miriam would announce a new promotion, a salary increase, or an acknowledgment in the academic or historical community.

It's hard to say why Miriam felt she could confide her sexual escapades and betrayals to Zoe. In truth she often worried Zoe was judging her for the poor white trash Miriam believed herself to be. She sometimes couldn't bear to tell her the truth for fear Zoe would be disappointed in her or ashamed of her. She'd use her sense of how badly wronged she'd been by Johnny, Al or Roy, as vindication and justification for taking a lover or having a one night fling while away from her home and children.

Though Zoe, too, was a mother, there was never a hint of sexuality about her. Attractive, but not overtly sexual, Zoe listened attentively, never betraying shock or judgement, approval, applause or scorn. She asked Miriam if she thought her behavior had been "rational" or "responsible" in a way that suggested to her that she felt it wasn't.

Miriam would expand voluminously on the mistreatment she'd received at the hands of whatever husband she had at the time and leave out the part where she'd reacted by indulging in a casual sexual fling. She behaved with enormous defensiveness and denials when accused by the offending husband. Miriam wanted peace, though. She craved sanity all the while she acted insane. Finally, she had to quit lying to Zoe. Not wanting to disappoint Zoe over the years, served to improve Miriam.

Over time she began to understand that her own lack of self-respect was at the heart of the problems in her relationships.

Zoe put it this way, "It's similar to that thing about if a woman doesn't love and know her own body she can't expect anyone else to. But this time it's about self-love and respect. It's become a near cliché now, but the truth is still there. If you don't love and respect yourself, it seems, you invite a similar response in others."

Miriam didn't want to believe her failed marriages and relationships were her own fault. They weren't, entirely. But, she had never learned that she deserved respect, kindness, tenderness and compassion. She hardly knew what they looked like. These qualities had not been modeled for her. She didn't know to seek them out. Throughout the years she'd sought counseling and the comfort and rescue it provided at times of crisis. Once the crisis of the moment passed, she moved on to the next, never willing to look at the pattern of her life. She would reach a point where she felt okay and was functioning reasonably well and determine there was no point spending her hard-earned money on therapy.

But the pattern of her life was not missed by Zoe. She'd watched Miriam fist fight her way through three marriages now. Miriam had two daughters who were impacted by the homes she'd brought them into. She was aware Miriam felt thoroughly broken and alone in her departure from Roy. That she was ashamed she'd ever let him into her life and ashamed to be leaving yet another husband.

Obvious questions hung in the air for Miriam. "How can all of these bad marriages always be the fault of someone else? Why was I choosing to wrap my life up with these men I ultimately needed to leave?" All the while she blamed and raged at the men who hurt her, who didn't love her the way she wanted to be loved, she blamed herself and believed deep in her heart that she deserved nothing but hurt and unhappiness.

Miriam always felt something about her was "all wrong" and her father and husbands felt perfectly comfortable confirming that impression. When they worked her over she thought that's what she deserved. For the most part, it's all she ever experienced.

Oh, there was the relationship with David. The wonderful intimacy of feeling her soul was embraced by another's, was a dabbling in something so powerful, yet so foreign to her, she had to run from it. It was too calm, too quiet and safe to be love. She thrived on crisis. She could create it through selfish and destructive behavior. She could engage her husband in the crisis and, once again, feel she was in the territory of love the way she knew it best.

Miriam's was a cruel and self-defeating cycle. She seemed to be on automatic programming that kept her in the spin of this circle for decade after decade.

Her sessions with Zoe offered her books to read, seminars to attend, support groups to join. She alternated trying to be what and who she thought the husband she loved or her parents or friends or therapist wanted her to be, with an all out dangerous leap into rejecting all rules, restrictions and responsibilities. Who Miriam actually was and its significance was a complete mystery to her. She was in a constant state of turmoil and reaction.

Occasionally Zoe would ask Miriam about her family history, family of origin, grandmas, grandpas, dad, mom and so forth. She would give surface responses that said very little. Though, over the years of regular visits to Zoe, she became a practicing and published historian, in her personal life, she behaved as if the current concern or crisis was of the utmost importance. She failed to see the bearing her history or that of her family had on her life in the here and now.

After Roy, Miriam needed Zoe's help more than ever.

When she left Roy a black terror descended on her. She felt she'd used up what little patience her friends and family might once have had with her. She hated to admit she'd failed in yet another marriage. Now Zoe was all she had. It was time for her to face herself and the truth behind her mask of successful living, blighted only and always by some "him" or other.

Miriam managed to pull together a professional, public persona for lecture tours and meetings with her classes. She'd been so dogged in her pursuit of the disguise of a life well lived, that she had a backlog of research and publications to fall back on. Her public lectures and course syllabi could carry her through at least a year of continued disguise of her broken personal life.

Storm was sixteen and living the typical life of a popular and athletic teenager. She spent much of her time in the city with her friends and her dad. Miriam couldn't hide from her the fact that her marriage to Roy was over. Though she must have felt confusion and maybe some concern, her attitude was easy for Miriam to interpret as "Okay Mom. Whatever." She didn't want her life disrupted. Didn't want to be bothered and didn't want to have to deal with a mother in anguish. Miriam tried to keep her as far away from the truth of her terrified and broken state as she could.

With Jane it was harder. Returning home from work each day Miriam would switch quickly from her professional mask to her good mommy mask. Her acting skills came in handy for the few hours before Jane's bedtime. She told herself Jane wouldn't notice the perpetually full glass of wine in her hand from the time she entered the door until the time she tucked her into bed at night. Miriam sipped slowly, never quite tipping the edge into full blown drunkenness or sleep prior to pulling the covers up under her little girl's neck and singing the repertoire of songs she'd sung to her from the time she was born.

But Miriam fooled herself where both girls were concerned. Jane had lived nearly every day of the years her mother spent with Roy in the volatile atmosphere in their home. She and Storm were both there nights when their mother would have to wake them and seek escape and shelter from their step-father. Jane lived in fear of Miriam's marriage ending. It was humiliating to her that her mother had divorced twice already. Another divorce would be an added embarrassment. She feared the loss of her friendships if they were forced to move to another school district to get away from Roy.

Both Miriam's daughters knew their family's future was uncertain. Already, Storm was continuing in a school miles from where her mother lived because Miriam hadn't wanted to disrupt her life when her marriage to Al ended. Now Jane worried she would no longer live where her friends lived.

Miriam made promises to Jane. Promised her that if they had to move, they would find a place in the same school district and in a neighborhood that would offer her easy access to her friends. Jane joylessly accompanied her mother on a search for a house or apartment. The home they shared with Roy was expensive, extravagant and compatible with the homes of her affluent friends. The thought of moving to this or that affordable and tiny house or apartment humiliated her.

She'd benefited from her step-dad's role in a summer camp she came to love. She built many of her teenage hopes and dreams on the summers she would spend in the company of her friends at that camp. She dreamed of becoming a counselor there and carrying her love of the place through her college years. The end of the marriage shattered those dreams.

Miriam didn't realize at the time how alone and afraid Jane was throughout that marriage. Miriam was so blinded by her own survival instinct or need to cope or maintain her disguise, that she failed to see her daughter's fear and pain. She recognized her anger. She didn't understand it. She thought her own cover was working. Jane had a beautiful home, a comfortable bedroom, any clothes, toys and equipment she wanted. If she wanted sailing lessons or to learn horseback riding, Miriam's answer was always yes. She excelled in school and Miriam never missed a parent-teacher conference, award or sporting event. She thought she was providing Jane with a childhood where she always knew she could count on her mother.

Jane missed her sister, busy in her away from home activities. And Jane wasn't blind to the turmoil at home. She was exhausted with concern for Miriam's safety and well-being.

The days and nights Jane spent with her dad, at the home of friends or at summer camp, Miriam allowed herself the privilege of being as broken as she felt.

Both her daughters knew she was in therapy and she imagined that provided them some comfort. They didn't have to take care of her. She insisted they not concern themselves with her feelings. That was not the responsibility of children as far as Miriam was concerned. Even her desire to protect them from the knowledge of her pain caused them harm.

She didn't fool them. They knew she was in pain. They were all lying to each other about their feelings.

Storm was hiding her fears by staying away from home as much as possible. When she was with Jane, she manipulated her to lie on her behalf. For this favor, she would grant Jane the much craved pleasure of her company. When Miriam thought Storm was watching out for her younger sister, she was often putting her in danger. Storm drank too much, smoked marijuana, broke curfew, lied to her dad and to Miriam about her activities and generally put herself in harm's way.

If Zoe didn't fear for Miriam's children, she may have never insisted, as she ultimately did, that she quit deceiving herself and everybody around her. It frightened Miriam to have Zoe insist she slow down and take a good look at herself and the part she played in bringing all these disastrous relationships into her life. Miriam feared she, too, had lost patience with her.

Years before, Miriam's mother and father had told her they'd had it with her mess of a life. They wanted to stay out of all but the superficial and grand parenting aspects of dealings with her. They loved her, they said, but they needed to live their own lives and couldn't be expected to be rescuing their grown daughter at every life crisis. They'd given up on Miriam ever making a responsible decision when it came to men. It was obvious to them these men were perfectly acceptable husbands. Miriam's expectations were way too high. Always had been. Her mom said Miriam never was able to realize how good she had it. Always focused on the sad times, the unhappy times. That she should accept the fact that this is the way men act and, if she didn't want to spend her whole life alone, she should learn to compromise.

Miriam spent a lot of energy, after Roy terrorized her by taking Jane, rationalizing her love of him and her choice to marry him, to friends who loved her and were concerned about the downward trend of her life. She didn't listen to their warnings. She dismissed them. She grabbed for the crisis filled life that to her spelled passionate love. When Roy became abusive in the context of their marriage she couldn't admit it to her friends. She feared the "I told you so's." Feared the lack of sympathy and understanding.

Zoe was her sole confidant. The only person who knew how bleak her life had become. The only person who knew, better than she, the level of danger she was in.

She made Miriam look at her history. She told her the same thing Pastor Paul told her almost twenty years before.

"It did too hurt you, Miriam, and it matters very much."

Miriam looked into Zoe's eyes and saw before her a cliff's edge over an endless, gaping black abyss. Hot tears filled her eyes and throat. She ran from the room and reached the bathroom just in time to become again, her shaking and small self, head in the toilet, vomiting.

Chapter Eighteen

"Where's Mommy? Where's my Mommy? Help me. Help me. Oh Mommy, where are you?" Miriam struggled to make the sounds come from her open mouth. But she was dreaming. Dreaming herself as a child. She was tied with long white strips of sheeting to a parent-size bed in a huge and cold bedroom. Dusk filled the room and created a sense of hazy fog. She could feel the cold and mist through her thin cotton dress. Her legs and arms were splayed full width across the bed with each limb tied to one of four dark bedposts. Her mouth was filled with toilet paper and she couldn't swallow. Could barely breath but for the breaths she forced in a tearful snort through her nose. Her eyes burned and she struggled turning her head from side to side trying to dislodge the toilet paper.

A man — her father — hissed commands into her face. She caught a fleeting glimpse of her mother as she filled the doorway, then turned to walk away. She noticed her mother's shining black hair and the dark frames of her eyeglasses.

Again Miriam squirmed, struggled and tried to force the gag from her mouth. "Mommy. Mommy." She willed her voice to make its sounds. "Help me!" She screamed with all her strength and found herself, sweating, awake and fully grown in a hospital bed in a pale green room. She looked and saw the concerned face of a nurse.

"Miriam, Miriam. You were whimpering and asking for your mother. You screamed, 'help me!' Are you all right? Do you need some medicine?"

Miriam couldn't answer. Couldn't believe her own terror. "What was that dream? What did it mean?"

The nurse turned to leave and Miriam said, "No. No, please don't go. Please." She returned to Miriam's bedside. Miriam took the collar of her white jacket in her hand and pulled her face close. "I . want. my. mom. Can you get me," her voice broke, "my mom?"

After garnering every ounce of strength she could muster to leave Roy, Miriam found herself running fast and hard. Full adrenaline survival mode was her single gear. She believed if she stopped running, stopped controlling every move and moment of her life, Roy and his threats would catch up with her and she would die. She knew her pace and her activities were dangerous but she had no choice. She had to out run, out distance her terror.

Every night since she insisted Roy leave she'd been visited by night terrors. Dreams of being chased, cornered in dark alleys and basements, dreams of suffocation, dreams of someone and their bone-crunching, vice grip exerting ever more pressure, twisting and pushing, creating unendurable pain. Always the overwhelming need to cry and vomit simultaneously accompanied these night terrors. Silent screams turned to near crazy yells in the night and she awakened to find herself alone in the dark. Under siege.

Her parents were ashamed she'd failed at another marriage but seemed to understand she was suffering pain and humiliation. Her father made an effort to be kinder to her than he'd been when she left Johnny and Al. Both those divorces resulted in her parents providing comfort and support to the abandoned husband rather than their daughter. Deep down her self-hatred caused her to share her parents belief the divorces were all her fault. She believed she brought about these failures through her immaturity and selfishness. Miriam had never, in their minds, considered anyone but herself.

But Miriam ran from them in their condemnation of her with the earlier divorces. She stood up for herself. Said it was her life and if they wanted any part in it they would have to quit judging her.

She didn't believe for a minute that they ceased their judgement. Her dad took every opportunity to bemoan her heathen state. Made the point repeatedly that all his other children had Jesus Christ at the helm in their successful marriages. She was certain her mom shared her dad's belief but didn't want to feel alienated from Miriam so she didn't criticize. She promised not to condemn Miriam but insisted their conversations would have to stay away from these topics of the disappointment Miriam had brought to her life.

Miriam had a reconciliation of sorts with her dad when he had open heart surgery a couple years into her marriage to Roy. She'd felt such need for a real family. Such need to put the past behind her and a need to feel accepted and have her father's approval. She went to him — surprised him by being there in his hospital room the day before surgery. He looked vulnerable and afraid in his thin cotton hospital gown.

They'd had very little to say to each other after her divorce from Al. He still believed her behavior and bad decisions could destroy his ministry. He didn't want her to come around his parishioners and have them know his daughter was a non-Christian and a divorcee. He seemed to think her failed life was a personal vendetta against him.

But Miriam had two children. Two little girls who wanted a grandpa and grandma in their lives. She decided her personal differences with her father had to be set aside so her children could feel they had something of a normal family.

Miriam loved her mother almost to the point of worship. She counted on her love for her, believed in it even when her mother rejected her. Miriam blamed herself, felt deserving of this rejection. Didn't feel worthy of her love. Miriam thought it made sense her mother was ashamed of her. She was thoroughly ashamed of herself.

So when Miriam's dad became ill, and there was a chance he might die, she went to him. Her mother was there when her dad turned from the window to see she'd come to him. Elizabeth bowed her head and cried as daughter and father fell into each others arms and held on as if their lives depended on it. All the past seemed to fall away.

"Oh my beautiful Miriam," he said, "I forgive you everything."

"I'm sorry Dad. I'm so sorry." She said, holding him, weeping and feeling thoroughly responsible for all the pain in his life and her mother's.

So, this time, when her mom told her dad that Roy and Miriam had separated and told him how Roy had hurt and threatened her, he determined he would be kind to his daughter.

Miriam was at home alone, Jane away at summer camp and

Storm on a mountain climbing trip in Colorado, one night when the phone rang. She'd had a terrible time sleeping because of the nightmares. She was exhausted but afraid of sleep. She'd dozed lightly as she tried to read to distract herself alone in her living room. Her hand reached for the phone but her voice wouldn't work to say "hello."

"Miriam?" A man's voice was saying her name.

She lost her breath at the sound of his voice. "Who is it? Why does that voice frighten me so?"

"Miriam. Miriam, are you there? Is that you?" said the single most frightening voice she'd ever heard.

Very carefully she set the phone back in its cradle without saying a word. A lightening bolt of burning hot pain shot through her whole body. She held herself in her own inadequate arms and rocked back and forth, back and forth, sobbing and saying aloud, "It was Dad. It was Dad. It was Dad."

She slept and fell into a nightmare in which she was three years old. The shadow of a man or adolescent boy, back-lit by a window opened to the summer night, stood over her as she slept on the top bunk in the darkened room. The menacing shadow held his penis in his hand and Miriam's small face was wet and hot. The shadow came closer to her face. The adult Miriam came into the room to find the three year old and take her in her arms. The three year old said, "I'm sorry. I'm sorry, Mommy. I didn't mean to." The adult held her and shushed her telling her everything was all right. Telling her she didn't do anything wrong. Miriam asked the little girl what happened. What upset her so. She opened her eyes wide and rubbed her fist against her mouth which she clenched shut with all her strength. Miriam lifted her smaller self from the bed and carried her away from the room. "Don't tell Daddy, Mommy. Please don't tell Daddy. He'll spank me, Mommy. Please, please," she pleaded, "tell him I'm sorry."

Miriam awakened herself crying the words "I'm sorry." She tried to move from the couch. It was daylight now and she knew she should get ready for work. Her legs wouldn't move. She put her head back against the cushions and tried to think. "Who can I call? What can I do? I can't call Mom because Dad might answer the phone and I can't, simply can't hear the sound of his voice." She couldn't call her sisters because they would never understand why their father evoked this kind of terror in her. Calling Roy was out of the question.

She felt utterly alone. Wanted to lose consciousness, find some way to have a dreamless sleep. She was so tired. So terribly weary. She couldn't move to go to the liquor cabinet. She had no drugs in the house even if she'd been able to stand and go to the medicine cabinet. She thought about the life insurance policy she had for her children's security. Everyone she needed or could have possibly turned to was completely fed up with her. She wanted to disappear and never face their condemning faces again. If she could have willed her death at that moment she would have.

It occurred to her then that her children would not get her life insurance if she harmed herself. They needed her to stay alive. They knew she was having some problems but had only witnessed her Hercules act since Roy left. They thought she was okay. That's exactly what she wanted them to think. They were away and wouldn't be home for at least two weeks. She could allow herself a two week breakdown.

Miriam reached for the phone and called Zoe. When she heard her voice on the other end of the line she was able to stand up. Miriam said, "Zoe, I'm in bad shape and need to stop pretending I'm not, or die."

"Miriam. I'm going to arrange for you to spend some time in the hospital. Can you meet me there or do you want me to come and get you?" she asked.

Miriam felt guilty for bothering her. Didn't want to impose. Felt herself a constant imposition to everyone from the day she was born. She couldn't impose. Couldn't tell her no. "I'm okay," Miriam said. "I'm okay now. I'll meet you there."

Miriam didn't tell anyone she was in the hospital at first. She made up some story to reassure her children and sent them each postcards. She phoned work to say there was a family emergency and she'd get back to them when she could.

The doctor prescribed a sleeping medication in the hope of curing Miriam's exhaustion. She slept and dreamed one black and terrifying dream after another.

The nurse called her mom and told her she was needed. She drove through the night and came to Miriam early in the morning. She took her daughter in her arms and rocked her. Miriam felt her tears soaking her hair and the shoulders of her pajamas.

"Here you are Mommy. Here you are. I always wondered where you were and here you are. You're here with me, Mommy." Miriam's words and voice were those of a child.

Zoe came to the hospital and sat on a chair across from Miriam's bed where both she and her mother sat. Together Zoe and Miriam told Elizabeth how Earl's cruelty and abuse had dictated the course Miriam's life had taken. That all the hurt and pain had returned to crush her. They told her they thought the possibility existed that Miriam's father's abuse had been sexual as well as physical and emotional. That the worst part, the part that's essential to understand, regardless of the form of the abuse, is the harm and debilitation Earl's resentment, anger and hatred of Miriam had caused.

Miriam watched her mother fold into herself. Watched as her mother became the hurt child. Elizabeth drove home that very day, promising she would hold her husband accountable. Instead she found a doctor who prescribed tranquilizers and became so sick and broken herself that she had nothing to give to Miriam. She walked straight back to her husband's arms. He convinced her he wasn't the monster Miriam described. Convinced her their daughter was delusional. Couldn't she see it? "We've always had trouble with Miriam. She was born to make trouble."

Miriam's mom called her at the hospital. "I'm very sorry you're having such a hard time honey. You know I am, but, well, Dad and I talked with one of the parishioners who has a degree in psychology. He advised us to take good care of ourselves. He told us you are an adult now, Miriam and it's best if you stand on your own two feet."

Miriam stayed in the hospital for three weeks, ultimately having to let her children know where she was. She missed parents day at Jane's camp. Jane felt humiliated admitting to her friends her mother had a breakdown and was in the hospital. Alone at camp Jane felt helpless, confused and afraid. Miriam tried to reassure her in her phone calls and letters, but wasn't able to provide her with the comfort to calm her fears. Kids asked her if her mom went crazy. Wondered if her mom tried to kill herself. Miriam wasn't able to protect her daughter from the effects of Earl Blackwell any more than her mother had protected her .

By the time Miriam left the hospital she had regularly scheduled appointments with a psychiatrist, a hypnotist and Zoe. She was a participant in an incest survivor's support group and had a renewable prescription for tranquilizers.

Chapter Nineteen

Miriam sat cross-legged in the debris of myriad dissected photograph albums and a near mountain of tiny torn paper circles. Jagged edged circles, each one different from the other, like so many grotesque snowflakes. They were snowflakes formed of the head of her father. Severed from hundreds — no thousands — of photographs. The room was cold and gray and smelled of winter.

For more than forty years Miriam's preoccupation with ridding herself of her father's dangerous presence served only to pull him closer to her. His presence crippling, debilitating and forever disapproving.

He loomed, bulging, enormous, floating huge above and around her. Like in a Macy's Thanksgiving Day parade Miriam walked, tiny and bare-limbed, an umbilical cord attached at one end to her vital organs; the other supporting the giant, air-filled Dad, who bobbed and careened above her — threatening to collapse around her and crush her to a suffocating death.

This was not her first attempt to rid herself of his powerful hold — this disemboweling the photo albums of his face, every aspect of his image. Oh no. She tried many times and many ways.

All these years of death-defying motion. Would she ever be able to look closely and without terror at the truth of the years gone by and the damage done? Look, not only at the damage done to her, but by her? She rose from the floor dripping severed heads from her lap. Groped her way to the view beyond her window where the street below showed her no parade of any sort, but the empty, frozen color of solitary confinement.

She looked through the front window of her third floor campus apartment. Forty years old and Associate Professor of History at St. David's College on the Luster River a few minutes walk from it's confluence with Lake Superior. From her window she could just manage to see where the river and the ocean of lake met.

It was nearly winter. November. The final days of yet another hurricane season, and though, for years now, she'd lived far inland from hurricane country, her body forever carried a stormy memory of the season. In the summer and spring she couldn't see beyond the leaf bearing trees to the water outside her window. Always, though, she felt the waves. Felt the claim they had on her. The force they exerted. Always a nearness to the water created in her, for good or worse, a sense of nearness to home.

The forward and backward motion of the waves — the moving in to shore and away from shore, forward and backward in time. At times the waves seemed to stand still. At times they cavorted in a whirlwind and whirlpool, in a downward motion threatening to suck her from the surface, from the safety of land and down into blackness. Sometimes she became the wave itself, and was propelled forward in a white rush, all around her a sense of light.

This ultimate forward motion, her belief in its constancy, was Miriam's solace. It was the forward motion of the world and of the generations that would follow her.

"For how many generations had the young believed they would move far beyond the paths their fathers, mothers, grandfathers and grandmothers set?"

She wandered the chilly rooms of her apartment, thinking. "All human beings are implicated in this forward motion. It's a fact of nature, isn't it, that the young dismiss the generation that came before them? Yet once we mature, and for some this is in youth and some in old age, we crave the knowledge, the information we earlier dismissed. The information that perhaps could have propelled us further up the shore line."

Bare feet walking over and through her father's paper heads — Miriam's thoughts came and went with the distant waves. Thoughts about the legacy she would leave as ancestor to future generations. She knew so little of the lives of her own ancestors.

"And oh yes," she told herself, "for years now, I've studied history. For years now I've industriously unearthed the history of women whose stories were buried or never written. I've written, published and lectured about the essential nature of understanding backward in order to live forward. But it has all been so completely intellectual and academic. I've turned my childhood fantasies, my childhood escape into a legitimate career."

But these women whose lives she revealed were other women's ancestors. Miriam thought she knew just enough about her own family to know there were no stories to be told that had significance for her future or the future of her progeny.

Leaning against her windowpane she thought about her children. She'd been a mother now for close to eighteen years. Motherhood awakened in her a fierce strength and an appreciation for the female animal. Both of her babies were conceived at a time in her life when she willfully, and with a sense of great personal strength, took life into her own hands. She determined it was her woman strength, her instinctual animal knowing, and the wild richness of her living that she could offer these babies.

"And yes," she thought. "It was a selfish act, and yes it dismissed the importance of the father. I didn't know the importance of the father. I struggle with it still. These babies were mine and mine alone."

"Would I deny them their fathers?" No, she somehow knew better than to do that. Knew there was much about having a father that could benefit her daughters. But with each of her babies she became a lone, protective she-animal. She removed herself from society. She left the noise behind her. Left the talking lips, the seeing eyes. She went to live with her animals in her cathedral, in her holy place, in the log structure overlooking the waves.

Young, impulsive, wild, ignorant of so much. Still, she sensed the power, the importance of conception, birth and giving life to the next generation. Oh and for Miriam it was a supremely sensual act. And it was an act of love. But it was a love, separate somehow, from the man who fathered the child.

Central as her lovers were to conceiving children and giving life she had no way of knowing how central the father would be in the lives of these children. In her ignorance she tried to protect her children from the danger of the father. It was a danger she found life threatening. It governed her life and put her in jeopardy into which she brought her children. In her ignorance — in her failure to face the truth, she harmed her children. These were the truths that continued to haunt her in her half-lived life.

She turned and walked away from the window. Extracted herself from the pull of the waves beyond the trees. She put a cup of water in the microwave and leaned against the oven as the water heated. She dared the radiation to wreck havoc with her body, give her something visible, tangible to send her to bed and relieve her this ponderous responsibility she'd set herself. The responsibility to seek her own history. To take stock.

"Bzzz..."

"Damn, still intact — nothing blew up. The cocoa's ready and I have hours ahead of me." "And," she thought, "Isn't that what I've always said and thought I wanted?"

She remembered her mom saying, "Be careful what you wish for. You might just get it." Well, here it was, what she'd wished for — time and space to think. Time and space to make sense of it all. She took a big, scalding gulp of the cocoa — a little pain to distract her — and she started. She set to work.

Like a pianist she approached the computer keyboard, head down, eyes closed. Her fingers came down on the keys with a force that surprised her eyes open, her head up.

Head lifted she turned her face side to side in a gesture of no, no, no. Suddenly she was whipping her head back and forth, back and forth and tears like little icy bullets hit the walls she felt closing in on her. "Bum, bum, bum, bum...bum, bum, bum, bum…" the music began. "Bah, Bah, bah, bah , bah, bah..." Shit! It was that insipid Tschaikovsky piece her dad always used as an accompaniment to slide shows of their trips to Niagara Falls or Fort Ticonderoga. It was that piece that accompanied a raw and stinging pain that left her cold and hot and tired and too, too awake all at the same time.

The music she was trying to make was about the truth of her experience. Her own history. "Why should this be so difficult?" she wondered aloud. "I'm a historian, for Christ's sake." But the music bangs and smashes and explodes. It makes no goddamn sense to anyone and it is damned, fucking hard to dance to.

She wrote what she knows. She knows it hurts. Knows she felt, still feels, discounted. Feels she doesn't count — didn't matter, was beaten, yelled at, dismissed, ridiculed, molested. That she was not treasured, protected, delighted in. That she felt and feels betrayal, abandonment, derision, darkness, suffocation, despair. If her siblings were subjected to the very same atmosphere, emotions and circumstances she was, they are not aware of feeling the way she feels.

Miriam stopped writing. Shame and guilt overcame her. "How much self-pity can one person dish out?" she asked her fingers, still for a moment but resting against the keyboard. She hated herself for every piece of truth she'd just written. "Get over it, Miriam. For Christ's sake. You are forty fucking years old!" She stood and walked back to the window through the carpet of her father's severed heads.

She wondered if she was making too much of it all. Maybe, she thought, it's that she simply did not fit the common denominator approach to child rearing — that everything hurt more, felt more intense, mattered more to her, than to the average child. She was able to see some of that in herself from time to time even now. She felt herself to be one of those "skinless" human beings. She wept easily, laughed harder, louder than most. Touch her skin, her hair, her taste buds — she moans, can't help herself. That fresh breeze coming off the waves feels like a personal gift of ecstasy straight from God. That rudeness, insult, dismissing, denigrating comment — that blood and guts scene from an adventure film felt like penetrating stab wounds and left her shaken, crying and craving comfort.

But really, was the issue whether or not she should feel traumatized, hated, discounted and in pain? No, and this is where that bottom line thing came in, if she could ever let go of the hatred and shame she felt for feeling such pain and broken-ness. The truth is she got lost and left alone in the rush. She was forgotten and fell into the hands of unkind, cruel, sick caretakers who sneaked into her room, pulled her panties down and whispered threats in her sleeping ears. Threats that paralyzed her while the "caretaker" covered her body with something hairy, smelly, scratchy, dripping, cold, slimy, pokey and confusing, confusing, confusing.

She believed he would slit her throat, cut her head off, as he did nightly in her dreams. That a huge, soft bellied, big, tooth-filled red, dripping mouth alligator slowly climbed her body and she couldn't breathe, she couldn't breathe, couldn't cry out. She couldn't do anything but go away, shrink into a coma, turn all black and dried up and not know truly, to this day, what actually happened.

She stood, left the keyboard and grabbed a blanket from the couch to wrap herself in a comforting cocoon. Aloud she said to no one at all, "I'm so weary. Enough of this for now." She reached for the brandy bottle and poured herself a warming snifter. Later she would walk the path along the river to where it reaches the waves. There she so often found solace and wisdom from a distant voice.

Chapter Twenty

Miriam came to the realization of the effects of her childhood on her adult life simultaneous with a national controversy raging over repressed memories of child abuse. In her case, the abuse by her grandfather was confirmed by her parents. Many people knew her father had been a harsh disciplinarian.

Her nightmares revealed a depth of damage far beyond the level expected to result from so-called harsh discipline. Sharing the content of her nightmares with the psychotherapists who led her incest survivor group as well as with other group members, resulted in her coming to believe her father must have sexually as well as physically and emotionally abused her.

The depth of her fear and depression as well as her father-specific terror was considered to be a strong symptom that she had repressed memories. Everything she read and heard and experienced, even sessions in hypnosis, seemed to confirm the diagnosis of traumatic stress syndrome induced by repressed memories of childhood sexual abuse. All symptoms pointed to her dad as primary culprit. She had a monster for a father. She had to stop fooling herself.

She was cautioned to stay out of harm's way. Her mom and siblings felt great compassion for her father in their knowledge he was being wrongfully accused. For Miriam, the experience was much like losing her entire family in a burning plane crash or a train wreck. She was the lone survivor with no one left to share her pain.

She was experiencing what many other women and men were

experiencing in therapy and support groups. It was essential to walk away from the family whose proximity left her feeling hated, crazy and afraid. She didn't want to lose her mom and sisters. She wanted her family's love and support. They'd all seen so much, lived in the same house with the same father, surely they wouldn't think she'd lie — make up something so horrible? Why would anyone subject themselves to this kind of loss if it wasn't true and necessary?

She lost her family. Her children lost their grandparents and aunts. She knew her ability to stay alive was dependent on her staying away from her father and the people who considered her, best case "crazy," and worst case "out to get Dad."

Oh, but she was in agony. Agony she could no longer disguise from her children, colleagues and students. She tried to bury her feelings and continue to function as she always had. Her therapists told her she had nothing to be ashamed of. She was searching for the truth and telling the truth as she discovered it. It was a truth that could save her. She was consumed with guilt. She felt more selfish than ever before in her life. She hated herself for what she was putting her family through. She couldn't bear the shame of how sick this accusation was making her mother. She felt fully responsible for causing damage to her children and their relationship to their extended family.

Her depression got worse as time went on. She was drinking and taking anti-depressants. She couldn't face the morning and would lie catatonic and in a fetal position, unable to call in to work. She began to feel her children would be better off without her. That, if she didn't exist, their fathers would take good care of them, and they wouldn't be burdened by a sick, non-functioning mother, unable to provide for them.

She determined she could never return to the hospital and hope to keep her job. The hospital had been her last resort and she'd used that up. This time she was able to move her legs. This time she did have drugs in the house. She craved unconsciousness. She wasn't set on suicide but she didn't care if death took her.

On a Saturday morning when she knew her children would be away until the next afternoon, she took two strong tranquilizers and washed them down with a full glass of wine. She lay down and reached for the "New York Times Book Review" on the coffee table in front of her.

"Beware the Incest-Survivor Machine." The title to the first page article leaped off the page at her. The author talked about the issue of degrees of trauma and the attempts of the current psychotherapeutic community to find and apply answers to the question "Why do I hurt so badly?" The article was about the repressed memory controversy.

Having still not arrived at a time and place where she deeply trusted her own perceptions, reading the opinion of the expert, social psychologist who wrote the article, caused her to feel like an exposed, lying and/or vindictive fool.

She wanted, more than ever, to dissolve in the unconsciousness so close to her now. She was too near oblivion to read the whole article or process what little she'd read. She slipped into deep and long sleep and didn't wake up until Sunday morning when Roy came to get her signature on an agreement that she would not hold him responsible for further payments on the house.

She came to, feeling guilty for any blame she'd placed on anyone, ever. Came to, feeling, once again, it was all her. All her fault. But — she did come to. She was still alive. Roy took the opportunity to berate her for being a useless drunk. Roy's presence brought out the fight in her. She knew she didn't have the courage to kill herself. She knew her only choice, then, was to live.

When Roy left she emptied the wine bottle in the sink and put the tranquilizers down the garbage disposal. She showered and went out into the morning sunshine. As she walked, warmed by the sun, happy she could move her legs, and strangely happy to be alive, she asked herself some serious questions. "What do I know about my history? What are my clear memories? What do I still need to understand?"

When she got home from her walk she made herself a cup of tea and read the rest of the N.Y. Times article. The "expert" community was strongly divided on this issue of repressed memories. The social psychologist who authored the article reviewed the list of symptoms of repressed memory of sexual abuse as presented in The Courage to Heal, and concluded it would be a rare person (abused or otherwise) who wouldn't exhibit some or many of those symptoms.

Miriam feared she'd been a fool for falling for this rush for answers that told her that the level of trauma and despair she felt — the feelings in her body, her terror response and sense of intimidation and powerlessness, her dream imagery — all of it, she'd been led to believe, stacked up to one plain and simple truth. Her dad sexually as well as physically and emotionally abused her. The real memories, they assured her, would come later. Pay attention to your body, your pain, your reactions to everyday places and things. Keep track of your dreams. Your subconscious knows and will tell you when you're are ready to know the truth.

She was urged to disassociate entirely from her family of origin, the family that harbored this "monster" Dad. She had to stay away because it was necessary to be in a state of denial to be part of the family system that thinks it's really okay to treat a child (or adult for that matter) the way she'd been treated.

So she backed away. She cursed every last one of them for not being there for her, for not believing her and holding her dad accountable. And, not one of them had been able to care. She accused them of denial, defensiveness and said their presence in her life caused her to not have a self or, worse yet, caused her to hate the self she has.

In their presence and to fit and get their love she had to not feel how much she hurt, had to behave (as they did) as if she didn't matter. Had to be willing to be the black sheep, the scapegoat. She was a black sheep because she rebelled always, even in the face of pretty extreme consequences, from her dad's version of the "truth." Her dad's version of love.

But the pivotal thing here had been her accusation of sexual abuse. That's what sent them all running, wasn't it? That's what had decided it once and for all in their minds that she was a liar and not worth dealing with except with a certain distant, head-shaking sort of compassion. They felt for her, of course, but it was all pity. It saddened them that her dementia had reached this all time, disastrous and tragic low.

Miriam wondered sometimes — what if she'd approached it differently — not told anyone about her suspicion that her dad was also sexual with her? What if she'd said she needed distance and time and would let them know when she felt safe coming home? "But no thank you, I really don't need or want, it might be harmful to the work I'm doing" — you know, with great care and gentleness, thinking only of them — "to have contact with you." Then, maybe — do you think? — there would have been occasional expressions of concern for her well being?

There were those expressions from her father — support and frequent phone calls, when he thought he knew she was hurting from the tragedy of her last marriage.

Since his rejection of her after her divorce from Johnny he'd been coerced by emerging liberal standards, even as far as Christianity was concerned, to play a more active part in his broken daughter's heartache.

She had begged her dad and mom to come to a therapy session with her when she was in her early 30's. She'd attempted then to hold them accountable for at least part of the disaster that was her mental health.

Earl never took any responsibility accept to admit she was right in thinking he hadn't felt love or tenderness for her. That he'd felt she was deserving of any punishment he dished out. The therapist explained to him that not all fathers beat their daughters and deny them every kindness and consideration.

Still, he left the session believing he was entitled to his prior actions toward Miriam, and that by merely attending this session, he was vindicated even if by some odd chance he had been wrong. After the session she felt so guilty for having put her mother and father through the trial of knowing how deeply she hurt that Miriam took them out for ice cream sundaes, made extra nicey-nice, and took it all back, apologizing for any unhappiness she'd caused.

They felt vindicated. Felt they'd done the right and modern thing for their daughter. They went home. Her mom called a few days later and said, in no uncertain terms, "That's it Miriam. That's the last time you drag us into this. You have no idea how deeply you hurt and humiliated your father."

"I'm sorry Mom. I know it must have been hard for both of you. I'll be all right now. Hey, I'm a grown up aren't I? I'll handle my own problems from now on. Sorry. Can you forgive me?"

"It's not a matter of forgiving you, honey. You're our daughter and you obviously thought all this dragging up the past would help you feel better somehow. We gave it a try. I truly hope it helped. I'm not sure but what it did more harm than good, and I certainly don't want to go through anything like that again ... Well, so be it. You just concentrate on taking care of those babies of yours now. I think it's probably all this self-absorption and women's liberation stuff that's put you in this state. You always have been selfish and had too high expectations of life. No one ever said life would be fair or you could expect constant, non-stop happiness. Anyway, we do love you, so you can just put any fears to the contrary to rest. I have to go tend to your father now. He hasn't slept a wink and is having terrible stomach pains ever since you subjected him to your accusations. I'll talk with you later, honey."

"Okay Mom. Well, I am sorry. Good bye." She hung up the phone and let her head fall into her arms on the table in front of her. Consumed with guilt, addled with confusion, the heat and burning came up through her body, into her face and eyes, and she simultaneously had the need to vomit and the need to cry.

This time when Miriam tried to separate from her family, Ariana, broke through the barriers she'd tried to create and insisted she'd be there for her. She begged Miriam to trust her, and, frankly, believed her and felt all the shattering devastation appropriate to the discovery of her abuse at the hands of their father. Then, Ariana did some work on herself, visited a therapist, underwent hypnosis, did some research, and after, told Miriam she simply could not believe their father had abused her.

Ariana said she did believe Miriam hurt like hell. That it was possible that almost any level of atrocity was committed against her small body. Ariana just couldn't see, she said, what that had to do with her. "Why," she raged, once it became more than she wanted to bear "why, should we all give up our family? Our Dad? Because you've had a few vague dreams and memories? No way. I won't do it! You're on your own, Miriam."

Months into Miriam's search for the truth and her guilt for all she'd brought down on the heads of her family members and children she found herself propelled between two realities as she thumbed through the daily news paper. Her eyes, mind and emotions were struck by two distant ends of the spectrum of the Abuse Memory controversy. Side by side in the Variety section she came upon Gary Trudeau's "Doonesbury" and Louise Erdrich's comments on the lives of the characters in her fiction.

Miriam felt caught smack in the middle of the false memory, repressed memory, visual, emotional, recall memory, false accusation controversy. She personally felt tremendous shame and embarrassment at the possibility of being identified with those who would label the slightest insult or absent minded infraction on the part of parent, teacher or priest as abuse. She felt SHAME, SHAME, SHAME at the media circus surrounding people seeking help — The various forms of help offered to would be and/or real victims; help that ranged from the silly, obnoxious, syrupy to hard-nosed "lock 'em up and throw away the key" court cases, to honest-to-God, legitimate psychotherapy offered by professionals who know the pervasiveness of child abuse and the life long debilitation and, yes, threat to society such abuse poses. Happening on Trudeau and Erdrich, Miriam at once felt red hot shame, guilt, helplessness, compassion, empathy and understanding.

The "Doonesbury" strip was the one where the defense attorney says to his client "And you were ABUSED, too, weren't you?" ". . . and, by a Priest wasn't it?" and the baffled, caught off guard client hops to and says "Abused? Yeah, sure, — abused? Hey, why not?"

Instant guilt and humiliation washed over Miriam and, again and always, the knowledge that no one will ever believe her and why did she ever open her mouth to expose her own childhood experience? Then, not more than a page away, Louise Erdrich, whose work she appreciated on a level equal to that of Trudeau's. Erdrich was saying how she, not having a tragic or abusive childhood, recognizes the unfixable, life long damage done when children are abandoned, neglected, un-cared for and abused by those they should have reason to trust. She invents, "recognizes" the childhood rape that has formed the stories in the life of her character June. " It's a great treasure to me that I had a secure childhood." Erdrich said. "But I see in people who are my age now great gaps and absences because they haven't . . ."

"June [Erdrich's character] is an intelligent woman but she is unable to make up for what she missed as a child to heal herself. She is a wounded person all through her life. She has enormous wells of 'rage and despair'. . . The thing that becomes apparent throughout life is that when you have terrible things happen to you, sometimes people don't really recover." [Erdrich by Kay Miller, Variety, Star Tribune]

In that roller coaster three minutes on Miriam's emotional clock she shared Trudeau's outrage at the courtroom and media circus; shared his disgust and shame that some so greedily seek the easy money, easy notoriety they picture available through victim hood and false accusation. These are crimes without witnesses and it is not politically correct to disbelieve a self proclaimed victim. She resented the fakery of those who intentionally and falsely accuse. She felt sympathy and regret toward the falsely accused. And God, she would swear this too, she shared, felt comforted in, Erdrich's compassion for people damaged in childhood. Her recognition of the effects of such hurt and she was reduced to tears as if Erdrich was her long lost Mommy taking her in her arms to say "It's alright, baby. I won't let anyone hurt you."

So when Miriam cringed in a kind of shameful empathy and appreciation when her hero Trudeau made a mockery of the fakes; and she burst into tears and felt heard and understood at the words of other-hero Erdrich, and both reached her at her very soul, she knew there were two true stories there.

There was the truth about falsehood and fakery and the truth about actual and harming experience. She knew then as she knows now, that we can't allow the revelation of falsehood and trickery to intimidate to silence those who reveal true experience. Trudeau told it true. Erdrich told it true.

Miriam's personal discoveries were having an impact on the nature of her professional work. She began to take an interest in the stories of the relationships historic women had with their fathers. Djuna Barnes, Anais Nin, Virginia Woolf – parts of their stories had already been told. How many women's stories were buried? How has the silence about the truth of women's experience affected current and future society?

She continued to struggle with depression but threw herself into a program of physical exercise, yoga and meditation to combat the fear and pain. She continued her sessions with Zoe. She hadn't communicated with her father since the day she heard his voice on the phone and collapsed. Fear of him continued to have a hold on her. She still couldn't pick up the phone and call her mother. She feared he would read her letters if she wrote to her mother. Finally Miriam decided she had to be clear with him. She had to tell him goodbye and she wanted to tell him why.

Chapter Twenty One

Miriam worked with renewed vigor in her profession as historian. Was now teaching in the history department at St. David's College. She'd initially been hired as the first of their faculty to offer courses in women's studies and in a cost-effective move to acquiesce to the powers that dictated affirmative action regulations. She welcomed the job, though the starting salary was barely a living wage. Many new Ph.D.'s were having trouble finding appropriate positions. It seemed so much the right position for Miriam though, with the college's proximity to her treasured woodlands, waves and the granite stage where so many times she'd felt a nearness to home.

St. David's was a pretty campus with buildings constructed of limestone and sandstone from Minnesota quarries that thrived in the late 19th and early 20th century. The school had limited enrollment and offered an environment, in its idyllic setting overlooking the river, conducive to reflection and intimate discourse among colleagues and students. Miriam's was not the grandest of the offices on campus, but she had a great view. She liked that her office was up high, on the fourth floor. Though it was tiny by comparison to offices occupied by senior faculty, one enormously tall, narrow window could be thrown open to the fresh breezes that blew off the Lake. The building interior was dark, aged and musty but she brightened her surroundings by, weekly, bringing in a super market purchased bouquet of fresh iris, lilies or freesia, flown to this cold and flower-inhospitable part of the country from gardens in the South and West. She put them in a favorite, ancient, salt jug on the window sill. When pouring over a research paper or her lecture notes she would live in the springtime the flowers provided.

Having made the decision to tell her father good bye, she left work early on a day in December. Arriving at the water's edge she sat on that jutting, granite stage, legs pulled close to her body. Again, she heard the whisper of rescue. A voice — still living voice, that told her when she was quiet, when she was attentive, that she does know the answer to the questions that haunt her.

That whisper in the waves, in the breeze through the trees, the sun, just then, so tentatively visiting, said to her "Let it go, honey. Say goodbye." The voice challenged her to test her strength. Challenged her to put the longing and unfinished business behind her.

She returned to her apartment, poured herself a glass of wine, lit a fire, opened the window to the coming and going sounds of the rain and the distant waves and started a letter to her father.

She worked on the letter off and on for five months. She finally sent it to him enclosed in a card. The card's cover showed a beleaguered and quite ugly, straggly-haired woman, digging a hole and trying to bury something in it that keeps seeping out even as she shovels the dirt over it. The card said, "Mad woman trying to bury delicate feelings for the last time."

Miriam wrote a brief, begging-for-love sort of note, to her older sister, Ariana, and enclosed a copy of the letter to her dad. She wrote to her two younger sisters and her mom explaining she had determined there are some tragedies short of death that are as unfixable and irrevocable as death and that her experience with her father is and was one of those. She sent them all copies of the letter. This is how she said goodbye:

> April 15, 1994
> Dear Dad:
>
> What to do with this mess I've got myself into in regard to you. Beats me if I know. I've been following a path that maybe, maybe, maybe offered some rest, some peace. That's not where it has taken me. I want out of this longing. None of this is meant to be, perhaps. I didn't mean, never meant to hurt you. I don't know why the first forty years of my life came back to me with full nightmare force and left me near death and why it seemed to be you who was to blame —

you I had to flee. I still want to stay away. My biggest hurt right now is longing for a sense of comfort that I increasingly fear (nobody's fault) will never come and the guilt I feel for wanting to stay away. I believe you have no more need for me now, than ever, except maybe for me to say "its all done now — I'm sorry to have troubled you," and I am. I don't have any more answers now than I ever did. I only know it was all so black and dark and terrifying, that I never want to go near its reminders again. And, from what I hear and guess, you are well — undiminished by my accusations I think. Middle-age is making me want to grab all the life I have coming and taste every tiny morsel of it. Certainly the way my childhood was lived, was experienced by me, has much to do with who I am now and how I behaved between eighteen and forty. I tried all those years to make sense of so much that seemed indecipherable; still seems indecipherable, so, in the end (or maybe, if I'm lucky, this is the middle of my life) all that I have and know for certain is experience. One experience after another and even those change so in retrospect. It's the ones piling up as we speak and on into whatever future I have ahead that I want to grasp, look at, hear, feel, not run away from. So my intent is to live in the here and now. I'm certain it appears the last few years I've spent living in the past and what was the point, you probably wonder. Well, I wasn't really living there so much as I was trying to visit a place where I spent a childhood in a kind of zombie-like, sleep walk state when I wasn't screaming at the top of my lungs for escape. The time I've spent visiting there, when I've been able to stay awake, not go numb, and not run and hide in the closet has taught me much about why I experience the here and now as I do. Maybe the best thing is for me to try to put all this in some kind of perspective. Overall, and in this day and age, I can expect maybe seventy five, eighty years of life. The first five or six, they say, are pretty critical in regard to how well equipped one is to handle the next seventy five or so. But, I didn't really know that in a personal way until I was nearly forty (halfway, you see). So, that childhood stuff, which was pretty confusing, lonely, crazy and scary, never got set right in the next twelve years when things in my life maybe weren't so awful in the larger scheme of things (given the horrors of the lives of some children in that age range). It's mostly that I couldn't seem to make any kind of an impact by being alive. My existence didn't seem to make a whole lot of difference to you, Dad, and I think this is, more than anything your fatal flaw as a father. Kids need acknowledgement, need a sense it's okay if they take up space, to grow up feeling like they do exist, aren't invisible, someone hears them when they talk, and, generally, that's okay. You didn't let me be visible. The more I'd rage against you and your attempts to silence me and get me out of the way the more you'd let me know how insignificant and troublesome I was. It never seemed fair or right somehow but everyone else seemed to be doing okay with it. Part of it, I think, is that people really do have their limits. My push up against yours, I'm quite sure, was my untimely birth in the life of a very young couple who was dirt-poor and already had a brand new baby girl. Maybe you thought you'd adjust but found out you just couldn't and I was pretty powerless to assert my will on my own behalf. Well, I understand how relentless the demands of children on parents can be. Children truly are an interruption in the life of someone who has aspirations beyond parenting. I don't think you knew anything much would be required of a Dad by a girl child with a stay-at-home Mother. And it probably would have been alright, not so devastating if you really were an absentee father and I'd had my Mother's devotion to be both a mother and father to me like in those "broken" homes. But you tried to protect Mom from the inconvenience of me. If she was inconvenienced with the attention I demanded, that tended to take away from what she had to offer as your wife, lover and friend. I know a little about that, too. I've done that balancing act between my desire to lie with my head in my husband's lap or vice verse and my children's need to have attentive, alert, guiding grownups for parents. Kids just can't make it all alone so the grown ups have to get up and listen to them, take care of them, show them the way. Contrast that with a kid who can't get heard no matter how loud she screams, she can only get beaten harder and ultimately, to survive, she has to find somebody who knows she exists and matters to help her grow up. She proves to be an embarrassment to her parents because she's always trying to attract attention from near to complete strangers. She acts up in school; she acts up in Sunday school; she's loud and boisterous and doesn't know when to keep her mouth shut. Life gets to be a constant battle to silence this little loud mouth, doesn't it? I sense you're still angry about that.

What did you give me to believe in? How did you expect me to feel safe? You knew Grandpa had sex with me. You knew I hid in closets and sucked three whole fingers until I was twelve years old. You knew I'd been beaten with the belt before going to school some mornings and came home to find out I'd said something that meant my evening would start with getting my mouth washed out with soap. You knew I kept trying to run away. When I threatened to go you told me you'd help pack my bags. “Good riddance,” you'd say. Then when you'd come to get me to bring me home you beat me with the belt again. You didn't really want me at home because you enjoyed my company or anything. You were just afraid of how my mouth might be flapping when I was out there, out of your sight. I stayed away from home as much as I could. I liked overnights at other people's houses. When I had girlfriends over you never thought I acted right and you'd threaten me with the belt right in front of them. Humiliating to have my girlfriends know my Dad acts like that, feels that way about me. Anyway, what seemed to work out best for me, starting at about age nine, was becoming boy-crazy. I craved their attention and affection. I lived in the dream world of romance and would risk any punishment from you for the touch of one of those sweet little boys who thought I was mighty cute. That's why I think life wasn't so awful once I hit adolescence. I found admirers. I also had a few experiences that told me some teachers thought I was pretty bright and clever and that was a help. Really, a form of rescue.

Basically, it's a life of confusion, running and chaos — a lot of yelling in a booming voice (you) that I remember. I don't have a single memory of feeling welcome, restful and peaceful in your presence, let alone feeling loved, delighted in or any availability of either refuge or comfort. I'm at the middle of my life at least, right now. I can't generate feelings of longing for the good old days. I am sorry.

I want to cram my life with beauty, peace, rest, connections and understanding and I don’t feel, truly don’t believe that’s possible between you and me. I wish you well. I wish you peace and rest, people who understand, appreciate and delight in you. I forgive you any mistakes, errors, hurts, deprivations toward me. I want you to forgive me for not wanting to come home.

With Hopes You’ll Have
a Long and Happy Life,
Miriam

Hard to say what Miriam’s expectations were, but having put the letter in the mail, she did feel she’d finished something. She’d finished something that was blocking her from moving on. Finished something that was weighing her down with guilt and confusion. She could tell it was finished — for the time being anyway — because she ceased to wrestle day after painful day with “What to do? What to do?” as she’d been doing for the last years. And this feeling of being finished, it felt like something else, too. She felt the bruises and dents from her father’s more than forty year grip on her arms becoming live, pink/gold flesh with muscles pumped full of blood and vigor. And she felt she was no longer walking away sheepishly, guiltily looking over her shoulder. No. No. Miriam was running. She broke for a sprint on a fresh, uncovered, red-clay road through a sanctuary of sun-sparkled leaves all the brilliant colors of cut glass. She left her father. She headed for home.

Chapter Twenty Two

As for the place Miriam called home and where she slept at night and ate her meals, it wasn't really her own, though its proximity to the river and therefore to the lake was a comfort to her. It was a little modern for her taste and possessed only a gas fireplace lacking the scent and crackle of a wood fire. Still she could gaze from her balcony and in the distance, an easy walk, see her beloved Lake Superior. She surrounded herself with treasured books, rugs, a goose down comforter, cups she loved to drink from, large globe crystal wine glasses, a linen table cloth and napkins and several small pieces of original artwork to keep her company.

Storm was in college. Jane had insisted she was miserable sharing a home with her mother and, though Miriam begged and pleaded with her to stay, she had no clout to keep her from moving in with her father. Miriam missed her terribly. Felt she'd lost her far too young, but knew she had no choice but to let her go.

In many ways Miriam treasured her solitude and for the first time since giving birth to her daughters, was un-haunted by secret guilt about not being available to them. She knew they would be drawn, at least occasionally to the lake. The love of its comfort and sanctuary was one thing she and her girls shared in common and it had the power to bring them together around a roaring, shore side fire to share a near primal intimacy.

The lake was, after all, the birthplace of each of her daughters, and their knowledge of that beginning and their mother's relationship to the wild places along the shore, Miriam hoped would feed them each with a primary sort of knowing about being a woman. It was nothing they would consciously acknowledge as a gift their mother gave; still, when they were there by the shore she believed they felt at home in a way they seldom felt anywhere else.

Soon after Miriam sent the letter of goodbye to her father, Storm came north to be with her and share the sanctuary of the lake.

They poked sticks into the fire as they talked and digested the marshmallows they roasted to a golden and creamy turn. They watched the flames and the glowing coals.

Storm, keeping her eyes on the stick poking business before her said, "Mom, I've always seen you as a sort of pioneer. You're the one person in your family who dared to take a stand. You're such a rebel. You took on new and frightening territory and said what you saw, experienced and felt."

"That's why," Storm said, "people are both drawn to you and afraid of you. You stir things up. Make people look at their lives and their commitments in a new way. It scares people who just want to live life without thinking much about it."

"A pioneer?" Miriam said, surprised and pleased her daughter saw her as courageous

"Is that why I feel so drawn to the days of westward ho the wagons and the long, dragging in the mud and dust skirts of those women and their unflagging spirits?"

She and Storm talked about how rarely, in the pioneer days of American history, marriage served as refuge for a woman. It was, perhaps, a noble life-calling. It was a calling to hard labor in the face of the siege of nature and change and force of war and conflict. Sure there were the elite and privileged classes. There were daughters born-to-wealth who would, after leaving their father's home and its pampering servants, reign as queen of their own servant staffed households. But those women were few.

Who were these women whose homes were the wagons and the crude huts on the prairie? Who among them twirled in dance in the circle of sunlight the early day projected on the dirt floor of their one-room cabin?

Who among them had a soul and mind that soared with the possibilities before them and yearned toward all they would become — all they would teach and leave to their children? Who among them left signs and words and songs from which we can learn to live forward? Live forward rather than be stopped dead in her tracks at the obstacles life would throw in the way?

And those early days in this country that belonged to its natives rather than Miriam's and her children's ancestors were fraught with obstacles to calm, peaceful and secure living. Their grandmothers strode over and through those obstacles, they threw themselves in front of and on top of their babies and defended their lives and homes.

Working and living by the lake at this time in Miriam's life, allowed her freedom from the daily domestic and emotional demands of the role of wife and mother.

Increasingly her work, her professional life, reflected her personal search. Increasingly she advocated "enough to go around . . . so . . . children [would] grow up to be neither the destroyers nor the destroyed," to paraphrase words that often crossed her mind. Words from Barbara Kingsolver's Animal Dreams that struck her as so appropriate to her new attempt to know what she hoped for and to live inside that hope.

Her research took her beyond the attics and basements and dusty library archives. Took her into the search for an understanding of what causes certain children to grow up and become creators and contributors and others to destroy their own lives and create damage in the lives of those who love or need them. Miriam found particular insight in the work of Alice Miller, a German psychoanalyst, nearly contemporary with Anais Nin, Otto Rank and her own grandparents.

Miller's work spelled out the effects of childhood trauma on creativity and destructiveness. It was not a new field entirely. Much had been assumed and theorized and even researched about what circumstances create a criminal and anti-social human adult. There was general understanding now that children who are mistreated, abandoned and brutalized often — more often than not it was said — grew up to repeat the behavior to which they'd been subjected. Circumstances like poverty and neglect were held responsible for a sense of hopelessness and lack of compassion. Neglected and abused children sometimes grew to be adults desperate to fill an awful void and played out a need to cause destruction. Examples of these wounded children include tyrants like Hitler and Charles Manson.

Miriam received an increased recognition for her work and was invited more and more to discuss her findings and speculations at seminars and lecture series for criminal justice professionals and school administrators and educators.

Professional journals and the occasional popular periodical published articles related to her work. Of course she welcomed this recognition. Her increasing notoriety offered her the chance to travel extensively and always she relished any engagement that would take her to one coast or another or to England or Scotland where the sea was never more than sixty miles away in either direction. Wherever she went, the sea, the river, the lake or mountain spring seemed to feed her.

Individuals searching for their own histories and understanding of repeated family behavior patterns pursued her. That particular outcome of recognition was hard to welcome.

She knew why these people called her and wrote her letters. She had great sympathy for them in their attempts to find the puzzle pieces to their own histories and family stories. She had received some press for her research in both oral and written histories of families of the American South. Prior to her contribution to this area of historical research there had been considerable emphasis placed on folk traditions.

Emphasis was placed on stories handed down, generation to generation about the heroic men who settled the hills and tamed the swamps, forged the rivers and streams, traded with the Indians and ultimately founded cities that have become the modern metropolises of late 20th century America. Her research focused on women's stories, women's histories. Her research led her to the archives of literature on the women's movement on the East Coast and information that chronicled the 1870 women's conference in the Catskill Mountains of New York State. She studied the lives of Djuna Barnes, Edith Wharton, Sarah Orn Jewitt and Anais Nin.

As a product of the post World War II baby boom, Miriam had arrived at young womanhood during the sexual revolution of the 1960's and participated in the re-kindled women's movement of the 1970's. She was unable to rest easy with the content of history books. The historical literature was largely written and edited by males from the generations who came before her.

There was, for one thing, a tremendous lack of information about women's lives and their impact on history. Even the lives of men were described in superficial terms. There was little sense of the intimate and emotional lives of men; how they felt rather than how they acted. Actions that built buildings, created inventions for industrial progress, committed crimes and assaults, behavior that won the West: these were the stories told in the history books.

How did it feel to be a man or a woman coming of age in the early part of this century, Miriam wanted to know. Men, then as now, she presumed, didn't talk much about their feelings. Stories and poems told a great deal but many of them had been lost to posterity.

With her love of history, it was only natural she would seek answers beyond what the textbooks provided the general population. As she came to adolescence, young womanhood, and full adult womanhood she played out the same battles each generation before her faced. She challenged societal norms and requirements. Her young woman's body and soul told her she could be — could do — anything. She became increasingly disillusioned with the information, maps and guides given her as legacy from her parents, grandparents, teachers and the books she combed for truth on the shelves of the public library.

Sure, there were books written by women and about women but the ones that really told a story she could identify with were fiction. Pretend women, often created by men. Men were published more often than women. Men's voices outnumbered women's by thousands of percentage points.

The women created by D.H. Lawrence, Thomas Wolfe, Henry Miller, J.D. Salinger, Henrik Ibsen, Herman Hesse, Flaubert, were women of blood and soul; passion driven women. There were the fictional women created by Virginia Woolf, Louisa May Alcott, Jane Austen, Edith Wharton and Charlotte and Emily Bronte. In these women-written books care had to be taken to be proper, careful not to fly in the face of societal expectations.

There was the widely accepted idea that women from poverty and working class and farm circumstances were illiterate because they were not permitted to attend school. It's true the literature coming from women with these circumstances is greatly limited, particularly if one looks to published and recognized works. What Miriam couldn't get over, though, the older she became, and the deeper she dug, was this sense that basic humanity doesn't change that much.

Where were the stories of women who led everyday, average lives but had hearts and souls of great depth, wisdom, passion?

Where were the stories of real, live women who didn't quite fit society's expectations? The question often came to her as she read the free-thinking philosophy and fiction written by men in the 1920's and 1930's. What women did these writers know who were motivated by dreams, a quest for knowledge, personal freedom and passion? These are the women of male-written fiction. Could it be that real, live women inspired these characters?

Miriam considered her own grandmothers who became women and mothers in the 1920's and 1930's. Women whose lives seemed to revolve around repressed emotion and secret keeping. Shamed women — though they led, by society's standards, proper lives.

She couldn't see any clear connection between the woman she'd become and the women who preceded her in her family. The questions — Why am I who I am? Why am I the way I am? — haunted her. She felt no affinity to these women and no acceptance of her nature in proximity to them. She felt herself an anomaly in a long line of women who were content with the lot dictated by religious institutions. Her predecessors, as far as she knew, were content with the expectations to be good, proper, safe, responsible — as in, timid, fearful and hidden. It made little sense to her.

Did a long line of truly timid and frightened women really spawn the likes of Miriam? Where had her strong will, spirit and drive come from? Her biblical training told her there was nothing new under the sun. She imagined the lives of the women she held as heroes; May Sarton, Adrienne Rich, Anais Nin, Virginia Woolf.

She imagined their mothers and grandmothers had been spirited and free thinking women who quite naturally handed on this spirit as legacy to their daughters. The affinity she felt toward these women, all of them much older than she was; some of them many years dead, told her there was a great deal more to learn about the generations of women who preceded her.

She refused to believe there were no records, journals, diaries, stories in existence that would reveal to her the lives, dreamed and realized, of everyday American women.

During Miriam's years as an undergraduate she explored as far as possible the fictional accounts of the lives of women, written by women, who had the good fortune to be published. The Awakening by Kate Chopin described a woman destroyed by her desire for free choice and her passionate sexuality.

Emma by Jane Austen seemed to look with contempt and loathing and a silly sense of romance on the life of the wife and mother. Austen gave great credence to the life of the mind available to the spinster daughter who relied on the income of her aristocratic father for financial support.

Fascinating and romantic stories like Jane Eyre and Wuthering Heights described spirited women all searching frantically and making great sacrifices for the sake of love, romance and marriage.

Virginia Woolf's women were introspective, reflective, deep and suicidal. Miriam discovered the diaries of Anais Nin. Her stories and novels were lyrical, fluid, dreamlike, but she too, kept secrets. She wouldn't (couldn't) tell all about what it was like to be her. She served as highly effective muse to men she loved and admired and her own literary work took a back seat to the work she inspired in others. She seemed to have worshiped and needed men in the extreme.

Nin was really the one that awakened Miriam to the possibility that her own grandmothers and great-grandmothers lived among women much like herself. Where were the stories of these women's lives?

Miriam's doctoral thesis and all her master's work had focused specifically on attempts to find the missing stories of American women who were coal-miner's wives, school teachers, spinster daughters, farmers, merchants, flappers, free-thinkers, muses to psychologists and writers and painters. Where were the Alice Neels, Georgia O'Keefes, Anais Nins, Djuna Barnes and Virginia Woolfs in her own family and the families of other women of her generation?

She'd been getting a lot of harassing calls in her office and at home as well as some negative media coverage over the past several weeks after a letter to the editor she authored was published in Harper's. Some of her research gave credence to the prevalence of incest and child molestation as well as child slavery that's a part of the history of pretty close to every family she'd researched. Where she'd been unable to find actual documentation and specific allegations she found hints and cries for help. She found women and girls trying, in their secret diaries, to figure out if what was happening to them was normal but they couldn't ask anyone and they couldn't tell anyone for fear of losing their very lives.

Miriam was getting a negative reaction because her research

came to light simultaneous with the controversy over repressed memories. Theories about repressed memory had large numbers of the population of the United States, assuming and guessing and dredging up maybe/maybe not memories of sexual abuse and incest as an explanation for all the emotional ills they suffered as adults.

People everywhere were seeking answers to the question "why do I hurt so much"? Some people flat-out knew they were molested, assaulted, raped, abused and who did it and when and how. The damage that resulted was obvious and on display on every seedy or reputable talk show on radio and television and in all the sensational newspapers and magazines in the country. The accused were running in defensive circles and swearing they "loved her, couldn't do that, never laid a hand on her" — that sort of thing. The people who seemed to be similarly damaged to these victims of documented abuse, and were seeking answers to the source of their pain as well as seeking heeling, were recipients of a range of explanations and theories that talked about repressed memories.

Some authors, themselves victims of childhood abuse, but with repressed memories, had published laundry lists of what signs to look for that you've been abused. Women and men alike were checking off these lists by the thousands and signing up for therapy and support groups and carrying with them a favorite childhood toy; undergoing hypnosis to uncover the truth of their tortured and sordid past. The accused, in this case too, was running in defensive circles and swore "I loved her. I could never lay a hand on her."

Families were tearing apart at the seams. Miriam's research came about at a time when people were down right exhausted with the whole topic. They were sick of it. They didn't care anymore. Her research came at a time when Time Magazine published an article trashing "incest" literature as tiresome and sensational and at a time when Harper's published a similar, though more complete and scholarly, article written by a recent female Harvard Ph.D. Nobody wanted to know the truth except the lost, scared and confused men and women running around leading lives filled with excruciating pain.

There were those who denied the harm of abuse, remembered or not. There were those who said un-remembered abuse was the most harmful form abuse could take — there were no collaborators. Its victims felt alone and crazy in their sense of the harm done.

Miriam felt women were once again being encouraged to be

silent. Encouraged to keep the truth of their feelings and experiences and searches to themselves. She reacted by writing a letter to the editor of Harper's, and since its publication the letters and phone calls were constant.

> Dear Editor:
> Like Katie Roiphe ("Making the Incest Scene," HARPER'S), I've begun to feel the "incest fiction" is much too much, and same-old, same-old sensationalism. But I can't help wondering how these stories, so frightfully common to the lives of so many of us, will get told if we disparage this particular genre. Roiphe blasts even those brilliant authors (Jane Smiley, Margaret Atwood, Toni Morrison) who have written these stories, resounding with truth, powerfully and well. She seems to speak fondly and wistfully about male authors who treat the subject more abstractly and with delicacy (Shakespeare, F. Scott Fitzgerald); careful to present incest in less vivid, graphic and jarring terms. I fear the truth of children's lives will be silenced by outrage such as Roiphe's. The telling of a story that allows one to look candidly at the truth of one's life experience is cathartic: it is healing. Reading a story that shows incest as a common occurrence in the lives of children sheds light on a societal truth and offers us a valuable piece of wisdom. These stories offer insight and comfort to those who have shared in this all too common experience. Yet Roiphe's opposition to incest as entertainment is understandable. Can future fiction, perhaps, start at the reclaiming part of a character's life and skip the graphics? I mean, simply assume damage and trauma, abandonment and alienation in childhood and tell a story of beating the resulting giants, dragons and monsters?
>
> Without contributions such as Smiley's, Atwood's and Morrison's, can we ever hope for a revision of Beauty and the Beast; one in which the beast has to shape up and become a responsible and communicative and accountable human being, or be rejected rather than embraced? All of this incest and child abuse is the result of a society willingly embracing the beast. It is the result of our believing we can love him into other than beast. We merely propagate the

species. Our daughters lie down with beasts and their children have beasts for fathers. But we are a society fascinated with beasts. Incest is common and society (critics such as Roiphe, anyway) apparently so bored with its prevalence in current fiction, that we run the risk of being unconcerned about the truth these stories tell and about the damaged lives incest leaves in its wake.

In Roiphe we have a highly educated woman (no less) telling predominately women writers to "can" this ho hum, same old, same old incest literature.

In 1965 Harper's published "Silences" by Tillie Olsen, in which she exposed the many ways women's voices have been silenced throughout history and urged us to speak the truth of our experience. Now, some thirty years later, it seems we are re-visited by a silencer. Authors of fiction are being asked to say what has to be said about incest, nicely, or not at all. Incest makes boring reading for Roiphe. Too common. Everybody is doing it. Write about something else.

Now that there is less freedom for men to openly suppress women's words we have a newly educated generation of women ready to attempt to silence their mothers' voices. It smacks of an adolescent arrogance that says, "Quit whining about your insignificant life, Mom." It is a familiar and frightening voice and spells something very sad for the silence-breaking legacy we mothers wish to leave to our children.

Respectfully and With
Concern,
Miriam Blackwell, Ph.D.
Department of History
St. David's College
Luster River, Minnesota

Roiphe's article caused Miriam to realize, again, how completely she had separated her professional life from the personal. After saying goodbye to her father she'd felt it essential to run from her history to survive and had failed to see the importance of facing its reality head on.

She wondered if she would only be able to overcome the torment by ceasing to run from it — by letting in as much truth about the forces that shaped her as she could find. In the months that followed, she began to take, for the first time, her own expert advice. She began to search for and attempt to face her own history.

Chapter Twenty Three

Looking straight ahead at the bleak ramshackle house whose porch had long since slid into the dust that used to be called the front yard, Miriam reached one hand behind her to the only rock almost big enough to make a seat. The rock was much lower to the ground than she expected and she lost her balance landing lopsided with one leg draped over the small hump of basalt, her bottom parallel to the mesmerizing fallen porch across the street. She didn't laugh, though she supposed it was a slap-sticky sort of situation. A grown woman making her way across this ghost town, desert highway where everything tasted like dust and smelled like dust and you can barely see through it to anything recognizable. She wondered, anyway, if there was anything to see no matter how hard she might try. "Why did I come here?" Miriam asked herself, then told herself it was a good question, an important question. Told herself she knew this was true. She repeated out loud, "Yes, this is both a good and an important question." Then told herself what she also knew to be true, that she sure didn't have anything like an answer.

Miriam sprawled there in the dust — thin, bedraggled and starved. She wanted to scream, to cry out "s-t-a-a-a-a-a-r-v-ed, starved, starved". Parched and cracking apart. Thirsty without end.

The only moisture in this land was now running down her cheeks making rivulets through the half-inch of dust her face accumulated in the short walk from the bus stop at Borley.

It was early August, 1996, and the academic year at St.

David's, ended in June. She was on summer break, and she didn't have to start next season's classes until late September. Miriam was on what she hoped would be the final quest for the truth the experts said would set her free.

She'd been the only one on the bus after it left Tallahassee and she sat two rows from the back, alone and ashamed and wishing she didn't have to share space with the driver who would surely think she was a lunatic.

She fully looked the lunatic part. She wore a 1930's mama-style house dress made out of some too-crisp, shabby cotton. She picked the dress up at Woolworth's for $6.99 as an act of contrition and humiliation because she'd always cared too much about how she looked for her own good. Everything she was, had been even, seemed somehow obscured by how she looked. Always had been. People thought they could see her. Thought they knew her. Imagined they knew who she was and where she came from. But nobody, Miriam could tell you, in her new self-knowledge — "no-fuckin'-body has a clue".

Her looks had meant her survival time and again. Her looks were a suit of armor through which she could clang and batter her way to places of relative safety and security, since all the world, you know, loves a pretty face. Yes, she had used, as they say, her looks. Always she felt a mixture of shame and pride from this truth. Her trim, tan body, her brown-black hair that shined in a billowy luster of curls around her face — were part of the picture that took the breath out of many an on looker over the years since high school. But it was her eyes, they told her, gray/green and lit from within — her eyes gave her a look that was either interpreted as "evil/ a devil's eyes" or, for people who saw her in a more positive light, an old-for-her-age look of wisdom.

No one at home ever saw her as cute or pretty. She was proud, vain they'd all said, assumed. At Sunday school, though, and at the houses of her friends she was told what pretty eyes, lovely hair, tawny and glistening skin she had. Mothers held her up to their daughters as an example of how a little girl should look. All through junior high and high school the boys chased her and she chased right back.

If she was particularly bright or talented as a child, she never really knew it. She came to believe it was her looks doing all the right tricks for her. And, really, what she craved so, always, was someone to love her. Someone to treasure her.

If she were to look back on her life she'd have to admit she'd used some sweet boys rather cruelly out of her need for a sense of control. Certainly, she'd acted without clear motive, without conscience — and, sadly, without compassion. As an adult she pursued the attention of married men without consideration for the harm she did their wives and children. Without concern for the pain and disruption she would bring to the women and children who believed in their husbands or fathers. She acted selfishly, thinking only of her own deep and aching need. She took their hearts from them, unaware they needed anything in return.

It started way, way back when she was little. Probably, it started when her mother thought she miscarried Miriam and mourned her for dead. When she turned up born and alive, her father felt put upon rather than compassionate toward the sickly child. Not much of a model for compassion was exhibited to Miriam in her childhood home.

But after all these years, and having finally taken the necessary step toward making a commitment to look closely at her past, and having said goodbye to her father — though she'd felt free of a terrible weight at the time she sent the letter, the consequences had been brutal. No one in her family wanted to have anything to do with a daughter or sibling who dared reject her own father.

Miriam had left her marriage and lost her friends. Her daughters tried to be supportive, but suffered so many losses of their own as a result of her actions that she was left, once again, utterly alone.

There in the Florida swamp/desert, having slid from her rock and landed in the soft brown dust, face to face with the porch that shared that dust, she felt the hopelessness of her situation. Felt the full reality of her solitary and lost state.

She lifted her head to see the fallen front porch of the house that had been her first home. She felt the porch was talking to her. Trying to tell her something. Felt that similar fallen porches had, for years been trying to reach her with some kind of truth. All along the way in her travels through derelict areas of the country she would see these porches, nearly fallen off or straight out already hanging off a house and laying right there in the weeds of what used to be some family's front yard, and something would happen. That porch, those porches mocked her.

There she'd be, in her comfortable car, with her comfortable income and just right clothing, makeup, hair and book-learned parenting skills. Life was good, she might be thinking. The future lies ahead, can only get better. And then, another monument to some other family's good-times-future-can-only-get-better, lying there like that family and its future never really did matter.

The future did not get better. Didn't get worse either. Just was. Just went by. Hers, for example, happened to her while all the time she was trying to mold it, control it all, make it fit somewhere pretty and peaceful and calm.

"Hah!" she breathed the words aloud. "This rock facing this fallen porch is where it was headed for a half way mark. Half off, half on an almost-rock across the street from a half on, half off, not quite porch anymore, on some planet that sure doesn't feel like home."

"God, could I be more self pitying than this?" She thought, looking around to be sure she was alone. It was a rhetorical question not nearly so good or important as the one about why she came here, what landed her here in the dust in the first place.

For a long time now, she'd thought she might make a fear-facing, mid life journey when Jane turned eighteen, graduated and she might not be needed so much at home. She felt far too necessary to everyone and everything — kids, ex-husbands, career, her mom, dad, sisters, nieces, nephews, the National Women's Caucus, the Women Against Military Madness and any and all causes related to the preservation of women's experience. She'd felt necessary to the three times a week aerobics classes, two time treadmill personal workout and the two walks around the park followed by coffee in a trendy Seattle-type cafe. She'd been necessary to her own image of middle class, educated, enlightened, liberal motherhood, friendship, daughter-hood, and so on.

Necessary as she'd felt, she had pretty much always wanted to leave. Felt she couldn't keep up this lie of good health and self-confidence, though she knew this was what she needed to model for her daughters. She knew, from her therapy sessions, it was a self esteem thing — her self-hatred clouded, she hoped, from others.

As she sprawled there across from the fallen porch she felt something like a sense of arrival. A sense she had waited a long time to be in this place. Felt perfectly suited to sitting right here, half on, half off, solid, thick with dust, barren ground. She didn't try to get herself up and centered on that rock. As a matter of fact she just lay back with one leg to each side of the rock like she planned to make a snow angel.

Fully aware of the penetrating heat of the cushioning dust beneath her and the dust hazed sun beating down on the skin of her face, throat, arms and legs, she opened the bottom buttons of her dress. She spread the wings of its faded pink and turquoise geometric print skirt far out to the sides and away from her thighs. From this angle her thighs reminded her of their much younger selves. She thought, "Will I always look good lying down? Have I ever looked this good standing up?"

"Now, maybe," she thought, "just maybe, this part is getting sort of funny." Funny, sad, pitiful. Was she amused, grateful for this desolate and barren bed or was she unbearably alone and lost? Lying here in the dirt, having fallen off a six inch rock, all sorts of feelings washed over her. She felt a warm rush in her body. Touched by the sun, her thighs looked golden-pink, almost copper and she felt she could almost fall in love with herself. Almost felt ready to tickle her own thighs with her dusty fingertips. She wanted to see the shiny black curls where her thighs meet. Her mouth filled with moisture. Now her very pretty, shiny black curly place leaked a moistening tear and she went to a place she knew well. The yearning place. The longing place. The unrequited place. She was born there and no one and nothing ever quite brought her home. That's what her journey is about. About finding home.

Now her own two legs, strong because she trained them to be so, had carried her away from all the places she tried to name "home" through all the forty-some years of her youth. Here she was — at the scene of the crimes of her parents' youth. The birthplace of her own crimes.

The house with the fallen porch, forever haunted by creatures she guessed only she had seen and experienced as a child, now housed desert and swamp lizards with tough, impenetrable armor. Armor she could have used during the days she lived here as a child. Now she was drifting. A small, so-what? kind of smile turned to a sobbing sort of laugh. She closed her eyes, exhausted, nearly hysterical and drained.

"CRACK!" came a terrible sound out of nowhere and all around her at the same time.

She shot up. Her heart pounded all through her head and she couldn't catch her breath. Her legs wouldn't let her stand. She whimpered, clammy with perspiration, hands and knees navigating a small circle in the dust as she sought refuge, shelter and escape. This place was the middle of everywhere and nowhere at once. Her mind flashed on the danger of snakes, spiders, reptiles of every kind and no shelter, no where to hide. She was drilling a hole there, spinning faster on hands and knees until, like a nesting turtle, she found herself sunk in a soft and cool womb in the earth. But it's a trap and a grave.

"Help me, Mommy!"

"What's the matter?" Harsh voice. It's her dad. (no pause) "You look fine to me."

"I know I look fine, but, I'm not!" She screamed and stomped her foot. "I want my Mommy! Where is my Mommy?"

"If you're going to scream I'll have to spank you."

(Screamed, cried, red-in-the-face, stomped both feet, threw herself face down on the floor.)

"Get up off the floor or I'll get my belt!"

(Stood, screamed, cried, her face, her whole body hot, clammy. Stomped into her room. Slammed the door, hurled herself face down on the bed.)

"Whirr, whirr, whirr, CRACK! (pause) whirr, CRACK! (pause) whirr, CRACK!

CRACK! CRACK !"

The door closed behind him. She heard his footsteps as he walked away.

Silence then. Her doll lay near death on the floor. She fell on the floor when Miriam was trying to escape the cutting razor-bite of his belt. She held her dolly close to her and told her that he hurt her and she hated him. She asked Milly to run away with her. Milly didn't say anything, but Miriam knew she understood. Knew they both lived in that place where they couldn't be heard and no one thought they mattered.

Still sunk and huddled in the little nest she'd made there in the Florida dust, she let herself be carried by her grief, by her memories of home, to that dark place she lived so long ago and that was still so very much alive in her. She floated, thinking of a book she'd read the month before she left on this journey. A book in which hopeful Jews, seeking refuge and shelter, bid farewell to loved ones with the words "Next year in Jerusalem".

Since she was not a Jew, she wondered if it was some kind of blasphemy to feel such a connection to the devastating plight of the Jews. But never had a phrase brought the tears and despair, sense of rage and loss to her heart... oh, yes, and a bitter sweet sense of hope, as the words uttered by the Jews under siege, then and now. "Next year in Jerusalem."

"Perhaps there's a phrase right for just my particular set of circumstances," she thought. "Something like . . . Next year in safety and acknowledgement. Next year a sense of self — next year a treasured child." So sad that many Jews who spoke those words never had a chance. Same with some of Miriam's un-treasured peers. She'd read somewhere that when you find someone who was brutally victimized, left for dead, literally or figuratively, and who is managing a relatively healthy looking life — look for art just pouring out of that person. Look for songs, stories and pictures.

Miriam drifted on, there in the Florida dirt. She thought, "what would my songs, stories and pictures be about?"

Oh, fantasy stuff. Pure fantasy. A smiling Daddy? — Oops, but no, on closer scrutiny that's a weird smile isn't it? The kind of smile you didn't know was sadistic when you were three years old (because you didn't know sadistic was a word — or even the word for smile, for that matter). Does the smiling Daddy picture have a big, black, scary sky in it and all the furniture is tumbling and the windows are breaking as he undoes his pants, whips off his belt and gets closer and closer to you? Do all the lights go out and everything looks bloody and frightening? And you are so little and the Mommy picture has on a pretty cotton dress, her hair looks nice and shiny and she's stirring the fried chicken. It smells so good and Mama doesn't see the black sky, the falling furniture, the breaking windows, his falling pants, the belt in his hand — Mama sees, knows for sure the Daddy is just, plain and simple, no harm done — SMILING!

And what about those songs? Really, all kinds. Sometimes when she really looked at the smiling Daddy and everything got dark and bloody she sang a little song (more like a cry) . . .

> "My Mommy told me something a little girl should know. It's all about the devil and I learned to hate him so. She says he causes trouble if you let him in the room and he'll never, never leave you if your heart is full of gloom —

So let the sunshine in, face it with a grin. Smilers never lose and frowners never win...
SO LET THE SUNSHINE IN
(everybody sing now...)
FACE IT WITH A GRIN...
(LOUDER NOW...NOT LOUD ENOUGH...THIS ISN'T HAPPENING...CAN'T BE HAPPENING)
Open. . . up. . . your (broken) heart. . .
and let the sun … shine … in-n-n-n!"

There, he was gone. She didn't cry. As a matter of fact, she smiled. But now God sees her. She was sick, her face was red and hot and she knew she was going to die and go to hell because she was not only frowning — she was crying. She was crying so hard it made her throw up. She was on her bare, cold knees in her little short sleeved dress, her head was in the toilet and her vomit was mixed with tears and snot and it all stinks. She couldn't stop and her daddy yelled at her to "hurry up, you're not the only person in this house who has to use the bathroom, you selfish little girl."

So Miriam wiped her face on a towel and got it dirty and she knew Mommy would tell her that was really inconsiderate of her, that they don't have very many towels and it is a lot of work to wash them. Miriam walked past Daddy and into her room. He looked at the back of his daughter and sneered with disgust. But her face, how much it hurt, it just didn't matter to him. She might as well have been invisible. She went into her bedroom and lay face down on the bed, hands holding her warm crotch. The afternoon sun faded away. Her room filled with gray dusk. Now, dinner was ready. What a bad dream she had and it's all her fault. She put her elbows on the table to hold up her head at dinner. She couldn't keep her eyes open. A new nightmare began.

"The itsy bitsy spider went up the water spout . . ."

Her bottom was bright red and all the skin has been beaten off it. It burned so she had to lie on her tummy. She faked being sick so Mommy would let her stay in bed with the lights off. If she imagined it was a cold coming on she would rub Miriam's chest with vapor rub and sit close to her for a while. Miriam imagined her mother's hand, warm on her chest, on the heated towels she tucked in her pajama top. Occasionally her mother's hand went to Miriam's hair and, softly, she brushed it from her face. Exhausted, comforted, Miriam went to sleep — safe until she'd have to get up and Daddy would come home again."

* * * * *

There in the hot Florida sun, she spun in an out of consciousness. In and out of memory, denial, despair and longing.

From somewhere so far away she felt she had to reach for it, she heard a voice. Was it another memory? Another dream that would take her down? It felt different though. Sounded different. She made the stretch toward awareness and heard it again.

It was a voice saying, " Hey, are you all right?"

Was this real or more of her crazy reverie? She felt like she'd passed out and come-to on "Quantum Leap" or what was that TV show where Michael Landon played a handsome, sexy, robust angel and everybody's dream-Daddy-rescuer-lover? She couldn't bear to lift her head for fear this voice, the voice of a man, was coming from the mouth of someone real and he would see her — was standing there looking right at her now.

She wanted to hide, to burrow deeper and cover herself in the dust, leaving him to think her presence had only been in his imagination. She knew this was going to be a hard one to recover from with any discretion. She found herself dazed, reaching through the thick mist in her brain. "Oh God, oh God, oh God. What do I do? What do I do now?"

She'd thought to be truly alone, truly hidden and then, to be truly herself. She'd always moaned about invisibility. In trying to be grown up and acceptable she created an image, an idea of herself, for people to look at, listen to a little, take somewhat seriously and move on, go away, convinced she was all right, taken care of, their attention was perhaps needed more elsewhere.

But always she wanted to be pronounced normal. And always, she'd had no idea what normal was. So, who was this guy? Where did he come from? How long had he been watching her? Did she need rescue or was she really in a reasonably safe situation considering the nature of her quest?

This certainly wasn't the first time she'd completely lost it and found herself whirling and digging and scraping and terrified of what she didn't even know. Clearly she had to get up. Had to acknowledge this voice and make some kind of explanation.

Hands and knees in her would-be grave, she cowered lower and moved only her eyes upward. Nice shaped foot, about a size ten, she thought for no reason at all. He was down on one knee, hand extended, wore sandals like her daughter Jane wears.

But she couldn't make herself take this stranger's outstretched hand. She couldn't look at him. She brought herself, after what seemed an eternity, to a squatting position with her hands on the soil between her knees and pulled herself to an upright position by making something like a frog jump. Her head swam and she fell face forward, vomiting, at the feet of a stranger.

* * * * *

When next she open her eyes she lay warm under fresh washed, sun dried linen sheets. A chiffon curtain, she could tell was home-made, blew away from the open window, where she could just make out a sky the color of a robin's egg. The breeze felt like, smelled like, autumn on the river near the sea. It smelled and tasted like safety. Somehow though, she knew there were no golden leaves, no red sumac lining the banks of rusty brown swirling river water. Knew she couldn't possibly be there safe in her autumn cathedral in the woods above the water. Safety couldn't have come as easily as that. Not after all these years.

She leaned on one elbow and lifted the curtain away from the window again. "Where am I?" she wondered. Now the view from the window was revealed to her. She was no where near home. The terrain through the window couldn't have been less like her holy forest and sea place. It was lovely, but it was not home.

She lay back on the pillows, realizing the stranger had brought her away from the fallen porch. Away from her humble beginnings. The memory of the fallen porch and her self-dug grave came clearly to mind and she felt ashamed. Ashamed and terminally tired.

Household sounds brushed her ears from somewhere far off. She dozed feeling somehow comforted believing it was her mother whose quiet noises came to her from a kitchen somewhere.

She pictured her mother then, 25 years old, tall, slender, beautiful green eyes and nearly black hair cut in a stylish bob with little bangs in a sort of crescent shape over one side of her forehead. Mom, Elizabeth Barrett Blackwell. In her dozing dream, there was no one else at home. Wouldn't be for hours. Maybe never, if she wished hard enough. Maybe she could have her mother all to herself now. Maybe she would sense her little girl was awake and she would come into the room softly in her canvas wedgie shoes.

She would come over and place her cool, dry hand on Miriam's forehead and her daughter would pretend to sleep and feel her mother looking at her and loving her, her sleeping child.

There in a stranger's bed, Miriam could almost taste the steaming Campbell's tomato soup and the burnt little buttered squares of toasted Wonder bread her Mama would bring to her along with a cold glass of milk for lunch.

It dawned on Miriam that she was in and out of dreaming and she had thoughts of Jane. Thought of what she would say if she knew where her mother's dreams were carrying her. She'd say, "Yeah... that's right, Mom...Then you woke up!" and go laughing off snapping her fingers and shuffling her feet to the tune of the Violent Femmes spitting out with a sound of something like despair, "Why can't I get just one fuck?!"

Thoughts of Jane, grown now and on her own, made Miriam smile and distracted her briefly. She missed Jane. Had been missing her off and on since she was nine years old. Maybe even before that. Her love for Jane was another longing and unrequited place she was too tired to visit now.

Miriam let herself drift back to the thoughts of tomato soup and toast; the sounds of her mother ironing and giggling softly to the sounds of Arthur Godfrey on the radio. Soothed and floating on mother love, Miriam slept.

When she awakened again she felt cold, exposed, naked and in desperate need of a toilet. "Where are my clothes?" she looked around her.

She'd packed a little knapsack kind of a thing and couldn't make it out anywhere in the room. "And, by the way — Where am I?"

Again she had this sense she'd come to life in a TV program. Again, Michael Landon was the star. This time she could swear she was in the "Little House on the Prairie."

The bed was pieced together from some raw, rough hewn pieces of tree but was frankly cushy with pillows and an overstuffed feather bed on top of what seemed a rather ordinary mattress. There was a small chest of drawers made of old cherry stained maple that was all pitted and scratched either for effect or for real, she couldn't yet tell. A small wood-framed mirror pretending to be an antique was hung by a nail over the chest of drawers. A linen doily sat dead center on the top of the chest where there lay, bristles up, she was sure, her Grandma Ginny's porcelain and gold hairbrush. The very hairbrush Grandpa used to brush her hair as she sat in his lap so long ago.

Scooching herself to the bed's edge she tugged at the sheet until it came loose from the foot of the bed. She wrapped it around her holding its two ends tight to her chest. Feeling cold and like a sneaky criminal type, she stepped across the age-darkened wood-plank floor and stood on a circular rag rug in front of the chest.

She felt dream-clutched. That kind of dream where she really was in the place where she was sleeping but a whole other life happened as she slept. The kind of dream where she would get up, go to the light switch and couldn't make it work. She'd open the door, go into the hallway seeking another light switch. It didn't work either. All the world feels chilly and, in the dream, she walked as if in heavy fog. She was deep in that kind of dream-clutched place when she saw her Grandma's hairbrush.

"And, why the impact of this single object?" she wondered. "A hairbrush. And it can't be Grandma's because she died so long ago, over twelve years now, and that hairbrush had only mattered to Grandpa and me and he was dead too, even longer than Grandma. And she had never told anybody to keep that hairbrush, "hang on to it. It is very precious and I want to keep it." Though she wished she had.

She lifted the hairbrush from the white doily and ran its firm, almost rough bristles across the palm of her hand and landed herself in a wooden rocker still wrapped in her linen sheet cocoon.

Rocking, rocking, not really seeing anything. Lost back in a time and place where she had tasted the possibility of home. As she rocked she began to stroke her own dusty hair with Grandma's hairbrush. She imagined herself little again, bare legged, bare footed and it was summer. She climbed into her Grandpa's lap. His big hands supported her wrist where her hand was full of hairbrush.

She was all bones and he was much muscle and tobacco smell

and warm strength. She straddled his lap and he took the brush from her hand. Without a word she rested her cheek against his white shirt spread thin and cool across his smooth, strong chest. He brushed, first with one hand, then the other, stroking the place he just brushed in a rotation like climbing higher and higher toward the most peaceful place ever.

"Where are you now Grandpa?" She said this aloud.

She was shaken from her reverie by a gentle knock on the door and a voice that said, "You're awake, huh? Hey there, I was starting to think you might sleep forever. Wondered what kind of a fix I got myself into by bringing you home."

He came into the room and chatted amiably while straightening quilt and curtains. He didn't quite register physically for Miriam. She couldn't quite bring herself to look fully at him. She hid from him like a kid who puts her hand over her eyes so no one can see her. He was clearly there in the room. She felt his presence but it was only his feet that made themselves visible. She looked up without really seeing him.

Finally, she summoned the courage. She lifted her eyes to look at him. "Just a man," she thinks. "Strong hands. Strong feet. Calm demeanor. Calming presence. A stranger. My closest friend."

"I'm afraid I need a toilet," she said and turned her eyes away.

He opened a door before her, bent to his knees and slipped thick ivory wool socks on her feet all the while tilting his head to look into her eyes, asking questions without words. He stood and took her by the hand to a little closet sized room just across the hall.

He pulled the door closed between them and told her to let him know when she is ready for a good, hot bath. "Can have a tub ready at a moment's notice," he assured her.

She still didn't know where her clothes were or where her knapsack was but as she perch on the toilet she noticed a bath robe hanging from a hook on the door. She let her head fall into her hands, elbows on her knees, as the interminable stream of urine and relief flooded from her.

When she finished peeing, she bent double and cried until her insides were empty from both ends. He came to check on her after awhile and she signal something through the closed door, letting him know she was okay. She flushed the toilet, still sitting there unable to move, unaware of the features of the room. Aware only of her aching emptiness and shame, she reached for the robe, her sheet dropping around her feet, and let the robe pull her from the cold, white tunnel that threatened to swallow her should she linger too long.

* * * * *

Away again in some unconscious place she rides a horse. Her thighs soak in the rich, red-chocolate shimmer of smooth and surging flesh. Bent double, breasts to the striding stallion's back — gliding, gliding. One smooth stride as on wheels of air past fences, fields, rivers and trees toward the perfection of cotton ball clouds precisely decorating the periwinkle sky. Riding, floating, gliding. Pure, powerful wild animal heat. Pounding. An African drum beat. Her land. Her home. Her heart. Pounding, rhythmic and nearer, nearer the surface.

"Don't you want to get cleaned up a little miss?" At the sound of his voice she stuttered and stammered herself awake. She tried to pull herself together and show some semblance of human decency to this man to whom she'd spoken exactly two sentences. Still, she was so groggy, in and out of sleep, and she didn't know where she was or why or how she got there or who he was or how long she'd been there. She only wanted to hide. Only wanted to disappear.

She sat up on the bed and said, "Soon. Soon. Yes. I should, shouldn't I?" She touched her hand to her dusty hair, feeling supremely awkward. She didn't know what to say. "Who is this man and why am I here with him?"

Did she need rescuing? She'd started out on a journey, a knowledge quest, a quest for the Essential — her essence — the essential Miriam. May Sarton would be proud of her. She thought if she didn't look for the Essential sooner rather than later, time would run out and she would never be, or rather, never know herself as anyone other than the image she'd had to make up to stay alive even this long. When she left St. David's on her quest she'd felt so full of strength. Ready to see, accept, maybe even embrace her history as she'd urged so many others to do.

She certainly couldn't blame this complete stranger for thinking she needed rescue. She hadn't exactly stood on her own two feet, assured him of her independent mobility and moved on in her self-propelled (compelled, compulsive) journey had she?

She looked up at him now. His face was new to her though she supposed she'd been looking at him off and on now for, how many days? His presence was familiar to her, but everything seemed to be happening as if in a dream. She was not at all sure he wasn't a figment of her imagination. "Have I really been riding a horse? Was I in a hot, dusty, lifeless place when he found me? What seasons of the years have I lived and in what country or state?" she wondered.

She looked at him, truly taking in his face for the first time. A smooth, hairless face with bold, chiseled features and a muscular neck marked him as a physical, athletic man. He was neither tall nor short, fat nor thin. Nicely proportioned. His body reminded her of Bruce Springsteen's; his hair and face were a handsome combination of Mikhail Barishnakov and Michael Douglas.

His light hair, a mixture of silver and light brown, fell in a loose wave across his forehead and he looked seventeen and forty five all at the same time. A beautiful boy and a wise man, she thought. He'd worn a navy blue long sleeve shirt, more of a chamois jacket, that hung out over his jeans, when he helped her to the toilet. Now he wore a white tee shirt and she could see that his well shaped forearms exhibited traces of moisture and soap bubbles. She could hear, somewhere, the sound of water running into a bathtub. She became conscious she was staring at her rescuer.

He looked at her, his eyes questioning, and repeated, "Would you enjoy a bath? I'm just getting one ready for you now."

She had no idea what shape she was in. She hadn't looked in a mirror for days and was beginning to have memory flashes of sickness and sweat and choking dust.

Still finding it hard to speak she managed to say, "Yes. A bath would be wonderful." She felt the thick, terry cloth comfort of the robe adding warmth next to her skin under the slippery cool of the polished cotton down comforter. The ivory socks had been almost too much under the covers and she'd reluctantly discarded them, leaving them within easy reach on top of the covers.

The room with the rocking chair, the open window and chest of drawers were all real, not some dreamed-of place that would leave her alone and shivering or in a fever on desert soil on awakening. She looked around the room for Grandma's hairbrush, but, not seeing it, determine it was never there. She realized she'd been going in and out of dream/reality for some time now.

"How long," she wondered, "will it take to sort out real from dream, lies, and true experience?" She caught herself, about to ask about the hairbrush, but thought better of it. There was so much she didn't know, didn't understand. Maybe there would be time later for these questions.

Maybe this would be all the time there is and in that case a cleansing, steaming bath was the way to live the moment. "Carpe diem," was her thought. Always for her, this conflict between the examined life and seizing the day. Perhaps one day, she thought, she'd seize the day to examine her life.

She turned her body toward the bed's edge, bringing her knees close to her chest like the fetus she still wanted to be, making a snail-shell shape there on the bed, warm in her cocoon or womb, or maybe the back of some well-protected cave.

She felt utterly fetal-stage, cave-baby — awakening to a new world with eyes too new, too full of glare and daze to grasp where she was or why. What forces brought her here, at her supposed age of maturity, she didn't know — feared to learn. She lifted her armored-snail body on one arm and cautiously let her legs do a slow, sliding ease down the side of the bed.

The robe covered her nakedness against the eyes of the stranger but let the cool breeze from the open window whip around her calves and ankles. She looked down at her feet, shades of pink touched by a new blue cold. Her toes reached beyond the few inches of bare wood floor toward an oval rag rug, rich with royal looking purple, green, and burgundy strands, hand-woven — how long ago, Miriam, the child, the historian, wondered.

The pair of socks she'd left on the covers seemed nearly alive the way they appeared suddenly in her hands. She felt stiff and awkward as she lifted her leg and attempted to put the sock on her foot.

"Here, let me help you with that." He kneeled at the bedside holding the weight of her foot and leg on his knee as he slipped the socks on first one of her feet, then the other. She couldn't help but notice how strong and muscular his thighs looked. It pained her, brought on some bitter sweet sensation, to see a man, so strong, physically powerful, in an act of such simplicity and tender kindness.

He looked up at her face, and though she felt exposed, too visible somehow, still, she couldn't move her eyes away from his gentle face. She wanted to reach out and put her hand on his cheek. "But, no," she thought, "I don't even know him. I don't even know his name." In a sudden flush of discomfort and self-consciousness, she averted her eyes, looked for a place to rest them where they wouldn't betray her embarrassment. She looked just past his face at the chest of drawers where she thought she'd seen Grandma's hairbrush.

"What's your name?" she asked him.

He stood quickly, shoved his hands in the pockets of his jeans. "Oh, didn't I even tell you my name? I can't believe it. Rude." He looked at the floor and scratched his head. He seemed embarrassed. Shy. "I'm sorry . Dumb. I didn't even introduce myself. It's Erik. Erik Newland. I'd ask you yours, but I already know. Miriam, right? Miriam Blackwell?"

His knowing her name threw her a bit. Created a fog, a memory of sorts. Was it anonymity she wanted or was she looking to be found? Had she come here because she was lost or had she come to lose herself?

Erik asked again if she was ready for a bath. She nodded yes and he signaled her to come with him. He led her to a lovely room where the tub was a deep and wide old porcelain model with four little claw feet, reminding her again of Grandpa Blackwell's comforting bathtub. Erik opened French doors onto a patio where the sun shone on red hibiscus blooms. The scent of gardenia filled the room. As the steam cleared she saw the heaven-white blossoms and black-green satin leaves in a salt-fired pot on an old oak dry sink. The dry sink was positioned right next to the head of the tub and she would be able to see the blooms and let the scent fill her head all through her bath.

"Intoxicating," she thought to herself, still feeling too awkward, too grateful to say much of anything out loud. Besides, she felt herself to be in some kind of spell. A spell she was not at all sure she wanted to break with casual, who-are-you, where-do-you-work, sort of every day conversation. Paralysis seemed to seize them both.

Did he want her to say something? He wasn't going to just stand there in the bathroom while she dropped her robe, removed her socks and climbed into the bath in front of a complete stranger, was he? Had he forgotten they were strangers? After all, how long had she been there, in his bed, his house?

What and who did he imagine her to be? Did he see her as an innocent, or as a wild woman? As a baby, an invalid or a wounded animal? — Someone or something for whom there is no nakedness? She looked at him then to see if his face offered clues.

He suddenly seemed to recognize the intimacy of the situation, grinned a quick, whoops! kind of grin and brought his right hand up to stroke the side of his face.

"Oh, sorry. You'll want to get in that bath now, won't you? You probably wonder what I'm doing standing here like a dummy. I'll just leave you to it then. Anything else you need? Well then. I'll — um — I'll just be out here in the other room. Holler if you need anything, okay?"

She smiled and nodded holding the door with one hand as he turned and left the room. She watched after him for a few seconds. Why did he touch her so? Such a combination of grace, strength, confidence and shyness as she'd never before experienced in a man. She closed the door and turned to welcome again the intoxicating sights and scents of the room. She hadn't noticed before, while the water was rushing in its hot downpour to fill the tub, but noticed now, the babbling river sounds of a fountain just beyond the hibiscus that crowded the patio in a profusion of bright red and green.

How she loved the sounds of the river. Any water, really. Pounding waves, a waterfall from a small mountain stream, falls from the highest cliff, rippling wind-blown sounds on a lake — loved them all.

It was where she wanted to go. Needed to go. To the water. To the river. Water led her where she felt she must go. Was it because she'd been so long consumed by a thirst that finally overcame her common sense, that she was here now? Here in Florida where sea meets desert, wild meets tame — She could hear the water, feel its beckoning, but was still half choked by salt and sand.

Erik left her a folded thick towel the color of shaded grass as a cushioned seat for her on the tub's edge. She sat on it now and eased the socks from her feet. These socks offered such comfort it was difficult to part with them even for the greater comfort of the bath. A deep sigh escaped the empty cavern of her insides as she sank in a slow swoon letting the water cover her so that only her nose and mouth met the air.

For the longest time she floated there as if there was no such thing as time. She let the water sounds carry her back, back in time. . . Back to the waves, back to the lake, back to the hurricane visited places of her entire life.

In thinking back on that marvelous lake, the freedom and wildness and safety it offered, she couldn't help but think it played a big part in saving her life. She was mighty little when she first met the biggest lake, where so many miles of river merge, but she, even as an adult, kept going back to it in one way or another. A rainstorm took her there. The stinging, refreshing water against her skin as she showered and lifted her voice in a song of still here, still alive, still healthy — maybe there's still time — took her back to the lake's saving wonder. The pounding river of her own blood through her own veins led her there. The current of all the rivers of her life runs through her.

Now in her life at St. David's, she lived a stone's throw from the place she first found that richness of safety and solace. Surging, swelling waves lifted her high above the drowning and murderous din that served as the greater portion of her childhood days. They led her back to that question of what she was doing out here in these dirty, dusty, ghost town-strewn miles of history.

She came to her senses, the water turning cold around her, a familiar sense visiting her. That sense of "not normal," "got it all wrong," "ungrateful," "unworthy," "it's all my fault," and, now, yes, "insane." She couldn't face her rescuer. Was more than ashamed at the imposition she was. She had to go. Had to find a way to escape.

* * * * *

"Nowhere to hide." She thought. She dried herself scrubbing harshly at the skin on her belly and legs. She watched her face, not seeing anyone she liked, in the mirror. "He probably thinks I'm completely insane. I must have scared him with that crazy bit by the old house. What's he going to do with me, anyway? He's got to be struggling for a way out of this. If I were him I'd just wish I'd turn around and the crazy person would be gone. I'm sure I've shocked him somehow and now he wishes I'd just disappear."

She bent her head to fiercely rub the towel to the depths of her scalp. In this position the welts from her fingernails through the towel showed purple on the skin of her belly. She couldn't feel a thing.

She rubbed harder and harder. She slapped her face. She pinched her wrists, twisting the skin and digging her fingernails into her flesh. She needed to feel, physically feel, something. Something. Even if what she felt was only pain.

Her thoughts came in rapid succession. They matched the rhythm of the slaps and gouges she inflicted on her body.

"I just knew it. Always it comes to this. Always, sooner or later, the decision is made that I'm not worth the trouble, not worth the saving. What is it this time? This time when I left and didn't need anyone or anything. It's his own fault. I didn't ask him to rescue me. I didn't want rescue."

She screamed silently, "I don't need you. I don't need anyone." She slumped to the floor, crying. Finally feeling again. Head in hands, she whimpered and thought to herself, "I can't need anyone. I can't."

Minutes later, drained from her sobs and self-abuse, she pulled herself together, put the robe back on and sat for a moment on the edge of the tub. "I know, I see, I understand," She told herself. "Of course. To the untrained eye I suppose anyone crouched down on all fours swirling in a circle digging a trench with her own bare hands, feet and knees — yeah," she thought, "I guess that would look like I needed rescue. But what I felt, believe it or not, Erik — was freedom. Crazy, huh? Freedom to be who I bloody well am. Freedom to be my animal and mineral instinctual self without all those eyes watching me, afraid of me. Afraid for me. Pitying me."

"Enough of this now." She wrapped the towel around her hair, sneaked back to the bedroom, catching on her way, a glimpse of the back of him, hand to his hair-flattened crown, coffee sloshing brown, apparently cold and unnoticed onto his jeans, his bare feet. Clearly he hadn't heard or seen her come out of the bathroom.

She felt relieved to be invisible. She detested being pitied and ranted under her breath, "Goddamn it. I'm alright. Go away. Don't watch me. For all your looking you've seldom seen me anyway and I've been your slave, been a slave to how you need me to look, need me to behave. That's what I gave up. That's what I left. There is no rescue without a price to be paid. Always after rescue there is the expectation of gratitude. Gratitude and loyalty. Gratitude, loyalty, trust, and then, abandonment. No more. Don't tell me anymore. Don't show me anymore. Real, sane people are not like you. You have to leave now. I have to leave now. If there is to be rescue, I'll do it myself. I cannot bear you any longer. Your kindness. Your tender eyes. You are too much of a good thing which is a bad thing. You are far too much of a bad thing." Miriam made her silent, departing soliloquy.

She tip toed to the bedroom and searched the room for something, anything, to wear. She found some one-size-fits-all rubber floppy sandals and a pair of his jeans that were too big for her. She put on a T-shirt from the top drawer of the chest, grabbed her little bundle, package/bag and was out the window and beyond the hibiscus and gardenias and warm little bed before Erik could possibly have broken through his apparent reverie. She left through the open window in the bedroom. She told herself it was not ingratitude. She told herself she wanted to spare Erik the agony of ousting her — she who can't be rescued anyway. "The crazy woman from the dust is forever on her own in the rescue department." She said to herself as she started down the dusty road away from Erik.

* * * * *

What time is it? Where is the road? Which direction to anywhere? She walked aimlessly, one foot in front of the other. She consciously sought the hazy sun and headed north fearing south or west could mean the increase of desert. Though north was certainly the direction of her beloved lake, there in Florida north is also the only direction that would lead her further from rather than closer to the waves refreshing motion.

Lord knows how long she'd been walking, dazed and unseeing, before she caught the scent of cars on a dusty highway. She followed her nose. When she reached the road she saw beyond it to trees and rain clouds far in the distance. A family in a camper had pulled off the road not far from where she stood. The door to the camper stood open and Miriam saw a woman and a man with two children eating lunch on the fold down table inside. She poked her head in the door.

"Sorry to bother you," she said. "You happen to know where I might find a grocery or road stop café in this area?"

"Yeah." The man quickly swallowed the bite he'd taken off his sandwich and nodded his head.

"There's a town between here and those trees in the distance. It's a good long hike, though. We'd give you a lift but we've got a deadline west of here and just came from that direction." The kids, a boy and a girl, probably six and nine, moved their eyes up and down over Miriam, apparently trying to discern what she was about. The mother seemed eager to be rid of Miriam. She didn't say anything.

"No. That's fine. I appreciate your help. I'm fine walking. Thinking time, you know." She pulled away from the door, pointing her finger at her brain. As she started to walk toward the trees, the woman came down the camper steps with an apple, a banana and a handful of tortilla chips. She reached her hand out to Miriam.

"Thanks." She smiled as she took the food from the mother's hands. "I really hadn't intended to beg."

Miriam could just barely hear the kids taunting their mother from the trailer, "No, Mom. What are you doing? We didn't even get our share. . ."

The mother shook her head and rolled her eyes in apology for her kids' rudeness. She smiled at Miriam and said, "Hey, I hope you find what you're looking for."

Miriam nodded toward her food-filled hands and said another thank you. She walked away feeling the woman understood something about what she was looking for and she wouldn't find it in a grocery store or café. Refreshed and with the hope of green trees, a river bank and a small town in her future, Miriam walked on.

Her thoughts were of rivers. Of "swirling streams." She remembered Adrienne Rich talking about the sheer necessity to thrust deeper and deeper into the swirling stream. What were her words? They'd meant so much to Miriam. ". . .history, nightmare, accountability . . . the current angrier and more multiform than the surface shows: There is fury here, and terror, but there is also power, power not to be had without the terror and the fury. We need to go beyond rhetoric or evasion into that place in ourselves, to feel the force of all we have been trying — without success — to skim across." Yes, that was it, wasn't it? And here she was. Thrusting deeper. "Is this bravery? Is this courage or is this evasion?" More questions Miriam couldn't answer.

Where was her hand in the deep and swirling stream? She felt that angry, multiform current. She showed and spoke only about the surface. Her conversations were dialogue with the brave, the dead, the fictitious.

This journey she was on — it was about capturing and bringing the angry, whirling tornado of truth to the surface. These conversations in her head — would they ever pass her lips, travel to the ears of another, and receive welcome? The words she dared utter through her conventional looking (dazzling, beautiful — they used to tell her) smile. Those words told lies.

"I'm just fine!" "Don't I look fine?" Most would concede she did, certainly, look fine.

Sometimes she had deeper conversations behind her smile and in her head. She would hear some voice from far away. The voice came to her through the words and remembered lives of the women in the generations before hers. She became adept at conversation with Adrienne Rich, Anais Nin, Tillie Olson, Djuna Barnes, Virginia Woolf, women of her grandmother's age. Having so much to share with these women and their words she wondered why she'd felt so little affinity to her own grandmothers and great grandmothers. For all Miriam's success in uncovering the lives of other women's grandmothers and great grandmothers, she knew very little about her own ancestors.

Prior to the necessity to say goodbye to her father, Miriam had tried, off and on, to get some answers to questions about the lives of her ancestors. Hers was a history deeply tangled in secrecy. Her grandparents shared little with her parents and their parents, Miriam's great grandparents told them nothing about their heritage. Miriam simply didn't have the necessary professional distance from whatever answers she might find, to thoroughly research her own past. Her work as historian grew from the seeds of childhood fantasy and escape that, for many years, served to protect her from the reality of her past.

But in these conversations with her dead heroines, words flowed like rich seminal syrup between Miriam and these women, her soul-mates. It was conversation that validated the sanity of the fury, the terror and the power of her own experience. The voice she so often heard from a place she couldn't name urged Miriam to press on. Plunge deeper. Listen, look and remember.

She sat for a minute on a rock at the road side. The sweet taste of the apple brought tears to her eyes. She ate the chips enjoying the sound of their snap in her teeth. She stood, wiped her hands on her jeans, peeled her banana and lodged big bites of it, one in each cheek. No one was there to see her. She felt her full animal self. She scratched under her arms and made moves like a dancing monkey. She laughed out loud. “If I’m crazy,” she sang to the heat of the desert air, “I’m crazy alive!”

Chapter Twenty Four

Energy and hope renewed she walked the sun and sandblasted shoulders of the county road the travelers said would lead to Whitley. She knew her dad had pastored his very first church in this town and wonder what ghosts awaited her arrival. She'd seen a few odd pictures of the place, black and white photos taken with Dad's first professional Yaschica. The kind of pictures you see in Life Magazine, of a town dust strewn with a lone sage brush floating down a human-empty Main Street. The next shot would be a dirty, bare-footed little girl, hair in her eyes, her dress torn, looking for all the world like an orphan in some doorway of a house that was no home.

Miriam must have walked three or four miles beyond the rock where she did her crazy monkey dance. Now her spirits flagged. She felt the sweat and grit on her face, arms and sandal-clad feet. Her hair hung in her eyes and she smeared mud on her forehead and cheeks when she tried to clear her vision. She kept getting herself confused with the imagined dirty little orphan girl in the doorway. The little girl's eyes wouldn't let go of Miriam's. Miriam felt she was searching for that little girl — felt compelled to find her.

Whitley wasn't quite big enough to be considered a real town. Miriam knew she'd arrived when she saw the tilted sign, "Whitley Township," probably damaged in some long-ago road accident.

Just past the broken sign and along the asbestos strip road, before she saw any other signs of the town, she saw "First Baptist Church." Housed, as it was, in a pre-cast sheet metal structure, it was hard to tell from a warehouse or storage building. Her dad's church. She recognized it from the pictures. Looked like attempts had been made to keep it standing, freshly white-washed, in recent years. There was a scrubby-looking man-made pond out back of it that she remembered her mom telling her the deacons had to keep clear of alligators for the monthly baptismal services. Out that way, too, was an orange grove, accessed by a dirt path that wound its way between ramshackle migrant cottages whose windows were mostly broken if they ever existed. If Miriam could see that far down the dirt road, she thought she'd probably see a hot and dirty little girl standing in one of those migrant hut doorways right now.

Briefly, Miriam left the paved road and wandered among the derelict huts. Rusted-out cars; couches, broken and bereft of upholstery; useless refrigerators and stoves as well as general trash lay scattered throughout the yards like the discarded carcasses of road kill. The sight wearied Miriam.

She returned to the main road, hoping something more like civilization and its comforts would greet her soon. She spotted Jan & Jimmy's Café, but felt hesitant to show her face to the group of local strangers she imagined seated at the counter there. She walked slowly past the wood frame structure that looked more western than southern with its low, wood plank porch and horse railing. Big windows stood to each side of the door. There was an inside door made of solid wood that stood open letting the screen door fill the door jamb, swing back and forth loosely, flapping open and closed and probably, she thought, always slamming when it shut.

She walked on, trying to get up her nerve to enter Jan & Jimmy's. The town was nothing but a few scattered, one story buildings put up in the forties and fifties after the land and brush were cleared. A crew of hard-hats with rolled up t-shirt sleeves with a pack of Camels tucked in them must have laid down a strip of black top and named it Main street. Whitley's brick post office is across the street from the now closed public library — a low white building of stucco with deep green trim. Both the post office and library sport American flags hung from diagonal metal poles mounted just outside their front doors, but the library flag had clearly gone untended for some time. There was a Congregational Church next to the library that could only be recognized as a church because of the cross mounted to its flat roof. It had a sign out front bearing the name First Whitely Congregational Church and telling the Pastor's name and the times of services. Miriam sat for a minute, leaning her weight against a thick wooden post that marked the pastor's empty parking space. The town seemed deserted, except for a Jeep and a couple other cars parked by the café.

Weary as she felt, she knew she couldn't just sit there against a post for the rest of the day or she'd fall off, land in a lump and find herself either humiliated by another rescue or abandoned to die. She wasn't sure which fate would be more dreadful. She stood and took a deep breath, prayed a little "forward motion, one foot in front of the other" type of prayer and walked back toward the café.

She couldn't see much beyond the screen door and into the restaurant as she approached. She felt self-conscious, imagining the sight of herself to anyone inside who might be looking. She was sure she filled the screen door with the image of a tee shirt and over-sized jeans clad woman who look tired and worn. Her face was smudged with sweat streaked dust. She barely had the strength to push the light weight of the screen door away from her body. Surely she looked to those inside, likely to fall right through the door.

This time, Jimmy, ran for the door in an attempt at rescue, but she actually managed her entrance all right. She fell past Jimmy (later learned it was him, the restaurant owner), felt around and sat, collapsed really, into a vinyl chair next to the Formica and chrome table closest to the door.

She looked down at her lap and her filthy hands, shook her head to clear it of embarrassment and turned her eyes upward. Jimmy, who had returned to his post behind the counter stood drying a milk-shake glass, looked at Miriam but asked no questions and certainly got no explanation. He turned to fetch the lid off the pot of lentil soup about to boil over on the stove behind the counter. Miriam knew it was lentil soup because the "Specials" board outside the door said so.

A gray and white flecked Formica counter top, guarded by red vinyl stools ran the full length of the inside wall of the cafe. As a kid, Miriam loved to sit on stools like that and turn in endless, dizzying circles. The usual plastic food display cases claimed the counter space and contained stale looking pieces of cherry pie, broken and oozing lemon meringue and a dry looking pale chocolate cake whose frosting was cracked like a dry river bed. A few donuts looked left over from the day before or even the day before that. The place smelled of grilled hamburgers and french fries, a scent that cheered Miriam for some reason.

The floor was covered in beige linoleum that had imbedded in it little speckles of brown, black, gray and cream. The kind of floor people install because it won't show dirt. After thirty years or so it looked pretty badly scuffed and imbedded with dirt even though Jimmy looked like the type to scrub it faithfully every night at closing time.

It was that kind of American café famous for its double thick malts and milkshakes. Centerpiece on the stainless steel food prep area along the wall, and behind the counter, stood the majestic mint green milk shake machine. Next to it were stacked stainless steel cups big enough to hold two full servings of extra thick shake. She wondered if Jimmy served the extra along side of the tapered malt glasses, long spoon slid in next to a maraschino cherry. Looking around the place, she felt awash in nostalgia for the kind of times she wished she'd had as a teenager. Double dates at the malt shop. Juke box music playing "Soldier Boy," "Johnny Angel," or "Johnny Get Angry," or better yet, her first and favorite hit, "Poetry in Motion." She drifted off into fantasy land, part in her imagined past, part still there in Jan and Jimmy's about to place an order for a double chocolate malt, don't spare the whipping cream …

"Hi, Miriam." It was a voice she knew. No longer the voice of a stranger. It was Erik's voice. He was there in the café and she hadn't even seen him. Hadn't really noticed anyone after sitting down and letting the nostalgic dream engage her senses.

She lifted her eyes and spoke to the button on his shirt pocket. "Hi." Without turning her chair she swiveled to rest her elbows on the cool, bare tabletop. She put her head in her hands.

Erik pulled a chair up to the table. He leaned toward her, lifting her face, his hand gentle under her chin.

"Hi yourself," he said.

Now she managed to look in his eyes. She couldn't help but smile.

"Hungry?" he said.

She nodded, unable to speak, then finally said, "Yes. Yes. I am. So, so hungry, Erik." Still she held her head up with one hand.

While Miriam downed one of the best bacon cheeseburgers and double chocolate malts she'd ever tasted, Erik talked to her.

He told her how he felt earlier in the day when she disappeared through the open bedroom window of his house. Said that hours after he discovered her gone he was unable to take any action.

He told her about his life on his small ranch. About his writing. About the job he used to have at the Whitley Library. Said he'd felt lately, that without the discipline of daily employment, that something was changing inside him. "And another thing too," he said. "Age. I'm experiencing aging like it's something that matters for the first time ever." Always he'd been blessed with vigor, good health, and an omniscient, infallible sense of longevity. But now, he said, that's wavering. It wasn't about appearance. "Not about the way I look. No. I really don't care much about that. It's something I can't quite put my finger on. You know, the passing of time … places where you spend that time. It's about picking and choosing or something."

Erik had never given his appearance much thought but knew he'd been regarded as handsome, athletic, a "good catch" in high school and in college. He never had much use for superficial conversation or socializing — found it made him lonelier than actually being alone.

Lost and alone was a fairly complete description of how he felt right then though, he told Miriam. Just in these last few hours since she'd been gone, especially. "Lost, alone, filled with self-pity and self-loathing" he said.

"Yee — uckpituey! Like you really need to hear this… Forgive me, Miriam, it's just, well, this is way more than you want to know I'm sure. Anyway … after awhile I just couldn't stand it anymore." He described slamming his coffee cup down sloshing its contents on his bare foot, putting his shoes on right over the goo and heading for his jeep not really knowing where her intended to go.

He just knew he needed the assurance right then that he was not entirely alone on this planet and he didn't care who he might come across to help him prove it. He had always asked for a fair amount of depth in the people he spent time with. He'd always been quick to judge if a person was worthy or unworthy of a significant amount of his attention.

Sometimes he chastised himself for this and tried to see deeper, beyond the surface of people whose lives looked so nothing-full. "What's that line from that poem? Full of sound and fury, is it? — and signifying nothing? That's not quite it. Lots of chatter. Lots of busy-ness. Moving around as if by instinct. Led by their sniffing noses toward the plastic and tinsel emporiums that scream "Buy now. Pay later. . ."

Erik told her he just couldn't grasp the pleasure so many people seem to gain from accumulating stuff upon stuff. Having to work so endlessly at jobs they hate to have the money necessary to buy stuff, until they're left with no concept of stillness, peace, reflection. "A good goddamn view, for Christ sake!" he went on.

"It's not that I'm into absolute asceticism," he said. He had possessions that were very important to him and felt it had been worthwhile to work for them. What he valued most, though, among those things money can buy, was a chance to settle himself for periods of time in a variety of countries, landscapes, seascapes, mountainsides and open prairies. All those places where whatever it is that feeds him — God, Art, The Muses, could visit him.

That's where he lived now, he said. "That's what my home here in the almost desert/mostly swamp, is about."

Miriam wondered, as she listened to this new friend confess his beliefs, his loneliness, his search, if there wasn't a purpose beyond her own need for rescue that brought her to this particular place and time. So many of his words echoed her own feelings and the voice she heard in those silent moments by the sea.

He shared with her his love of the night time and why he held it so precious. Gradually, over the years, he said, he'd come to think of the night almost anywhere in the world, as the one place he could lay claim to that place where god and art visit. Now he was engaged in writing a novel about a place he thought of as the country of the night time.

He told her that before she showed up at the door to the café, he'd been reminiscing with Jimmy. Jimmy played the bartender-like role of listening to, but not questioning the occasional customer who'd come in from a solitary life just to know they were not alone. Like Erik, they seldom wanted his opinion, just the sense he was there, another living, breathing human animal in that place that alternately fed their souls and stood up and hit them in the face with its god-forsaken-ness and their own.

Erik told Miriam he'd spent a fair amount of time sitting on a counter stool at the Cafe but still didn't feel he knew Jimmy very well. He said he trusted him though. "Folks around here do. He's better than the library in town had been for the wealth of information he can provide and he's quite a talker."

Erik stopped his confiding long enough to order a cup of soup and sat staring into its depths as he stirred it to a swirling cyclone of steam. He licked the spoon and set it on the saucer.

"Miriam?"

Fearing he was about to change the subject to her, but knowing it's time she did some explaining, she managed a hesitant, "Yeah? What is it Erik?.

"I was just wondering — do you trust me enough to tell me a little bit about what's going on with you? I've pretty much talked your ears off here. I mean, well, I guess I'm trying to let you know… Oh hell. I don't know. I'm sorry, I don't mean to pressure you. But, well, here's the thing … I just think there's a reason for things … Do you? Am I just crazy here?" He ran his fingers through his hair. His face wore a look of apology.

Miriam did trust him. Wanted to thank him. Wanted to reassure him of both his sanity and her own, though she still had grave doubts about herself.

"What is it Erik? I'll answer you if I can. It's not that I don't trust you. It's really not personal, I mean, not really anything about you at all. It's all pretty complicated — what's going on with me, I mean." Jimmy brought Miriam a cup of coffee somehow knowing without words it was just what she wanted. She caressed the warm cup and let herself have a momentary thought of Adrienne Rich's "swirling stream" as the steam from the coffee rose in the air between the new friends. She reminded herself of the necessity to plunge beneath the surface.

"No, Erik. I think you're right. Maybe there's a reason. I'll try to talk to you — try to answer your questions. Maybe it will help me find some answers."

He leaned closer to her and they both stared at the swirling steam above the coffee cup she held in her hands. "I really don't want to push you. The last thing I want to do is make things worse for you. But, maybe I'm supposed to help. Maybe we're both supposed to understand something here. You know?" Now they looked at each other. Miriam nodded.

Erik relaxed his back against his chair and asked, "What's the story on those old, empty houses outside town? The place where I found you? It's clear something pretty powerful went on for you out there." His face showed worry again that he'd gone too far.

Maybe he had. She didn't know. What did she dare to tell him? What did she dare acknowledge herself, for that matter?

"Oh Erik, I wish so much I knew what to tell to you. I don't really know what I'm doing here. I will confess I left home and came here on a search."

"A search? Hmmm. Miriam, forgive me if I'm prying. I don't mean to make you uncomfortable. I don't know, can't really explain why, knowing you so briefly — really, so little about you, but, like I said before, I feel we met for a reason. It's none of my business, but I want to know you if you'll let me."

"Is it something you lost? Is that what you're searching for? Something I might be able to help you find?" Now he leaned toward her again.

"I guess I'd better talk awhile. I'm worried your soup will get cold if I keep you guessing and waiting a whole lot longer."

Erik ate a spoonful of soup and said he had asked Jimmy if he knew anything about the place where he found Miriam the other day. He said Jimmy was somewhat of a gossip if not a true historian. When he got to Jimmy's he was still thinking of Miriam, he said. Said he couldn't get her off his mind. Why the hell had she been out there so far from anywhere civilized, digging herself a little cave, an early grave, a place to call home or to curl up and die?

"What is it about you?" Erik asked her then.

She shrugged her shoulders and nodded her head. She felt the familiar sense she was an imposter in a setting that didn't need the disruption she might bring.

Erik went on talking about his conversation with Jimmy who'd said 'Hey, funny you should ask. I was just thinking about that place, that old family, a couple of days ago." Jimmy had said he and Jan were just talking about it recently. "Said there seem to be a lot of stories about the place — the families — one family in particular. He said it really used to be almost a neighborhood out there. A few houses. Never much green stuff. You know, grass, trees. Just those little swamp tufts that come up in the sand. Some scrub brush and a loner tree from time to time. Used to be an orchard out there I guess.

Jimmy said no one who lived there ever had any money to speak of. Said some eerie stories have come out of that place's history and he wondered, sometimes, shouldn't they just burn a place like that down and start with something new and fresh or just go back to dirt and swamp."

"But this is the part that got to me, Miriam. Jimmy said, 'It's nothing but a memorial to some poor kid's terror.'"

"That really got me. Is that kid you? Is that why you're here?"

"Oh Erik. I just don't know anything for sure. It was all such a long time ago. What difference does it make, I wonder? Yet, here I am. A historian. I believe in the past. I've built my professional life on the belief the past has everything to do with the present and future. Took me this long, though, to take that belief personally. And now — God … I just didn't know what a big deal this would be."

"So, you're a historian, huh? So, are you saying this search of yours is in the nature of professional research?" He seemed a bit relieved. He said Jimmy commented on the stories he'd heard. "Jimmy said he often wonders what becomes of people like that."

"People like what? Did he explain at all?" she asked Erik.

"Well, that's just what I asked Jimmy. He said the most recent folks who lived there, must be more than thirty years ago now, had a few little kids. There was a lot of secrecy and pretense, creepy smokescreen kind of attitude this "kid-preacher" — he called him — wrapped around his pretty wife and the little ones. Said he never thought much of it when they were living out there. That in those days they all had pretty much the idea that a family's got its problems they're best to keep it to themselves. 'But,' he said, 'that guy! Poor as dirt. Nothing to show for nothing and seemed to think he was something pretty special.' Said people like that always make him think they got something to hide. 'Hard to trust a know-it-all kid like that.' He said. 'Can't tell 'em a thing. You worry some about the damage done to little kids and maybe even that young wife of his with him being such a smart aleck. Hard to know, though, what stories are real . . .'" Erik's voice trailed off and he looked away like he had an important picture in his mind.

Miriam watched him looking at that picture and suddenly felt naked, exposed. She pushed her plate out of the way and put her head in her arms folded in front of her just like she used to do in kindergarten. That's how she felt too. Small. Small and tired.

"Miriam. Miriam, what did I say? I went too far didn't I? I'm prying. "

She lifted her head and supported it with one hand while she looked at Erik.

"We don't have to talk about this anymore. Stupid of me. This is not a professional mission you're on at all, is it?" He looked uncomfortable, like he didn't know what to do with his hands. He rubbed his hands, wadding a napkin between them, set it down, straightened the knife at the side of his saucer and picked the wadded napkin up again.

Miriam reached her hand to calm his frenetic hand-dance and said, "It's okay, Erik. You're not prying. I think I could probably use a confidant. I — you have to understand, though — I don't trust easily."

"I understand. Or, at least, I'm trying to. What about this historian business though? Tell me about your work. What kind of history are you interested in?" He relaxed a little with the subject less personal, less emotional.

Miriam felt more her comfortable, competent public-self when discussing her work. The frightened little girl crept back inside the darkened doorway and closed it quietly behind her. She knew Miriam wouldn't welcome her intrusion now.

"Well, I've done a lot of writing, speaking and research about the women who preceded women of my generation. When I was in school there was so little written by and about women, what their lives were really like. How it really, truly felt, on every level, to live the life of a daughter, wife, mother, lover — to long for a career, for example. To fight for dreams that mattered and have those dreams blocked at every turn . . ."

"Do you teach then? Are you Professor Miriam Blackwell?" He smiled. Impressed.

"Yes. Dr. Miriam to you from now on, Erik. I'm not surprised you didn't guess my professional calling, the state you found me in."

"Yes. I teach at a small parochial college in northern Minnesota. I'm quite lucky, actually. I get to do what I love for a living and live near Lake Superior. A very wild, Atlantic Ocean, North Sea kind of a lake that keeps me (mostly) sane."

"What's your calling Erik? What do you do for a living here so far from the hectic pace of civilization? I mean, I know you said you're working on a book, but do you have wage-earning work that distracts you — the fate so many artists suffer?"

"Yes, there are financial needs, income earning needs, that distract me. But, really, I'm quite fortunate. I love gardening and landscape-design and get hired often for that sort of work. Like I told you, I was the librarian here in town until they closed that down. Truth is, my parents left me pretty well off and that gives me a great deal of freedom. I get paid for some freelance writing and the column I write for the community paper."

"But, listen Miriam. I don't know about you, but I feel we have an awful lot more to say to each other and I'd feel a whole lot better if we could get cleaned up, settle in somewhere and give our conversation the time and space it deserves."

"Yes. Yes. All right. I'd like that. Would you mind giving me a ride to a nearby motel or rooming house or something? "

"Tell you what. We know each other a little better now, right? Would you be uncomfortable just coming back to the house with me? You left some of your things there. I have that spare room. There really isn't a need for you to get a motel room. I promise to be a gentleman."

"Okay. I guess, given my history with you so far, I can risk that. And, thank you. You are very kind."

"My pleasure." He stood making an "after you" gesture, and ushered her to his jeep.

It was a night when two strangers became friends and confidants. Miriam learned he was a marvelous cook and took the same pleasure in drinking a good wine and eating simple, fresh delicious food as she.

Late that night, as the fire warmed the cool night air and they watched each other in shadows and bright, fire-lit eyes, he shared the secrets of his solitary life on his small, flower filled ranch.

He sat, staring at the fire, one leg draped over the arm of the poinsettia leather library chair. He told her what the chair means to him. How he'd claimed this chair as his own (how many years ago?) when the Whitley Library where he'd been librarian was forced finally to close its doors and give up its soul to the powers of a budget crisis.

He held a mostly empty coffee cup dangling from the index finger of his right hand. He told her he didn't have a clue what he wanted from her that had left him so disappointed at her departure. What had he wanted to happen he wondered aloud to her. So many years determinedly alone. The library's closing had meant his freedom, he said. Now he lived his long-craved dream of the writer's life, supported partially by publication of an occasional essay or short story, partially by the income from a substantial inheritance. He liked to work with his hands and took every opportunity to do handiwork like gardening, carpentry or ditch digging. Sometimes somebody would need a new coat of paint on their house. Career-wise, he told her, his life was completely fulfilling.

He helped out with the local weekly newspaper and occasionally The Sarasota Herald published an opinion, commentary or editorial and listed him as a "regular contributor" to their pages. He considered himself a full time writer and worked steadily on a novel he hoped to publish one day.

For Erik, it was a truly satisfying life. To a great extent, his was the life he always dreamed might be his.

He told her that that morning when she left, he'd been staring straight ahead, unseeing, wandering the house with his cold coffee in his hand, alternately pacing and collapsing in his chair, ever since he'd looked to find her gone. He looked right at her then, in the light of the evening fire, and said he couldn't figure out why it bothered him so. Why everything about her bothered him so. "Moved," he said. "That's how I felt. Still feel. Moved. Deeply moved." Now he took his eyes from hers and stared into the fire.

"I can't get you out of my head, haven't been able to all day, yet I've no idea who you really are or where you came from or what circumstance put you in my path. Forgive me if I'm too bold, Miriam, but I couldn't shake your image, the sound of your voice."

He told her he'd helped other people out over the years. He was just that kind of man. No reason not to lend a hand where it was needed. It had always been easy enough and really just a fleeting gracious gesture that relieved some of his guilt for avoiding the usual path of wife, children, an active social life, he figured.

It's not that he'd been happy when the library closed, he said. It had provided a perfect arena for his love of knowledge, of literature, of research. Had fed his endless hunger for discovery and the written word. Fed his imagination too. Enough to inspire a weekly column in a regional philosophy, politics and arts rag which allowed him the comfort of being regularly published — regularly heard; not a total recluse whose words and thoughts fell all around him in suffocating silence.

Miriam felt safe there with Erik. It felt right to her to confide in him. She told him hers was not a purely professional search as he already surmised. She told him she'd come to Whitley, feeling brave and ready, to face whatever ghosts her birth home might hold. She told him about her daughters, Storm and Jane. That the answers she was seeking had to do with the legacy she wanted to leave them. A legacy that would say there is enough hope and safety to go around.

Miriam told him about the solace of nature she finds in the woods, by the water — the essential power of nearness to the shore, its silent calm, its crashing waves. She said, "The water is to me what the night time is to you."

Chapter Twenty Five

Monday, March 6, 1995
Owl's Head, Maine

Dear Diary,

First night alone in my bed in the woods by the sea since Dr. Damon informed me my heart is losing interest in life. Today dawned a lovely and brisk sunny day. I fed Delilah, Widget and Scandal, our cats, yours and mine. I dressed in a thick Scottish wool sweater and carried my thermal L.L. Bean coffee mug down to the rocks and sat directly overlooking the sea for a time before driving to Camden for my appointment with the doctor. I guess I already knew he would tell me my life would end soon. The wind and water, the coming and going of the waves, engaged me, warmed and comforted me somehow, in spite of this knowledge I held in my breast. I have known for some time now, always, really, that life cannot go on forever. I didn't expect to escape this particular human fate, did I? And I slept well last night. Comfortable, fearless. The moon lit the night sky and I basked in the luxury of a moon bath, my aged body bathed in blue light.

I've always felt that here in Maine there is a quality to the light that reveals. It's a clarity so unusual in these modern times. Clarity and revelation. The stuff that nurtures and sustains my life here on this beloved rocky cliff overlooking the sea. Ah life! Here's to you!

And, did I tell you? Today, when Dr. Damon looked me in

my eyes, his eyes heavy with the words he had to say, and told me my heart is failing, I asked, "My heart? It's my heart? Is there any old woman more fortunate than I?"

"But Julia," he said, "I don't understand. I've just given you terrible news. I've told you that you haven't long to live! How is it you consider yourself fortunate?"

"Oh Doctor," I said, "I am more than ninety years old. You know I've seldom been sick a day in my life. My mind, body and heart have served me well all these ninety years. And now, it is not a painful cancer, or a mind-eating, strength eating disease that will take me. No, I am blessed. You've told me my heart is likely to take me soon. There is nothing to be done for it but to go on living until that final moment."

"Yes. I see," the youthful doctor said — though, clearly, he did not.

But you understand, don't you dear diary?

I've lived deeply — fully. My affairs are in order. Years ago I found my granddaughter, Miriam and all preparations are in place for my presence to be revealed to her after my death. You know, I've been tempted in the days and years since discovering her to rename you "Miriam" — to call you, dear diary, by her name, because all I write here is (has always been, really) a message to her.

And now, I face my death and the time is approaching when my long held dream of connection with Miriam will be realized.

She will know how I've lived my life and why I've made the choices I've made. Perhaps knowing I've cared for her over the years and miles will help her make peace with her own past and future.

There is much I cannot know, of course. Will she understand my silence all these years? Will she forgive me for abandoning her father — an act that in many ways set her fate in motion?

Ah, but truly, I am at peace. I leave for her the truth of the life I've lived. I leave her the home where I've found sanctuary, wisdom and rest.

Yes, I am fortunate. I will busy myself now with appreciation of the moments left to me. Ah sweet life! Leave me at your will … This poem I'll leave for you today.

<u>Sunset</u>

Sunset, take me with you where you go
Striped in lavender, gold

And blue
I can't stay here a single hue.
Just now you've lit me with your fire.
You tease. You beauty queen.
So brief, so grand.
You bounce
Once, then twice
You slip behind earth's platform.
Take me down with you tonight
Let me rest where all is light.
Bring me with you the next dawn
I'll burn
Unending Sun song.

Chapter Twenty Six

Miriam stayed in Erik's house for three weeks. She set aside her search and reveled in the refreshing company of a newfound friend. She ventured, almost daily, to the beaches and parks along the Gulf Coast. She lay soaking in the warmth of the sun, wandered along the sand, felt the slap of the mounting waves as another hurricane season approached. She gathered strength.

One morning, nearly three weeks after Erik found her, she awakened knowing, though she'd found a friend, her search remained a solitary one. Though she'd shared many secrets of her heart with Erik over the days and nights since they'd met, she hadn't risked everything. The story of the life she'd led, the confusion and heartache she felt — carried with her endlessly, in spite of professional success and how "okay" she looked to the rest of the world — remained a source of deep personal shame.

Erik was still sleeping when she went to the kitchen to make coffee. His home was so lovely. His gentleness and generosity beckoned her to ignore her quest to find the source of her sorrow.

While the coffee brewed, she showered and dressed, then, returned to the kitchen and sat at the table drinking her first cup. The stillness of the room around her, the silent morning garden beyond the open kitchen door, deceived her into thinking she was alone.

Cup still in hand she arranged her arms to rest her head there. "I'm so ashamed," she said to the air between her arms and the cold table top. "So very. . .very . . . ashamed," she spaced her words between deep sighs.

"Miriam." She wasn't alone after all. Erik placed his hand on her hair. His voice, no longer the voice of a stranger but that of a friend. Still she didn't lift her head aware Erik had heard her self-confessed shame.

"Miriam, will you come with me?"

Now she lifted her face to his, nodded and stood to offer him her hand. He led her outside where he opened the driver's side of his Jeep and she slid behind the wheel, then on over to the passenger side. She didn't, couldn't, say anything. She looked out the window on her side of the car.

"Let him take me where he will," she thought. "At least he'll know where we are, where I am — and maybe that means I'm not lost after all."

"Ashamed." She'd said it because it was the one absolute truth she knew. She was ashamed. Is ashamed. Was "Shame Itself" for all she knew. The embodiment of the concept and the reality. Ashamed she is beautiful. Ashamed she is not more beautiful. Ashamed she is smart. Ashamed she is such a stupid fool. Ashamed she is so naive. Ashamed she is so fucking aware, informed, enlightened. Ashamed she is dirty. Ashamed she is hungry. Ashamed she is lonely. Ashamed she is afraid. Ashamed she is helpless and powerless. Ashamed she has so much. Ashamed she has so very little. And certainly, most shameful of all, is her very Shame. "Shame on me for being jealous. Shame on me for wanting to be alone. Shame on me for leaving. Shame on me for sitting right where I am and not trying to find out where I'm supposed to be. Shame. Paralysis. Let me sleep." She thinks. "Knock me out. Somebody, please."

Paralysis. Tied to a chair. A voiceless, stopped at the throat scream in a dark room echoes back through the deep cave of her charred black, heart and soul. "Leave me alone! Leave me alone!" Her silent scream echoes off the cavern that houses her brain.

Erik pulled the Jeep to a stop. Miriam looked up to see the fallen porch through a screen of sagebrush. Barely able to pull herself back to reality from her voiceless daytime nightmare, she opened the car door, walked across the would-be yard, mounted the fallen porch and entered the house through the opening that used to be the front door of the first house she ever lived in.

Once inside, she didn't know where to rest her eyes. She felt terminally tired. With effort she raised her voice to ask Erik to bring a blanket please, if he happened to have one in the car. He came in with a little whisk broom in one hand and an old Navajo blanket over his arm. He looked like a Prince Charming if ever there was one. She watched him as he swept a place clean in a corner and spread the blanket, smoothing it on his hands and knees. She smiled weakly and slunk to blanket level where she stretched out on the floor. She looked across the room and up at the bit of sky she could see through the glass-less window. Erik slid down the wall at the opposite corner of the room and sat, hugging his knees to his chest. He was silent.

"Am I afraid?" Miriam wondered to herself. "Am I now completely broken? Or, perhaps, on the mend? So much rush to live, to stay alive, rushing toward some illusion of safety. Where has it all landed me in my most certainly half-lived life?"

She sighed deep, shuddering at the end. She fixed her eyes on the sky beyond the window where a lone, tall treetop accepted her into its fluttering leaves and offered the first possibility of peace, acceptance and rest. She didn't remember such a tree from her earlier visit. It was an oak tree, probably thirty or more years old, and obviously buffeted by many storms and droughts.

Now she felt ready. Ready to think it all through — maybe even ready to be accountable for her own part in the chaos, confusion, rage and despair that threw life so entirely out of whack, not only for her, but for the people she loved and who loved her.

In recent years she'd often tried to pick a segment in her life, her childhood, and comb through it for the memories and for some answers to her lost and ashamed condition. She never really managed to reconstruct a chronology that might offer a bit of balance, a bit of perspective. She always felt herself enormously selfish even in her fragmented attempts to remember, to name names and to understand what forces and events formed her. Such attempts just added to her shame.

In her guilt she would lash out with great gushes of defensiveness and tirades of rationalization her inalienable right to live her own life free from the claims of others on her mind, body, skills, space and time. These great gushes would wash all comers aside and away, send them scattering and confused and talking among themselves — muttering about "gone overboard," "off the deep end," and "overkill."

Oh, she was strident. She was vehement. She was articulate in her outrage and the justness of her cause. She made herself her primary cause and focus. She thought it was about finding "normal," finding "healthful," in spite of a lifetime of lessons that offered anything but. One of the important pieces she discovered was missing from her was an ability to value her own perceptions. To believe there was value to her point of view. She couldn't trust herself to have a reasonable, sane or intelligent perspective.

When challenged she'd fight like a tiger, at first and briefly. Then, she'd fold and know she was stupid and wrong and unworthy of an opinion. She'd recently come to understand that missing this piece — she actually visualized and almost felt it physically; this big, gapping hole, quite black, nearly filling her torso — made her different from others. Missing this piece made it hard for her to understand people who were whole and made it hard for whole people to understand her.

Self help aficionados said that knowing the problem, that is, knowing this piece is missing, was half the solution. But for the longest time after the discovery she was testing and researching: "Is it true? Am I different? Isn't everybody like this?" Then there had been the shame of walking around so clearly different and everybody else knowing it all the time and thinking she must know it too. But here she was, forty-seven years old and just finding out what everybody else must have known all along.

Still stretched out on Erik's Navaho blanket, Miriam let the sounds and sights and smells from outside the dusty house lift up the parts of her she knew were there; the parts of her she knew were really her. She told herself, "I know sensation. Oh God — I do know beauty. I know skin and nerve ending touched by blue sky, warm sun, bird song, fresh breezes and, somewhere, please God, let it not be far, river smells, swells, rushes, flows, wanders, meanders calmly, always arriving exactly where its intended to be."

She thought of the freedom of the river. The river was free, not because it had put up just the right fight for its life, its place and its freedom. The river is here. The river simply is. It exists. Ah, the rivers, oceans, mammoth lakes . . . So volatile, aren't they? So inconsistent. Always changing. But, in truth, always running the same course and going the right way. Beginning to end. Front to finish. The waves, ripples, currents don't change their course, turn themselves into a still and quiet something they're not meant to be, or get out of the way when society decides it likes roads and concrete runways better than water. The runways and highways have to coexist with the river in its flow to the lakes and sea. The river knows just where its going whether or not anyone thinks it should go there. And this was it maybe. The clue she needed to begin again. Again she heard the voice that whispered to her always in the river, lakes and ocean waves. Like a river enthusiast, a river historian, she listened to the voice telling her she must go to the headwaters.

"Thrust deeper," she heard Adrienne Rich whispering again, reminding her — how many times . . . how many years now?

In all her years of struggle to survive, her attempts to find answers, she'd never really started at the beginning. Only plunged deeper at moments along the way, then feeling the "current more swift," felt the danger too near . Too ready to pull her down, suck her under. She feared she wouldn't have the strength, the will to stay afloat as the wild and knowing water whirled around and through her.

Perhaps now, though, she was ready. Maybe if she started at the shallow and calm headwaters and allowed for the balance of turmoil and calm, drought and flood, ripples and rapids, there would ultimately come a whole picture of some sort. Observance, awe, worship, honor.. Would she know wisdom someday? Peace?

Energized by this reverie which she knew as guidance, she bounded to her feet. She brushed her bottom, slapping it hard with both hands. She picked up the blanket and folded it quickly with the precision of a true homemaker. Laying the blanket across her left arm she extended her right hand to Erik and pulled him to his feet not quite two inches from her beaming face.

"M-i-s-s-i-s-s-i-p-p-i!" She spelled in a quiet but urgent whisper. Erik's eyes received her completely. They held each other only with their eyes and only for a moment. He touched her hair and brushed it from her cheek. Quietly, slowly, he spelled " g-o-o-d-b-y-e, beautiful."

Miriam leaned to kiss his cheek and whispered in his ear "goodbye, beautiful." She watched through the door and beyond the fallen porch as he left. She watched him, admiring the strength of his stride. He climbed into his jeep and drove away, wheels kicking up a cloud of dust. She stood, just so, until the dust cleared. She walked outside and looked up at her tree and her sky one more time from that particular vantage point. She packed the image firmly in her brain for safe-keeping. She turned to say "Goodbye for now, old porch." She walked toward the place where she would begin at the beginning.

Chapter Twenty Seven

Miriam returned home with several weeks available before classes were to start in late September. Her trip to her birthplace had threatened to take her under. She thought she was so strong. Was determined she needed no one and nothing but herself to face her demons. She learned it was essential to her survival and her search to seek out places of safety and refuge rather than enter places of darkness, danger and harm. She'd been moving too fast. She used her professional life to outdistance the fear this time. She'd forgotten the lesson the waves, the sun through the trees and the winding rivers tried to teach her time and again. She forgot to listen. She forgot to pay attention to a truth she already knew.

She stopped briefly at her office and apartment to pick up any phone messages or mail that accumulated while she was away. She made a couple phone calls and secured a log cottage with a small stone fireplace some forty miles up shore from St. David's. She packed warm clothes, aware of the early occurrence of autumn in the North Country. She packed candles and matches as well as an empty cooler she planned to fill at the grocery on the way up shore. She put her mail in a grocery bag and threw it in the trunk of the car.

The cottage was set close to the banks of an iron rich river that flowed into Lake Superior less than a tenth of a mile away. It hadn't been cleaned in a while but there was a broom and dustpan and she tidied the place quickly before building a fire. Already, in late August, the temperature hovered near freezing certain times of the day unless they were blessed with an Indian Summer. She fixed herself a cup of hot chocolate, wrapped her down comforter around her and sat on the floor staring into the snapping and licking flames. She waited. She listened. She paid attention. Miriam felt safe there — found somehow. Warmed and embraced by a rescuing and comforting presence. Her mind wandered to the kindness of Erik. Such a gentle man. So understanding. He asked nothing in return for the rescue and care he provided a complete stranger. She raised her cup to the memory of his face and hands and smiled her gratitude into the golden flames.

She slept a long and dreamless sleep that night, rising early to walk in the woods by the shore.

She brought with her a tuna fish sandwich, carrot sticks, low fat potato chips and a bottle of water. It was a fall day glorious like none she could remember. The leaves had already turned to their stained-glass autumn colors. It was warmer than when she arrived yesterday. The silence of the forest, the dry air, sun-filled, lent an exaggerated crunch to the leaves beneath her feet. When she arrived at the perfect spot where forest meets “sea,” she held her brown bag in her left hand, her bottle of water in her right then crossed her feet in front of her where she stood.

She looked at the ground under her feet and let her bottom drop all the way to the ground. Her crossed feet kicked at the air and she rocked forward to a sitting position after gravity rocked her backward with the fall. She laughed to think someone well hidden might have seen her but she was quite certain she was alone.

The sky was ridiculously blue. Like a toy. Unreal. And the trees! The leaves gold/green against a silver-gold-white sun that pierced and punctuated the tree branches as they stirred in the slight breeze. A willow tree bent to the river reminded her of the willow she loved as a child in suburban Lansing. Reminded her too of a line she’d recently read in a novel. “Weeping Willows bending down in their perpetual thirst.” “Explains my affinity for the Willow,” she said out loud.

Suddenly she had an urge she simply couldn’t resist. She held tight to her bag and bottle, put both arms out to her sides, spread her legs as far as they would go, and lay back in the thick, crunchy leaves to make a pre-snow angel. She was so full of this day and this place she couldn’t think why she’d bothered to bring lunch. And a "comfort" lunch at that.

She'd started the day feeling empty and lost. She'd determined to make herself her favorite picnic lunch and find a place she could name her own.

Sitting there in the woods she remembered a time she visited Missouri on a lecture tour. It was a rural town with a small college and an eighteenth century French heritage. She took an opportunity for a walk when her lecture was over.

She hadn't expected to walk so far. She started down the river road just a couple blocks from the old inn where she was staying. A mile or so outside of town she took a dirt side road and discovered a flood damaged car junk yard. The cars were old model Ford and Chevy trucks and coupes. The latest model was 1956 if that. The rust and black colors of the decayed cars camouflaged them among the fallen leaves and empty black tree branches. Grave yard. Car bone yard. Old bones. Old souls. Souls wrapped in leaves the color of rubies. Hard and cold and caressed by beauty. The waters had receded. Harmless now. Had they ever truly caused harm? Had the volcano been a disaster? The Flood, The Volcano and the Earthquake? Were they about disaster, tragedy and the end of the world? Were they, rather, about change and passion and wild and true life? She felt they spoke to her, much the same as fallen porches did. Rocks and bones and graveyard headstones had a story to tell that she wanted to hear. Oh yes. It would break her heart, send tremors through her so very temporary body. The story would be about those who came before and about those who would follow.

On that Missouri day, full of beauty and sunshine, it was an odd exercise to focus on decay. Maybe then, it shouldn't be called decay. Not decay, but transformation. The story was of temporary tragedy leaving beauty in its wake. A story of attraction to the forever gone moment and its transforming power. The importance of monument in helping us value the present moment. The upset and devastation of man made life as we know it shook Miriam deeply, but there was a certain beauty to the scene before her.

Certainty is something she'd always sought. Only now was she coming to terms with the no-such-thing-as-certainty truth of human life — human control over nature. But the flood that destroyed these cars was back many years now. People had moved on touched by other natural and not so natural events that ripped and tore at the security they craved.

But now, lying there in her fallen angel position in the woods by Lake Superior, she caught the scent of a wood fire. Was it a campfire or the hearth of someone's lake side home? She lay there on her back, lunch still in hand, and let the full comfort of the solitary day wash over and through her

"It's true," she thought. "The sky never was bluer than this bluest (true bluest) sky today. Summer — even Spring — they have not left me yet. Here they are, precious, treasured bundles — soft, yet substantial in my arms. Warming my lap and chest. Moving in syncopated time with my breath and my heart beat." She breathed deeply through her nose trying to take in the combined freshness, decay and fire warmth her sense of smell offered.

She closed her eyes and felt tiny rivulets of tears running from the corners. She turned her head to the side and tasted the ocean salt of her tears as they crossed her lips and moved over her face and neck.

It was cleansing rather than sorrow she felt. She would sleep here if sleep would come. Instead her thoughts wandered to the boy who grew to be her father. Her nemesis.

It was all right, though. Safe in these woods along the riverbanks she could let what she knew of the life of that little boy and his years of growing to manhood, present itself to her.

From this point in her life and at this distance and in this moment of relative safety, she was able to generate a sense of compassion for her father. She felt sorry for him that he had caused enough harm to mean he could not delight in the woman his second-born daughter had become.

Felt sorrow that her retreat from him had kept him from knowing what magnificent grand-daughters Storm and Jane were. At times when this compassion touched Miriam's heart she felt tempted to call him and sob out her concern and longing for him.

At times like this she would imagine him capable of understanding and feeling sorrow for the harm he'd done. She imagined him wracked with a sense of loss and guilt and wanted to relieve him of his pain by taking him in her arms and telling him he is forgiven. It was at times like these, when her heart filled with compassion for her father, that he visited her in dreams and reminded her again of the danger of letting him near.

As Miriam sat eating her comfort lunch on the banks of this

country's greatest lake she felt aware of the sensual, creative, river and ocean fed aspects of her being. She found comfort in her growing affinity to the women of her grandmother's generation. She felt that affinity most when she was near the water. She stayed and listened to the waves as they built with a growing wind. As she listened, a voice inside her reminded her again of what she already knew. Yes, memory is important. The truth of what is remembered, yes, that's important.

But Miriam may never know the whole truth. She may never unearth her true history. And something else. Something else required her attention. That something else, she realized, was communion. Communion she understood at that moment, could be hers if she knew her history or not. She watched the place where the river meets the fresh water sea. "Confluence," she thought. "A coming together. A communion."

Chapter Twenty Eight

The wind picked up and brought with it a fine, cold rain. By the time Miriam returned to the cottage her hair and her brown lunch bag were soaked through. She took the bag of mail from the trunk of her car and set it on the floor next to the stone hearth. She built a fire quickly and put a kettle on the stove for coffee. As the water heated and the fire grew, she towel dried her hair with one hand and stooped by the fire to sort through the full bag of mail with the other.

Lots of junk. Catalogues, special offers. A few bills. A stack of letters from people whose names she'd never heard, presumably fan mail or criticism. Since there was nothing from either of her daughters she set most of the mail aside to open later. As she put the mail back in the brown grocery bag, an ivory business envelope with gold embossed insignia of a law office located in Cornwall-on-Hudson slipped from her hands and onto the floor. Cornwall-on -Hudson was a place about an hour north of New York City, a place she knew to be packed with history of fascinating lives. She remembered a small book she'd first seen at a lodge in the Catskills when she was only a girl. In it were pictures and profiles of women who made mention of the artists and writers who lived in this town along the Hudson River.

She looked the envelope over carefully. It was quite thick so it had required a second postage stamp. It was addressed to Dr. Miriam Blackwell and sent to her office at the college. Perhaps an invitation to lecture, she thought.

Her coffee was ready so she fetched herself a cup before settling on the sofa in front of the fire to open this curious communication.

She wrapped a towel around her head and put on an oversized red and black hunter's plaid shirt that covered her to her knees. She pulled on some fleece sweat pants and a pair of red wool socks and settled on the couch with her cup of coffee. She examined the envelope for the longest time. She didn't know why it took her so long to open it. Didn't know why it seemed so mysterious to her. It seemed important though. Seemed to require her full attention and energy. She set her coffee cup on the end table and ran her finger under the seal, tearing the envelope open. She cut her finger on the paper and when she went to put it to her mouth to suck away the sudden pain, a photograph of a woman fell onto the sofa.

Miriam picked the picture up and held it close to the light of the lamp next to her. In the black and white image the woman wore a man-style dark suit and a crisp, open collared white shirt. Her black hair was pulled away from her face and caught at the neck in a beaded clip that held it above her neck and shoulders. Miriam looked at her face and saw her own eyes looking back at her.

She caught her breath and looked closer, harder, at the image. "Is this a picture of me?" But Miriam had never worn clothes like that or seen that beaded hair clip before. And the picture looked old, like it was taken in the times before color photography. Miriam's twin stood on a rocky plate where tall firs surrounded her and waves curled and smashed in the sea behind her. She turned the photo over and saw in faded, penciled script, the words, "Julia Rousseau, 1950, Owl's Head, Maine."

Miriam picked up the envelope to see if there were more photographs. She found a color image of the back of a woman, white hair piled loosely on her head. The woman stood in a room with a stone hearth and huge windows looking out on a sunset over the very same rocky precipice in the old photograph. There was yet another picture, again, recent and in color, of a weathered gray house, clearly the house containing the room and the woman who looked out upon the roiling sea.

"I've seen that house," Miriam said aloud. "I know this place. Have I only dreamed it?" Who was this woman who could be her twin? Miriam felt she looked at her through eyes that knew her to her very soul.

She took the folded pages of stationary from the envelope and saw a script that resembled her own handwriting.

My Dearest Miriam,

I am your very own, personal, missing woman, and I can tell from all I know about you, that it is about time I am— found. I am quite certain that after all your searching this letter will come as a surprise to you.

My name is Julia Rousseau. I am your grandmother and I must beg your forgiveness for my absence from your life. I would not have eluded you all these years if it had not been for the promise I made upon the birth of your father when I was a young girl. I am your grandmother. Your father is my son.

I never knew the name and place of the parents who adopted your father — whose son he became. They never did know my name or where I was or anything about me, really. It was part of the agreement and certainly the way of the times to protect the child and the parents who would raise him as their own from the possibility of the birth-mother determining she had made a mistake and then wanting the child for her very own.

It was the way of the times to swear your own identity to secrecy under threat of exposure, humiliation and possible lawsuit. Always pig-headed and so sure I was right in doing things my way rather than the way prescribed by society — I thought in this one area it was of the utmost importance to try to do right by your father and the parents who would raise him.

I fully meant to keep my promise and to never let anyone associated with my son know my identity. But then, there was you.

Not only you — but you looking — I felt it from the day you were born, for me. Maybe you know and maybe you don't, but a woman who has a baby out of wedlock and subsequently gives up that baby has to move on with her life. Has to move forward. Often times, when delving fully into my own life I could nearly forget that I was a mother or at least the vehicle by which a baby came to life.

I would be lying to say I ever completely forgot I had a son. But I was a thoroughly modern woman, for my time — I believed I had done (was doing) the right thing. I had never meant to have children. Had never had the craving to bear and raise my own family and knew my boy would be better off with a family who really wanted a child to call their own.

I don't know what happened to your father as a child. I know very little about him as a man. I kept my promise to not keep close tabs on him. I hope he was loved. I hope his parents did not hold against him the sullied reputation of his birth mother. There was little leniency toward childbirth outside marriage in those days.

However that was — however that is — so be it. Life brought with it forces outside my control while I was busy or engaged in trying to control something I thought required my hand in it. Other things go on; things I should have been aware of, but wasn't. While I tried to do right, to create forces in this world for the good of women, I did harm and I am to blame.

So you, grand daughter-mine, to all appearances, noticed some missing pieces. Oh, don't misunderstand, I've not been privy to the details of your personal life. Your personal search. Perhaps I'm assuming too much, perhaps I've mis-guessed the message behind your published work — your taped lectures. But, if I have not; if I'm right, you have been looking for me and I want to show myself to you in hopes this puzzle piece will aid you in putting together your history and, thereby allow you to live fully a life of peace and rest.

I once heard you, in a public lecture, quote Kierkegaard, "Life must be viewed backward but must be lived forward." So true. So very true. I've heard it said living in the past steals precious time from the present, but without a knowledge of history and our place in it, we lack the perspective that can enrich and lend meaning to our present moments.

Women in your generation, as in mine, are offered so few clues; far too few models of strength, stamina, personal freedom and safety in living independent of the male of the species. It is right and good, and perhaps I flatter myself here, but I think it also a sign you are a woman descended from me, that you have devoted your professional life to bringing the hidden lives of women to the surface and are casting on them the full light of day.

What forces shaped and hindered the women who came before you and your generation? This is the question you, in your public life as Dr. Miriam Blackwell, have put forward and attempted to answer.

What I've wondered though — What I've attempted to guess from reading your words and listening to you talk, is this: How much — to what extent has my absence shaped your life and ultimately shaped your contribution to the lives of others? Your impact so visible and, I think, therefore positive. Mine, hidden from your sight and, therefore keeping you lost and in the dark — maybe even unprotected.

I left your father in uncertain times in an uncertain world and to an uncertain future. Your advocacy toward women wounded in childhood, women whose fathers were absent or cruel, your obvious search for solid ground to stand on to keep the tide and current from carrying you away or under, tells me you, too, have been wounded. And I fear it was your father, my son, who played a role in that hurt.

Oh, I don't mean to say its obvious you feel lost and broken, like those you defend in your essays. But your level of compassion, empathy, encouragement and your dogged perseverance in exposing the danger hurting a child poses to the future (not only of that child) but to generations beyond — this is what I have noticed.

So, on the one hand, I have regrets. I have to take responsibility, first, for doing harm in taking so little responsibility for the life I created, and second, for giving life to a son who subsequently may have done harm. For that, I am so very sorry.

On the other hand, or to take another view — that you are here, an open-mouthed, refuses-to-be-silenced and urges others toward full-voice woman, as the result (to some extent) of the harm I've done — is a singular blessing that has come of my living and your father's life.

You, my living progeny, are the one of my so-far descendents, who has carried on, unbeknown to you, my legacy. A legacy of making the unseen visible. A legacy of living out loud and in defiance in the face of fear. A legacy of the examined life and the personal life lived deeply.

How I've wanted, how many times I've wanted, to come to you; call you and embrace you as my own, my grandchild. But it was pride and maybe folly and I couldn't know but what I would cause further harm in breaking my promise. With your father still living, how could I impose myself on your life or his and not create a maelstrom? Well, be that as it may; I've come to terms and determined my existence will not be lost to you.

Only, you will wait to know me and understand what you are to me, until after my death. All for me — yes. I am selfish to reveal myself and selfish in not revealing myself. Maybe you'll resent my not revealing myself sooner when we could have sat for hours in front of my fire, watching the waves and knowing, fully realizing the depth of our kinship. But I don't truly believe that path was ever open to us; open to me. I can only hope that good, rather than further harm, will come to you from my revealing myself now.

For that matter, it is only now when it is late in my life that I've been able to see myself clearly: been able to recognize something like the nearly whole picture of who I am and what my life has been.

I've lived a life of impulse and passion. Of dreaming and feeling entitled to the realization of those dreams. A life many would say, and perhaps rightly so, was selfish and in which I cared only for my own pleasure and satisfaction. Perhaps in the end the only true good I've done will be the part I've played in your existence. But, I (perhaps self-flattery again here) think that is not true. I think there is a goodness and a service I have performed for those who've known me and been influenced by me.

I have tried to leave evidence for you of all that I am. Evidence and documentation as well as practical, physical relics of the good and the harm.

All in all, it has been a life, for me, of vastness and richness beyond measure. Though I possess no faith in God, I do believe in grace. I believe in epiphany and blessing. You, your palpable, out-there-in-the-face existence, have been my epiphany: my visitation with grace. And you, my beloved Miriam, have been my blessing.

As I started to say earlier, I believe I've sensed harm was done to you. What I must say too, is that I see that for you there has also been rescue. I don't know where you are in your personal search now, but wherever you've arrived, whatever you've learned or remembered, I want to urge you to notice the times and circumstances of rescue. A life of utter and non-stopping harm creates damage so debilitating as to render its victim dead in life. Wrecked and ruined. No, for you, if I'm right about the harm and the hurt — for you, there has been rescue as well. Someone, a presence in some place or, perhaps several people over time and in just the right place, has believed in you. Believed in you, and yes, maybe even treasured you.

A person needs that treasuring to thrive. One can survive without absolute treasuring. One can survive with merely occasional support and encouragement, but, not thrive, no. No, never can one thrive without being first, at some time, in some way, by some one — treasured.

In my own life, which was certainly storm-tossed, I felt treasured in my early years by my father and my mother. When I no longer had my father it was my mother, forever championing me, urging me on to live fully and boldly; telling me the soul and art restriction society imposed on so many women could be disregarded by a girl with my gifts; a girl with, according to Mother, my extraordinary character. And so, I flourished and I felt entitled in a way so few of our gender do.

I will never know if you knew of my life before this letter. Though my work was not that of historian so you would not have encountered the name Julia Rousseau in your particular field, you may be aware of my minor reputation as a writer documenting aspects of the lives of late nineteenth and early twentieth century iconoclasts. I spent a great deal of time in and around New York City and came to know Cornwall-on-Hudson as a place of great inspiration and communion. Still my business affairs are handled by a law firm there. They will, no doubt, be the ones to contact you when I'm gone.

Contemporaries like Virginia Woolf, Djuna Barnes, Anais Nin and Peggy Guggenheim were my living heroes, and, after the influence of my mother, had considerable influence on the direction my life would take.

But, no, this is not what I wanted to say, and there will be time later for you to learn the details of my life. I wish you to know who I loved, who I admired and the kind of life I embraced. It was then, as it is now, a world out of control. It was then, as it seems now, a world bent on self-destruct. Wars and rumors of wars, ever expanding industry and technology, a mind-numbing pace of growth. The world becoming an increasing hoard of humanity and the sense, even in that hoard, of being inexorably alone and alienated. There existed a loss of faith and a concoction of faith built on a desperate need for meaning — for sense of purpose. Each generation in succession screaming "Is that all there is?" with only a few embracing what is and feeling it as blessing and grace.

And life, as you clearly know, is over and over again a lesson about cycles and circles and history repeating itself.

You will by now, no doubt, have read the words of the writers of my generation. In your quest for lost lives, (no, not lost, hidden is the word isn't it. . .) you will have discovered (just as I've discovered the words of your generation and that of your father's) the fears and sins of the fathers visited on the children. You will know by now that, in my generation, as in yours, there were pacifists and activists for peace. There were those who decried racism and who extolled women's rights. There were those who despaired the artistic desert, the superficiality, the mad, meaningless, heart-less and soul-less rush to busy-ness of capitalism and every-man-for-himself. Get rich quick stole the spirit and the other-connectedness from us and pitted us against each other in a ruthless quest for "its mine. I was here first." It was, as it is today, a society without enough to go around. Some thing so very hard to figure out in a world of plenty. (Where, truth be known — there is still plenty — and, still and also, no where near enough to go around.)

I wonder if you read the work of your contemporaries and imagine that you do. I found such poignancy and meaning in Barbara Kingsolver's words in her "Animal Dreams" and (though you probably have them already) want to offer them to you here and now as I try to leave you anything and everything from my life that might serve you in yours and in what you leave for the children who follow you. She says this:

> *"The very least you can do in your life is to figure out what you hope for, and the most you can do is to live inside that hope. What I want is so simple I can hardly say it: elementary kindness. Enough to eat. Enough to go around. The possibility that kids might one day grow up to be neither the destroyers nor the destroyed."*

There is something more I leave to you. I leave you this home I have loved and in which I've found sanctuary and a true sense of communion for so many seasons and years of my life. If I know your search as I believe I do, you have a yearning toward home that would ultimately have brought you here without my sending this letter. If home is what you seek, I pray you'll find it here. I'm sure the lawyers will take care of all practicalities in regard to my passing and provide you with all necessary assistance in coming home.

I am undyingly grateful for your existence, Miriam. Your very life affirms mine. Bless you.

Grandmother Julia

The envelope contained a brief business letter urging Miriam to contact the law offices of Tyler, Burnes & Dunson, for further information. She folded her grandmother's letter, put the pictures with it back in the envelope and put it in her purse. She put out the fire, packed her belongings and returned to her apartment to make a phone call.

Chapter Twenty Nine

"Thanks for calling 872-8974. Can't get to the phone right now, but if you'll leave a message and the day and time of your call, I'll get back to you right away." This was only the mechanical version of the voice Miriam wanted to hear at the other end of the line.

"Erik. Erik, please. Tell me you're there. Tell me you're just screening your calls . . . It's me, Miriam. Remember me? Oh, please, pick up."

"Miriam. Miriam, it's you? I didn't expect to hear from you. Hi. I mean. Hello. Yes, I'm right here." Ah, his real voice.

"Hi Erik. Oh, I can't tell you how glad I am you're home. I have news I simply can't contain. I need to talk to you. I want to see you. Can I come back? Or, no. Can you come here? Can you possibly? No, that doesn't make sense does it? Tell you what. I'll come there. I still have time left."

"Miriam, what is it? What's happened?"

"I've found it Erik. Or, rather, it's found me. Home. I'm going home!"

"That's great, Miriam, but, where, who, how, what happened?"

"Can I tell you in person Erik? There's so much to say. So much to feel, I can hardly get my breath. I want to see your face. My friend, my rescuer. I can be there tomorrow. Will you meet me in Sarasota? I'll fly in."

"I'll be there. Can't wait to see you. Can't wait to hear your news. You sound so good. So well. You've been well, then?"

"I have and I haven't, but I'm flying right now. I haven't really processed this yet, but I feel something so right is happening for me. I'll go now and get my tickets. Thanks for being there, Erik. See you tomorrow, all right?"

"Okay, Miriam. Till tomorrow. Safe journey."

She set the phone down and took a look at herself in the mirror over the phone stand. This mirror was supposed to keep her from being a total grump times when she was home and unhappy about answering the calls she couldn't escape. Sometimes she needed to give herself a good talking to. Like now.

She couldn't quite figure out if that had really been her, running home, not thinking twice about who she would call or if she would call anyone... It was automatic! Her grandmother's letter said to accept rescue. "Rescue is essential," she'd said.

But where was Miriam's usual crap load of self-loathing, guilt and shame that made her so sure she was an imposition on anyone and everyone? Where had all of that gone?

"Well. Gone? No more? Better take advantage. A friend. A friend. I haven't had a friend in so very long." She said to the face in the mirror. "Oh. And a family! I haven't had a family in so very long!"

She got her things together for the next day's trip. Called and booked a seat on the earliest flight, which sadly, wasn't until eleven in the morning. She hardly slept that night picturing the possibility of home. Picturing the possibility of a true friend. Knowing, so brief and new, the reality of family.

Next morning she was up early, full sun shining in the bedroom window. Now it was time to take advantage, do a little thinking. Live these moments of now even though they were so packed with anticipating the future.

Miriam dressed and walked the dirt path to the confluence of the river and the lake. Yesterday's rain had soaked the streets but the temperature dropped during the night leaving the road smooth and rubber hard, solid beneath her boots. She walked through a clear light like she hadn't known in years. The thick gray, opaque rubber mask was gone from her eyes. Every sense was sharp and keen. A babbling brook along the road's edge fairly laughed accompaniment to the rhythm of her feet on the path.

The rubber robe of anguish hadn't fallen away all at once, but bit by bit, piece by piece. It's muting of the light, sounds, scents and taste of real and true living and noticing the moments had perhaps made the moments of terror survivable. The mask gone, something of great importance was left in its place. Acceptance. Acceptance that life does hold some tragedies, short of death, that remain unfixable. Some can't even be remembered with clarity, but the effects linger on. The search has to continue. It's the search that matters. "It's about knowing what you hope for. Yes. Like Julia said. Like Barbara Kingsolver said." She reminded herself.

Miriam knew what she hoped for. She hoped for confluence. She hoped for understanding. She hoped for communion.

* * * * *

The day was lovely, the flight was on time and Erik was there at the gate when her plane landed in Sarasota. He came toward her, flashing his handsome smile, his eyes bluer than she remembered. He wore a white tee shirt tucked into blue jeans with a linen blazer. Coincidentally, her own clothes were a slightly feminine version of his. They instantly noticed they'd dressed like twins and nodded their mutual pleasure and approval.

Neither of them knew what to do with their hands. Should they fall into each other's arms? Shake hands? What?

Erik settled the confusion by reaching his hand to tuck the hair behind Miriam's ear and quickly leaned to her face to kiss her cheek.

"So, so good to see you, Miriam," he said. He stepped back, sliding a hand in the pocket of his blue jeans. "I like your outfit."

"Erik, I can't tell you how much it means to have you here. You look great. Healthy. Great! Just great!" She couldn't take her eyes off the man. She realized she must have hardly seen him when she was here having her breakdown several weeks ago, so blinded was she with the past.

"Let's go pick up your bag, Miriam. I'm dying to get out of here and find out what this is all about."

"My bag. Oh, yes. Oh, I didn't check it. I carried it. . ." She looked around. "Oh. No. I didn't carry it on. I was going to. It wasn't that much. Just a little black wheelie bag." She kept looking around her but it was beginning to dawn on her she'd left her bag in the trunk of her car back home.

"Erik. You won't believe this. This is simply going to give you further proof I'm a total nut case, isn't it? Damn. You know what I did?"

"What? Where's your suitcase? Did you leave it on the plane?"

"I wish. No. It's in my car at the airport." A thought occurred her and she quickly looked in her purse. "Oh, thank God! It's here. The letter. The envelope. I did bring that. That's all that's important, really. Let's go." She took his arm. He looked baffled but came along as she hurried him through the door.

As soon as they were seated in Erik's Jeep he turned to her, "Okay, Miriam. I can't wait any longer. I've been going absolutely nuts since your call yesterday. I've wanted so much to call you since you left, but I just didn't know what would be right. I knew so little except you were suffering pretty bad when you were down here. I know you decided you weren't going to find your answers here and decided to go back and continue your search from where you live. But, here you are. Tell me. Tell me, Miriam."

"Erik." She looked at him and touched his face. "I'm, I'm having trouble finding words. There's so much, so many years, so many questions still. But something absolutely amazing has happened. I believe it with all my heart and soul and I can't believe it at all." She didn't quite know how to begin to tell him.

"Before I came back here to visit my birthplace, I'd been rather accomplished at keeping my personal and professional lives separate. I was an advocate for the raised voices for truth concerning women's experience. I believed strongly in the contribution I was making to a true historical perspective that included the truth, not only about the lives of the men who preceded us and built this country, but the other half of that story too. The story of the women. The uncovering of whatever legacy they left for their daughters and sons and grandchildren."

"But my personal search to understand my own beginnings and put them in a context that would bring me some level of rest — Turns out I opened a can of worms that would damn near kill me." She leaned her head against the back of the seat and continued.

"My birthplace reunion didn't offer answers but I don't regret the journey. No. That journey, the black pool into which I stumbled, the rescue and the friendship — you, my friend acted as catalyst of a sort. I was beginning to see the relevance of all my years as a historian to my need for resolution in regard to my own history. I was beginning to understand the importance of always holding before me a yearning toward the truth even when the details evaded discovery."

She turned to face Erik again. "It was this yearning toward truth and the forward motion it brought to my life that created a richness and vibrancy in living each moment. Yeah. There were huge chunks, enormous pieces of mystery that, if I could uncover them, might aid me in avoiding further spinning in cataclysmic circles. To a large extent, through therapy, I'd already put words and feelings to the experiences that held me hostage to destruction for most of my adult life. Looking at those experiences and at the child who'd been hurt, rather than running from the horror, had rendered me free in a way I'd never known or felt prior to going to the depths of that abyss that was the truth of my childhood. I was much healthier for hitting bottom and surviving to continue my search. At least that's what I've come to believe."

"Believe it or not, I was in pretty good shape and had a reasonable support system in place before I came here and collapsed alongside that fallen porch"

Erik smiled a look of reassurance. "Go on, Miriam. I want to listen."

"But, this is such a long and convoluted story. Let's find some place we can really talk. I will tell you though, the reason I called and the reason I'm here. I've been found. I'm going home for the very first time. You had to be the first to know. I don't know for sure why. But I do know and trust with all my heart, that that's the way it has to be."

"I'm listening, Miriam. Can't say I really understand all you've just told me. But, you're right. We need to find a place to really settle in and talk. Let's get ourselves near the water. We need water sights, sounds and smells for this one, don't you think?"

"Oh, yes. Yes. Yes. Take me to the water my friend." She turned to face the front of the car and sighed. Her body felt chilled and drained with the enormity of all that had happened and the possibilities before her. She reached to put her hand on Erik's as he steered them toward the next place they would go.

They decided a meal at a nice place on the water with a nearby waterside inn would be just the thing.

Erik wasn't particularly familiar with Sarasota and neither was Miriam so they pulled up to a pay phone at the Super America where a weather battered yellow pages dangled from a cord, occasionally wrapping itself like a tether ball around the post that held the phone. She found a number for Tourist Information and Erik called. They recommended "Butterlick's Bistro" and said it was less than a block along the shore from a comfortable B&B. They booked two rooms at the inn and made reservations for dinner. They had one hour to find the place.

Their matching outfits weren't quite the things for the elegant restaurant so they located a Famous Footwear and a Dillard's department store on the way to the shore.

Miriam concocted an impromptu shopping list and named the items aloud as she jumped from the Jeep, held the door handle to be sure her side was locked, and came around to the front of the car to meet up with her shopping buddy. "A sweater, a sleeveless top for when it warms up, a skirt that can go casual or dressy (depending), shorts and maybe some khaki's. Yes, I think khaki's that will go with a black tank top or a white shirt. Yes. Oh, and shoes -- ummm -- sandals that can look dressed down or up. How's that sound to you Erik? Have I got all potential weather conditions covered?"

"Sounds fairly comprehensive to me. Plus, we have our twin outfits. We can go almost anywhere in these. Did you, by any chance have the jeans and tee shirt you stole from me packed in that suitcase you left home? I so hoped those weren't a permanent loss. They hold some interesting memories for me, you understand. I don't know a whole lot about you, my friend, but you seem to run into a lot of problems related to clothing." He said all this as he steered her through the double glass doors of the department store.

Their shopping spree could have appropriately been accompanied by some kind of Beatles era music video. Reminded Miriam of the foursome in "Hard Day's Night," the way they primped, careened and cavorted. They tried on every variety of clothing, hats, scarves, necklaces and earrings (one tiny cubic zirconium stud for one of his ears and one for hers perhaps?) They modeled for each other and in front of the three way mirrors throughout the store.

They suddenly remembered their dinner reservations and the seriousness of their mission and got quickly down to the business of shopping. She found a simple, tee-shirt fabric black dress that was comfortable, soft and fit beautifully. It was only ten dollars so she snatched it up. She bought a black tank top (close fitting, soft, tee-shirt fabric again), khaki slacks, a crisp white cotton shirt with long sleeves she could roll up part way and feel just like Meryl Streep in "Out of Africa." She found a button front khaki skirt and a light weight, sort of flowy, flowered skirt too. She picked up a few necessary pieces of underwear. All this primping and selecting took under forty-five minutes. She passed by the jewelry counter on her way to see what Erik had found, and picked up a pair of two inch pewter hoop earrings that fit her mood precisely.

Erik saw her coming up behind him in the mirror. He turned and spread his arms, turning this way and that to see what she thought of his white, collar-less, long-sleeved shirt tucked into a pair of taupe slacks. He held his natural linen blazer from his extended right hand. Miriam folded her arms across her dressed for dinner chest and nodded her head with approval. "My, but this man is a handsome one," she said to herself.

* * * * *

The weather had warmed with the evening breeze from the South. They found the restaurant easily. It was just the kind of place she'd hoped for. Not too touristy and not too much of a local hang out. Butterlick's Bistro had a terraced and canopied deck extending within mere feet of the sand and the waves of the Gulf of Mexico. The sun had set long ago by the time Miriam and Erik arrived for dinner. Candle light flickered on each table and the smartly dressed young people waiting tables knew how to be just helpful enough without intruding on intimate conversation.

Erik pulled out a chair for her and she smiled up at him as she accepted his courtesy. He chose a seat where he could easily look at her face as they talked but that wasn't all the way across the table from her. She leaned into the table with her body supported by arms folded in front of her.

She lifted her chin and breathed the night air, the Gulf air, deeply, until it filled her. She looked at Erik and smiled. "Would it be presumptuous of me to treat you to a bottle of wine?" She'd anticipated something, white, crisp and dry as she dressed for dinner.

"I'd be delighted and honored, Ma'am. Thank you, yes." Erik settled back in his chair not taking his eyes off Miriam's face.

When the waiter came she selected a French Sauvignon Blanc (not too dry, not too sweet) and asked for a plate of roasted garlic, chutney and crusty bread for an appetizer to share.

The wine came and she lifted her glass to Erik in a toast-like gesture. "So much to say. So many thank you's. Too-soon-goodbye's. A second 'hello.' To Erik Newland. To you."

"Oh, Miriam, where did you ever come from? I've known you always, haven't I?" Erik leaned close to her face and held her eyes in his very serious gaze.

She leaned back in her chair and put her feet up, crossed at the ankles on the chair across from her. Erik's feet shared the same chair. Miriam lifted one arm up and rested the back of her head against it like she was stretching out in the warmth of the summer sun. She closed her eyes and breathed a deep and satisfied breath.

The waiter brought an earthenware platter, wood-fired and glazed to a polished obsidian turn. Red-brown swaths of color, painted Japanese style, decorated the surface of the sixteen inch circle that bore an arrangement of delectable, appetite arousing roasted garlic of a pale ivory/gold hue and a sphere of creamy Gorgonzola on a tender bed of arugula. An obsidian tea bowl filled with spicy/sweet, cranberry colored chutney was positioned to one side of the arugula arrangement. The sight and scent of this presentation forced Miriam to bring her napkin to her lips to prevent an unseemly line of drool escaping her mouth.

Erik slathered a toasted round of baguette with the creamy, warm garlic and spooned the ruby chutney in the center of the circle. He held one hand under this aromatic, mouth watering circle as he reached it toward her lips.

They took their time savoring every bite and swallow. Their conversation became richer, deeper and more intimate as the meal increased in sensuality.

As he offered Miriam the first bites of their meal together, and their eyes met over the taste and scent of creamy garlic and pungent chutney Erik said, " You've let me in pretty far today, you know. Your toast, the 'too soon good-byes' part — what do you mean?

Are you going to run away again? Is tonight a nice way of saying goodbye without really saying it?"

"No, Erik — or I don't know for sure. I'm here because I knew I had to come. I can't predict exactly what will happen. You may as well be a friend I've known all my life. I know as I've never known anything before, that my trust in you is not misplaced. The 'too-soon-good-bye' was for the time before when I left. You've been so exceedingly kind."

"I was terribly confused by what happened when I was here last time. I felt ashamed and embarrassed to be so confused. I keep telling myself I should have myself and my life sorted out by now. Hell, Erik. I'm about as middle-aged as you can get unless I'm going to live to be more than a hundred years old."

"I've botched so many friendships and relationships during this lifetime of trying to create myself. Trying to make myself into a person whose life makes sense. Fits someplace. A person whose life doesn't have to end just because, in the early days, it was treated as so insignificant."

"Listen to me. I'm doing it again. I hate this. I'm getting all deep and vague and I'm avoiding telling you anything. But, really — are you sure you want to hear all the trials, tribulations and middle-aged whining of a vagabond you happened to stumble on out in the dirt?"

"I'm here now, Miriam. You called me your friend. I'm not going anywhere until you tell me why you've come to me. I feel pretty strong and grown up right now. I haven't always felt that way, and I've done my fair share of running away and hiding, myself. I want to know whatever you can tell me about what's brought you here. What have you lost? What are you looking for? Home has found you, you said. Tell me, please."

"Okay, Erik. All right. I'll try to begin to tell you. But it's such a long story and I don't know if it holds any interest for anyone but me. I'd really rather you see the surface me. The me who cleaned up pretty nice for supper and didn't run away and hide this time. I want more than anything to look 'together,' mature and healthy for your eyes. But, too, I want more than anything to be acceptable as I truly am. No masks, no lies."

"I want to believe I'll never feel as broken again as the day you found me. The truth is, and you've probably already guessed it

— that brokeness, what you found and saw; that's no where near the most broken I've been. It's no where near the first time either."

"I never would have come here to start looking for — whatever it is — if I thought I was still in such a bad place. Can you believe I felt strong and ready for whatever I'd have to face coming here when I left Minnesota?" She propped her head in one hand and looked into her wine glass.

"Miriam, I wish so much you dared look at me as you say these things. I don't know why — I don't have any explanation for why I want so very much to know more about you. To learn your story — maybe even help in your search. But I do. I am interested and I want you to feel you can talk to me. I promise I won't think ill of you. You know I understand brokeness myself." He paused. "I told you quite a lot about me when you were here last and you gave me a little sense of what your search is about. But now, it's time for me to hear your story in detail. Can't we start tonight? What better setting? I've got nowhere I have to be. Damn it, Miriam, there is nowhere on earth I'd rather be at this moment than right here where I am. Please talk to me. Please."

"Okay. Okay, I will. But . . . I'm going to need another one of those garlicky things just oozing over with Gorgonzola and chutney before I even attempt this." She was making light now and smiling, stealing the odd glance at Erik's face and eyes without daring to hold on. She fixed another garlic toast and did away with it in two bites. She gulped, wiped her face with her napkin and lifted her wine glass in a salute-like gesture before taking a deep drink of the fortifying golden liquid. She swallowed hard, slapped her hands together in a gesture of getting down to serious business, and began.

Miriam kept her head tilted and propped on her left hand, elbow on the table and let herself look at Erik. "Here goes. How can I say this . . . you know, get it right? It's about — well, in a way it's about my grandmother and Henry Miller, Anais Nin and Erica Jong — or, no . . . maybe it's about the cyclical nature of living. Maybe it's about 'there's nothing new under the sun,' Ecclesiastes, you know." She gave him a questioning look, a kind of crazy smile/ frown like look that said "am I making any sense at all — no, I guess not" all at the same time.

"Go on, go on. You've got me curious . . . What do Nin, Jong, Miller and your grandmother have to do with each other? Or. . . is it with you? What do they have to do with you? And, Ecclesiastes? You mean how history repeats itself but we humans never seem to learn much from that past?"

"Yes. That part about Ecclesiastes. That's what I mean. I feel rotten about wasting my life thrashing and flailing about without a net; without any sense of who and what came before me. Who and what formed me?" She leaned closer now, concentrating on some thought that seemed to rest there in the depths of the obsidian platter before her. "You see, what I've not been able to understand is that I don't seem to be very much like anyone else in my family that I know or have been told about. I've always felt 'odd man out' or 'odd woman out', 'odd kid out', whatever. . . I've thought maybe I'm sort of like my mother but it seems impossible to know what lies at the very heart of her — because, she's always seemed cowed and cowering. So damned timid: she's — whoever she might really be (or might have wanted to be) has been lost way down somewhere where I can't see her or find her. She's all just this outside view. The proper preacher's wife. Never raising her voice in opinion or descent. Hardly ever raising it even in song — though, I do think she loves music."

"Sometimes, when I was small she'd give me a glimpse of a playful, childlike spirit — maybe she'd break into a run into the lake. Or, sometimes, she'd show this extraordinary tenderness toward me, however briefly. But, before I could catch any of that spirit and hold it to me and embrace my mother, that one she'd showed me, it would be gone. She'd retreat inside her so proper, quiet, inoffensive self."

"I'm not explaining about Nin or Jong or anything am I? Well, I told you this could be long. I guess I should have said how convoluted it is too. Besides, I've really never put it all down or said it to any one else. I don't really know what I'll tell you or how I'll tell it. Are you sure you don't mind getting into this tonight?"

"Miriam. We've already settled that. Please go on. We'll try together to make sense of it all."

"Yah! Okay — soooooo. Where was I? Um. Um. My grandmother et. al. Well. Can I have a little more of that wine?" Erik filled her glass to the very brim and she laughed and bent her lips to sip quickly before it overflowed the glass. "Thank you." She gulped trying to hold the wine in her mouth and wanting to laugh.

Erik put his chin on his fist and looked her straight in the eyes conveying his all ear-ness.

A gentle rendition of Handel's "Water Music," wafted out over the terrace from the interior of the restaurant. The only music they'd been hearing was that of the waves as they rolled and broke in a sudsy foam upon the few rocks that guarded the terrace from the Gulf. The music brought a lovely, lulling sound. A sound both safe and freeing. Miriam went on.

"Here's the thing. There are a lot of mysteries in my heritage. I know that's true of most families. And, maybe I won't be able to uncover all the secrets. It's probably not necessary. But there are some questions that I've just had to believe have answers that are within my reach. So, that's why I came here in the first place. I was looking for answers to certain questions."

"Like. I'm sure I told you my Dad was adopted? My Grandma and Grandpa — the Grandpa I adored, by the way, and who went and died on me without explanation when I was eight — well, they were Dad's adoptive parents. And, I guess, I mean, from what I can tell, they weren't very nice to him."

"Both Grandma and Grandpa worked at the shoe factories all the time Dad was little and vague rumors say he was left with a pretty nasty disciplinarian of an aunt (about whom I know zippo) while they were at work. As much as I worshipped my Grandpa and thought Grandma was certainly OK, it seemed they didn't pay each other much attention. Grandma always looked put upon and martyr-like. She seemed kind of disgusted with Grandpa and they only slept in the same room together (and then had separate beds) when we came to visit. I think it was a pretty loveless marriage and I doubt they did a lot of coordinated and careful child-rearing."

"I maybe told you. No. I don't think I did. This was another thing. I just learned, I mean only very recently, that my Dad was adopted. This was another one of those secrets. And, why? Why couldn't I be told this? I learned it as a result of confronting Dad with some of the lies and denial going on in our family about how healthy and happy we were, are, had always been. It came out in one of his excuses for being such a bastard, maybe I should say son of a bitch, maybe just a jerky creep so I don't place the blame on his parentage. It was like, 'Well, what do you expect? My own mother yelled the truth one day in a rage when I seven years old and never gave me any further information in her entire life-time of 90 years!?' I guess his dad wouldn't talk about it either."

"Another interesting break in the heritage connection is that my Grandmother, Dad's adoptive mother, was an illegitimate child whose mother none of us ever met, and whose father was never mentioned, even when Grandma was questioned with great intensity. Again, this woman lived to be over 90 years old and carried whatever information she had about her own and my father's heritage to her grave. I can sort of forgive Grandpa (though I probably shouldn't, but I did adore him) because he only lived to be sixty and his son had given up asking questions by about ten. I, of course, at age birth to eight years old, didn't have any curiosity about these things prior to his death."

The waiter brought crisp, red/gold game hens, skin sizzling, fresh from the rotisserie. Red baby potatoes and asparagus spears, were brought on plates and placed before them. They breathed deeply, hands in laps, ready to lunge for knife and fork immediately after the waiter turned and walked away. A fresh bottle of wine was presented, opened and tasted. Miriam pulled a fragrant drumstick from her game hen and bit into its crusty cover to pull away a mouthful of dark meat. She poked the tines of her fork through a small potato and brought its meat into her mouth to accompany the flavor of the hen.

"Mmmm. That is so good. Isn't this delicious? Oh — the pleasure. I hope this is as pleasant for you as it is for me. I know I keep saying this, but, well, thanks." She took another bite, cramming bits of each delectable treasure into her cheeks at once and swilling the delightful and refreshing white wine after each swallow.

Erik's mouth was too full for him to form actual words. He sat, cheeks bulging, his hands holding his fork to one side of his plate, his knife on the other, arms stretched full length allowing plenty of room for his muscular torso to reign there over the table. He looked very much the satisfied Scheik. Garbled oohs, ahhs, ummm, uh huhs came from his closed lips as he chewed the food that gave him such obvious delight. For a few minutes they let themselves be absorbed in the singular pleasure of sharing the meal.

"Erik, why don't I just do the make a long story short bit here? I'll get to the general crux of stuff and we can get back to the gory details another time. I just don't want to waste this chance to get to know you by doing nothing but talking about me. So, if it's okay with you — is that okay? I'll try to just be brief now and you can fill me in on what's been happening for you since we last talked."

Erik nodded, "Sure, Miriam. That's fine as long as you promise not to run away before you tell me a whole lot more. I'll be happy to tell you some stuff about me if that will make the evening more enjoyable for you. But, you can't stop now. Your Dad, then is adopted and his adoptive mother is illegitimate. I still don't get what this has to do with Ecclesiastes, or those other folks you mentioned."

"Well, Erik. Here's the big thing you have to know. I have to tell you this one thing before I pop. Yesterday I opened an envelope from a lawyer near New York City and out fell a photograph of a woman who could be my twin! Her name was Julia Rousseau. Julia was my dad's birth mother. She died recently, but wrote me an incredible letter, also in the lawyer's envelope. Erik, she said her house on the cliffs above the ocean in Maine is my home. She said she's believed this ever since she knew of my existence. She's left me everything, Erik. Everything. More than I ever had right to hope for. That's why I called you. That's why I'm here."

"Whew. Jesus Christ, Miriam. That's incredible. Amazing. It's a pretty heavy search you've been on. It's no wonder you've kind of fallen in under the weight some times. And this Julia. This grandmother. How did she find you? This is fascinating."

"Isn't it amazing though? I still haven't processed it all. I had a good walk this morning and realized I've reached a level of peace and acceptance I'd almost given up hoping for. I was getting there anyway, but this letter, this revelation explains so much I've always wondered about. I feel absolutely set free. But, frankly, this stuff, as you said, is pretty heavy and I'm feeling drained. That was enough of an introduction to get me pretty riled up. Let's see if we can't lighten up for awhile and live this moment right here and now."

"Shall we live this moment with or without dessert, do you think?" Erik asked her.

"With dessert. With dessert. Definitely, yes, yes — with dessert!"

It was getting quite late and the waiter had been most gracious and patient with them; a couple who didn't seem to take even a small break in the intensity of their conversation, so he could offer them further service. Erik turned and waved to him. As he approached, bending near, Erik looked closely at his name badge and asked, "How's the tiramisu here at Butterlick's, Sean?"

"The very, very best, Sir. Will that be two?"

"Oh yes, two," Miriam said. "If it's that good I think we'll each need one. And, let's see — espresso Erik? Shouldn't we have espresso? And, oh, yes — two snifters of warm brandy would be lovely, Sean."

Sean invited them to come inside to have their brandy and espresso on the sofa in front of the fire. The hour grew late and they talked as if there was no one else in the world until the fire died and Sean came to tell them it was closing time.

Chapter Thirty

The next day they drove to Erik's inland home outside of Whitley. All the way they talked, sharing the circumstances of their lives and their hearts' secrets. They talked of what they hoped for. Miriam read him her grandmother's letter and showed him the photographs. She read him what Julia said about rescue. She asked him to help her to go home.

Miriam spent the next five days in Florida. Erik served as her confidant, counselor and support. During the days she talked with the attorneys in Cornwall-on- Hudson and made the necessary practical arrangements. At night they sat by Erik's fire and she told him all the places life had taken her. She came to know Erik as he confided in her the circumstances of his life.

Erik's life had been one of peace seeking ever since his life of calm and upper-middle class ordinary nice-ness had started to fall down around him. Ever since, at age seventeen, he had been orphaned by the death of his mother following only three years on the heels of his father's early death. His childhood, before then, had been happy and secure. His father was a successful architect with a love of art and literature. He was a loving and devoted husband to Erik's mother. He adored his boys, Erik and Jeremy and though, like many fathers, he worked long hours he did make his family his priority and instilled in his children a love of learning and discovery.

Both Erik's mother and father championed their boys and urged them gently and with love and a solid belief in their abilities toward self-esteem and confidence. It had been many long years now since Erik had felt familial obligation of any kind. He and his brother kept in touch but had vastly differing interests and thousands of miles between them. His brother had found refuge after his parents death with a wealthy family whose influence was toward financial success and all things material. His brother had been ten when their father died a slow death from pancreatic cancer and he pulled debilitatingly close to his mother after that loss. When his mother died quickly from brain cancer just three years later, Jeremy was devastated. Erik had felt responsible for his little brother but resented the disruption in his senior year of high school of having to be so grown up; so alone and so much all that Jeremy had left. Erik did his best to go on as if nothing much had changed for him. His parents left both children in great financial shape. Erik had two cars, the money from the sale of their nice home, a considerable college fund and proceeds from significant life insurance from both parents.

Jeremy wanted for nothing as he finished school and Erik comforted himself in that practical knowledge and left Jeremy to develop a sense of family in his new home. Erik would be away in college the following fall and unable to be there in a day to day way for Jeremy anyway, so he told himself he and Jeremy both might as well get used to it.

Erik moved into a spare room in the home of a family who had been close friends to his parents. It was the home of his best friend in high school. It was a tough time to go through the loss he suffered. He couldn't believe he had lost them both.

In the first months after his mother's death he had numerous experiences of feeling absolutely driven and compelled to the cemetery where his parents slept side by side.

He told Miriam a story of one such visit. He'd felt positively ripped wide open, could practically feel the jagged edges of his chest showing past the place where his shirt hung open letting the bone-chilling, Michigan wind rip through the front of him and grab hold his seventeen year old, orphaned heart.

"A day not fit for man or beast." Erik nodded his head slowly from side to side in emotion-stirred remembrance. He looked up, shaking his head clear in recognition of Miriam's presence, "God, Miriam, it really wasn't a day to be outside at all, but, for me, inside was no better place to be. I couldn't figure out where or how or who to be for that matter. I wasn't a man really. Couldn't any longer lay claim to childhood. Felt fully wild, instinctual, wounded and ravaged animal." Here Erik stood, walked the few steps to the mantle and leaned looking into the flame as he shared the story of that day of reckoning.

He was seeking shelter, that day, he told her. "There wasn't any. There just wasn't any." He had left the house that wasn't home, he didn't know how many hours or minutes before. He was vaguely aware of the changing light but it was no where near nightfall yet. As he entered the cemetery he felt the first chill. It dipped and swirled into the space inside his coat collar that a forgotten scarf would have protected. The chill was another symptom of his motherless state.

"Maybe I was alone there at the gate to the cemetery. I didn't know. Certainly couldn't realize any one's presence — kind, cruel, benevolent, or otherwise. But, yeah," he said "Oh, yeah. I was alone in every sense that it really mattered."

"I kept walking that day, hardly knowing how — stumbling forward really, blindly falling toward the two, far too new headstones, side by side. They read, "Beloved" and "Devoted." The sky was a dark and threatening shade of green and the air held the slightly sour scent of decaying leaves feeding the hungry brown earth. There was no snow yet to cover the fresh dirt of my mother's grave. My father's grave beside hers was a mound of fall-faded and chilled sparse grass-covered dirt."

"I threw myself, face-down, in the little valley there between the separate mounds my mom's and dad's bodies formed. The ground felt warm to me. I pressed my cold face into the dirt; pressed my clean white T-shirt against the ground and let the swirling, whistling wind render me deaf to all but the soft, consoling warmth of Mommy's silence and Daddy's silence." Erik was quiet for a while. He rubbed his eyes with his hand, remembering.

Then, "As I lay there I became their three-year old son snuggled safely between the warm mounds their bodies made on the Saturday morning bed they shared since before I was even born."

"God, Miriam," he said, "Saturdays had been so special. So different from every other day in the week when everything was about busy-ness. On Saturdays my mom and dad would sleep in. I couldn't, though. I felt them. I swear I felt them there in the next room. The coziness of their bed, blankets and bodies drew me like a magnet from my own lonesome bed every Saturday of my life.

That is, until I was obligated to be that big six year old who had to go it alone and learn to love his own company on those weekend mornings. But from way back as far as my memory goes and up until the big boy demand reared its ugly head, I'd entered their room, pajama clad and bare-footed. I always put one bare foot on the little shelf of the foot board and swung my leg up and over making my parents both bounce when I landed smack in the middle of their sleep. They usually moaned, pulled the covers over their heads or hid their heads under their pillows. I tugged and pulled at the blankets until I could see their tousled hair and their closed eyes feigning sleep. I'd stick my little face right up close to Dad's and with my thumb and forefinger lift one eyelid and say 'Peek-a-boo, I see you.'"

His Dad snapped his eyelid shut and made a snoring noise or two just before lunging, like a mad-man, like Erik's much desired morning monster, from the covers. He grabbed Erik by the waist and made monster noises, and chewing noises while nuzzling his little boy's ecstatic neck.

Erik remembered lying there between his parents' graves, arms spread — one arm wrapped over his Mom's grave and one over his Dad's. He lay there like that for the longest time feeling washed clean by his tears. Washed clean so his sorrow was fresh and new, bare-naked and skinless. He recalled talking to the silence, saying, "Dad, I made it, you know. Or do you? How does this death thing work? Are you in any position to know any more? — Anyway, if you can know, I want you to. I want you to know I got my first acceptance letter. But, if you can know, you probably knew that already. So, it's from Michigan." Here Erik broke his reverie and told Miriam that Michigan was his dad's alma matre and he knew he'd have been so proud. He said he talked to his dad's grave, saying, "I suppose you know I really want Princeton, Dad. That's my first choice. I don't know who to ask, though, what's really the best place for me. I'm kind of winging it here. Don't want to impose too much on these people who have their own kids to counsel. I'm trying real hard to do the right thing. To be honest, I'm trying real hard to just manage to get up in the mornings and keep on with my life." He told Miriam how blind and clumsy he felt. Like every body was looking at him and wondering when he'd fall. "Not that they really wanted me to fall. I don't think they did. I think they wanted me to show them it's perfectly fine and great to lose your parents. Most of them seemed pretty busy trying to ignore their parents; convincing themselves parents don't matter once you've learned to tie your own shoes and drive and stuff."

"Hey, Dad." He'd said there in the cold cemetery. "Do you and Mom get to see each other, or talk or at least kind of know the other one is there with you now? Probably not. I don't suppose so. You don't know I'm here either, do you?" He said he noticed the ground becoming colder; much more like the dirt it was than the imagined warmth of his parents bed. He kissed his Mother's dirt; gave it a little pat and said "Happy Thanksgiving, Mom." He stood up and buttoned his shirt and coat. He pulled his collar up and, holding it close around his neck, walked toward the cemetery gate and back toward the house that wasn't home, but where a twenty-one pound turkey, with stuffing, biscuits, gravy, mashed potatoes and squash awaited his orphan hunger.

Erik described squatting by an old gravestone, picking up some dirt and letting it run through his fingers. He felt warm there with his parents. Just what he needed. Communion of a sort. That's what he missed most in his solitary life.

By the time he started college he had forced himself to become numb to need of family. There was a girl he had loved and confided in all through high school. A lovely, compassionate and gifted young woman, he said, but, she too had started college far from home and far from the school he attended. She needed to be free. She had felt unable to say goodbye to him even when their love turned primarily to a sense of obligation and ultimately she grew to resent his need for her. Unknowingly he had required her to fill the place his mom played in his life.

It wasn't fair. He was sensitive enough to know that. But, oh the need. The intolerable need. His first semester, he said, he must have spent a thousand dollars on long-distance calls just to assure himself Natalie would always be there for him. When they were both home for Thanksgiving she finally broke down and told him she felt utterly harassed and didn't want him to call anymore. "She was sorry, she told me, but she felt my need for her was dictating her life and she just couldn't make that kind of sacrifice — didn't think it was at all good for me either." They parted friends — vowing they would always, deep down, mean a great deal to each other. First love for each of them and, they both believed, that counted for something.

He stopped calling. Once she felt sure he had his need for her under control, she called him and they continued to correspond and their friendship took on a much healthier tone.

It was never again like it had been in the beginning though. They were never lovers again. "I treasure her memory. I think of her sometimes and wonder how her life is. She went to medical school. Excelled there." He said. "She married a mutual friend and, last I heard, was happy and had two little boys of her own."

Unlike Miriam's life, Erik's early life had been made of the stuff that builds strength and inner confidence. He was loved unconditionally by his parents in the crucial years of his life and that love set him on a path of healthful living.

There were no secrets and there was no shame to haunt him. Nothing for him to run away from. Even the tragic loss he felt when his parents died was not something he denied. He looked at the truth of his experience with wide open eyes. It was too real. Too much his very own for him to deny it.

Because he believed in himself he was able to accept the reality of his life circumstances. The early loss did something else for Erik though. Something absolutely critical to the person he is as a man and critical to the work he does.

The loss taught him his time to live life might not be long. Wasting time was something he would not do. It was responsible for his discernment about how, where, when and with whom he would spend time. It was responsible for his believing deeply that, if one is very fortunate, they might just experience in life a few truly symbiotic relationships. Might just get a crack at a sense of real and solid connection to one other, very right person. Because of this belief, Erik lived his adult life carefully picking and choosing. He set up for himself a life that satisfied his soul and felt whole and complete. There had been women toward whom he felt affection, and women he desired. There had not been a woman, though, who was the soul's companion with whom he could share his life.

His friends analyzed his unmarried state as a fear of commitment resulting from the loss of his parents. He told Miriam he thought there was probably some truth to this, but the driving force in his living alone all these years was his resistance to wasted time.

He never had developed a belief in God but had some sense he would certainly know when and if he found his true love. And, yes,

Erik did believe in true love. He knew in a way he knew and believed little else, that he had it in him to deeply love and commit to the right woman when he found her.

Erik was born and grew up in a prosperous suburban community near Detroit, Michigan. Family vacations consisted of trips to Disney Land, Mexican beach side resort retreats, trips of educational value to learn the history of America and the occasional rental of a lake side cabin where his dad would make manly attempts to teach his boys to fish and water ski. Erik's athletic ability was apparent when he was quite small and by the time he entered junior high school, his father and uncles had determined his would be the life of a football hero. He played varsity in ninth grade and distinguished himself throughout high school to such an extent he was offered a scholarship that paid for college. He lost interest in football though, when his parents were no longer there to applaud and cheer him on. He stayed with it as a sort of dying-wish-type obligation until his junior year at Michigan when he determined it was a demanding and dangerous pursuit and his interest in distinguishing himself as a writer and journalist was much more compelling.

After college he took a job managing the art library at Cranbrook. Having no demands to support a family he was able to travel extensively and spent much of his travel time jotting notes and musings in a notebook that ultimately fed his writing. He worked as archivist and librarian at several small colleges until a colleague from Florida phoned to say there was an opening for a small town librarian "down here not too far from the Gulf."

It was more or less a "hey, why not" decision and it landed Erik in near ghost-town Whitely, Florida. After six years he still hadn't quite figured out if it was the place for him. The laid-back, rural quality to the place gave him a sense of freedom he hadn't felt in and around the city. And, certainly he loved the place he built and called home. He could nurture his darker nature, darker dreams and cowboy-esque leanings there on his sandy almost-ranch type property. He became quite the gardener too. It was a vocation one could only pursue year around in a climate like Florida's. It had been a good decision for him and, really, nothing held him there should he be offered more compelling circumstances.

* * * * *

In the days and nights with Erik, Miriam shared the details of her history and her search. The time came for her to leave for Maine. It had been a little more than a week since she'd found Julia's letter when she arrived at her heart's home, her first ever and only home. Hurricane season. Her season of arriving. Something in her knew that home had always been within reach. She marveled, now, at how very long the journey home had taken.

She and Erik talked almost daily as she learned the life her grandmother lived. She left Miriam so much more than a place to call home. Her diaries told Miriam her experiences, her dreams, all that she'd feared, all she'd lost. Through all she left for Miriam she was able to begin to piece together the puzzle that became her father's broken life. Pieced together the hurt that led him to love so poorly.

Being found by Julia was not the answer to all pain and fear. What became. apparent, though, the more Miriam learned of Julia's life and example, was the treasuring this unknown grandmother had sent to her across the years — across the waves. How, through all the years of knowing Miriam was alive in this world, Julia worked to leave for her a legacy of that treasuring. In this way, Julia Rousseau rescued her granddaughter.

Chapter Thirty One

October 12, 1999
Owl's Head, Maine

Dear Storm and Jane,

Last night I saw my father in a dream. He rowed a sinking, weather-worn fishing boat in a slow circle of black water. A sliver of a moon cast the only light. No one was there to rescue him but the unwilling dreamer. Beyond the pirouette of his boat, a matter of feet, maybe an oars length from shore, the fog obliterated the distance. Only what was near, moments from rescue or drowning, suffocating, never-to-be-revisited-silence — could be seen. The only sound the subdued and useless slap of the oars as first one then the other cut the water in the rhythm of a dying heartbeat.

All day long I've wandered the house, unaware of my surroundings. Uncomforted and holding only this image before me and in me in its glossy blackness. A blackness that repeats itself in a bottomless, black lake in the depths of my stomach. I feel I'm carrying this death dance here in the water that sustains my very life. I know now, only I have the power to end this dance.

The room's colors slide to muted shades in the dying daylight. An edge of cold penetrates the cocoon that has warmed and cradled me since I first settled here in the ancient tapestry chair. A subtle scent of burning leaves, dying embers mixes with the ever present sea smells and quietly announces summer's end. Autumn's arrival.

Here on the Atlantic Coast it is hurricane season, alternating violent, calamitous thrashing with exquisite calm.

I am mere days beyond my fiftieth birthday. Each year this season brings reminders of my calamitous birth during a hard-hitting hurricane that battered my birthplace, the Gulf shore of Florida late in the summer of 1949. Today, as I approach a new season of the year, and this new season of my life, I sit looking silently out to sea.

It is early evening now. The setting sun casts a gossamer veil that lifts and sways colors in a transparent dance of violet, silver, and rose. A dance of shifting veils alternately hiding and revealing the answers I seek and bringing this uncommonly still day to a close.

But, I am home now. Home in this house on a rock cliff peninsula off Maine's coast not far from Owl's Head and Tenants Harbor. Home at last, having arrived only recently on this narrow spit of land that pokes its way out into the ocean and turns back to look at the shore, allowing both sunrise and sunset to color the complexion of my home. Home in this house first owned by, built by, inhabited by Julia Rousseau, my father's birth mother. That it is so much more than a house, that it is true sanctuary, is deliberate. Whether sanctuary in spite of, or because of its proximity to nature's forces, I cannot say. But it is a house forever at peace in its setting. Warm against the cold and bluster. Strong against the fiercest winds. On scorching, sea-calm days, an oasis and a refreshment, guarded and shaded by shimmering poplar, towering fir and spruce.

Built by the design and artist's hands of my grandmother of hand-hewn and weathered logs some sixty years earlier, the house perches like some magnificent bird atop a rocky precipice where the Atlantic Ocean performs its daily repertoire. A subtle wind blows wooden-flute sounds in and around a gentle, lapping silence that's come as an unexpected visitor to these rocky shores, where the night before cymbals crashed in a sky that was an explosion of lightening over storm-tossed, mountain-high waves.

Every room in this sanctuary looks out to sea, giving me a sense of being carried on voyages of the mind so powerful I'm rendered insensible of the land on which I stand. Insensible, too, of the customs and conventions of the time in which I live.

It is a place apart from time. Apart from day to day distractions from the essential. In the endless wash of the waves, the forever and always coming and going of the tide, it is a place of infinity, essence and timelessness.

But now, so many hours since I awakened from dreaming, my body (limp) has become the chair. My face, so often taut and sharp edged with searching, wears an expression of calm I can feel in my skin, in the muscles around my mouth. I feel changed somehow. Visited. My reflection, as I catch a glimpse in the darkening glass, speaks acceptance. No, it's more than acceptance. Mine is a face visited by grace. Yes. It is a grace-visited face I see in the glass. In my hand, hanging loosely over the left arm of the chair, I hold the pages of a letter I've read time and again in the three years since it found me.

It is the letter that brought me to these shores. The same hands that built my home, penned this letter. The hands of Julia, a grandmother I might never have known had she not broken a promise made in her unconventional youth.

In the years since Julia broke her promise I've learned it is her spirit, her voice that flows in me. That spirit that's sustained me, spoken to me so often in proximity to the waves, kept me afloat through the storms that threatened, time and again, my very survival.

I look out to sea beyond the window wall of this weather-beaten, fire-warmed log home. The fire is mere embers now. The sun is setting. The room's darkness heightens the effect of my nearness to the silver and swaying waves beyond.

I rise from my chair and walk to stand by the window. Deep breaths of air through the open window cleanse me of somber thoughts of my father and remind me of the rest and safety I feel here by the sea.

A sea gull appears suddenly, dipping, screeching a dissonant song to the approaching night. Jumping, startled, I look beyond my reflection in the window; cup my hand to my face against the glass. On the rocky platform beyond my wall of windows I see the silhouette of a man. He bends to light a match and touch it to the kindling and logs he's arranged for an ocean-side fire. The light from the match gives a warm glow to his face. He must feel me watching him. He looks up toward the house and smiles, drops the match into the flames and lifts his hand to gesture me to come to him. I smile, thinking how much the very sight of this man, Erik Newland, my very true friend, my life's love — moves me.

I sigh deeply, trying to breathe in the reality of his presence in my life, the sheer and absolute goodness of him.

Gathering, first, the few items we need for supper, I rush to him. I arrive breathless, my arms full, and confess to Erik's eyes that I've waited all day for this moment. Erik opens the wine and pours a glass for each of us. I set the spices and wine to heat on the fire. Now the fire light and the scent of mussels steaming in garlic and white wine mingles with the cold crispness of the wine we sip from Julia's hand-blown wine goblets. The sea air smells of fall and the coming winter. The occasional seagull soars overhead adding her music to the quiet lapping of the water against the shore.

The sky is black except for the nearly full moon and a few bright stars. I reach to touch Erik's face and pull him to me, burying my face in his neck. He smells of autumn smoke, firelight, and his day of working out of doors. He sets the wine a safe distance away on the rock, reaching his arm beyond the blanket, my face still buried in his neck.

The wind picks up and fans the fire flames. I pull my husband, my lover, my truest friend into my arms. The whistle of the wind through the fir and spruce and the waves increasing intensity muffles our voices. I hear him only when he speaks, so close to me, in whispers. So much of our connection, our communication, it seems, happens in soul-filled silence. In many ways we've spoken in whispered voices, a silent communion, over years and miles, not even knowing whose voice it was we heard.

Wrapped warm in the blanket Erik brought to the fireside, we talk about the day behind us, the present moment, all that's past and things to come.

I tell him of my dream-clutched day. Tell him how I held the letter in my hand for I don't know how many hours. We talk about my long search for rest, for safety, for home.

"Oh, but it's been so long, Erik. So very, very long," I admit, looking into the fire, my husband's arm holding the comforter warm around my shoulders. He rises to reach the coffee from the open flame and we sit close, caressing our cups in our hands. I let myself drift back in time, free from fear of what the memories may bring.

For so long my legs ran in anguished and near-dead weary motion. But running where? Was I running toward or away from something? Someone? What and who? I simply didn't know.

When was it my life became consumed with a need to know, a need to understand the forces that shaped me?

The answer, I suppose, was always. Always. Even before I knew to call it a search or to put names to my questions. Only in recent years had I ceased to run away.

Always I'd been in motion. Desperate and frantic, panicky, leg-kicking motion. Always. But that was the motion of avoidance wasn't it? There were occasional friends or older and wiser observers, visitors in my life, who looked at my motions and knew them as evidence I needed answers. Saw I needed a place to land that would not hold me captive to lies. Believed answers and a freeing truth might bring me rest and peace. Might stop me from my fearful and headlong dash from shameful secrets I couldn't acknowledge. Didn't dare look at face on. Always — I ran. I hid. I blamed. I raged.

I remember now there were rescuers, though I didn't recognize them as that at the time. Mrs. Brook, Mrs. Beach, Grandpa Blackwell ... Others along the way befriended me. Maybe even adored me. The healthiest among them, as I got older, I rejected. Unable, as I was, to recognize health and wholeness as anything other than an absence of passion.

Today, sitting by the sea, was a day of reckoning the past with present and future. The sea's timelessness weaves past, present and future into an essential moment that cannot rightly be called a moment. It is outside of and beyond time and measurement. But in the stillness of this day, in the knowledge contained in my grandmother's letter, I felt, again, the freedom of release from the terrifying grip of the past. All my years of dread, all the years of utter captivity washed over and through me. And I have not drowned. I am not gasping for air. I am not afraid.

And it's not really the truth that's held me captive all these years, but my fear that the truth would destroy me — And not only me. I feared the truth would destroy everyone around me. My whole family. The entire rickety foundation of their lives, our lives, built on lies.

Oh, I know, even believe with all my heart, that the people who harmed me did what they did without intention. I believe now, that I was most harmed by inattention. I was harmed, as so many are, by fear of truth and fear of failure in the face of responsibility. Those who hurt me, damaged me and set me on a path to do harm to others did not pay attention to their own behavior or surroundings. They acted blindly and dumbly like cornered animals unable to see what came before and what would follow. I know now these things it took me far too long to learn. I know this very fear and inattention, this truth avoidance, is the cause of the harm I've done.

For more than two years now I've been living the life I longed for throughout my life. A life of safety and refuge I tasted briefly when life's circumstances brought me to those places where the river meets huge and rolling bodies of water. Places where the trees sway and moan, calling my name, telling me they are my safety, my refuge. Life seemed to snatch me carelessly from the embrace of serenity and comfort of the waves and land me over and over again in a quagmire or swamp or desert of one kind or another. But now, and in these recent years — the years since I first read the letter I held in my hand today — I've felt the total embrace of grace and rescue.

I've found my home. Through all the years of running away, my home was seeking me. I heard home whisper my name on the rocky precipice by Lake Superior when I was a small child. I heard home calling to me from the glass surfaced lake of my youth. Home was there in the grove of trees in Grandpa's side-yard, and in the orchard by the swirling stream where I lived and played for so brief a time.

The desserts and swamps were a constant interruption to the song of home. Chaos, noise, tangled reeds and quick-sand were the places from which I sought escape. Yards bare of grass but for their tufts of weeds hiding dens of snakes; dark, coal-filled basements with rotting foundations that housed rodents, spiders and the snakes who fed on them: these were the places I lived where the whisper of home was silent.

I've stopped running away now, but I've not ceased to run. I have been and will remain in constant motion. Oh, not necessarily physical, busy motion. There is now motion, a forward motion, even in my stillness. I have set aside, for the most part, the unessential. I have taken up active participation in noticing my life as I live it.

I know now, that for some people, this awakening toward paying attention in a day to day, minute to minute way, to all that is in them and surrounds them, comes only when told they have only so much life left to live. A dreaded and terminal disease. A year, maybe two, then darkness. In some ways, I've always felt a death sentence hanging over me. A sentence that urged me toward experience and survival but wouldn't let me rest and be present in the now of the moments of my life. A sentence from which I tried to hide and escape.

Escape became my obsession. Years of my life passed with my noticing only how quickly they were gone without a trace. Noticing only how much pain was left in the wake of my running and batting away, flailing at the memories of youth that assaulted me and crowded my path with their horrors. Perhaps there was to be no peace for me. Perhaps rest would never come. Perhaps I would never feel a moment of safety.

But here I am. Whole. Alive. Fifty years old and thriving. And still my body and soul house a fierce rage to live. I am consumed with gratitude to find myself home. If this fullness of life is mine for another fifty years or if I am swept into the tides by an event that will end my life in the next fifty minutes, I will know that, yes. The answer has always been, yes. I will know peace and rest and I will know safety.

The past and its memories still hold the power to make me feel sad. I'm sorry the hurt ever took place. But, the past no longer has the power to break me. It's no longer something I have to bury or run from to live effectively as an adult.

I looked my childhood demons full in the face and they withered and cringed and crawled into a corner. The ability of my father to hurt or destroy me is no longer an issue. I will not be destroyed. The return to my birthplace did not completely lay to rest my past the way I'd seen it happen for other hurt women. Women who, upon finally daring to look in the aged eyes and face of their tormentor, are struck by the powerlessness of the dragon. No. It didn't happen like that for me.

For me that look in my tormentor's eyes still holds a kind of power that won't let me go. I remain and perhaps always will remain alone in recognizing the harm done. No one in my family who professes to love me, can understand that it was my father who inspired my terror and debilitation. It is disruptive, destructive and cruel of me, they believe, to look at the past — "After all," I hear them say, "look at us. Look at you. You're educated, healthy, financially comfortable . . . No harm done, right?"

But still, as I learned so recently after believing myself strong and ready, whatever it was that pulled me under, it always and forever wore the face of my father. I've never found home in proximity to him. I have to accept my true and safe home is a place far from my parents.

Those few short years ago, when my search led me to Erik, and I lay in the white cotton bed those days after he rescued me, I dreamed myself as a child. I was long and skinny and in a dress that left my legs feeling bare and cold. I tried to pick myself up off the ground where I'd fallen face down in the sparse grass by the lilac bush that never bloomed. And it was my front yard. I was maybe twelve years old. The house was set back a bit from the road and on a little hill.. I saw it all in a sort of slow motion. Still I wore the red, brown and white plaid dress that I know I could only wear up until age three or four, but somehow it's there and I'm wearing it and it feels too small. I feel completely uncovered and all wrong. My mom has just come out on the porch. Stephanie and Ariana are up close to the house. Ariana dutifully sweeps the porch steps and Stephanie chases a brightly colored beach ball into the bushes that line the front of the house. Dad has just swung the entire length and power of his right arm and knocked me for a loop and halfway across the yard to the spot where I'm writhe, humiliated. I lift my face slightly, my mouth full of dirt, my knees and elbows burning and scrapped, and turn my head to see if it's safe to get up. Dad is laughing. Mom and Ariana and Stephanie cast their eyes downward and go dumb and blind as if they've seen nothing. I want to disappear into the earth.

And now, in my true home, the dreams still come sometimes. The night terrors. But something else had been revealed to me since I was there in the home of a rescuer named Erik and since arriving in the home of a rescuer named Julia. I know now the source of my strength and courage was the spirit of my grandmother. For so many years she cheered me on and championed my search and my survival.

It was my grandmother's spirit alive in me that drew me again and again to those women's voices and the legacy they left that spoke to my own sense of truth. Those voices that touched my soul and with whom I feel such affinity.

And now, dear children, grown women that you are, I write to you as in a diary. You will know the story of the women who came before you. Your search will be different from mine but you have much to discover. I offer you the words of my search and my life *lessons as legacy and pray you will thrive.*

As always, with love and gratitude for your very lives,
Mother

Miriam closed the pages of her journal and tucked it into the drawer of the bedside table as on all the nights since coming home to Owl's Head. She turned to face her husband and he took her in his arms.

The evening spent with Erik so many years before, freshened by the breeze off the Gulf — the whole experience of visiting her birthplace, so devoid of refreshment, yet so near the ocean—had proved catalyst to send her back to fully adult life. And Erik, he was and is refreshment itself.

Once Miriam settled in Maine in the autumn of 1997, Erik joined her there for Thanksgiving and Christmas. She resigned her position at St. David's and conducted research and a lecture series from her home. The following summer, Erik came to stay. He completed his novel, <u>In the Night Country.</u> He returned the following Christmas and they were married in January.

Miriam faced her father fear. That fear that had held her back from taking her own professional advice— "Don't run from history. You can't out distance it. It has to find its place in you so you might live forward and away from destruction." Now she was fully ready to let it go.

A sense of peace, rest and acceptance of what *is* exists for her now. She accepted the reality of her past. She ceased her railing against it. It no longer mattered what could have been. She now lived in the rich and present moments of her life and followed the urgings of her grandmother. She put aside the unessential. And now, it was the next half of Miriam's life that mattered. She would attempt to live it with self-possession and a realization of the impact her life and spirit might leave on the lives of her children and her children's children.

Miriam would move forward. She would find peace on the wind blown shores where the river meets the sea. She would live inside all that she hoped for—Arrival. Understanding. Confluence. Communion. —And enough of each to go around.

THE END

About the Author

Deborah McWatters Padgett has been writing and painting her entire adult life. Her background includes a concentration in Literature from the University of Minnesota and a participating membership in the Loft Center for Literary Arts. Her instructors have included Alexs Pate, Faith Sullivan, Jonis Agee, Mary Gardener, Carol Bly and Patricia Weaver Francisco. She is a lifelong avid reader of literary and commercial fiction. Reading has served as primary educator to her writing.

Deborah's first novel, SOLVING LONELY, was published by LULU Press in 2011. Deborah's second novel, THE SEA IN WINTER was published in 2012 and is availabe at amazon.com. Her short fiction has appeared in SPOUT, GYPSY CAB and SING HEAVENLY MUSE. Her essays and articles have been published in national and regional arts publications, as well as, Ceramics Monthly, Ceramics Art and Perception, (Australia) and in the Minneapolis Star Tribune. She currently writes a monthly column titled "Living, Loving & Laughing…. Dear Deb", for Saint Paul, Minnesota's non-profit COMMUNITY REPORTER.

Deborah is mother to four grown children and grandmother to twenty-one. Her work celebrates the ordinary and attempts to hold dear the present moment in all its joy and sorrow. She lives with her husband, ceramic artist and emeritus professor of art, Michael Padgett in Saint Paul, Minnesota.

A STORY LIKE TRUTH is Deborah's third novel. Look for her online at:

www.padgettstudios.com and www.lulu.com.